Jack Deighton was born in Dumbarton in 1953. He has a Ph.D. in Chemistry and once worked in England as a research chemist. He returned to Scotland to take up teaching and now lives in Kirkcaldy with his wife and two sons. Pupils in Cowdenbeath and, later, Dunfermline have received his tuition with various degrees of willingness.

His short fiction has been published in *New Worlds* and *Interzone*. Two of these stories have since appeared in translation in the French magazine *Cyberdreams*.

He tries to keep fit by playing badminton and now watches less football than he used to.

A Son
of the Rock

A Space Libretto

Jack Deighton

ORBIT

An *Orbit* Book

First published in Great Britain by Orbit 1997

Copyright © Jack Deighton 1997

The moral right of the author has been asserted.

*All characters in this publication are fictitious
and any resemblance to real persons, living or dead,
is purely coincidental.*

A CIP catalogue record for this book
is available from the British Library.

ISBN 1 85723 452 9

Typeset in Sabon by
Palimpsest Book Production Limited,
Polmont, Stirlingshire
Printed and bound in Great Britain by
Clays Ltd, St Ives plc.

UK companies, institutions and other organisations wishing
to make bulk purchases of this or any other book
published by Little, Brown should contact their local
bookshop or the special sales department at the address below.
Tel 0171 911 8000. Fax 0171 911 8100.

Orbit
A Division of
Little, Brown and Company (UK)
Brettenham House
Lancaster Place
London WC2E 7EN

To Katrina

Acknowledgements

My thanks go to David Garnett for first taking a chance on me and for easing my path; to Colin Murray and all at Orbit/Little, Brown; to my agent, Antony Harwood; to the members of the Edinburgh SF writers' group, especially the core four, Paul Cockburn, Andrew Ferguson, Gavin Inglis and Andrew Wilson, for our many fruitful discussions; and to all those who gave me encouragement; but most of all to my wife, Katrina, without whose understanding and forbearance I would not have been able to complete it.

Acknowledgment

Prologue

As I look in the mirror at features rendered beyond familiarity by constant scrutiny, I question just what it was about him that was so shocking. He was only an old man after all. But at the time I'd never met anyone who looked old: I couldn't have known what to expect. Now I see at least one example every day.

It wasn't that he seemed strange, though he did; or different, which he was. It was because, to my culture-adapted eye, he looked wrong, inhuman, *ugly*. Nothing I'd encountered in my short life up to then could have prepared me for that.

At this distance, in time and experience as much as place, it's hard to remember how unusual he was. But every time I'm sipping down raki, thinking about Home, back come the memories of his unbelievable face and voice; and my mind brims with thoughts of Sile, forever young and beautiful.

PART I

Not the Hills of Home

I

Don't You (Forget About Me)

I remember the first time we really talked, when it was still relatively good; before Sile discovered what I'd just done, how badly I'd let her, and Sonny, down.

I hadn't wanted to broach the subject. Hell, I'd suppressed the memory for over half a young lifetime, hoping it would go away. It wasn't something you could broach delicately, and let's face it, I was scared. I didn't know what her reaction might be.

We were in the cramped cabin at the foot of Roodsland Quarry – bed, chair, sink, mirror, chemical loo in the doored recess off, rickety drobe leaning-to equally rickety thin partition wall, sound of some brash recorded VT entertainment or other from the communal viewing-tank next door coming through loud and exceedingly clear. I was perched on the edge of the chair – I wanted some distance between us for this, but not too much – Sile sat on the bed, listening.

Ludicrously, considering the intruding noise, I was whispering. But then everything we did in that hut was done quietly. Everything.

I'd recently been putting a foot or two wrong (just

little things: like us being there in that cabin in the first place) and I didn't want to lose her. But I owed her some explanation. I didn't know at the time it wasn't for any lack of candour but for my sins of commission that she would hold me to account. So, reluctantly and haltingly, I laid it out for her. My dark secret.

'I was seven years old when my grandmother was taken,' I said. 'And all I was left with were memories. She'd spent her adult life on Home, lived nearby, and had kept up a close relationship with my mother, even after Mum set up her unusual ménage with my father. Gran was for ever round the house, helping out, baby-sitting and so on. There was a great physical resemblance between them – you sometimes get that between mother and daughter – they had the same full face with high cheekbones, the same smiling blue eyes, the delicate mouth with upper lip that pulled down when they talked, making the nose move in an attractive way. They might almost have been twins. Some people couldn't have told them apart, except that they cut their hair differently.

'Gran quite often stayed over, so I didn't think much of it when one of her visits was longer than usual, even though she'd spent the last few days closeted away. I'd just got in from school – they're strict about that on Home, none of this accessing Edunet from your own little terminal; socialising with your peer group was a must for deprived two-parent kids like me.

'I'd passed a green and white hovervan outside, with small lettering declaring it to be from the "Elder Hospice", but at the time I had no idea what that meant.'

I paused to assess the effect my story was having on Sile but she just regarded me attentively from the bed, legs crossed under her, hands resting between her knees.

'The house seemed full of strangers,' I went on, 'patrol procs from the local coronal's office making numberless enquiries, Hospice employees in white trimsuits, a couple of medics with those medpouches they always carry, clasped as if to let go would strip them of their mystique – all talking in hushed tones. Mum and Dad were like zombies; ashen-faced, wooden. It was the first time I became aware of them as less than omnipotent. They might have been sleep-walking, they were so incapable. Anyone asking them a question had to repeat it two or three times before they seemed to understand. After I'd been told to run along, my questions brushed aside, I was totally ignored: everyone was too preoccupied to concern themselves with me.

'I went into Sis's room to see if she knew anything, but she was as much in the dark as I was, and soon chased me out. I hung around for a while, upset at the disruption to my routine, perturbed by my exclusion from the disturbance around me, a bit resentful at having to mumble excuses whenever I got under someone's feet in what had previously been my domain. After a while the medics' confab ended, they went away along with the procs, and a woman in a blue trimsuit embroidered with yellow – she had blonde hair in the stacked style that was fashionable at the time – produced a thumbpad, got my mother's assent and started issuing orders.'

I sighed, then; got up from the chair and started to pace the small area of floor. Sile leaned back on the bed, taking her torso's weight on outstretched arms, breasts bulging her Titefit, distorting the image it depicted of some feral animal suckling a pair of human babies. I was reminded of the strange fascination her father had bestowed on her, matching her exotically spelled name. I'd long got used to calling her Sheila, though. Her gaze followed me about the room, drawing out the rest of my story.

'A posse of Hospice workers entered Gran's room along with Mum,' I went on. 'There was a muffled conversation, followed by a voice that sounded like Gran's, but thinner, wailing, "No. No." Mum came out and stood with her back pressed to the wall, eyes closed, head bent upwards to rest gently against the support. She was crying. The blue-suited blonde reappeared and, catching sight of me, said, "Clear the child, this won't take long." Dad hustled me into the nearest room. There was the sound of feet passing, the drilling of wheels on concrete. The last view I had of Gran was snatched through the window. All I could see was a pathetic bundle, obscured from view by Hospice coverlets, being trundled into the hovervan before it sped off.'

I could sense Sile had guessed, but she wanted confirmation. 'What was wrong?' she asked. 'Was she just ill or . . . ?'

I hesitated. 'She had that genetic fault,' I said, watching her carefully. 'The one that meant she had a reaction to Euthuol. She'd had less than half her expected lifetime, and she'd aged prematurely, in only a few days. She was faced with senility, and a life of isolation, at an age when everyone else is still vigorous and active.'

'Oh Alan, I'm sorry.' Sile stood up, put her hand on my arm. I hugged her tightly, not really wanting to let go, but I'd repressed this for so long that now I'd started talking about it I couldn't stop. I stood back a little, arms still round her, hers resting gently on mine.

'It was as if she'd had a premonition about it,' I continued. 'She was always staring into mirrors, checking her appearance – that's where I picked up the habit – looking for those first fatal flaws, the wrinkles round the eyes, the tell-tale flecks of grey in the hair, the cut or bruise that won't heal quickly, that mean the end of normal life and the social death that comes before the body's.

'I kept asking if she had died, in an accident or something, and when I was told she'd had to go away, it was best if I didn't see her again, she wouldn't want that, I took it badly. Gran had been such a fixture in my life that I couldn't understand her sudden absence.

'She used to take me off my parent's hands when I was very young, going for "walks" – she walked, I was conveyed in buggies of one sort or another – and she would point out and name the bits of indigenous wildlife that graced the neighbourhood – things like Homebirds, hammertits, coarsegrass, pantaloon trees, yellowleafs, redhearts, the cotton-easter which draped its white wisps over the scrubby hillsides every spring, quickrabbits, spiderflies, even the occasional batfox, as well as the gengineered Homewheat, Sturdicows and geep that inhabited the surrounding farmland. Home isn't very heavily populated, and not all that mineral-rich, its land use tends to be varied. There are even some conservation areas where the original landscape has been left intact – the tourist income makes a large contribution to the Gross Planetary Product. You'll like it when we get there.'

'Is that a promise?' Sile asked, probably trying to distract me.

'Yes,' I said. Her response had been better than I'd expected, she hadn't drawn back at all, and I felt easier. The words flowed.

'When I was older I was given one of those old-fashioned pedal cycles – "for the exercise" – and Gran took me further afield. We'd visit the huge excavation which was my father's responsibility, move among the monstrous wonder of the machines, alert to the danger of the juggernauts, darting on and off the paths they'd worn. I used to pretend they were dragons and that I had to protect her from them; joust with them with my cycle as a trusty steed, keep her out of their way, save her for a long life. It's strange, and I know that I must be wrong, but somehow nothing I've come across since compares with my memory of Dad's quarry. What I saw a few days ago at the Hole seems tiny beside the pictures I hold in my head from my youth. And Paczai wasn't as good a companion as Gran.

'She took me and Sis on day trips to see the sights; to adventure parks, Wildlife zones, out boating on the lake that was only a few kayem away, swimming in the sea. My parents did too, of course, when they could, but there was something more carefree about those days with Gran; I could just be myself, I wasn't burdened with the expectations and demands of my parents, the constraints they placed on my behaviour. Don't get me wrong, they weren't harsh or anything like that; it was just part of me felt stifled when they were around. I repressed aspects of my personality that I didn't feel I had to when I was with Gran.' Sile nodded in agreement at this. I guess she'd had much the same experience.

'I remember the first time she took us hill-walking,' I said, 'stumbling over rocky outcrops, through brush and low-lying shrubs. There were some long, low crags overlooking the town, naturally terraced affairs like giant steps, tailing away into the promontory which housed Dad's quarry. From the top you could see right down to where the sluggish estuary widened out into the sea, and along the valley of a faster flowing river to Squat Thrust, the local landmark which dominated the lake it sprang from; a broad-shouldered peak looking, from a distance, like two smoothed-off regular trapeziums, the smaller symmetrically capping the other.

'It was an easy walk along the ridge to the quarry's rim, and I can see us yet, staring out over the edge like reluctant bathers at the sea-shore, safely elevated from the mysterious to-ings and fro-ings of my imagined adversaries, those excavators which were scaled down now, made less fearsome by their apparent smallness.

'Perspective's a funny thing. It's a long time since I've thought about any of this; but being with Sonny yesterday, staring into that quarry up there, brought it all back. It might almost have been Gran I made the promise to.'

'So what happened?' Sile asked.

'You know. I told him what he – and you – wanted to hear.'

'Not that. I meant with your grandmother.'

'Oh. Finally she died. It wasn't long after. I found out later she'd wasted away – refused to eat for a time, before they force-fed her – but she'd lost the will to live. The one thing Orth culture holds out as a universal benefit had been stripped from her without warning, so I guess it's not so surprising.

'They still wouldn't let me see her. The coffin lid was nailed down tight so all I could say goodbye to was this over-polished, wooden box with gleaming metal handles. There was none of my grandmother in that. It was trundled away impersonally behind the folds of an automatically drawn curtain to the accompaniment of that ghastly music that for some reason is deemed appropriate for such occasions but only makes the whole thing worse. Nobody came.

'And afterwards no-one spoke of her. It might almost never have happened, with Gran never having existed. It was the shame of it, I think, and the fear. But I couldn't let go. It was so unreal I couldn't believe it. For months I woke up in the mornings thinking, "This is the day she'll come back," until finally I stopped hoping and began to forget.'

I'd started parading up and down again, occasionally gripping the back of the chair and wrestling with it. Sile watched me carefully, craning her head round when I walked behind her.

'It had affected Mum too. She walked round in a daze. I'd catch her looking at me or Sis in a strange way; find her and Dad talking in whispers, only to break off their conversation when I entered the room. I guess they wondered whether or not the defect had been passed on and if Mum, Sis and I would suffer the same fate, but they never let on. Too delicate a subject for young ears.

'She'd had us quite late and taken her youth shot straight after I was born. It must have seemed her useful life was facing a cul-de-sac. She took to Gran's habit of mirror-watching; pulling and pinching her face, massaging it with creams, searching for grey hairs, stoking up with pills of all shapes and sizes, enduring bizarre diets and strict exercise regimens. She was prey to every sort of quackery and willingly embraced each fad that came along. None of it brought her peace of mind.

'She couldn't be sure, do you see? Her potions and crazes might be working, but on the other hand she might be normal after all, her youth shot not a potential danger to the life she had planned for herself. It made no difference: the effect her palliatives had, if any, couldn't be measured. The result would be exactly the same as if she was normal and had nothing to worry about. She was quietly going mad, I think. Her work suffered, and Dad's. It wasn't a happy house for a while.'

'Poor Alan,' Sile said. 'It must have been hard.'

'It wasn't so bad for me,' I said, 'but it would have been easier if they'd just talked to me about it. That was the awful thing, knowing there was this great big hole in their lives and not being able to help them with it. It was worse later, when I knew what had troubled Mum so much, realising that I had actually added to her worries, just by being her son and subject to the same fear.'

'So what happened to your mother?'

'Well, she was stuck with it. She had a one-in-two chance of inheriting the problem. Her genalysis record was inconclusive; the tests are for parenthood, they're not designed to pick out tiny subtleties. Why worry about something that may not happen? She took counselling and that seemed to help, but I don't think she felt truly free till two years ago. Then she passed the age Gran had been when she was taken, without mishap. But you can see why I'm uncomfortable with Sonny. My genalysis looks okay, but there's still that one-in-four chance of being like Gran. Do you think I want to be reminded of that?'

I was wrung out. I'd never talked about any of this before; for years I'd never reflected about how I felt. Maybe I was becoming more mature, our encounter with Sonny making me more aware of my own mortality, or maybe Sile was getting under my skin, loosening my guard.

'I don't suppose so,' she said, 'but if you take Sonny as an example, he hasn't done so badly. It's not as if he's helpless or anything.'

'But it's not right. He's all alone; he looks grotesque and his lifestyle is horrible, so squalid . . .'

'It isn't,' Sile objected. 'You should try to understand a bit more. He's not horrible or grotesque. He's just different.'

'But I don't want to be like that,' I said. 'I want to be happy, not to end my life a poor man, friendless and hidden away.'

Gazing through my window, lifting my eyes to the hills which remind me so much of Home, I think of those other hills, in whose shadows the cabin stood, her decades-old words coming back to me as clear as – maybe clearer than – if they were spoken today, right now.

'Well, if you play your cards right,' she said, staring at me with those knowing blue eyes, 'you'll always have me.'

'Is that a threat or a promise?' I joked, feebly.

'Both,' she said.

2

Forgotten Sons

'There's a man over there,' I said.

'Don't be silly,' Sile answered. 'There can't be.'

We were on an evening scramble over the rocks just off the main quarry area, partly for the fun of it but mainly to escape the oppressive atmosphere of work surrounding the camp. We also wanted some privacy, Sile especially. She was one of the few females ever to visit the place and the burden was weighing on her.

We'd chosen that spot because, while reasonably close, it wasn't part of the workings and we were unlikely to be disturbed. When I saw the light from his fire, filtering through the trees obscuring the clearing where he had made his lodge, the sight wasn't entirely welcome.

'There, look,' I said, pointing.

'Oh, shit, so there is,' she said.

Sile seemed to be as mystified by his presence as I was. 'Why would someone else be out here?' she asked.

'Yeah,' I answered. 'And why the fire?'

As we came closer and the details of his situation

unfolded in the firelight, our puzzlement grew. His clothes were obviously not those of a quarrier. Even though he seemed to be wearing protective headgear, bright in the light, the rest of his garments were dull, unlike the highly reflective trimsuits that were standard issue on Copper. Behind him, there was a curious construction, vaguely cubic in shape, with rod-like extensions at each of its four upper corners, covered in some more dull fabric, parts of which were hanging loose and in need of repair. To his side lay a bundle of logs and the carcase of a medium-sized animal. The wood must have been very dry because his fire was virtually smokeless with none of the white clouds and carbon-laden smoke that water and the consequent inefficient burning give to a flame. A joint from the animal had been removed and was cooking on a spit suspended over the blazing logs.

When we finally caught a glimpse of his face he was so unlike anything we had ever seen neither of us was willing to believe it.

'What the Hell is that?' I said.

'I don't know,' said Sile. 'I think it must be a native.'

'I thought they cleared them all out before they started blasting.'

'They can't have. It certainly doesn't look like it.'

Apparently unaware of us, he sat cross-legged before the fire, regarding it intently, as if entranced by its patterns, the only sound to distract him the crackling of the burning wood or the occasional spit and fizz as droplets of fat from the joint were consumed by the flames. Fascinated by this oddness, we moved closer, trying not to disturb his reverie.

It was his ugliness that startled me most. It shouted

at me in myriad ways. His hair, which for a time I had thought to be a hard hat, was white (white!) on both head and chin; his dry, leathery skin hung in loose, crinkly folds about his face; his sunken eyes peered out from under a heavily creased brow; prominent bones emphasised his hollow jaw-line. His hands were knobby and gnarled, the fingers seemingly unable to straighten properly; his arms were so thin the tendons and blood vessels stood out clearly. Large brown discolourations dotted the visible areas of his body.

Highlighting each further grotesquerie, the flicker of the flames from his fire cast alternate light and shadow on his features as he sat motionless, taking in the warmth. It all made a stark contrast to the sleek, smooth, almost flawless appearance of Sile by my side, and to all the other people I'd met in my twenty-two Orth Standard years of existence.

He was an echo of childhood nightmares, an affront to my settled world-view, an irritant, like a piece that didn't fit into a previously ordered puzzle. The effect was heightened by the wind which was tickling the trees, making their leaves give off those whispering sounds that almost seem to contain meaning; as if they understood his secret but were unwilling to reveal it directly.

I shivered involuntarily.

'What's the matter?' Sile whispered.

I wasn't sure, then, if I could trust her, and I didn't want to risk it, so all I replied was, 'It's horrible.'

'I know,' she said. 'No-one should have to live like this.'

'I didn't mean that,' I said. 'It's disgusting. Hasn't he heard of youth shots?'

She looked at me witheringly. 'They've probably

'never had them here,' she said, adding, 'and why should he bother? They'll not do him much good now.'

'Well, if he must look like that, he ought to keep out of sight and not frighten innocent people.'

'God, Alan. You can be a right bastard sometimes,' she said. 'Perhaps if you spent less time admiring yourself you'd be able to appreciate someone else.'

I grinned, trying to make light of it. 'I appreciate you, don't I?' I said, reaching out to stroke her cheek.

As was usual round that time, I'd misjudged her mood. She flinched and batted my hand away. 'How come you're so crass?' she said. 'Come on. I want to get back.'

'I thought you wanted to get away for a while?' I asked.

'I've changed my mind,' she said.

So, I was young, arrogant and used to getting my own way. I had a lifetime to pursue women and I might stay handsome for ever. What the Hell did I know?

Before we left, I contemplated his appearance again. As I watched, he turned the spit and fed a log onto the fire. Its crackling increased as the pent-up gases produced by the heat released themselves suddenly through weak points in the wood's structure. The flare of the fire lit up his face more brightly, throwing the curvature of his nose and jawbone into sharp relief, emphasising his alienness.

The panic I'd not felt for years had been building slowly, bubbling to a climax. Now its pangs broke free from their confinement, rose to constrict my throat. I was glad to hurry away, to try to find a way to suppress the once familiar symptoms; to screw the lid back onto the box in my stomach from which it seemed they'd just escaped.

'What are you going to do today?' I asked. I wiped the last of the Depilcreme from my face and arched my back in an effort to relieve the ache a night on the floor had produced. My reaction to the previous night's apparition had angered Sile and she had kept distant, insisting on sleeping alone. I wasn't sure I understood hers, but I didn't want to push it, hence the disturbed night, tossing and turning on the hard boards, trying not to think about what I'd seen. I suppose it might have been different if I'd been willing to unburden myself to her, to disclose my blighted inheritance then, but that thought was still too new and uncomfortable.

I stared at my reflection, comforted by its familiarity; firm jaw-line, grey eyes, short dark hair, trim nose, tight skin, brow smooth, lips not too thin, cheeks sheened blue where the hair that would need removed the next day continued its slow march from the follicles. For the first time in over a decade I wondered how my face would look in old age, criss-crossed by folds and creases, skin hanging loose, muscle tone lost, and why anyone would choose to look like that if they could avoid it.

From the bed, Sile said, 'You're a big-headed sod, you know. You're at it again. Get away from that mirror.' I glanced round. She was propped up on her elbows, holding the coverlet to her torso with one hand, revealing only her shoulders and bare arms.

'I was thinking about a youth shot, actually,' I said, before realising this would only confirm what she was thinking.

'But you've not fathered your kids, yet,' she objected, before adding vehemently, 'And you needn't look at me. I'm not in the market.'

I turned back to the mirror. 'I only said I was thinking about it, not that I was desperate,' I replied. 'Anyway, I'm in pain.' I arched my back again.

'You deserve it, pig,' she said.

I shrugged.

'I suppose I'll follow you around this dump. Again,' she said, picking absently at the duvet. 'There's bugger all else to do.'

'It was your choice. You didn't have to come. I told you it would be boring.'

'I wish I hadn't, now. But I didn't have anything better on hand, did I?'

I laughed. At least she was talking to me. 'There's no need to get up,' I said, stepping into my trimsuit. 'Just laze around, it won't harm you. Or you could stay in bed and wait.'

'What for?'

'What do you think?' I grinned, and made for the door.

'Pig,' she said to my back as I left.

Imagine the interlocked fingers of two hands, not clasped over each other but each inclined slightly from the vertical, making an angle of about 20 degrees between them. Turn the fingers into hexagonal columns of basalt two em wide and several hundred high, crystallised from the molten rock of some millennia old eruption. Countless such hands are laid one beside the other, each containing hundreds of fingers, the interlocking digits stacking to form a small mountain. Their tips and the sides of the stack are eroded into smoother shapes by the action of wind and, sometimes, rain or frost. Stray plant growths cling tenuously to the external faces, splashes of dull colour in the pervading redness of the soil.

A huge gap has been torn from the stack's midst so that the mountain is an amphitheatre; a hollow bowl one part of which is razed to the ground. A succession of vehicles nuzzle at the internal walls like insects in search of food, slowly wearing away the structure, before departing through the opening to the outside world. Every so often all the vehicles withdraw, like sheep scurrying from danger, and an explosion rips further huge chunks from the hill's interior, tumbling down an avalanche of rock, throwing up a curtain of fine, grey dust to add to the pall which hangs over everything, mixing with the windborne soil particles, penetrating the smallest spaces, settling slowly out only to be churned up anew by the actions of the trucks which constantly wend their way in and out of the bowl. Like an outlined tongue lolling obscenely, the path leading up to the gap's mouth is marked by whitewashed boulders. Two canine pinnacles of rock rear from the underlying jaw, sabred teeth waiting to spear the careless.

Beyond lie some light brown, dust-streaked buildings made from corrugated aluminium, supported on stilts where they abut the hill's side. Long narrow tunnels span the air between them, conveying rock from one to the other in a continuous flow. A series of hoppers of increasing size, fed by the conveyors, waits to discharge their differing loads into haulage vehicles, the first step on the long trip to the crushed rock's light-years-distant destination.

To either side, obscuring the base of the hill from

view, its eviscerated bowels are heaped up in mounds of gravel, tamped down into roadways where bulldozers have forged paths to the top for the dumper trucks. In some cases the mounds have grown to a height that overlooks the hill itself.

At a decent remove, but still not far enough to evade the dust's depredations, squat the low, rectangular living quarters, spartan huts made of weathered plasterboard, hugging the ground like waiting predators eyeing up their prey. Only in the distance, along the banks of the two depleted rivers which meet a kayem or so away, is there a wash of greenery to soften the harsh landscape.

This scene was Roodsland quarry, finishing school and home for a couple of weeks. I'd only been there a few days and I was fed up. I could sympathise with Sile's disenchantment.

Paczai was the site manager, my tutor and temporary boss, a man with a small, round face, blue eyes, dark brows and moustache and, like all the quarriers – though some had made an effort to smarten themselves up once they realised Sile was staying for a while – a seemingly permanent covering of the grey-red dust. We were standing on the lip of the quarry inspecting the activities below, Paczai pointing out areas intended for blasting.

'Who's the weird guy up over the ridge?' I asked him.

'That'll be Sonny. He's our token Cuprite. Did you meet him?'

'No, just saw him from a distance, and that was enough.'

He laughed. 'A shock, was it?'

'Just a bit,' I replied.

'Don't let it worry you. He's harmless.'

'I thought all the natives got shifted,' I said. 'What's he still doing here?'

'Most of them did, but he was a member of some sort of weird cult that didn't want to move. They revered one of the hills around here, or so they say. They called themselves "the Sons of the Rock". That's how he got his name – his real one's probably unpronounceable; we just use Sonny. Their numbers have fallen off over the years. He's the only one left.'

'But isn't he a nuisance?'

'He keeps himself pretty much to himself; doesn't interfere with the mining operations. To tell you the truth, mostly we forget about him. I suppose we'll get round to removing him eventually, but he's not a problem just now.'

'How did he get to be like that?' I asked. 'Why wasn't he given youth shots?'

'I don't know. I guess he was offered them. He must have refused. You know what cultists can be like. Look at the Femazons. All that crap about one side of the body being sacred – just an excuse to flaunt a breast if you ask me.'

'I thought you liked that sort of thing,' I objected. 'What about the pictures in the cabins?'

The walls of the workmen's huts were decorated with representations of women of all shapes and sizes, in various states of undress – not to mention a diversity of peculiar positions. Prominent among them were posters defiantly displaying the esoteric paramilitary garb of the Femazon sisterhood. The severe style of tonsure, totally shaven at front and crown, with a curtain of hair over the nape falling sheer to the shoulders from a meticulously horizontal line just above and behind the ears. The plucked eyebrows, left eye encircled in green, painted red streaks arrowing in from head, ear and cheek. The unshod feet and V-shaped stance they habitually adopted. The bodies whose naked right halves, save for a single strand at the neck and another on the hip, their garments did not clothe. A bizarre mixture of tantalising austerity and celebratory abandon, it was a perverse choice of wardrobe for people dedicated to the notion that men should be held aloof, and one which, along with the other pin-ups, I found distasteful. Still, I guess the sisterhood made money and converts from licensing the posters.

I had made my feelings known when I first saw the pictures, but my motives had been misconstrued. I had avoided mentioning them since.

'The men like them,' he explained. 'It's all right for you. You've got a woman here. The best they can look forward to until they go home is a visit from the *Merkins* every few months. It's as well wages day is coming up. That should deflect some interest off her.' I bore the implied rebuke in silence. My back was also feeling it had been a mistake to bring Sile here.

'Even if I do enjoy their pictures,' he added, 'it doesn't mean I don't think they're crazy. The universe is full of nutters. What about that group that went mad about the Alban migration a few years back – funny clothes, elaborate tasting ceremonies for that drink . . .'

'I tried that once,' I interrupted. 'It was foul.'

'Made you feel good after, I bet,' he said.

'I suppose so, but I prefer raki, myself.'

He shrugged. 'As long as it gets you high, who cares?'

It was a point of view, but not one I shared. I've never

liked the experience of being out of control of my body, especially when the side-effects involved vomiting.

Paczai was continuing with his diatribe. 'Some of those fanatics even carved their faces to resemble Alban outcasts. Crazy. And what for? You never hear of them now.'

To get him off the subject I said, 'Alba's an agricultural planet, isn't it? I've not been there.'

He removed his hat, revealing that at least part of his head was dust-free under the covering. He rubbed his forehead with the back of his wrist and said, 'It's got some quarries, but not many. Nothing like Copper.' He paused. 'We're a bit of a backwater here,' he said. 'You'll find the Hole a lot more lively. I'll be leaving sharp for the visit, remember.'

'I wish we could just go now. I've been looking forward to it.'

'Sorry. I don't have a break in my schedule till the day after tomorrow.'

'I'll be ready, whenever,' I said.

The Hole was the largest single mine on the planet, which meant, since Copper was the primary source of raw material for much of Orth civilisation – dotted with virtually nothing but mines and quarries extracting countless quantities of silicates, aggregate, metals, stone and minerals – it was the largest anywhere; and it had promised to be the highlight of my trip. Despite my immersion in the realms of theory this would be my first field experience of the cutting edge of mining technology. Besides, if I'd missed it my dad would have killed me.

I was on what I called a 'Grand Tour', sailing up the western spiral arm, taking a break before I got down to the serious business of working for a living. I'd been to Mildenbeck, Astrakind, Helcynth, April, Wemadeit, Maratak, Novymir, Shestri and various lesser staging posts in between. But my father had insisted the trip wasn't all pleasure (well he was, through his position with Orthrocks, instrumental in setting it up) and I was beginning to feel I'd visited every mine and quarry in the known universe.

Copper was my last stop before going home. A fountain-head of precious stones and building materials, Copper was also a metallic treasure-house containing gold and silver, platinum and palladium, oxides of lead, aluminium, titanium, manganese, tungsten, chromium, molybdenum, tin, zinc, nickel and zirconium, alkali metals galore – half a Periodic Table of useful elements; not to mention the iron ore that, from space, gave most of its land surface the burnished brown colour for which it was named. Just about the only metal it didn't have in reasonable quantity was copper.

It was also the test-bed for the very latest in mining techniques, though I wasn't sure they were much improvement on the crude, brute processes that had always been in use. So far on my tour I'd found one mine much like the next and every quarry just a hill with a gash torn out of it. I was hoping the Hole would be different.

3

Tongues

Sile had always had a soft spot for waifs and strays. She latched on to me, for one thing. But I remember once on Helcynth – or was it April? I barely knew her at the time wherever it was – we'd come across a bird, stunned in some way, lying on the ground in the middle of a road. It had probably flown into a passing vehicle; birds there weren't as agile as on Home. Whatever had happened to it, it wasn't moving. At first I thought it was dead but she picked it up and said it was warm and could feel its heart beating. I warned her to beware of fleas or other parasites but she ignored me.

'What should we do?' she asked. 'We can't leave it here, poor thing. It'll get squashed or eaten by something.'

I looked around. The area was fairly built-up, with few trees. Pointing to a jumble of rubbish beside the nearest building, I said, 'We'll just have to put it over there; cover it up a bit and hope it isn't too badly hurt.'

The bird made small, quivering movements in her hands as she stroked it. All the while she whispered gently in an effort to soothe it. When she laid it down it hopped around a little and then flopped down exhausted.

When we came back that way an hour or so later, the bird was gone.

'Do you suppose it's all right?' she asked.

I tried to reassure her. 'I expect so,' I said. 'It probably got its strength back and flew off. There's no sign of feathers lying about. I don't think it's been eaten.'

Judging by her expression, she was still worried that the bird might not have survived. Her concern touched me. It was then, I think, that I began to form the opinion that she'd make a good mother – once she decided whose seed she wanted to help create her two children – provided, of course, that she wanted to rear them herself. Not that I'd have told her this to her face. Twenty-two years is more than enough to learn that some women can be sensitive about certain attributes.

Knowing her to the extent that I did, I wasn't too surprised she wanted to learn more about Sonny. It was the strength of her interest that bothered me. 'It must be awful for him up there all alone,' she said. 'He must need looking after.' Despite my misgivings, I knew I wouldn't have been able to dissuade her from further contact with him.

Not wanting to alarm him by appearing suddenly, we deliberately made our presence known by talking loudly during our approach to his fireside that next evening. The animal's body had now been skinned, its hide was stretched out on a wooden frame near the fire. Sonny was clad in furs from similar skins and the sides and canopy of his square tent were covered with further, overlapping pelts. I hung back a little to begin with, letting Sile perform the introductions.

'Hello,' she said. There was no reply. He sat unmoving as if we weren't there.

'Do you mind if we stay awhile and talk? My name is Sile and my companion is called Alan.'

He finally gazed up at us lingeringly. It was difficult to tell from his expression whether he resented our presence or not, I couldn't read emotions on such an unfamiliar face. I might as well have been trying to decipher the feelings of a lizard. It was hard, too, to resist the temptation to stare. I shifted uncomfortably, averting my eyes.

'Good day,' he said at last, from a mouth of blackened teeth and ragged stumps. 'The Rock greets you. You are welcome.' He gestured to the empty space around the fire. 'Sit, and share the Rock's blessings.'

The first time I hadn't been sure, but on the repetition there was no doubt. When he said 'Rock', it was with a capital R.

His unfamiliar accent made him difficult to understand, until I got used to it, and he phrased things in peculiar ways. He spoke Orth capably, which surprised me. But then I thought, well he'd have to, there was no-one else left who could use Cupric; he would need some means of communicating with the people he encountered. His voice was thin and delicate, like the stem of a very fine glass; beautiful in texture but fragile, always seeming to be on the point of breaking yet bearing its load without apparent strain.

Paczai had been right; Sonny's real name was unpronounceable. Both Sile and I had to gloss over it, using honorifics to evade the embarrassment of our inadequacy. We were already trespassing on his privacy; it was only proper to avoid additional slights.

The first exchanges were awkward.

'Forgive us for the intrusion but we were curious,' said Sile. 'It's an unusual lifestyle you have.'

'I know no other,' he replied, evenly, addressing Sile.

'But how do you subsist? It must be difficult for you to find food, what with the quarry and the noise. Don't any animals stay away?'

'The Rock provides, as it has always done,' he said. 'The Rock is good.'

I asked, 'Are you comfortable? Your belongings seem rather . . . basic.'

For the first time he turned his attention directly on me. The light of his countenance was as inscrutable as if he was still regarding Sile. Once more I experienced the discomfort I had felt the previous day, like a shadow across my soul. My conceptions of what was right and proper were under threat. He was like an errant formula in a chemical equation, unbalancing the whole. How could anyone exist like this? Why did he spurn the consolations of civilised life? I was agitated, struggling for a clue to the unknown factor which would allow the equation to be resolved.

'I live the life of my forefathers,' he said, as if my question was meaningless.

'Don't you get lonely?' Sile asked.

With a kind of finality, he replied, 'The Rock is with me always.'

'I think Sile meant do you lack companionship,' I said. 'We believe you were once part of a larger grouping?'

'The Rock had many children, but not all were true Sons.'

He remained polite but distant, apparently indifferent to our questioning, but parsimonious with his words as if they were precious and not to be wasted. I wondered if his grasp of Orth was an illusion and his vocabulary was actually limited, or whether he was in a different mental realm entirely, only half-aware of us, parading down some beguiling byway of memory. Or, the thought struck with a sense of dismay tinged with foreboding, were the old always like this? Was it just differences in culture and upbringing that made him so peculiar or was there something deeper, more fundamental, some different structure of the brain that afflicted his reason? Was this why the old were usually shunned, hidden away unmentioned, taken at the first sign of ageing, before rapidly advancing senility destroyed their faculties? There was so much I didn't understand, and maybe didn't want to learn. That he would have had difficulty comprehending me was a factor beyond my youthful ken. At the time I assumed he'd had a wide contact with Orth culture.

The obliqueness of his answers certainly made the conversation stilted. It was like speaking to an oracle. His Delphic utterances, a cipher for which I had no key, began to grate on me. I was about to suggest to Sile that we were wasting our time when he produced what for him was a burst of eloquence.

'Now time has borne all Its Sons away and I alone am left here on the cold hill's side. It is the Rock's will.'

'Shall I put some more logs on the fire?' I said.

'Idiot!' hissed Sile, 'He's not really cold. It's just his

way of speaking.' Turning to Sonny she said, 'Yes, sir? What happened to them? All the Sons? Where are they now?'

'They have rejoined the Rock,' he replied, 'or they were not steadfast and have strayed from the old ways. The Rock's punishment is upon them. The Rock's blessings fall only on the faithful.'

He stared straight ahead in some sort of trance, apparently oblivious to Sile and myself, rocking back and forth, beginning to mumble and hum. He switched to singing in what I supposed was Cupric.

'*Jiljippytup,*' it sounded like. '*Woseyhoneh.*'

'What was that?' Sile whispered, catching hold of my arm.

'*Honehwosey. Jiljippytup,*' he went on.

'It's some sort of ritual incantation, I think,' I told her.

'*Oowah fonkee dong. Jiljippytup.*'

'What do you suppose it means?'

'I don't know. I've never heard this language before.'

'*Behenn. Astorree. Urst'e weesh e'ze.*'

'It could be anything,' I said.

'*Nehsee. Hoojaree. Urst'e weesh e'ze.*'

'Quiet, Alan,' she said. 'I want to hear this.'

We squatted down as comfortably as possible on the bare ground, and listened. His singing slowly mutated; became a series of long slow cadences interspersed with higher-pitched faster passages punctuated by clicks, plosives and guttural phonemes. Rhythmically complex, metronomically precise. And I could feel the power, as if he were in truth tapped into a well of energy beyond himself, a residuum of Godhead.

But, on Mildenbeck, I had seen the Trevi in their orgy of glossolalia; and its lack of effect on the unchosen few who went about their business as usual, totally unconcerned among the babel. Is not conviction itself the source of power, and ritual its means of summoning? There are many capable of speaking in tongues, but only the believer does so.

'It's okay,' I reassured Sile, who had begun staring at him in alarm. 'It'll pass. I've seen this sort of thing before.'

'But what's he doing?'

'The technique is simple enough.' I said. 'It's a form of auto-suggestion, self-hypnosis if you like. But it does give the effect of a spiritual high. Charismatics call it rapture. If it's accompanied by strange contortions and wailings then you're "touched by the spirit". Old-fashioned preachers produced similar results in their audiences just using oratory. Didn't your father ever mention this sort of thing?'

'He's more interested in the nature of stories than the effects they have,' she said. Continuing to look at Sonny she asked, 'What if he hurts himself?'

'I shouldn't think it'll come to that. These trances never last.'

I told her about the frenzy-inducing mantras of the Trevian babblers and the equally peculiar behaviour, implacable as stone, as blind in its way as that of the faithful, of those Trevi who refused to acknowledge the power of their compatriots' deity.

'He seems to be enraptured, rather than possessed,' I said, inclining my head towards Sonny. 'He's not moving around much. But if it'll make you happy we'll hang around till he snaps out of it.'

Sonny's litany became soothing, his chanting lulling us both into a reverie. My thoughts floated slowly round each other; dark, shadow shapes writhing sinuously inside my closed eyes. Seemingly great truths flitted elusively at the edge of comprehension, momentous concepts grasped dimly and then forgotten as they were replaced by new dreams dancing and slipping through my mind like flying dolphins. It may only have been for a few minutes but it seemed we drowsed for hours before waking from the dwalm. Only the memory of the revelations remained, any meaning they might have had vanished from consciousness.

. Sonny's singing had taken on a harsher tone, driving towards a climactic coda. Sile looked shaken by her experience but I wasn't perturbed. Suggestibility is enhanced by lateness of the hour and tiredness. How many times have the deepest secrets of the universe been discovered in sleep, or drug-related stupor, only for dawn or the hit's evaporation to dismiss the revelations as awesome drivel, their interconnections tenuous and internal logic meaningless? Having done with youthful experiment, the only drug I still used was old-fashioned alcohol, and it wasn't a regular habit. I preferred my speculations rooted in reality. Sonny's mantras had induced a mind-altered state, but their effect was as short-lived as any, and as unreal. But I knew that wouldn't be how it seemed to him, or Sile.

When he had finished, silence descended for a few seconds and his head fell, chin resting on his chest, as if he had fallen asleep. I signalled to Sile with a movement of my head that we should go. As we were rising from our positions, he was roused from his somnolent state by a sudden crackle from the fire. He took a deep breath and opened his eyes. Seeing us, he appeared agitated, looking round quickly from Sile to myself, then announced abruptly, 'You must eat now.'

I looked at Sile as he rose slowly, haltingly, and

began to make his way towards his tented dwelling.

'No, that's not necessary,' I said. 'We've already . . .'

She waved me to silence. 'Thank you,' she called to him. 'We would be honoured.'

His walk was slow and he had difficulty entering the tent, having to stoop while simultaneously holding back the flap that covered the entrance. When he emerged he brushed the cover aside more easily but he had problems straightening to an erect posture again. It was as if his back was incapable of smooth movement and could only adopt certain intermediate positions, jumping from one to the next in a series of jerks. He was cradling a metal bowl which he carried over to the fire and placed directly on the glowing embers. Inside the bowl, slices of plant root marinaded alongside strips of a brown leathery substance in a clear, thin soup. Light reflected in orange-tinted rainbow streaks from the greasy surface of the broth. In that painfully slow way of his, he sat down and stacked extra logs around the bowl.

'Those who seek the Rock's guidance must partake of Its bounty. It is the way,' he said.

I managed to say, 'But we don't seek . . .' before Sile kicked me. I subsided.

We sat in silence, staring at the patterns in the flames, watching the warm air rise above them, carrying its burden of tiny particles of unburnt wood. In the background, trees and stars shimmered as minor density fluctuations in the hot air-stream continually altered its refractive index. Over the ridge, the quarry's lights threw a curtain of illumination into the sky, shielding the galactic core's aura from our sight. Only the brightest or nearest of suns could penetrate the artificial glare. One of them, I knew, was Home; but which point of light that was, I couldn't have said.

The pot boiled for several minutes before he began to remove the solids with a knife, methodically placing meat then vegetables in alternation onto three skewer-like sticks till the bowl contained only liquid. Wordlessly, he passed over two of the sticks and commenced eating.

Despite its tough appearance, the meat was tender and tasty, requiring little chewing before slipping down the throat, filling the mouth with sweetness as it did so. The vegetables were a different matter. Fibrous and tasting of iron-rich soil, they stuck in my gullet. Sile, too, gagged on the woody chunks. Sonny seemed to suffer no such predicament, attacking meat and vegetables alike with zeal, finishing his meal quickly for one apparently so frail.

'This is delicious,' I said, to cover my difficulties. Pointing to the hide on the frame, I asked, 'Is it meat from this animal?'

'A dumbuck,' he said, using its Orth name. 'Yes. The Rock's gifts are plentiful. The dumbuck were once scarce, but now they are many in number.'

I said to Sile, 'I suppose that's because there are no Cuprites but him left to eat them.'

'Alan!' she said, in a tone of outraged disbelief.

I glanced at Sonny. A fierce light had kindled in his eyes. He gripped my arm with bony fingers, surprisingly strongly for such thin appendages, and said, 'It has not always been so. Once the Sons of the Rock were a force in the land, carrying all before them by Its grace. The Rock provided many gifts and the living was easy. But the source of that ease was confused with virtue, and the ways of the Rock were cast aside, Its gifts defiled.

'The Rock has taken a terrible revenge. Even those of Its Sons who held good suffered Its displeasure as It tested them; and many could not sustain their belief. But while one of us remains, the Rock endures; the old thoughts do not die.'

He stared at me even more intently, as if gazing into my essence to calculate its worth. 'You are a Son of the Rock, now; as mediated by the rite,' he said. 'To you will fall the task of preserving the Rock.'

I regarded him with stunned incredulity. Switching my gaze between him and Sile, I saw incomprehension mirroring my own on the one hand, and placid imperturbability on the other. 'What?' I finally stuttered. 'Me? You're joking.' Through my bewilderment I felt a vague sense of being unfairly singled out. 'What about Sile?' I demanded. 'She went through the rite, too.'

'It is on you that I lay this burden,' he said. 'If you wish to share it, that is for you to decide.'

I could not tell whether he was serious or if his statements were motivated by some desire to get back at me for my earlier irreverence; or for revenge on anyone to do with the decline in the numbers of his precious Sons. My amazement was now turning to anger. Who the hell did he think he was, with his revolting appearance and curious habits, to put the stamp of his crackpot religion on me? 'I think we'd better go,' I said to Sile, 'before I do something I might regret.'

She was strangely quiet, taken aback at the turn of events, no doubt afflicted by the same uncertainties as I was. But she was looking at me in a peculiar way, as if she had suddenly perceived a quality in me previously lacking.

He gave us a final benediction as we left. 'May the blessings of the Rock be with you always,' he said.

'Weird bastard,' I muttered to myself. I clung tightly to Sile all the way back to our hut, glad to have something familiar to hold on to.

That night, Sile made love to me with an ardent passion I hadn't met in her before. At first I thought it was because she was as upset and disturbed by the night's happenings as I was, that she also needed reassurance that things were as they had always been, and sought the same comfort. But there was more to it than that. There was a hunger to her promptings, a wildness, an animal lust that was new, to me at any rate; and I found it unnerving.

Her tongue and hands darted and flickered over every inch of my body, teasing and compelling, entering places known and unknown, seeking as yet undiscovered pleasure zones. I repaid the compliment in kind, stroking and kneading, licking and thrusting, fondling and groping; smelling her scent, tasting her pheromonal glow, kissing and tonguing her feet, arms, back, fingers, breasts, thighs, buttocks; every savoury orifice and none. She took me into her in various ways, sweat rubbing between us, mingling with the flow from elsewhere, while my hands and tongue did what they could. Each time she would bend to her endeavours again, patiently working to restore me to the state she desired, moving above me, tracing patterns on my chest with her fingers. When she finally came – after a succession of lapses on my part – it was with a concentration of inarticulate sounds, legs pressing on mine from above at a dangerous angle, nails dug deep into my back, tongue savaging my throat, lips bruising in their vigour. Her body was wracked with a series of convulsions so severe that I thought I would lose my manhood, squeezing me ever tighter within her so that it seemed inevitable that damage would result to one or other of us, yet providing an intense charge that drove me into spasm once more.

I was incapable of functioning further, the pleasure and the pain having drained me. Sile, satisfied at last, drifted off to sleep and the dreams of the righteous. I tossed and turned again, troubled by the new aspect of our relationship, thinking about Sonny and the apparent curse with which I had been endowed.

4

Rip It Up

The Hole lay a few hours' travel distant through the unfamiliar Cupric landscape. For the most part parched desert, Copper's land surface was ribboned with lines of green lancing and probing from the mountains of its high central plateau, merging and growing as they followed its rivers down to the single huge ocean. Here and there small seas gathered together rainfall in a temporary mass before it ran once more down-hill on the long gravity-driven journey to its lowest point. Surrounding the seas and the few landlocked large lakes, a profusion of plants fought for the available water, daubing the countryside with roundels of colour, splashes of paint on an otherwise dull canvas.

Seen from orbit, or on a map of vegetation, the effect was of an abstract design in which the eye sought pattern but could find none. It was as if a set of disembodied brain cells, stained for the microscope slide, were caught reaching out to each other with feathery tendrils in an effort to avoid being drawn into the gigantic tumour they would eventually feed.

One mighty river delivered its moist cargo in a series

of massive loops through the only low-lying plain. It was served by a host of alternating tributaries, giving it an aspect like the bone structure of a malformed snake when viewed from above.

We came to several lesser streams, with their associated vegetation emphasising the intervening patches of desolation, as we climbed ever higher on our oblique path to the Hole. The first signs of nearing water were the scrub grasses and succulents which could survive in the outlying regions, leaves and stem adapted to minimise loss of moisture. Large shrubs would then appear, giving way in the distance to the barrier of lush greenery – and the plethora of animal life which depended on it – guarding the banks of each waterway.

As we approached the first of these I asked Paczai, 'How will we cross the river?' The road was an ill-defined dirt track, not a major thoroughfare, and the extent of the vegetation suggested a substantial body of water was up ahead. I didn't fancy a bath.

'There's a pontoon,' he said. 'All the deep rivers have been bridged just for as long as we're using this part of the planet. When we're done, the bridges get shipped elsewhere. Most of the later streams are fordable.'

The bridges varied in size – spanning broad, slow-moving masses, deep, narrow-gorged rapids or burbling rivulets – but were otherwise the same, displaying a trapezoidal superstructure with triangulated support trusses, and transverse struts carrying the roadway. The smaller, plashing brooklets presented little obstacle to the ground-jeep's wide wheel-base. Once safely across each watercourse, whether dry shod or not, we recapitulated in reverse our journey through the habitat zones surrounding it, soon emerging once more into the seemingly lifeless blasted heath.

On one of our traverses through these wastelands Paczai said, 'Don't let all this fool you.' He gestured at the barren surroundings. 'It may look stone dead, but it isn't. It's all there, just waiting for the right conditions.'

The deserts could bloom in an instant, he said, whenever a chance downpour saturated the ground temporarily, allowing the organisms which lay dormant to quicken for a moment, racing against time and the deadly evaporation which would frustrate the urges of their genes to take a shot at immortality. Plants threw up shoots, flowered, set seed and died; animals hatched frantically, fed, grew and reproduced; all in the space of a few hours, living out their brief spans in an orgy of speeded-up metabolism, before descending once more into a quiescence that might last centuries. Evanescent carpets of growth swept hectares in an eye-blink and winked out again almost as quickly, as the land returned to its usual barren state.

The rivers narrowed in our progression – climbing, always climbing – towards the Hole, the green interludes in the landscape becoming smaller in extent. The table-topped line of crags that lay in the distance grew gradually closer.

A lilac flash suddenly suffused the cloud-laden horizon ahead.

'What was that?' I asked. 'It looked like lightning, but it was a funny colour.'

'That'll be a laser-cutter,' Paczai said. 'There's about ten of them working the Hole. You'll see they're slightly different colours if you look closely enough.'

'How much further is it?' I asked.

'Just over those hills.'

Further laser flickers of ruby or purple occasionally

lit up the sky above the crags as we drew near, an impromptu light-show reflecting demonically from the smoke of infinitesimal rock particles which formed a colloidal suspension in the air above the workings. Small dots on the crest of the heights slowly enlarged into diggers with long articulated necks, bending to graze on the rock like mechanical camels. Trucks queued in lines to receive the diggers' tribute, filing obediently into place once their sated predecessor had moved off. A bulldozer crawled imperceptibly up the vertiginous face of one of the huge bings piled nearby, sculpting the heap's outlines into a regular shape, erasing the runnels and gullies created by a recent fall of rain, sending brown avalanches cascading down the slope. Rain was relatively frequent here, seeded from the atmosphere by the many dust particles which provided suitable nuclei for water droplets to coalesce. The geometrical heaps of waste rock were rendered less stark by the green covering this unusual level of precipitation encouraged, their baldness hidden under a crew-cut thin rug of vegetation poking through the soil.

We crested the peak into an unnatural flatness. I had expected a plateau, but one with the undulations and imperfections of a normal landscape. This was completely level, as if the mountain tops had been excised by a giant scalpel. It was as perfect as a well-made road, and without the camber – or at least as smooth as the tracks of the trucks and bulldozers which had dressed the cut allowed.

A couple of hundred em in, my perspective suddenly shifted. A cliff edge had appeared in front of us, extending to right and left as far as I could see. Approaching the lip of the precipice, the stupendous size of the Hole became apparent. The horizon vanished.

It was as if the world were truly flat and we were about to fall over the edge. To either side, the curvature of the Hole could only be glimpsed in the distance. In our immediate vicinity the drop's sheer edge seemed to be ramrod straight, stamped out of the land by a huge, regular die. Far, far below, a new world was barely visible; a jumble of rock piles and dun-coloured dust, filament-sized roads lacing over the pit like a spider's web, mite-sized haulage vehicles, miniature mine buildings small as fairies' toys. In those dizzying depths laboured men's mighty mine machines and their attendants, massive aggregations of metal and synthetics rendered paltry, dwarfed by the artefact they had helped create; but, like lethal viruses, ceaselessly working away, devastating their host.

Ahead, the Hole faded into infinity. Our height subtended an unusually large horizontal angle, making the junction of this huge pit with the sky, somewhere in the hazy, smoke-ridden distance, look all wrong. Through the smoke, a pulse of magenta light assaulted our retinas as a laser-cutter tens of kayem distant lanced its way into the cliff wall. Of the Hole's furthest perimeter, a great circle's diameter away, there was not a sign.

'Look at that!' I breathed. Home had its share of mines and quarries, and I'd seen them all in my travels with my father on his rounds of inspection; but there was nothing to compare with this. I'd been expecting something like Frierton, Home's largest, only more so: but this was stupendous. I knew the dimensions, of course; eleven hundred kayem in circumference, three hundred and fifty wide, four and a half deep from excavated floor to cliff top; but those were just numbers, they couldn't convey the impression. As well call it a million kayem round circle: the mind can't take it in. Until you'd seen it you couldn't really have any idea how huge it was.

'It's really something, eh?' Paczai replied. 'It hits me every time. I can never get used to it. You get the best view from up here. Down there all you can see is dust and rock and dumper trucks. You don't get the scale, even when you're working near the cliff.'

We turned right and motored along an em or so in from the edge. Different aspects of the Hole's infra-structure slowly came in sight, swelled, and slipped behind us. Set well back from the wall, groups of grey-clad aluminium buildings with the usual umbilical connections suspended in the air between them, were fed by a succession of trucks, and in their turn fed others. At intervals, those giant constructions named, rather quaintly, mechanical shovels – with their one shorter arm crossed over the other in a skewed 'X', cables strung tight to their chassis to take the load – hacked at the debris near the foot of the escarpment, gulping at the rock then swivelling gracefully to disgorge their morsels through suddenly dislocated jaws into the waiting lorries.

The pattern of roads below was concentric. Occasional thruways arrowing straight from the rim to the centre pierced the circular routes. As we went on, traffic on the curving roads became increasingly busy with dumper trucks passing to and fro on an endless round of fetching and carrying. The radial routes were more sparsely populated.

The vehicles' resemblance to scrabbling insects had been nagging at me. Remembering the diversity of animal life we had witnessed on our journey, it suddenly clicked. 'There's not really much foliage around, is there?' I asked.

'There's enough. A fair bit along each waterway,' Paczai said, 'and there's a few of those. But you're right. There's not a lot. There might have been more once, judging by the stuff we've dug through.'

'Where does all the oxygen come from, then? This is a class M planet. Nineteen percent oxygen. There aren't enough plants to account for that. And no sizable tropical forest.'

'You're forgetting the ocean,' he said. 'It covers nearly half the globe. The number of photosynthetic organisms is countless and it's almost the same for the fish that feed on them. The wonder is the air here doesn't have more oxygen.'

A small amorphous shape perched on the lip of the precipice ahead of us amidst a pother of smoke and dust, like an insect on a steaming jungle frond, slowly resolved itself into an immense ore-cutter, massive weights on its landward side for counterbalance, ranks of tyres searching for a firm grip on the flattened summit. Its giant blade – tipped with diamonds hewn from similar terrain elsewhere – whirled viciously, slicing the top few em of wall into cold cuts, carving off huge chunks which tumbled gracefully down the cliff wall like icebergs calving from a glacier into the sea. A single square eye set high on the landward side of the blade was the cabin, the operator a restless searching pupil. A laser flickered over the horizon, bathing the cutter in a purple light, giving it a malevolent look, like that of some carnivore with curious sideways jaws about to strike. We detoured to avoid this monster, yet still the noise was terrible; a grinding high-pitched screech which rattled bones and brain, underlaid with the whine of the turning blade, the hiss of coolant, the roar of the machine's motor and the rumble of descending tonnes of rock.

Paczai slowed the jeep to give me a good view, handed me some cowl-shaped headphones with radio-mike attachment and clipped on a pair himself. 'There are four of these babies here, each working their own section of arc,' he said, waving at the ore-cutter. The noise was still audible through the radio-link from his mike.

Thirty or so em long, its squat weights lumped in pairs of truncated pyramids above each of the four balloon tyres along either side, tank of coolant liquid planted incongruously on top, the cutter had a curious lop-sided appearance. Its blade, taller than three men, upper half covered by a semi-circular metal guard reaching almost down to 'ground' level, the whole supported on a swivelling boom jutting from the main body, stuck out partly into empty air. The blade's teeth chopped at the projecting rock outcrop where they extended below the guard's reach. Gouts of gasified coolant and dust spurted into the air; chunks of rock thrown up by the blade peppered the ridge-top like scatter-shot, some of them threatening the jeep. Hugging the cliff edge in its deadly embrace, the cutter resembled an ancient windmill lying on its edge, sails driven into a blur by a demonic wind. Stencilled onto its side in large white letters partly obscured by dust, was the single word 'Faith'.

I shouted above the noise. 'What's the "Faith" for?'

Paczai winced. 'No need to shout,' he said. 'The mikes are tuned to enhance speech frequencies.' He added, 'It's her name. She's called "Faith" because she can move mountains.'

I contemplated this in silence for a moment, then said, 'So what's the name of the fourth one?'

'The fourth one?' He sounded puzzled.

'Well, I presume two and three are "Hope" and "Charity".'

'Oh that's good,' he replied. 'We hadn't thought of that.' He chuckled. 'One of the others is "Mahomet", though.'

'Faith' continued her slow progress along the cliff top, grinding past methodically, chomping at the hill like a caterpillar devouring a leaf. Paczai engaged the jeep's engine and we resumed our journey along the ridge-top, discarding the headphones as the noise diminished.

A breach appeared in the cliff wall up ahead, a shape halfway between a 'U' and a 'V', with steeply sloping sides leading down to a horizontal bar at ground level. The Hole's floor was some way below this, connected to the breach by an earthen ramp. A huge radial road led to the ramp from the Hole's interior. This was fed by the outer perimeter circular routes at a junction near the ramp's foot. A stream of vehicles filled the road, pouring up and down the slope on their trips back and forth from the Hole to the shipment port. The stream would thin and spread as its components delved deeper into the Hole, like ants scurrying to their queen's chemical commands or fish to their spawning grounds, retracing their paths to the area which had yielded their cargoes.

'We're not going down this are we?' I asked, as we reached the vertiginous lip of the breach.

'Don't worry, it's not as bad as it looks,' Paczai said.

We made our way down the incline, Paczai weaving

the jeep carefully round the hairpin bends, and joined the flood of traffic descending the glacis into the Hole.

The sheer cliff wall, receding into the distance on either side, was stratified with layer on layer of lode-bearing rock, marbled with streaks and veins of differing colour. From this vantage point the further reaches merged into an amorphous smudgy mass. Close up there would be the reds and browns of iron oxide; manganese pinks, cobalt blues, nickel greens; the blacks and greys of shales and slate; with, lower down the face, the sparkle of quartz and mica and the glister of iron pyrites. Laid down and hidden over millennia, exposed in a michron of geological time, it was like a relic in some ancient linear script, with a message which could be discovered only by those who had deciphered the language. For some reason I was reminded of Sonny. Perhaps the creases and ridges on his face told a story, if only I could read the lines.

Further into the Hole there were deposits of translucent yellow topaz, shimmering green beryl, deep purple amethyst, red garnet, dark sapphire and the glitzy lure of diamond. The site was the scene of various different types of mining and the diverse techniques they required. The activity was ceaseless, with operations continuing round the clock. Floods stood over the road system's intersections, their trellised supports rising skywards like disembodied scaffolding. At night the mining and processing areas were bathed in their intense yellow light.

The pastel-green dumper trucks with which we shared the road and which had looked so toy-like from up on the escarpment, towered above the ground-jeep, each of their tyres more than the jeep's length in diameter and about half as broad. The loads were piled precariously high and shifted alarmingly, threatening to deluge us as the trucks lurched and bounced over the uneven surface. I was glad when the route we followed branched off from the main thoroughfare, even though by then the traffic had thinned slightly.

'I've been thinking about Sonny,' I said. 'Why would anyone want to be like that? Doesn't he know how repulsive it is? Doesn't he want to look normal?'

'I'm not sure,' Paczai replied. 'I don't think he knows the difference. Cuprites will always have aged that way, so I guess it's normal for him. He won't have thought much about it and maybe didn't believe us. To him mining would be young men's work. He'll be puzzled by your Sile.'

I stared at him as he said this, wondering how old he was. Impossible to tell of course. Since the discovery of Euthuol, everyone older than a minor tended to be caged in a timeless bubble centred about or just after the onset of full maturity. A few allowed the ageing process to drift a little beyond then, but none delayed too long, waiting only to sire their maximum two children before entering the long stasis in appearance and vigour that their now sterile lives would consist of till the accumulating side effects hit quickly, devastatingly, decades later. I knew only too well how people became obsessive searchers for that tell-tale wrinkle or greying hair that would signal the onset of first, social, and then actual, death. Others carried on blithely, not caring to waste the precious days of their lives in a hopeless quest to delay their ultimate destiny.

'He didn't seem to be,' I said. 'She got on well with him, I think.'

I approached this delicately, it wasn't really a subject you discussed freely. 'Have you had your youth shot?' I asked.

'Oh yeah,' he said. 'I've a son on Mildenbeck and a daughter on Shandra. I never see them but we keep in touch. You know.' I nodded. 'They'll be old enough themselves soon. I'll be a grandfather in a couple of years no doubt. Don't suppose I'll see much of the grandkids either.'

'Does that bother you?'

'I guess not,' he said. 'My life's here, really. I don't have time for much else. I thought we'd take in the ore-crushing plant first,' he added, changing the subject, 'then have a look at a laser-cutter.'

'Great,' I said, tacitly acquiescing. 'I've not seen one of those in action, yet. That's one of the reasons I came to Copper. Described its mechanism often enough, though,' I added, thinking about the tedious exams I'd had to sit.

'They're not very practical for smaller operations,' he replied. 'It takes something the size of the Hole to make them worthwhile.'

A cluster of buildings like those round Roodsland – of the same aluminium construction, only this time rooted on the ground and more plentiful – straddled the radial route we had taken. Servitor trucks plied back and forth, scooting around the complex like worker bees, depositing chunky stone from the cliff face onto belted conveyors and scurrying away to replenish their skips with further bounty. Other haulage vehicles waited in line, crawling forward at regular intervals to suffer deluge by precise, metered volumes of pulverised rock delivered from the crushing plant's hoppers in a swooshing rumble.

Paczai stopped the jeep before the largest building.
'You'd better put these on,' he said, handing me the
headphones and a face mask with goggles attached.
Filtered from the dust and noise, protected from flying
grit, we made our way inside.

On either side conveyors trundled their irregularly
shaped cargoes of rock to well above ground level
before tipping them onto a gentle down slope feeding
a funnelled chute which deposited the load onto the
flat-slabbed holding area. The impact of a colossal
tempered hammer with parallel rows of specially
hardened heads, dropped regularly from a raising
boom – to hit with a discordant tinny thud – began
the pulverising process. After several passes a huge
hydraulic ram pushed the debris into the first of the
ponderous trommels waiting to grind the rock into
further fragments, their gridded sheeting separating
the particles by size. These massive rolling mills filled
the hall, receding into the distance either side of the
central aisle, each feeding its harvest of progressively
crushed rock onto more conveyors to be carried to
the appropriate hopper.

'This place processes thousands of tonnes a day,'
Paczai said, proudly. 'All destined for some byway
of Orth.'

The hammer gave out its intermittent anharmonic
peal. 'Looking at that thing,' I said, 'I wonder if there
might be some better way to do it.'

'Mass and momentum versus inertia,' he replied.
'You can't beat it. All that kinetic energy has no place
else to go. It finds the weak points in the rock, and
Kapow!'

'It still seems crude to me.'

'Extension of the old engineers' principle. To make

it work, give it a wallop. Explosives are just the same idea in spades. Concentrated, focused spades, but the principle's the same.'

'I suppose. But wouldn't you really like to get your hands on a laser-cutter?'

He grunted non-committally. 'Maybe. It's all just thumping rocks with different forms of energy though, isn't it? When you think about it. You seen enough, here?'

'Yeah. Let's roll.'

We motored on round the circle, past successive clusters of buildings similar to those we'd just left, indistinguishable apart from their painted identifying codes, most of which were all but obscured by layers of accumulated grime in any case. I lost count of the number of intersections we crossed before hooking right on a radial road.

'Is there no end to this?' I asked, when we'd gone on for ages and the rim still seemed no more than an irregularly laser-flashed blip on the horizon. Despite my moment of awe at the cliff edge I hadn't really grasped how big the Hole was. An early start combined with the long journey had begun to tire me. The visual monotony didn't help. The endless vistas of blasted plain, the piles of rock and dust had soon palled.

'Only another half-hour or so,' Paczai replied cheerily.

I endured the rest of the trip stoically, prevented from dozing off completely by the rutted rigours of the road and the infrequent but brightening ruby-red flashes from up ahead. Paczai's mumbled, 'What's going on here?' roused me.

Three outsize blue container vans and a smaller

accompanying trailer, all blazoned with the unmis-
takable yellow jagged stripe logo of Orth Broadcasting
Network news, guarded the roadway in front. Groups
of figures with the same insignia of a reversed N with
extended uprights on their glittering trimsuits offloaded
an assortment of equipment from the vans, trundling
it away towards the quarrying operations beyond.
Paczai manoeuvred the ground-jeep carefully through
the bustle on towards the cutting crew, bringing it to
a halt by the site's administration hut.

'I'll just go and check in,' he said.

I took a stroll to banish the stiffness from my legs
and was circling back to the jeep again when I heard
a shout from behind me. 'Alan!'

A blond-haired man whose face I recognised but
couldn't quite place was hurrying towards me. 'It is
Alan, isn't it?' His trimsuit marked him as one of the
news team.

'Yes. It is,' I replied.

'I thought it was you,' he said. 'Frazer Barber,' he
added as a prompt.

Recognition dawned. 'Frazer! I can't have seen you
since Home, what, seven years now? How's it going?
I see you made it into the media machine.'

'Yeah,' he said. 'I've done okay. Made the dizzy
heights of sound engineer for Chelsea Monday, anyway.'

I nodded appreciatively. 'Chelsea Monday? Wow.
That's some job.' I couldn't quite keep the element of
star-struck voyeurism out of my next question. 'Is she
here, now?'

'No. She's not arrived yet.' He lowered his voice.
'Just as well. Between you and me she's a bit of a bitch
to work for.'

'I can imagine. But what about the perks?'

'What perks? Unlimited travel to Orth's greatest attractions? Like this one.' We both smiled.

'What are you doing here?' I asked.

'Shooting background material for an item on the largest man-made hole in the universe. "Part of an irregular series on the wonders of Orth," unquote. We've got the Crescent Pyramid, the Towers of Toron and the Frozen Ponds of Ich-Iken in the can already. We'll be off to Tokamuri's floating gardens on Aquarius next, unless something better turns up. You know Chelsea. She likes anything big or bold or off the wall. How about yourself?'

'I finally gave up on academia and got a job with Orthrocks. I'm just brushing up on some practical aspects. I start work proper in a month or so.'

I saw Paczai emerge from the admin hut and look around but fail to see me. He headed off towards the quarrying operations. 'I need to go now,' I said.

I suppose hindsight is always the perfect navigator. (It whispers maddeningly, insistently, if I'd known *this* and *that* I could have steered a truer course.) But perhaps it's as well that we never know the unmarked *Here Be Dragons* that will suddenly rear up and burn our boats with the breath of their passage. For what if we did and still made the wrong choice? Sometimes the consequences of our actions are unimaginable. For reasons of upbringing, outlook, experience (or the lack of it) – not forgetting arrogance, the blindest of sins – our expectations are limited. We cannot see beyond them.

I am not sure that if I'd known then what I do now I would never have uttered my next words. I was a different person then; likely I would have dismissed their ultimate outcome as absurd, which by all my youthful understanding it was. I can only aver that in the same circumstances today I would not repeat those words.

'I've got an idea that might interest you,' I said. 'Will you be around for a while?'

'The shoot should take up most of the day,' he said.

'I'll see you later, then.'

The business end of the laser-cutter was surprisingly small. A length of optical cable fed into each of the VT camera-sized boxes of the cutting head, which hung from a tracking crane mounted on a flat-bed. The cables looped back to where the beam generator's housing squatted along the offside of the flat-bed like a counterweight. A bank of infra-red orthometers pointed from the nearside towards the target, measuring the distance. Outthrust stabilisers arced from chassis to ground like knobbed claws. As the operator fed in the alignment the cutting head bobbed and weaved, a viper mesmerising its prey. The beams lanced out, momentarily splashing a deep ruby colour over the rock wall, obliterating its normal hues. The puff of instantly sublimed rock – rapidly condensing as it took to the air – was lost in the greater brightness. Backwash delineated the onlookers as the VT crew's quadrax cameras – positioned well back to avoid damage to their sensitive optics – caught the full glory of the display. The first whoosh of vaporisation was followed by a series of irregular popping sounds as bubbles of gas escaped from the superheated rock.

We stood in an arc abreast of the flat-bed; myself, Paczai and the site foreman, a stocky well-muscled man named Hechette, a little apart from the rest. None of us actually saw the flash except as a brief shadow. We watched through the mandatory goggles green-filtered to cut the appropriate wavelengths. Immediate injury from the backscatter was unlikely, direct impact of the focused beam on the retina would be required for that, but a stray reflection might be bright enough to cause temporary burnout in an unprotected eye. Too many of those in quick succession were more disabling. Our filtered eyes were able to discern the puff blossom as an evanescent greenish cloud against the lighter green of the rock face.

In theory, a laser can be tuned to the exact vibrational frequency of the molecular bonds to be broken. The lack of anything which could be called molecules in the nonetheless strong bonding arrangements which do exist, coupled with the flaws in most rock's crystalline structures means in practice blasting away at the stone at an average frequency using sufficient power to be sure that the consequent atomic turmoil will rip the stuff apart anyway.

Bubbling liquid oozed from the points of impact of the beams on the topmost step of the already well-worked face; molten rock welling out of the holes drilled by the lasers. Gentle streams trickled down the vertical face, congealing like wax on a birthday candle. The clear brown glass which resulted collected in tear-drop shaped dribbles.

The coherency reference detectors signalled the desired depth had been reached and the head went into reflux mode, jiggering up and down, blasting at the remaining interstices, cycling and recycling like a paper-jammed printer scanning the same line. The lasers cut off, revealing a ramrod straight edge; the head made a horizontal traverse and started punching more holes parallel to the first cuts.

'Just the back and bottom edges to do now,' Hechette said when the process had left another precise canyon in the rock, a thin glassy waterfall crawling from its mouth. 'It'll be easier with the rest of the blocks from this level,' he explained. 'Only three edges to cut on each of them.'

The tracking crane arced up, extending over the step; the head swivelled, lasers pointing down. Fountains of distilled microdust exploded from the new cuts as the slice commenced. Melted stone funnelled down the side gullies, adding further amorphous layers to the glassy debris, giving the rock the appearance of some strange slit-eyed creature weeping. For a moment my brain glimpsed a vision of Sonny's weird deity manifesting itself from its primal matter. Snapping back to rationality, I hurriedly dismissed the notion and saw again only inanimate rock yielding to the brute force of Orth technology.

The crane lifted up and away. Paczai and I accompanied the squad in their approach, crunching over the unwanted shards of glassified waste that littered the site. I inspected the smooth sides of the partly cut block, blemished with only a few easily removed minor encrustations, stood back to allow a four-toed grapple to be hoisted into place round the top of the block. The grappling arm was tensioned and we retreated to the flat bed.

The lasers peppered the stone once more, gouging out the final cut. A slitted mouth appeared below the block, the lasers licking its lips with tongues of fire. Vapours rose from the thin vents at sides and back, streamers of microdust emanating from the block like a full head of hair blown awry by a hurricane. A few wisps eddied upwards from the mouth, partially obscuring the view.

The apparition suddenly came into focus, too striking to ignore. I saw the full face of the Rock bearing on me, an ancient tired face, contorted as if in agony, dribbling glassy goo as it wrestled with the pain of its long, slow dismemberment. Its gaze held me rigid, unable to speak, the fiery vision persisting even through the end of the slice, the to and fro jigger, the last blasts of the lasers to clear the side channels of adherent debris, the solid clunk as the block broke from its connections and the grapple's slight swing took it into contact with its neighbour; until the soaring sweep as the untimely ripped cube was hauled up and out, and the spectre finally faded. Only a gap-toothed hole was left in the place where once the rock had rested secure and whole. The excision, from first cut to deposition of the block in the line for final polishing, had taken only a few minutes.

'Bet you've not seen anything like that before,' Hechette said. Still speechless at the fevered imaginings my mind had conjured from the ravings of an old madman and a few chance configurations of line and light, I could only nod. I stared at the newly cut opening in the top step wondering if somehow Sonny had slipped somewhere into his trance-chant a post-hypnotic suggestion to render me more receptive to his beliefs. But he had seemed too ingenuous for that, too open. The notion of deviousness did not sit with him at all. And, I reasoned, his culpability was likely to be unwitting. His litany had been handed down through generations. It would have been designed for maximum effect.

'Alan? . . . Alan!'

I looked up. Paczai and Hechette were halfway towards the stone polishing equipment, beckoning impatiently. 'Are you coming?'

I shook my head to clear it of my line of thought. 'Uh . . . Yes,' I said, and hurried to rejoin them, and the reassurance of normality.

But the tortured face in the rock and its implied hint of Sonny's god made manifest kept pushing into my thoughts for the remains of the day. Its images permeated my fateful rendezvous with Frazer, nagged at me when I contemplated the operations at the other sites Paczai and I visited as we continued our short tour of the Hole, superimposed their features on the occasional oddly shaped bush or shrub at a waterway during the long journey back, resurfaced with increased force as we approached Roodsland and, from this different angle, it bore in on me the excavated hill's forlorn resemblance to a single decayed molar, drilled out but not yet capped, like a negative echo of that sliced out gap back in the Hole.

The phantoms melted away only in the warmth of Sile's arms, which took and caressed them into fantasies more welcome, overwhelmingly urgent and pressing.

5

Ra Dancer

'Hello,' she'd said, taking the seat across from mine, disconcerting me with a cool, appraising stare. 'You look like you could do with some company.'

I ignored her for a moment and surveyed the rest lounge. A view-tank in one corner was displaying an episode of an interminable saga of colonising folk. Borealis had been rendered habitable in half a generation; 'The Mulns' had been running for at least three times that. The quaint accents were about all that made it bearable, the acting was appalling. Not even the unintended comedy of the script could lift it above the banal. Despite this, the tables were all arranged to allow obstruction-free sight of the tank. The mirrors set at dado height round two of the walls to give an illusion of space played tricks with the tank's image, offering multiple perspectives on the display. There wasn't anything I could do if I appeared scruffy, but I checked my reflection anyway. Not surprisingly, given the present quality of the in-flight entertainment, the place was empty apart from the bartender. And my new companion.

I returned her gaze, weighing the possibilities. 'Hello,' I replied, guardedly. I knew we were all supposed to be equal these days, but I'd never been approached quite so openly by a stranger before. Certainly not by such an obviously young, attractive stranger.

She had a smallish face, rounded, with full lips and a slender nose. A mass of dark hair cascaded in contoured curls down to chin level. Her colouring was emphasised by thick eyebrows and a thin dark line of facial hair above her compact mouth, which excited me a little – but my taste has always been for the unfeigned, the natural. Her blue eyes held a hint of sparkle, an amused knowingness which added to my discomfort. I wasn't in control here, and she knew it.

'My name's Sile,' she said.

'Alan,' I answered; then, 'Sheila? That's nice.'

'It's actually Sile. S.I.L.E. And I like it. It's unusual. It's from one of the old Orth languages. My dad is obsessed by antiquities.'

'Really?' I was surprised. Not so much at the name or the interest, as the fact that her father was obviously a fixture in her life. On Home I had been one of the very few children whose two parents even maintained contact. Like most Orth kids, my friends had only half-siblings and, at best, a single parent. Many, whose parents' busy lives left only time for the odd access visit, were brought up in the communal board-houses, supervised by career careparents. I was a curiosity. My sister was full-blood and, worse, my mother and father actually lived together.

'Mine is a mining engineer,' I said.

'Oh. I didn't mean dad makes a living as an anti-quarian,' she said. 'It's just a hobby. He's really a plant pathologist. He's part of a team gengineering disease-resistant monocrops for the agricultural worlds.'

'Mine's a mining engineer,' I repeated. No need to make it easy for the girl, was there?

'And you?' she asked. 'What absurd accident of fate has made us shipmates?'

We were *en route* from Wemadeit to April on the S-class liner *Strangeness And Charm* – this was long before the SHIFT made such long-haulers obsolete – twelve hours into a six-day journey of potentially mind-numbing tedium. Well, why else would I have been prepared to endure wall-to-wall soap opera?

But things were picking up. Now at least I had the prospect of numbing something much more interesting.

'I'm studying to be a mining engineer,' I said.

'The strong, silent type, huh?' she asked.

'Not once you get to know me.'

I decided to cut the pretence and suggest I was hooked, allowing my gaze to travel slowly down that part of her torso not hidden under the table's rim, taking in her bare arms and the delicate hairs which adorned them, the slim fingers with nails disappointingly varnished a pale peach colour, dwelling on the bulge her breasts made in the red top she wore. 'So what's a well-connected girl like you doing on a ship like this?' I insinuated.

She laughed. 'I'm a dancer,' she said, 'but I'm getting tired of it. Too much hassle, not enough reward. I'll see my contract out then take a rest. I'm due to perform on April, next week. I can get you a ticket if you're free.'

'Mmm,' I grunted. 'What sort of dancer?'

'Nothing exotic,' she said.

'Pity,' I leered. She ignored me.

'Classical, modern,' she continued. 'Pretty much anything really. But it's been mostly chorus work, bits of theatre to flatter singers' egos, things like that. I'm still waiting for my big break.'

'You've surely not been waiting long?' I asked.

She threw me a hard stare. Don't ask me how I knew she hadn't had her shot. I just did. There must have been something about her that spoke of inexperience – her light-heartedness perhaps. Immersed all my life in a society where everyone appeared ageless maybe I had unconsciously picked up the signals which bespoke true chronology. Or is it that years carry with them an unavoidable gravitas, a weariness about everyday life absent in the young?

'Not too long,' she said. 'I'm just impatient. And you're teasing me. You can't do much studying on a ship.'

'I'm visiting all the important mines and quarries in this sector,' I said. 'Final training before I return to Home. I've got five stops left, counting April. And I would like that ticket.'

'Done,' she said.

'I hope so. Fancy a potion?'

She smiled. 'What took you so long? I'll have a Bulayma Grand.'

I had to bring the hits back on a tray. The raki I could carry on two fingers. The Bulayma Grand, though, was a violent red concoction laid over a layer of white grains, in a special glass mounted on a cradle. The glass was an almost perfect globe, marred only by the two hollow stems pointing upwards and the projections of the cradle supports. It must have been a bugger to clean. A small burner and a set of igniters came with the device.

'What the hell's this?' I asked.

'It's Bulayma's contribution to the art of relaxation. I got a smell for it when I was there once on an engagement.'

'You don't drink it, then?'

'No.' She fiddled with the burner and took up the igniters. Making large circular movements with her hands she waved them in the air over the burner. It lit on her third pass. She then slid the faint blue ring of flame beneath the glass.

I had noted this essence of ritual about the use of intoxicating substances before; lips run round the glass, froth blown from the surface, a preparatory swirl, the elaborate procedures adopted for the snorting of various powders. Each person has their own particular favourite. Somehow the satisfaction seems less if the drug is not imbibed just so. The ritual itself can be the intoxicating agent; it is certainly so in the religious context. Her draught could have been supplied pre-warmed, ready to inhale, but that would not have sustained the mystique of the user, nor, I suppose, would it have had the element of delay that is a paramount requirement of the fullest pleasure, in any sphere.

A coating of mist shielded the contents briefly as the water from the flame condensed on the cold surface. It soon vanished when the gradually warming glass had gained enough heat to re-evaporate the water.

'It'll boil in a minute,' she said. 'You sniff the fumes through the stems. What's yours?'

'Raki. Plain old-fashioned alcohol. But it's in a dirty glass.'

'What?'

I waved my hand. 'Forget it. Try some.'

She sipped a little. 'Hmm,' she said, wrinkling her

eyebrows. 'Not bad; but it's not got much of a belt, has it?'

'It has if you take enough.'

'I guess.'

The Bulayma Grand was now bubbling merrily, small globules of gas emanating from the grains in a steady stream. The air above the liquid filled with haze. Rivulets of red ran like blood down the upper parts of the glass, coursing into the main contents in tiny striations.

'It's a bit vampiric, isn't it?' I said. 'It's not like any hit I've ever seen. More like a witch's cauldron.'

'It's wonderful,' she said.

She put her nostrils to the stems – I caught a brief glimpse of firm cleavage as she bent – and inhaled long and hard, holding her breath as she leant away again. After several seconds she sighed out deeply. Her eyes were watering. She sat composing herself, then lifted the glass, reversing it on the cradle. 'Your turn,' she said, pushing it towards me.

I sniffed cautiously, not willing to risk the full-blooded effect of a deep breath. A faint whiff of something sweet and cloying emboldened me. Breathing deeper, the subtlety of the concoction then took me by surprise. Mixed with air its effect was muted. Filling my nasal passages, it was as if all my olfactory receptors fired at once. My eyes started streaming as its pungency hit my sinuses. I coughed and spluttered, sneezing the alien vapours away too late. In the midst of this assault its other, more delicate fragrances struggled to assert themselves. The aftershock was a strange mixture of subtle odours, fleetingly discerned. I caught rose, patchouli, musk and the aroma of herica, the tiny ling-like shrub that occurs in such profusion above the tree line on the hills of Home. Through it all, slowly, came the sensation of numbness, spreading across my face and up into my brain.

I realised, later, that the concerted attack on my sense of smell had deceived me. The Bulayma Grand contained none of the ingredients I thought I had apprehended; the torrent of contrary signals sent as the nasal nerve cells switched rapidly on and off, had been misinterpreted by my brain, confusing it. But brain dysfunction is, after all, one of the desired features of a recreational drug.

'You might have warned me,' I managed when I had recovered slightly.

She shrugged. 'You're a big boy. You can take care of yourself,' she said, then began to explain. 'It works on two levels. There's a local anaesthetic – you should be going numb.' I nodded. '– And then the intoxicant. That takes a few more whiffs to work its way through. The anaesthetic allows you to keep sniffing without experiencing the side effects.'

She repossessed the cradle and breathed in the fumes once more. This time she kept the gases in her lungs for longer, and when she exhaled her eyes were clear.

I took a sip of raki and frowned. The usual sensation of warmth was present but it now had a peculiar flat taste. The aromatic content was missing, knocked out by the anaesthetic's effect on my nose.

'How long till it wears off?'

'The anaesthetic?'

'Mm.'

'About an hour.'

I thought – what the Hell, I'm not going to enjoy the raki now, anyway – and tried her potion once more. It went down smoothly, only a tiny tickle of irritation affecting my equilibrium. The gases' warmth caressed the back of my throat as they passed, in contrast to the usual cold rawness I associated with solvents. The numbness spread to inside my chest. I had a moment of panic as sensation departed, then relaxed as the drug began to take effect.

The VT was now running some sort of game show. An assortment of inarticulate contestants in bizarre outfits were answering questions (badly) on a diamond-patterned board resembling Shestrian checkers. The compère was remorselessly ridiculing every wrong response. The contestants didn't seem to mind: I guess they were happy with their five minutes of fame. Personally I could have done without the embarrassment, considering the prospect of continuous re-run throughout the spiral arm, but what's embarrassment when you're entertaining millions?

The bar had gradually filled up. (I guess once you'd sampled the delights of the discontinuum for five minutes you'd seen enough; or, rather, you hadn't.) There were singles, of both sexes, like Sile on the look-out for talent, or content to be alone. Business types taking a short break, immediately jacking-in the head-ups without which they wouldn't feel secure, draping them soothingly round their necks: 'I like to keep in touch. You know,' one of them had said, the first time I witnessed this performance.

As in most Orth locations, we were spared children. If there were any on a hyperspace cruiser like the *Charm* they would be in their own lounge somewhere, doubtless watching some frantic VT extravaganza, all primary colours and noise. I'd recently been subjected to some of these during my trip to Wemadeit when my hotel had been deluged by diminutive hordes with piping voices on some educational excursion and the communal VTs had been given over to pacifying them. I had no wish to repeat the experience.

Assorted couples in various degrees of intimacy now sat at the tables, some totally ignoring each other, some conversing animatedly; larger groups indulged in pangamic flirtation. Each of the customers assiduously sought the oblivion their own particular poison provided. A quick glance showed no-one else favoured the Bulayma Grand.

'So. What are we going to do for the next five days?' I asked, dreamily, some time later.

'We'll think of something,' she said.

I followed her out of the bar, taking the opportunity to size up the rest of her body. Slim hips, trim buttocks shown off by tight black leggings, nice thighs, bit too much calf – but then nobody's perfect, and she *was* a dancer. Her feet were encased in stout shoes out of which flowed thick red socks.

She glided along, her rear in attractive motion. The various chemicals running in my blood merged into a glow of impetuosity and lust. The trip wouldn't be as boring as I'd once feared. God knows what she saw in me.

At her cabin she paused. 'You're sure about this?' she asked.

'I'm sure,' I said.

'You'd better come in, then.'

Inside, she dimmed the lights which had automatically cut in when we entered. I made to kiss her. She put a hand on my chest. 'Wait,' she said, pushing me gently away. 'Sit down. I won't be long.'

She turned and headed for the other room. 'Fancy

anything to clear your head?' she said over her shoulder. 'There's Deetox in the cabinet, or coffee, if you want. Make yourself at home.'

I sprawled on the couch, wondering if I'd misread the situation, and scanned the room. She'd personalised it with various knick-knacks and a disarray of flotsam she'd managed to scatter, her bag, a bottle of scent, clothing, a hair-brush, PortaVee and discs.

I checked out the discs, hoping to find out more about her, or, failing that, unearth some decent programmes. They were dance stuff mostly, touching the style spectrum from classical ballet to the stylised flamboyant *estras* associated with the irregular rhythms of Novymir, and on to the gyrations of the Wemadeit Tremblers. A few discs were unmarked but I guessed she'd have recorded dance on those as well. I restacked them and returned to the couch.

On the wall she'd placed a picture of the Crescent Pyramid, Shandra's one and only claim to a wonder of Orth culture, a building whose name obviates further description, a huge, exquisitely proportioned construction, rising in ever shorter, gracefully curved tiers to an apical summit. More remarkably, it was a functioning building, housing the administrative headquarters of the Shandran commonalty.

'That's to remind me of my mother,' she said, from the doorway. She retained the leggings but had donned a gold Titefit bearing a circular design. The stretched fabric squashed her breasts, smearing them out across her chest almost into one semi-solid band, as if they were amorphous, structureless. 'She designed it,' she added.

'Your mother?' I said, disbelievingly. She nodded. 'Cassandra Tybolt, the architect?'

'Don't sound so surprised.'

'I wasn't,' I said. 'I mean, I was; but not by that. It's just ... Why did you want to be a dancer? I'd have thought with such well-connected parents you could have got into just about anything.'

'I enjoy dancing,' she said with an emphasis that meant I'd put my foot in it. 'Well, I did till the work got too repetitive.' She went on, 'I still enjoy dancing for myself. Anyway, I don't think kids should enter either of their parents' professions.'

'You don't?'

'Comparisons are too easy. If you don't do as well, then you're a failure. If you're really good, you demean any of their achievements.'

I thought about that. With both my parents working for Orthrocks, I'd never really considered anything other than mining. Even with a static population there was always a demand for building materials for replacement or repair; Orth's ever-extending cultural boundary provided new markets on the frontier planets plus the occasional surge of demand when one of the diaspora worlds was readsorbed; people continued to value gemstones and the supply of metals was a staple of industry. The employment prospects were reasonable. It wasn't something I'd questioned. 'You might be right,' I said.

She had removed her shoes and socks. As she padded across the room I checked out her toes. The nails were thankfully unadorned by artifice.

Make-up I can take (provided it is not too indiscreet), the removal of unwanted hair I understand, the varnishing of fingernails less so; but there is something peculiarly repugnant to me about the painting of toenails. Why decorate a part of the anatomy normally kept hidden? If it is to conceal, it signals a lack of trust in one's potential intimates, as if they will flee at the slightest hint of a blemish. If, on the other hand, it is to attract, it speaks of vanity and the shifting sands of subterfuge. Either way, it is a sign of insecurity on the deceiver's part.

She picked out a disc and inserted it into the PortaVee. A dance rhythm filtered out of the head set. She turned up the volume, tilting the ear-flaps until the sound billowed into the room.

'Want to dance?' she asked, turning around, beginning to move to the beat. 'It helps work off the drug.'

I shook my head. 'I'm not one for dancing,' I said.

She limbered up gracefully, flexing the muscles she would use. I gazed at her as she worked, watching the bounce and flow. The design on her Titefit rippled gently. Within its circle, a long, arched brow curved across her chest, with a single stylised eye below her left breast. A horizontal bar led from the eye across to her right, like a kite's tail streamed flat by the wind. Beneath the iris, a line in the shape of a scorpion's tail curled towards the bar, like artfully smeared mascara. A large, black tear wept downwards from the smudge.

'What's that all about?' I asked, indicating the logo.

She stopped, staring down at her chest. 'My father used to tell me ancient creation myths,' she said. 'This is one of my favourites. It's the symbol of the sun-god Ra. He detached one eye to look after his creations, and grew another. When the original eye came back, Ra wept because it was angry it had been replaced. His tears became the first people.' She looked up and her gaze held a kind of challenge. 'Sad, isn't it?' she said.

I shrugged. 'Yeah, I suppose so,' I said.

She inspected me for a moment then started dancing,

fluidly, each movement a caress, losing herself in the routine.

She increased her efforts, concentrating, immersing herself further in the dance. Despite the attractiveness of the display, I gradually realised it was not solely for my benefit. I had been dismissed, as if I had failed a test, was unworthy in some way. Though I was its audience, the performance was not directed primarily at me. She was working out some private apprehension, assuaging an inner need. I felt isolated and uncomfortable. I knew I was missing something, but couldn't think what.

Her motions became a blur, the shadows cast by her restless arms in the dim light distorting her features, falling over the image of the Crescent Pyramid like clouds, combining with her undulations to make the eye of Ra on her torso seem to blink. The Bulayma Grand and raki surged in my bloodstream, synergistically whirling through my brain, the dance track rang endlessly, the stroboscopic action of her movements flashed on my retinas.

Watched by the flickering eye of Ra, weeping the tears that would become humanity, I fell asleep.

6

These Are My Mountains

'You're not getting me up there again. The guy's horrible; he gives me the creeps. And he's a nutter. He ought to be locked up. What did he mean by all that Son of the Rock business, anyway?'

It was the day after my visit to the Hole and I had intended taking a break, lounging about with Sile, all thoughts of mines, quarries and strange visions banished. She was sitting on the bed, cross-legged, playing with the crystal of garnet I'd brought her from the Hole, turning it over in her hands, toying with the scattered light. Her hair was tied back, showing off her ears. She wore one of her Titefits over a short-sleeved sweatshirt; her leggings exposed the turn of her calves and the shadowy hollows of her shins. The skin on her legs was darkening a shade as its hair grew back in.

'You're not being fair, Alan,' she said. 'Just because he's different, there's no call to be rude. All his folks are gone. He's lonely. Nobody understands him. He probably wants to feel that there'll be someone after him to carry on his traditions. He was just passing you the torch.'

I regarded the mirror, stroking my cheeks, wondering if a beard would be less trouble, what difference it would make. Not for the first time, I decided against it: in a backwater like this, I had to conform to expectation. If I were truly part of the workings it wouldn't have mattered, but any attempt to ape the quarriers would have been resented. They might disparage me as too theory conscious, but out here, my clean-shaven face and short hair were indicators of status, marking me out from the men, even from Paczai, as much an expression of position and standing as their subtle differences in dress code were for Femazons, or the variant colours of the shapeless outfits worn on Wemadeit, or any of the other ways such distinctions were expressed throughout Orth. As badges of identity, these were important, but not as resonant as Euthuol, the binding agent of Orth culture.

By contrast, Sile had adopted confused and confusing habits, her leanings to the unconventional one of the many things that attracted me to her.

'Well, I never asked for it,' I said, washing away the pile of black-flecked cream that had collected in the sink. 'I wish he'd passed it to someone else. He'd no right, not without my agreement. He didn't even say what he meant by it.'

'You hardly gave him the chance,' she said, but I was beginning to weaken and Sile knew it.

'Come on,' she cajoled. 'You're not doing anything special. If we go to see him again you might find out.' She turned away slightly, placing the crystal in her bag, adding, 'I think he's nice. I had a long talk with him yesterday. He's really sweet.'

I turned and glared at her. 'You *what*?'

She looked up, startled. 'I had a long talk with him . . .'

'You mean you went out there on your own? Are you crazy? Anything could have happened.'

'Don't be silly. He's harmless. He can hardly walk. I'd have been in more danger here, the way some of these guys look at me.' She nodded her head towards the rest of the cabins.

'Who?' I demanded. 'If one of them's laid a finger on you . . .'

'Relax,' she said, standing up. 'No-one's done anything but look.' She gave a cheeky grin and put her arms round my neck. 'It's nice to know you care,' she said.

'Did you doubt it?' I asked, holding her gaze, stroking her back.

Her eyes widened slightly. 'Sometimes,' she said.

My hands moved to her shoulders, thumbs hooking under her Titefit. 'Well don't,' I whispered, leaning towards her.

Later, she asked, 'So what about it, then?'

'Again?'

'No. Not that.'

'What, then?'

'Sonny,' she said. 'I'm not spending all day cooped up in here. I've had enough of that.'

'Well, thanks a lot.'

'I didn't mean *that*. I want to do something. It's all right for you. You go off and pretend to be working. I have to sit here and climb the walls. I've run out of chocolate. I can't even have a shower! I'm tired of my discs; if I want entertainment there's only next door, where I have to be polite to the great unwashed.'

'All right, all right,' I grumbled, 'but if he starts

talking nonsense, I'm off. And I'm not eating any more of those vegetables.'

The wind had changed overnight, freshening and gusting a bit between the huts. We ventured out layered in extra clothing. Sile's feet seemed unusually cumbrous in her thicker shoes.

His fire was burning slowly, but he wasn't in sight. The stiff breeze fanned the flames, fluttering the dumbuck skin on its frame. The loose fabric of the tent flapped and slapped as if beckoning us forward.

'Hello?' Sile said. 'Sir? Are you there?' There was no reply.

'Do you think we should look inside?' she asked.

'I don't know,' I replied. 'Maybe he wants to be alone.'

'I don't think so,' she said. 'He seemed glad of the company yesterday.'

'You'd better try again.'

'Hello? Sir?' she shouted; with the same result.

'What if he's ill or something?' she asked.

'Did he seem ill yesterday?'

'No, but he could have caught something.' She took in her breath sharply, looking at me in concern, laying her hand on my arm. 'I've just thought,' she whispered. 'What if he doesn't have any of our immunities?'

'That's not very likely,' I said. 'He's been in contact with Orth people for long enough. He must have been given the jabs.'

'But he didn't take Euthuol!' Her voice was louder, now. 'Maybe he didn't take anything else either.'

'I'd forgotten that,' I said. 'Maybe we should take a peek.'

'We're coming in,' I shouted, feeling faintly embarrassed at the possibility of addressing thin air.

I pulled back the flap and Sile entered. I tucked the flap into a join in the tent fabric and followed her. There was room to stand in the central area, but not to manoeuvre. The smell was strong, overwhelmingly animal. The floor was lined with furs, more of which were stacked into a pile along the left-hand wall, some stitched together to form larger coverings. A carved table which looked as if it had been cut whole from a single piece of wood, stood to one side. On it were bowls of various sizes, each with their own decoration. An assortment of tools and metal containers occupied the nearer corner; the further contained a heap of the fibrous vegetables. Interlocked stakes supported the walls and roof, from which hung strips of dried and drying meat. Sonny wasn't there.

'It doesn't look like he's ill,' I said.

'No,' Sile replied. 'But where is he?'

'Well, he can't have gone far. We could scout around.'

We searched the area round the lodge, following a zigzag pattern through the trees, without success. Sile became increasingly worried, fretting about some possible disaster that might have befallen him. After covering the immediate surroundings, the ones within reasonable walking distance, I was becoming frustrated.

'Wherever he's hidden himself he's done it well. We're not going to find him. Let's go back.'

'No, Alan. He must have hurt himself. What if he's lying around somewhere? He could die.'

'But where can he be?'

'I don't know; but we must keep looking.'

Continuing the search, we broke clear of the trees near the base of the hill we'd been on the first time we encountered him.

'Well, I still can't see him,' I said, scanning in both directions. Sile grabbed my arm. 'Look,' she said, pointing upwards.

There was a figure on the crest of the hill, standing over the quarry like a flagstaff. Its non-reflective clothing and white head meant it could only be Sonny.

'How the hell did he get up there?' I said.

'I don't know, but we'd better go and help him. He might fall or hurt himself on the way back down.'

We scrambled up the hill, Sile's training showing in her nimble footwork, dancing between the small shrubs and over the stones, arms stretched, in perfect balance. My clumsier efforts brought me scratched limbs, barked shins and a badly turned ankle as I struggled to keep pace. I limped, cursing, up the final steps to where Sile stood a few em from Sonny, the whirl and commotion of the quarry mixing with a breeze now much stronger, to bring eddies of dust swirling theatrically round him. A walking stick grasped in one hand, stern gaze fixed on the organised chaos below, he resembled a sorcerer summoning demons to his will. His demeanour was such I half-expected a call, in imperious ringing tones, for the Rock to banish these interlopers from Its domain; but any movement would have revealed his many frailties as a vessel to channel whatever power his beliefs had once contained. Thin and etiolated, he stood mute, impassive, a proud figurehead, buffeted by the wind.

From his vantage point the immediate countryside unfolded, toy-like, to the horizon. The savage cut of the quarry lay below, an open wound in the landscape, excavators and lorries rummaging in its interior like rigid green maggots, the buildings in its mouth resembling inadequate plasters taped across the scar.

Beyond, the green strips on the larger river's banks meandered in harmony inland until distance merged them into a single undulating tail. Shepherded by a line of crags, the swift-running tributary mirrored this behaviour, funnelling back to its source lake in a series of treacherous loops. At the confluence, a lush triangle of land flourished between the flows. Standing over it was a peculiar double rock shaped like two upturned cones – one broad and rounded, one thinner and more pointed – joined amidships. For centuries the tributary had dashed against this bulwark before meeting its primary, thrown first to one side then the other as the silts accumulated. Downstream, the mingled waters spread, fanning out to fill the strath between the widening hills, losing impetus as they neared their destination in this round of the cycle from sea to sky and back.

'Are you all right, sir?' Sile asked, coming to stand at his left shoulder. I approached his right. He was about an em from the quarry's edge, swaying slightly as the wind gusted. Sile pulled a lock of hair from the corner of her mouth and curled it languidly behind her ear, concern for him apparent in her gaze.

'The Rock will care for me,' he whispered, almost as if unconvinced. 'It has little else, now,' he added. He turned to look at me. 'But It cares for Its Sons,' he said.

'Why are you up here?' Sile asked hurriedly. 'It could be dangerous.'

'Once this land was a shrine to the Rock,' he said. 'Trees bloomed, game abounded, and life was good under Its pleasure.' He stared at us in turn, slowly. 'But the Rock became angry,' he said, before looking back at the quarry. 'Then the men came, and the mountains moved away.'

for your companion, he lacks belief. The Rock will not flourish long beyond my death.'

'No, no! Tell him Alan!' she said.

'I . . .'

'It does not matter,' he told me. 'The Rock knows.'

'Tell him!' she hissed.

It was such a little thing, and she obviously needed some gesture from me. 'There is still you, and me to come after,' I said.

'Thank you,' she said, when we had seen him safely to his lodge and were heading for the huts.

'For what?'

'Saying you were a Son.'

'Oh, that. I didn't mean it, you know,' I said.

'I think you did, but it doesn't matter anyway. He thought you did, and that's what's important.'

'So now he can die happy his precious Sons will carry on, is that it?'

'Something like that. At least a little of his burden has been eased.'

'And what happens when we leave? Doesn't being a Son of the Rock mean staying here?'

'We'll tell him you'll take the Rock with you wherever you go. That might keep him happy.'

'Got it all worked out, haven't you?'

'Yeah,' she grinned, pleased with herself.

'Did I ever tell you I love you?' I said.

She stopped; turned to face me. 'You know you haven't,' she said.

'Well I do.'

It was some time before we crawled back to the hut.

7

All The Things She Said

It's strange how some people affect your life, mould it in ways you couldn't have foreseen, ways you maybe didn't want, might in fact have scoffed at had you been told about them in advance. All these years I would have said I had Sonny and his influence – or was it curse? – to blame (if that's the right word) for the course my life took. Certainly, if I hadn't met him, it would all have turned out differently, the pains and pleasures arranged in contrary guise. I would, I suppose, have proved my virility siring the statutory two offspring, taken youth shots, merged with the mass, latched onto every passing fad, tried to assert my individuality by aping the ways of others. I would then have been spared the wearying of my years tilting against the devouring giant that is Orth culture. But there would have been other irritations.

My life is less hectic, now. I have time to draw breath – a little shallower than once I did – and to reflect.

Sonny on his own would have been merely a curio, passing understanding – and quickly forgotten. The real catalyst was Sile. Warm, captivating Sile, of the wicked grin and gentle heart, who is probably out there somewhere now, as young and beautiful as ever, still capable of filleting hearts with an innocent, graceful gesture.

We were well matched in some respects – of all the women I've been attracted to she's the only one who had also been cared for in the one home by both parents, and the sexual aspect of our relationship just seemed to flow – though we were misfits too in our various ways. Neither of us gave in gracefully, a legacy, perhaps, of our individual upbringing, which made for a few lively encounters.

I do not know for sure, but I can't see her as an ageing woman. She will have taken Euthuol. She would not let all that vitality slip away early, let that smooth, unblemished skin become wrinkled and worn, those taut muscles loosen and sag. I would like to think so, anyway. I loved her as she was: trim, lissom and proud, enthusiastic, effervescent, and that is the picture I hold in my mind.

But then again, maybe she was just a bitch, worming her way into my affections with poisonous allure and ill intent. I had, for a while at the start, thought she was interested in me not for my body, but for some mercenary reason; and she did control the relationship, in the end as in the beginning. But as I think now of all the things she said, I cannot believe she was capable of such deception.

She had good reason to leave me. I never meant to, but I broke her heart.

I woke in a strange bunk, naked, covered only in a sheet, reminded exactly why I'd decided to stick to raki. My mouth felt scorched and I had to touch my nose to make sure it hadn't been blown off. A dance track rumbled through the open doorway. There was a curious hissing which resolved itself slowly into the sound of water in a shower as a soft voice began to hum in time to the music.

I sat up, wishing I hadn't, and looked around. The bedroom was similar to the one in my quarters. A fitted drobe took up most of one wall, a small bedside cabinet squeezed into the space left between the bunk and the other. My clothes were in an uncharacteristically neat pile on the floor, next to a collection of feminine garments I could only dimly recall. I flopped back down, waiting till my head and body agreed with each other. I wondered if I'd had a good time or not.

The sounds of the shower stopped, the run of water draining away as it gurgled into the ship's recycling system. The humming continued for a while, with an occasional enigmatic break, until it got louder and she appeared in the doorway.

I didn't recognise her, maybe because she had an effective disguise. Her hair was hidden, wrapped in a white towel which emphasised the flush on her face. She wore a knee-length yellow robe, knotted at the waist. She was biting into a confectionery bar. Lust kindled as I stared at her, more than aware of her imperfectly concealed naked flesh.

'Oh, you're awake,' she mumbled. She swallowed and held out the bar. 'You want some chocolate?' she asked.

I shook my head, grimaced. 'Uh-uh. Water,' I croaked.

She smiled mischievously. 'Water, huh?' She shrugged. 'Okay.'

She came back with a thin plystrene cup and no chocolate. As I was drinking, carefully, she said, 'You should have danced with me. You wouldn't be feeling so bad now, if you had.'

'Oh, yeah, right. The dancer,' I said, remembering. 'The one with the name. Sile, wasn't it?'

'Very good!' She sat on the bunk and patted my arm. 'You can't be too hung over.'

'Mmm.' I wasn't convinced. 'What the hell was in that stuff, anyway?' I asked.

'Don't worry. You'll live. It's nothing if you know how to work it off,' she said, dismissively.

'I'll take your word for it.'

'Some Deetox would have helped. I did offer.'

I looked down the bed. 'You've got me at a disadvantage, here,' I said.

'That's how I like it,' she replied. My loins stirred further. I took in the exposed flesh in the V of her robe, the curves of her breasts beneath.

'Did you get me into bed yourself?' I asked.

'Don't be silly. I called the steward. He helped carry you.' I felt vaguely relieved but it must have shown, for she immediately added, 'I undressed you myself, though.'

'Oh,' I said. She let her eyes stray to where the bulge of my groin showed up through the sheet. 'And you didn't look like that,' she said, pointedly.

'Well,' I said, looking into her eyes, I hoped suggestively. 'I didn't know what I was missing. I was asleep then.' I reached out to touch her knee. 'I'm not now.'

She moved my hand onto the bed. 'And my hair's wet,' she said. 'I'm never comfortable when my hair's wet.'

'What? Can't you dry it or something?' I knew it was a mistake as soon as I said it.

'No. Bugger off. You made me wait. Now it's your

turn.' She stood up, gathered together some clothes from various drawers. 'Come into the other room when you're ready,' she said, and disappeared out the door. The sound coming in the opposite direction diminished.

I lay there for a while, getting my head together, listening to her humming along to the music, trying to figure her out. Finally I summoned the energy to drag on my clothes and haul myself into the other room. As I rounded the door my optic nerves objected to the change in the intensity of the light hitting my retinas. My half-opened eyes saw her curled up on the couch, flaps up PortaVee perched on her head, still dressed in her robe, her clothes piled beside her.

'Can I have some coffee?' I asked.

'Help yourself,' she said, inclining her head towards the machine. 'It's a myth, you know,' she said, as I wandered across.

'What is?'

'That coffee relieves hangovers.'

'I need the liquid,' I said, 'and water isn't a stimulant.' I punched the buttons and waited for the beep.

Warily, I turned to look at her. She had tilted the PortaVee's screen up off her eyes so she could see me. That was a style I tried to avoid, as I'd always thought it gave the appearance of heavy-browed, half-blinded helplessness. Her legs projected smooth and shiny from the robe, the uppermost's calf and shin pressed into a shape like a hollowed-out canoe.

'I could do with a shower myself,' I said. 'Is it all right if I . . . ?'

'On you go.'

'I'll get the coffee when I come out, then. I don't like it too hot anyway.'

The shower stung. I let it beat onto my face, imagining it penetrating my bloodstream, washing the after-effects of the drug away. I rotated under the jet, allowing the water to play on my back and chest in sequence, lifting my legs into the flow. Through the clouds of condensation and the transparent half-screen I caught a glimpse of yellow.

'I brought your coffee,' she said.

Startled, I bumped my head against the shower head. She giggled.

'Do you make a habit of this?' I enquired.

'A habit of what?'

'Taking advantage of naked men.' Despite my annoyance, I felt again the stirrings of an erection. I turned away from her.

'Only some,' she said. 'You're not embarrassed are you? You shouldn't be. You have an attractive body. I especially like the dimples on your bum.'

'Well maybe I'm choosy about who sees them and when,' I said.

'I thought you liked me. You were coming on to me strong enough.'

'And you said you weren't comfortable with wet hair.'

'Silly man,' she said. As she kissed the back of my neck, I jumped. She slid her arms round me and I felt her breasts pressing into my back. Her hands moved down to cradle my balls. 'Mm,' she said, 'I was right.' Whatever confusion my brain felt, my body had come to a decision.

I turned again and studied her. Her robe was on the floor together with the towel from her hair. She had pushed the wet strands behind her ears, exposing a smooth, slender neck. Her breasts were full and round, nipples erect. The slight curve of her abdomen cut off any further view.

I embraced her, hands exploring the small of her back, the swell of her buttocks. My erection was squashed between our two bellies, arousing me further. Her mouth was soft and yielding, her tongue a strange, alien creature, warm and alive, her breasts a comforting pressure on my chest. She moved her arms onto my shoulders from behind, pulling herself up, legs straddling mine. She was hot and moist, enveloping, and I was hungry for her. Too hungry. I came almost immediately, exploding into her, knees buckling, staggering back into the cubicle wall. She eased herself away and shut off the flow of water. Swivelling back, she swept me with an appraising stare.

'Now,' she said, 'we do it again.'

She was methodical, and knew what she wanted. I was less impatient; explored the damp, dark tufts of her pubic hair, slowly, gently; nuzzled her ears and breasts; stroked her supple skin as her fingers walked all over me and her enigmatic tongue colonised its new-found territory. This second, longer time, she seemed to be satisfied.

Later, we removed our mingled sweat in the shower, delineating the extent of our new sensual landscapes, giggling as we soaped each other's bodies, washing them clean; watched our joined liquids run down arms and legs, to mix briefly before being sundered in the recycler's purifier.

Eventually, towelled and drained, I took a sip of the coffee. 'Shit. This stuff's cold, now,' I complained.

She laughed.

Beyond brief forays into the ship's hinterland in search

of food (I steered clear of more exotic concoctions) the *Strangeness And Charm* remained a blank. Not even an invitation to inspect the engines could have distracted me. My explorations lay in other directions, as did Sile's.

We got past the awkward moments discussing 'Prevent' and feasted on, and off, each other, living for the day. Sexual partners would be sterile if they'd taken Euthuol; but we were both as yet childless and had assumed the other would be responsible about it. Nevertheless it was as well to be sure; neither of us wished to throw away one of our two chances at reproduction on a casual basis, and there were stories of the treatment failing even if only one of a couple were unprotected.

Our shipboard union was scheduled to end at planetfall and we filled the waiting hours with as much mutual activity as we could muster. Between times, Sile danced and I was content to watch, till her glow made its siren call to my, less pure, athleticism. And we talked, slipping into an easy familiarity that belied our short acquaintance. But thoughts of the impending future occasionally broke in.

'I've got a couple of days' rehearsal and then a week of performances,' she said one time. 'What night are you coming to see me?'

'I'll not be able to get away for the first few days, so let's say your last night. Make a party of it, eh?'

'Fine,' she said, 'But I'm due to leave the morning after. Better not be too late a night.'

'Well, maybe the night before, then,' I said.

'You don't sound too enthusiastic.'

'No. No. I want to see you perform. But I'm going to be busy.'

'Doing what? What attraction does April have compared to my dancing?'

'Only some of the finest crushed stone known to Orth,' I said, archly.

She screwed up her face. 'Crushed stone?' she said. 'How romantic. I come second to crushed stone, do I?' I guessed she knew I was teasing her, and was replying in kind.

'I didn't say that,' I said, just in case, adding, 'And you ought to know better by now.'

She pretended to be unconvinced. 'Mmm,' she said. 'What's so fascinating about crushed stone?'

'Not a lot,' I admitted. 'It's used for building, mainly. Cement. Clay for bricks. Basic construction. But some of it has chemical and metallurgical applications or contains various other raw materials. You'd be surprised at the demand. April ships thousands of tonnes of the stuff every day.'

'You should hear yourself,' she complained. 'Can you only think in numbers? Size isn't everything, you know.'

'That's not what you told me earlier,' I replied, grinning.

'Pig,' she said; followed quickly by, 'and I wasn't really that impressed.' I shrugged.

Her expression turned quizzical. 'Isn't it all a bit wasteful?' she asked. 'If it's bulk you want, wouldn't it be easier just to cut up asteroids and shift them? It surely wouldn't use anything like the fuel that must be needed to lift tonnes of stone off planets.'

'It wouldn't; but you end up with all sorts of problems. Say you cut the asteroid up before shipment: then all the tiny lumps orbit about each other, drift apart, clump together. It's a bugger trying to keep track of them all. Shooting that at a target is incredibly difficult. A huge nearby mass would help, but then you've got to get it there and move the lot. It turns out you might as well ship from planet.

'Anyway, there might not be a suitable asteroid within a reasonable distance. And you can't fire one at an inhabited world – too much could go wrong; so again you're left with breaking it up. Even doing that in orbit round the target, you still end up with bits drifting off, falling free, and lumps landing where they shouldn't. It's much safer to work on planets, and with transport ships.'

She was now looking at me with that crooked grin of hers, eyes glinting their mischievous allure. 'It's nice to know you can think of other things,' she said, deadpan.

'You're a sly one,' I replied, sliding on top of her again. 'How did you get me on to that anyway?'

April came too soon.

I felt a brittleness to the last few hours, an uncertainty that crept into the relationship slowly, souring the previously carefree atmosphere with awkwardness, as if the intervening days had never been, and we were as strange to each other as if we hadn't met. Not enough time had elapsed to cement our liaison with the bonds of remembrance and shared experience, of the trust, that makes a parting only the unwonted prelude to a reunion. Our bond was, as yet, a fragile one, neither of us knowing if it would survive even a short separation; nor, perhaps, sure we would want it to.

'You don't have to, you know,' she said, as we prepared to disembark. 'I know you're not crazy on dancing. Maybe you'd like to spend your time off some other way?'

'No. I'll be there,' I protested. 'Just make sure there's a ticket waiting for me. I want to know how good you really are.'

'I'll get you a backstage pass, then; and you can tell me.'

The hoverbus that fetched us from the landing pad was a groaning relic winding its way between the transport ships, whining across the spoor of multi-coloured dust marking the routes the shipment trucks took over the tarmac. A dull ache grew inside me as we approached the bleak spaceport reception area. A grimy place, fly-blown, noises echoed harshly in its voluminous spaces. Few passengers disturbed its rustic tranquillity. The buildings seemed insubstantial somehow, like an abandoned set for a long-forgotten view-tank saga. Beyond them, a scattering of anti-quated cabs flaunted their 'for hire' signs, a deceitful promise of life further afield.

We caressed each other in the midst of that emptiness, her kiss not quite able to remove the corresponding bleakness from my chest. She said, 'See you,' and turned away. As I watched her walk away, enter one of the cabs and depart without a backward glance, the hollowness descended slowly through my guts, as if squeezing me into a much smaller space, leaving a cavern which only Sile could fill.

April was a cruel world, with a cruel reputation. Settled in the ill-documented dark ages of the diaspora, the col-onists had slashed out a meagre living from the dense jungles clothing the lower slopes of its rocky plateaux, augmenting their diet with a smattering of fish hardly wrung from its torrential rivers and capricious seas. Their initial struggle against the ravages of deficiency disease on a planet whose biochemistry supplied few 'normal' vitamins was eventually won by a combination of slowly adjusting metabolic pathways and use of Beribbe root, a tuber the settlers managed to infuse into a concoction which dulled the appetite and assuaged hunger pangs. Their cultivation system provided little else. The advancing wavefront of Orth's expansion took in a stable population with a fragile agriculture geared to April's needs.

The root's effects on unadapted metabolisms changed all that. A feel-good hallucinogenic with no unfortunate side effects, it rapidly became the most sought after recreational drug throughout Orth, commanding outrageous prices. Whole Aprilian forests were cut down and resown with Beribbe to supply Orth's thirst for novelty – and April's inhabitants with undreamt of wealth. Their peculiar metabolisms' inability to assimilate Euthuol fully was regarded by them as a typically Aprilish misfortune, with their new-found affluence some compensation till a way could be found to provide them with all of civilisation's benefits. They indulged in a frenzy of consumption, sampling the delights of Orth, patronising Arts and Sciences, hailing each new cultural icon with more fervour than the last, outdoing even the most avid high-brow aficionados with their enthusiasms. They built grand temples to the gods of Music, Dance and Progress, architectural extravagances perched uneasily amid the more humble structures they had recently inhabited. Some they sited in hitherto inaccessible areas of the planet, exploiting the new thoroughfares the expansion of Beribbe production had spawned.

The mines and quarries I had come to see were less celebrated, seen as a mundane addition to the gross planetary product, but April's geology had furnished ample quantities of workable rocks and there were few inhabitants to disturb. A handful of scattered sites supplied what was now April's only export.

For the planet had again fallen on hard times. Beribbe had been successfully planted elsewhere in Orth, nearer the spiral arm's trade routes, and blight had maliciously struck April's crop, devastating the vast orchards which had sprung up to meet the demand. The trees withered and fell, leaving behind hectares of dust or mud where jungles had once stood. The population dwindled; those who could – metabolisms readjusted to more normal functions and no longer tied to the land by the demands of their bodies – seeking to emigrate while their wealth remained; those left behind, though like their departed compatriots in being able to survive without Beribbe, echoed a previous existence by scraping a living from the planet's surface. At least this time they had the benefit of Orth's technology. And for a short spell, me.

Once you've seen one quarry you've seen them all; the only difference is scale, like with The Hole. There are differences in detail of course, dimension stone for building or facing requires a more subtle technique than the crude (though precise) blasting sufficient for infill or metal extraction; but basically you're just ripping hills apart. In some ways a quarrier is a bit like a surgeon – except that the aftercare is usually non-existent. The landscape's wounds are left to heal themselves.

April's quarries were unlikely economic saviours, small mainly, and providing relatively few jobs, but the stone was high-grade, pure, still much in demand,

and the work was steady. A regular stream of trucks ferried the crushed, eviscerated guts of April's mountains towards the spaceport and greater Orth. None of them detained me for long. I wouldn't have bothered with them at all if Dad hadn't expected me to visit every one. 'Go round the sites, son,' he'd said. 'See the different conditions you might have to contend with.' It was as well that April didn't present too many novelties, because my mind wasn't really on it.

The 'Terpsichorea' where Sile was to dance was a monument to April's good times. A titanium and glass dome designed to be visible from kayem below, with a seating capacity now far in excess of any likely audience, it clung to the slope of its plateau – amid the plethora of hotels, shops and houses which had sprung up to service it – like a maggot browsing on an open wound. The whole complex was a vivid slash through the otherwise green landscape, as if the damaged jungle were bleeding a slowly crystallising sap which wholly failed to prevent the spread of infection.

The aura of decay which hung over what was left of April's brief flowering was accentuated here. A cluster of lean-tos guarded the town's perimeter, stacking up the hillside like discarded wrappings. Within them, ghostly flickerings lit up the blank depths. A few bored men and women, none displaying anything but the vigorous countenances of Euthuol, lingered listlessly in doorways, making fitful conversation with their neighbours or idly ogling the viewing-tanks within. Further on, more substantial dwellings betrayed their owners' neglect with sagging roofs, detached flashings or dirt-streaked windows. The commercial streets were full of rooming houses apparently named 'Vacancies'. Shopfronts gaped empty, tattered curtains drawing grimy veils over the deaths. On the shelves of the going concerns the necessities of life were unattractively laid out for inspection; a smattering of other goods lay forlornly gathering dust.

I paid the cab driver and a couple of women leaning on the wall by the hotel entrance moved forward to show interest, making eyes at me hopefully as I walked past. The shutters were down on the hotel windows: and on a world going nowhere. Only the bright colours of the usual franchises and the tied houses of the licensed drug palaces, with their eternal call to recreational distraction, had leavened the dullness.

The receptionist was bright and efficient, making a good job of selling the place. 'Come for the Dance Festival, have you, sir?' she asked as she typed in my details.

'Ummm, no,' I said. 'I didn't realise there was one on.'

'Oh yes, sir,' she replied. 'The April Dance Festival is famous throughout Orth. I'm surprised you didn't know of it.'

I looked around the deserted lobby where a VT was riveting an invisible audience with curiously fractured, jerky images and said, 'It looks like I'm not the only one.'

'But we're almost fully booked, you're lucky we could fit you in.' My raised eyebrows brought forth a confidential tone, almost obscured by the hum of an ancient printer. 'Our clients prefer to sleep at this time, sir,' she added. 'Late nights you know . . . At the Festival . . .'

I nodded sagely. 'Is there something wrong with that thing,' I asked, indicating the VT. She handed me the hardcopy to sign.

'The lateral control has gone or something,' she said. 'There'll be someone round to fix it, tomorrow. Don't worry about it, sir. The one in your room works perfectly.'

'Oh that's okay,' I said. 'I don't watch much anyway.'

'You'll not be attending the Terpsichorea, then, sir?' she asked, reaching for my room key. 'It's worth a visit. I go as often as I can.'

'Actually I will,' I said, accepting the key. It was her turn to affect surprise. 'One of the dancers is a friend of mine,' I explained.

She paused. 'I see, sir,' she said, sitting back. 'Well, enjoy your stay.'

'I intend to,' I said. 'Oh. One more thing. Can you tell me where I can get some raki round here?'

'Raki, sir?'

'Alcohol-based stimulant,' I sighed.

'Alcohol.' She smiled. 'How quaint. There's not much call for that on April, sir. Perhaps the *Dancers' Arms*?' she mused. 'They get a lot of unusual requests.'

I wasted little time unpacking, pausing only to sort out my dirty washing and send it down to the hotel laundry before eating. As I came out of the dining-room the receptionist called over, 'Package for you, sir.' The nagging thought that Sile might have forgotten me was stilled. The package contained a ticket for that evening's performance plus a backstage pass.

'From your friend, sir?'

'Yes,' I said, showing the receptionist the ticket.

'Mm. Front row, Grand Circle? You are honoured. But then I expect a fine-looking man like you has lots of friends, sir.'

I looked at her closely then. Fringed hair, shiny and dark, cut horizontal above the ears then dropping to shoulder length behind them – a style long out of vogue in less back-of-beyond regions of Orth – trimsuit and matching bolero top emblazoned with hotel logo, hint of superiority in her unflinching green-eyed gaze. 'Enough,' I said, unsure of the meaning of her comment. 'Enough.'

I wandered over to the Terpsichorea early and, despite the pass, found myself having to convince the goon on the stage door I was invited.

'This is highly unusual,' he said. 'Civilians don't normally get in till after the show.'

'I'm only going to see one of the dancers. To let her know I'm here. I'll not be long.'

He admitted me in the end, grudgingly directing me to the appropriate dressing room.

I knocked three times and a small woman, round face made to look almost all eyes by greasepaint, opened the door.

'Hello,' she said. 'Can I help you?'

'I'm looking for Sile.'

'Okay. Come in.' She turned her head and yelled, 'Sile!' to the interior.

I walked in and glanced around. Several dancers in various stages of (un)dress were scattered over the room's area. I recognised none of them. Panic bubbled up as I stared at them in turn, striving to discern some familiar features. The room was lined with mirrors along one side, giving it the impression of greater width, and strewn with costumes and other dancing apparel. Each of the dancers had sized me up quickly and returned to whatever she'd been doing before I entered. I started checking my appearance in the mirrors, beginning to wonder if I'd forgotten what Sile looked like, when she emerged from behind a row of dresses hanging on a rail at the far end of the room.

'Alan. You got the ticket,' she said. She was wearing one of her Titefits plus the inevitable leggings. 'I might have known it,' she added. 'Admiring yourself again.'

I kissed her briefly and stood back to refamiliarise myself with her appearance. Her eyes held the same amused glint I had remembered. Her breasts swelled invitingly beneath the Titefit's constraints, distorting its logo, a sinuous creature covered with long feathers.

We kissed again, longer this time, and one of the others said, 'Mmm. Ruddy will be displeased.' Sile glared at her.

'What?' I said.

'Nothing,' Sile replied, quickly. 'She's just jealous. What have you been doing since I last saw you?'

'Oh you know,' I replied. 'The usual stuff.'

'But I don't know. I've never been to a quarry. Remember?'

'You haven't missed much.'

'I can believe that, but there must have been some-thing interesting, surely?'

'Not really. I pretty much knew all about it before I came.'

'Wasted journey, then?'

'Not quite,' I said, smiling stupidly. 'Rehearsals gone okay?' I asked.

'Yeah,' she said.

'Oh Sile's been enjoying it, haven't you, Sile?' said the same voice as before.

'I've always enjoyed dancing,' Sile said.

'It shows, believe me,' came the reply.

'Is there something I'm missing here?' I asked.

'Ignore her,' Sile said staring at her colleague pointedly. 'She might go away.'

The door opened and a small, sharp-nosed man breezed in, dressed in a gaudy of styles; tight-fitting florid trews, peach-coloured overtop, purple cravat. 'Hello girls,' he said, then, catching sight of me, 'Oh. Who are you?'

'I'm a friend of Sile's,' I said.

'I see.' He frowned. 'You shouldn't be here you know,' he said. 'These are artistes. The slightest disturbance to their preparation can affect their performance.' His hair was slicked over to the side in a manner I hadn't seen for years. As he spoke his hands executed little pirouettes in the air in front of him.

'So what are you doing here, then?'

He drew in a breath, raising his shoulders by a cee-em or so. 'I am the producer of the season's *divertissements* here.' He then essayed a small but theatrical bow which only emphasised the fact that his hair was set rigid, stuck to his head like a piece of moulded plastic. 'Caduceus Ruddy, at your service,' he said.

I looked at Sile incredulously. 'Caduceus?' I mouthed. She made furious eyes at me, warning me not to comment aloud. Ruddy saved me the bother.

'Unfortunately I must ask you to leave now,' he said. 'The performance will begin shortly.'

'Okay,' I said. 'I suppose it's all right if I come backstage after the show?'

'By all means,' he said. 'Be my guest.'

I turned to Sile, 'See you later, then,' I said, and made to kiss her again; but she shied away, pressing her arms against my chest in rebuff.

'Enjoy the show,' she said before I turned away.

'Yes. Do,' added Ruddy as I walked past.

'I'll do my best,' I replied.

The auditorium was a barn of a place, showing the signs of neglect which I had come to recognise as April's trademark. Fading paint, peeling decor and scuffed upholstery contrasted with the bright aura provided by the light streaming through the huge titanium and glass walls. The synthestral sound which boomed from enormous speakers below the layers of seats rumbled from woofer to woofer like a far-off thunderstorm, set up vibrating columns of air between the tip-ups and the punters' legs, echoing tinnily from the vast open spaces of the empty upper tiers – long since left to moulder due to the sparseness of the audiences. Whole ranks of dust-covered seating gaped forlornly towards the stage like the ghosts of a forgotten memory.

The stalls had accumulated a reasonable crowd, though the audience eschewed the peripheral aisles, huddling together in the central area as if seeking mutual reassurance in their choice of entertainment. I was one of the privileged few in the still open Grand Circle, with an unhindered view of the action.

It was a curious experience. My attention was centred on Sile and her appearances, not on the qualities or otherwise of the dance programme itself. I couldn't get to grips with most of it. A bunch of people waggling their arms and legs about in various postures, jumping up and down while careering all over the stage to no obvious purpose seemed futile to me. I could admire the technical aspects of it, the synchronisation, the dexterity, but it didn't touch me. I was shaken, by the music's volume, but I wasn't stirred. I don't suppose Sile was any better than the other dancers, but I recognised her instantly; something in the way she moved marked her out, some subliminally familiar aspect of her carriage or bearing.

The strange dimensions of theatrical presentation were also a puzzle. Used to seeing things in the round on a VT, to cutaways and backshots, closeups and dioramas, the unremitting single perspective from the auditorium was an unaccustomed challenge. I supposed that April's inhabitants had constructed the arena so soon after their regained contact with mainstream Orth that their previous aesthetic sensibilities had prevailed. It was probable that the decline in attendances at the Terpsichorea was in part due to an increasing reluctance by Aprilers themselves to accept such an outmoded convention. More state-of-the-art playhouses elsewhere in Orth featured central stages with all-around seating and performers swirling back and forth across the stage to ensure all angles an equal exposure (an echo of a prediasporic theatrical age Sile later informed me). A certain suspension of disbelief was necessary, in the absence of walls and so on, but the closer resemblance to what audiences had come to expect from VT was less discomfiting than the Terpsichorea's constrained vista. The VT was less work too. Here, I could choose on what to focus my attention, not merely accept what someone had displayed before me.

The evening wearied on, one incomprehensible sequence of cavortings following another, a visual muzak distracting me from the more pleasing symphony sound underground; and Sile. Each dance was greeted with great enthusiasm by the seemingly delighted punters, copious 'Bravo!'s and a deluge of out-of-season Beribbe flowers drowning the final curtain, quite unnecessarily I thought. But I was no judge: still amn't even all these years later. I fooled myself that Sile had bowed to me only, right at the end, then she was skipping off out of sight.

I found the dressing room packed with dancers, punters and various hangers-on, the wall-mirrors all but hidden by garlands of surplus Beribbe. Caduceus Ruddy was expounding in a fulsome manner, praising the dancers extravagantly, raving about the success of the evening's performance. As I watched, Sile accepted a further bouquet from a well-wisher. When she saw me, she broke off and laid it among the others festooning the dressing tables. Her eyes and face were heavily disguised under grotesque greasepaint caricatures.

'What did you think?' she asked.

'You were good,' I said.

'Don't sound so surprised.'

'I'm not. I mean it. You were good.'

'What about the rest?'

'They were all right, I suppose. But it's not really my thing. I wasn't paying proper attention. I only came here to see you.'

'That's sweet,' she said. 'Listen. We can't talk here.'

'Talk!' I interrupted, putting my arms round her. 'I was hoping to communicate some other way.' I glimpsed a suddenly arched eyebrow and a darting glance from the dancer behind her.

'Later,' Sile said, forestalling any further amorous overtures. 'Anyway, you can't stay long. We all need to change. We usually go to the *Dancers' Arms* after a show. Would you mind just slipping in there? I'll get over as soon as possible.'

'No problem. I was going to suggest something like that myself. I hear they even sell raki.'

'Who told you that?'

'Oh, I have my sources. Bulayma Grand is it still?'

'Good boy!' she said. 'I'll have you trained yet.'

'Don't bet on it.' She grinned mischievously.

I kissed her temporarily goodbye and the attempted contact slid off her parodic face. The unpleasant, waxy taste of greasepaint on my lips accompanied me out of the building.

The salon of the *Dancers' Arms* had filled up nicely – punters flamboyantly discussing the night's performance, dancers winding down from their exertions, the usual bored local ladies chancing but finding few takers and resigning themselves to each other's company, even some out-of-place strays in from the streets for a brief illusion of companionship and a dose of forgetfulness which they hoped would stretch the whole evening. A long-discontinued model of viewing-tank hung from the ceiling, plying its wares to the largely indifferent customers, seamlessly recycling archive dance programmes with hardly a flicker out of place to betray its age. The decor was faded but clean, the upholstery, although worn, was sound. The racks of intoxicants behind the counter sparkled their invitations to pleasure. Perhaps the proximity to the Terpsichorea ensured a steady core of clients and a degree of profitability. Whatever, the overall ambience spoke of a more prosperous establishment than the typical April enterprise.

I had commandeered an alcove booth, guarding it jealously till Sile's arrival. Fed up waiting, I was toying with an empty glass, the virgin bottle of raki I was intending to fill it with and an unignited Bulayma

Grand for Sile, testing their triple effect on the balance of the somewhat rickety table in front of me, adjusting their positions carefully in an effort to find a level point of equilibrium. The only pauses in my attempts came when I scrutinised each new entrant to the bar.

At last the door swung open to reveal a crowd of theatricals, Caduceus Ruddy at its centre, with his arms draped round a couple of the dancers. One of his companions was Sile. I half-stood, then collapsed again into the chair, my wave of greeting faltering as I suddenly fathomed the earlier barbed comments of Sile's colleague. Ruddy and his entourage paraded towards the counter. Sile detached herself from the procession and came over.

'Hi. Sorry I've been so long,' she said as she sat down.

A surge of fear and jealousy had thrown my stomach into my throat. 'That's all right,' I managed to grunt. 'I can see you've been busy.' I inclined my head towards Ruddy.

She looked at me strangely. 'He's the boss, Alan. He pays the wages. We're just keeping him sweet.'

'It depends how sweet,' I muttered.

'Don't you know me better than that?' she asked.

'No,' I said angrily. 'I hardly know you at all. I hadn't a clue how you behave off-ship, but maybe I should have done. I did think you might still have been eager to see me.'

'I was. I am,' she protested.

'I've only travelled round half a planet to get here, after all,' I added. 'By the way, that's for you.' I indicated the Bulayma Grand.

She grimaced. 'I'm a bit tired. I couldn't face one right now,' she said. 'Can I have something else?'

I spotted Ruddy wending his way towards us, still supported by a bevy of dancers, each armed with some potion or other. His was a bilious shade of green. 'Why don't you ask your friendly boss to buy it for you? I'm sure he'd be delighted.'

The producer's reedy voice whined over the background noise, 'Ah. Sile's mining friend.'

I looked back at her. 'Have you been talking about me?' I demanded.

'Only a little,' she said.

Ruddy sniggered.

'What's the joke?' I enquired, glaring at him.

He shook his head mildly, 'Nothing, nothing.' He planted his emerald tipple on the table, slipped into the seat opposite, sliding round to be at Sile's side. 'Sit down,' he said to his claque, gesturing them to fill the remaining spaces, then asked me, 'What did you think of our little show?'

'It's not my sort of thing I'm afraid,' I said. 'I couldn't possibly comment.' Pausing, I added, 'Join us why don't you?' Sile's elbow exploded against my ribs.

'I thought we already had,' he commented.

'Yes. Quite,' I said, massaging my side.

'You didn't find the show entertaining?' he asked.

'To tell you the truth,' I replied, 'I was bored. I don't really see much point to all that prancing about.'

His eyebrows arched and he said to Sile, 'I told you you were wasting your time with this one.'

'What have you been saying?' I accused her. 'And what's it got to do with him?'

'Nothing really, Alan,' she said. 'I hardly mentioned you at all.'

My frustration suddenly exploded. 'Right. That's it,' I said, standing. 'I'm out of here. I've had enough knock-backs for one night.' I picked up the bottle of raki and started to walk out.

'Alan!' she hissed. 'Don't be silly. Come back. It's not what you think.'

I turned and said deliberately, 'If you want me, you know where to find me.'

Sile caught my wrist as I made to go. 'Alan,' she chided. 'You're being childish.'

'I came to see you,' I told her, 'I wasn't counting on sharing your time with anybody else. If that's childish I'm sorry.'

'They're my friends, Alan. Do you want me to ignore them?'

'I thought I was your friend. I didn't expect to have to hang around on the off-chance we'd get some time together. And I'm certainly not going to play the unwitting foil of some florid dandy in a cravat.'

At this, Ruddy's companions bristled. He made no comment, just sat there grinning. I removed her hand from my wrist. 'I'm going back to my room now,' I said. 'Mainly to get away from him. You can come or not, it's up to you.'

It seemed a long walk to the door.

Waving my bottle at the receptionist in passing, I said, 'Send me up a glass,' and charged on up to my room.

When I barked, 'Come in,' to the knock, it was the receptionist who entered, carrying not one glass, but two.

'What the hell's this?' I said.

'I thought you might want some company,' she replied. 'They say you ought never to get high on your own.'

'Do they?' I said, grabbing a glass and sloshing it

full. 'Well I don't want to get high. I want to get low. And I don't need your help.' The glass emptied in three swallows.

'I think I should maybe stay around in case you get out of control.' She put her hand on the bottle. 'And we wouldn't like any damage to hotel property.'

'I don't want you here,' I said, wresting it away from her. 'Piss off before I call the manager.'

'I am the manager,' she said.

'Oh.' I thought about this as I refilled the glass. 'So who's minding the shop?' I asked.

'I do employ other people.'

'Do they take kindly to you consorting with the guests?' I sipped this time.

'They don't mind. It's a perk of the job. They get their share.' She took the bottle again and poured herself a tot.

'Don't you have rules about hitting on duty?' I asked. The warmth of the alcohol had spread through my upper digestive tract. Its earliest messengers would already be tumbling their dissolute way through my bloodstream, *en route* to wreak their mildly poisonous havoc on my brain cells.

'None I can't ignore.' She held her glass up to the light, squinted through it before sipping slowly. 'Mm. This stuff's good.'

'Well I like it,' I said.

'So what's the problem? Why do you feel the need to get blitzed?'

'None of your damn business.'

'You don't want to talk about it?'

'No.' I took another belt, felt the satisfying glow travel slowly downwards, imagined the oblivion to come.

'Let me guess.' She toyed with the glass, swirling it round, peering at the contents as if carrying out a divination. 'Your dancer friend wasn't as accommodating as you would like?'

'Don't you have something you should be doing?' I interrupted. 'Other guests to look after?'

'Not as many as I would like.'

'I thought you said you were busy.'

'I was exaggerating. Trade has fallen off a bit.'

'How much is a bit?'

'Let's just say you'll be kind of lonely at breakfast.'

'Well that's the way I'll like it. And I'd rather you found your amusements elsewhere. Leave please. Now. Or I will. And this,' I placed the bottle out of her reach, 'is mine.'

'If that's what you want.'

'It is.'

'Are you sure?' She placed a hand on my arm. 'I mean, I could stay longer if you wanted.'

'No thanks. I wouldn't be good company. I just want to get out of my head. Quickly.'

'There'll be an extra charge for that,' she said, indicating the bottle. 'Carriage.'

'That's okay,' I replied. 'And I promise not to damage hotel property.'

'As long as that's clear,' she said, turning to go.

'It's about the only thing that is,' I muttered.

She paused at the door. 'Shipboard romance was it?' she said, then shrugged ruefully. 'Ah well. You know what they say about spacefarers.' The door closed behind her with a soft click.

'Your morning call, sir!'

I struggled blearily awake, fighting off the dehydra-
tion demons that were battering the inside of my head.
'Not you again,' I groaned as my eyes focused, then,
'Shouldn't you have knocked?'

The manager was gazing down at me, a too-bright-
for-the-morning grin on her face. She had on a new,
body-hugging trimsuit, minus bolero top. 'I did,' she
said. 'You didn't seem to hear.'

I yawned and stretched. 'I must have needed the
sleep,' I said, raising myself on my elbows. I looked
her over again. 'Is this place a one-woman band?' I
asked. 'I thought you said you had some staff.'

She sat down on the bed and leaned towards
me, green eyes smiling invitation. 'There are some
things I like to do for myself,' she said. 'Waking
up handsome men is one of them. I know several
interesting methods.'

I'll bet you do, I thought, but restricted myself to
saying, 'Is that why you're here in person, rather than
paging me?'

'Naturally. Don't you remember last night?'

'I'm trying to forget last night,' I said, sitting up and
rubbing my head.

'I wondered if maybe you'd changed your mind,'
she added. 'And, of course, I'm checking for damage
to the room.'

'See for yourself.' I spread my arms expansively, then
thought better of it. 'The only damage is internal,' I
winced.

As she moved her hand to my chest I could see the
glint of varnish on her nails. 'You want to try one of
my remedies?' she asked. She leant closer, mouth open.
An unnatural gleam around it betrayed the smear of
lipstick. A hint of dullness to her rounded cheeks

spoke of further cosmetology. The remembrance of Sile's greasepaint mask of the previous night leapt into my mind. Pangs of loss and regret accompanied it.

'Eh, no,' I said, putting my hands up defensively. 'I'm still too fragile. A coffee would be fine, though.'

She seemed undeterred, looming closer; and I let her kiss me, feeling the strange slickness of her lips, the urgent probings of her tongue, breathing in the mix of animal and synthetic smells she exuded. Somehow none of it touched me. When she broke off, I drew back and said carefully, 'How about that coffee?'

She held my gaze for a second or so, then stood up and smoothed off her trimsuit. 'You'll find breakfast downstairs,' she said abruptly. 'We stop serving in fifteen minutes.' Her head twitched peculiarly as she turned to go.

I lay back and wondered why I'd turned her down. It wasn't just her attempts at artifice. My dislike of such contrivance hadn't stopped me with women before, biological urgings proving stronger.

Maybe it was simply the flashed reminder of Sile's appearance after the performance the night before and the painful recollections of her preference for Ruddy's company over mine, but that would more likely have prompted an eager acceptance of the manager's offer. Perhaps I was growing up, maturing beyond the contemplation of petty acts of misplaced revenge. Or was it merely the effect of the battering my head was still taking?

Something had changed, I thought. The woman just hadn't interested me. I was no longer the libertine, the avid notcher I had been since I first lost my virginity to Sorene Lerbu one sun-kissed spring afternoon on the wisp-clad hills of Home. In a sudden shock of love and regret I realised that I wanted only Sile and that I'd probably lost her by my selfish behaviour in the *Dancers' Arms*.

I managed to rouse myself, dressed and washed hurriedly, examined the effects of my over-indulgence in the mirror. The eyes were dull and hooded, but they would do. From the waste bin the empty bottle of raki silently mocked my scrutiny, pointing its finger of neck at me accusingly.

The manager was dealing with some sort of complaint as I approached the desk: voices were raised. A bolero once again concealed the contours of her trimsuited torso. She looked up from the exchange, giving me a disdainful stare. To my right, lurid green and purple arcs flickered across the lobby's viewing-tank, adding a further degree of surreality to the fractured images it presented.

I hovered, waiting for the dispute at the desk to end. 'As I said,' I heard. 'There will be someone round to fix it today. We're sorry if it spoiled your stay.'

'It did,' the guest responded. 'There's little enough to do on this backwater. Without a decent VT to pass the time it's just about intolerable.'

'If it's in more than one tank the fault is probably in the feed lines from the receiver,' I put in.

The manager glared at me. 'Who asked you?' she said.

'Sorry,' I said. 'Just trying to help. Breakfast?'

'Yes?'

'Dining-room, is it?'

'Where else would it be?' she growled.

Business couldn't have been as bad as she'd led me to believe. There were several bodies scattered about the room, gloomily consuming the hotel's fare. The coffee tasted awful. I couldn't face solids and the meticulous sculpting by the guest on a nearby table of some greasy cooked concoction into as perfect a design as possible before its consumption irritated me even more. I settled for some fruit juice.

I came into the lobby to find Sile waiting for me.

'Hello,' she said. 'Tantrum over?'

'What are you doing here?' I stammered. 'I mean . . . I thought . . .'

'What?' she prompted. 'That I'd thrown you over? You'd have deserved it. You behaved like a prick last night.'

'That too,' I mumbled. 'But I was more worried about . . .'

She began to laugh, creases of delight animating her face. Behind her, I saw the manager glance in our direction. 'You thought I'd taken up with Mr Ruddy, didn't you,' Sile said, emphasising the honorific heavily. 'Oh Alan. You can't be serious. He's a sleaze-bag. You don't really think I'd be interested in him?'

'Well that's the way it looked.'

'He'd love it, I'm sure,' she said. 'But I'd only ever be a minor diversion to somebody like him. He has too many other options. You now, you I can do something with.'

This contradiction of my worries of the previous few hours had me totally confused. And my brain was still not free of the hammering demons. I stalled for some thinking time. 'We can't talk here,' I said. 'Let's go into the bar.'

When we had settled down, each with a non-intoxicating refreshment to toy with – it was still early after all and I thought we both might need clear heads – I asked her, 'So why did you let me make a fool of myself? Why didn't you tell me any of this last night?'

'I tried, but you were too determined that you knew what's what. I thought I'd let you stew for a bit. And serves you right.' She sat back in her chair and sipped defensively.

'I'm sorry,' I said. 'I didn't think. I guess I was upset because I thought our relationship was in jeopardy. And you've become important to me.'

She flashed me one of her wicked grins. 'Have I?' she said. 'That's nice to know.'

I hadn't noticed the manager come into the bar. As she passed she stooped and said to Sile, 'You'll be lucky to get anything out of him, my dear.'

Sile looked up, startled. Turning to me she asked. 'What was that?'

I grimaced. 'That was the hotel manager,' I explained. 'She gave me the come-on last night when I got back here.'

'Did she now? Well it didn't take you long to get over me,' Sile said in what I hoped was mock indignation. 'I suppose I should have expected something like that,' she mused.

'I didn't say that anything happened,' I protested. 'I turned her down.' Sile nodded approval. 'She tried again this morning, though,' I added, off-hand.

A dangerous glint came into Sile's eyes. 'And?' she said, menacingly.

'Nothing,' I said. 'I told her to piss off.'

Sile relaxed. 'Good,' she said. 'I'm glad.'

'What is it with you women, anyway,' I jokingly complained. 'Can't you leave well alone? Am I marked out as unattached man in need of companion, or something?'

Sile began to laugh again, loud stomach-wrenching guffaws that drew disapproving stares from the bar's few occupants.

'What's so funny?' I asked. 'You'd better quieten down. You'll get us thrown out.'

'Don't you know?' she said through her convulsions. 'She,' she indicated the manager, 'thinks . . . you're not . . .'

I was becoming impatient. 'Not what?' I interrupted.

She got out, 'Interested in . . . women,' before collapsing in giggles once more.

'But . . .' I stammered, briefly confused. I thought about it and shook my head in vigorous denial. 'No. She can't!'

'Oh but she does,' Sile asserted, seriousness returning to her demeanour. 'She wouldn't have said anything if she didn't.'

'No,' I replied. 'She'll only be jealous.'

'Look at the way she's watching us,' said Sile. 'That's not jealousy. It's more like regret – with a dash of pity.'

I glanced over. The manager was gazing in our direction but I couldn't discern anything unusual in her stare.

Sile waved at her, and grinned. The manager's attention was suddenly fixed elsewhere.

'I'm going to talk to her,' Sile announced, getting up.

'What for?'

'To tell her she was wrong,' she said over her shoulder.

I rose to grab her arm but missed. 'You can't do that,' I hissed.

She stopped, turned to question me. 'Why not?'

From her expression I realised Sile thought I had something to hide. 'Em . . . I don't know really,' I said lamely.

Her gaze lingered on me appraisingly. 'Fine,' she said, eventually. 'I'll get on with it, then.'

She marched off and I sat down, watched the exchange. Sile's demeanour was insistent, with short demonstrative gestures. The manager's was at first defensive, then merged into startled disbelief before finally seeming to settle into a cold rage. When she was done, Sile bounced across the room to our table and settled herself with an air of satisfaction.

'What did you say to her?' I asked.

'I told her how big a mistake she'd made.'

'Is that all?'

Her smile broadened. 'And exactly what we're going to be doing shortly.'

'Ah,' I said. 'And what would that be?'

She leaned close and began to tell me.

We did. All of it. Several times.

It was that afternoon when she really surprised me.

'I don't think I'll bother going in tonight,' she said.

I raised myself on one elbow and asked, 'Why not? You're not feeling ill are you?'

'No.'

'So why, then?'

'There's not much point,' she explained, lying back, staring at the cracked ceiling. 'It's not getting me anywhere. I'm just a poxy little member of a mediocre dance troupe in a thoroughly poxy production in the back end of nowhere.'

'What brought this on?' I inquired. 'I thought you enjoyed it all. And I know I'm no judge, but you looked good enough to me.' I began gently stroking one of her breasts again. 'Even with your clothes on,' I joked.

She smiled deprecatingly. 'I'm not improving, Alan,' she went on, shaking her head. 'I can do that sort of performance in my sleep. I'm not getting any challenges.' She paused and sighed. 'I'm fed up with trying to please all the Ruddys in the business.' Shrugged. 'I've no more work lined up at the moment anyway.'

'So what are you going to do?'

She gave me one of her mischievous looks, the sideways kind I eventually learned to recognise as part of her attractions.

'I thought, maybe if you . . .'

'Yes?' I had stopped stroking.

She rose, kissed me briefly. My hand fell to her hip. She pulled back, blue eyes regarding me steadily.

'If you wanted company . . . I'm not trying to push you . . .'

'You won't be,' I said, with more confidence than I felt. I started stroking again.

'Well, then. I could give up the dancing.' My hand stopped once more. 'Go along with you on your trip.' Withdrew. 'We could get to know each other a lot better.' Moved to cup the left side of her face.

'Are you sure? I know how much dancing means to you. I don't want you giving it up just for me.'

'Yes. I've been thinking about it for a long time. I hadn't found anything else I wanted to do, though, till now.'

I was still grinning broadly, at a receptionist I hadn't seen before, when I signed out of the hotel. The manager emerged from her office during the transaction, scowled at us in passing.

Her voice, attempting to placate another guest, drifted back to us. As Sile and I were leaving, the last words I heard were, 'There'll be someone round to fix it tomorrow.'

8

Young At Heart

The caravan whined in along the road from where the rivers met; three huge dust-streaked pantechnicons, blue in colour, disfigured by the jagged stripe logo of OBN news, crammed with VT recording and editing equipment, ground station relay receiver/transmitters and other broadcasting essentials, and the trailer with all the necessary luxuries the highly rated crew demanded as their due when on a field trip. A scattering of off-duty quarrymen, alert to any diversion and eager to make the acquaintance of new faces, hurried to the juggernauts as they came to a halt amid dust-laden gusts dispersing from their collapsing skirts. Whistles of appreciation greeted the first of the newcomers as she descended from the hovertruck, sliding down its curved flank with a casual grace that spoke of reflex, or endless practice. Her OBN trimsuit glittered in the sunlight, its logo flashing streaks of gold as she moved. The murmurs of contentment grew louder as the trailer emptied and the assembled quarriers realised that half the VT crew were women. Each quickly gathered an admiring audience.

I scanned the male crew, rendered all alike in their standard OBN issue, quickly spotting Frazer's familiar blond crop. I walked over, arm extended, and we shook hands.

'Hello, Frazer,' I said. 'Glad you could make it.'

He grinned. 'Hi,' he said. 'Good to see you again,' and without stopping for an answer added, 'It's a bit of a dump, this place, isn't it?' as he looked around.

'Yes, but we call it home,' I replied.

'It's not like the Home I remember,' he muttered, with a grimace.

'Well, I'm only here for a couple more days. I can put up with it,' I said.

Attracted by the noise, Sile had emerged from our cabin. 'What's going on?' she asked as she came over. 'Who are all these people?'

'This,' I said, 'is Frazer. He's an old friend from Home. Frazer; meet Sile, my, ah, companion.' They exchanged greetings, Sile a little warily. This was one of the few times in our relationship I'd sprung a surprise on her.

Frazer smiled approvingly. 'You always did have an eye for the lassies, Alan,' he said. The intended compliment annoyed Sile. It wasn't the sort of remark she took kindly, unless she'd sought it out.

I hastily butted in, 'Frazer's a sound engineer on Chelsea Monday's OBN unit. The others are the rest of the crew.'

Glancing round, I said, 'I don't see Chelsea. Is she not with you?'

'Oh, she never travels with us,' Frazer replied. 'She'll be along later in a hired flier, once we get the equipment set up.'

'But what are you doing here?' Sile asked him. 'You

surely haven't come here just to visit Alan.' She turned on me, her quick intuition worming towards the truth. 'And what interest would Chelsea Monday have in a godforsaken backwater like this?' she demanded. She phrased it like an accusation.

'I told Frazer about Sonny,' I said off-handedly. 'I thought it would make a good story for his boss. You know. Stubborn representative of the old order hangs on until the last. Native Cuprite refuses benefits of Euthuol.'

'You did WHAT?'

Her vehemence startled me. I had expected a less extreme reaction, but she was staring at me in horrified disbelief. 'I, em, let Frazer know about Sonny,' I said, less surely.

'Oh, Alan,' she wailed. 'How could you? Do you realise what you've done?'

'What do you mean?' I asked. 'I haven't done anything.'

'Don't be so stupid. You must know what a huge intrusion like this will do to him.'

'What harm can it do for goodness sake? It's only a few pictures.'

'I think I'll back off here,' Frazer said. 'This is obviously not a good time.'

'Yes. Do that,' Sile snapped. 'And you can take that lot with you.' She indicated the trucks whose crews were now beginning to unload the first of their racks of equipment.

'I'm afraid that won't be possible,' he apologised. 'At least, not until Chelsea gets here.'

'And when's that likely to be?' demanded Sile.

'A couple of hours, maybe. She's sometimes a bit wobbly on the time front.'

'Well she'd better turn right round again when she does arrive,' Sile fumed. 'And as for you!' she added, turning her rage on me once more. 'I'm trying to think up some suitable way to repay you for this stupid, idiotic . . .' Her anger had built up until she could only growl, 'Uhhrrr,' shaking it out like a dog attempting to dry itself. 'How did I ever take up with such an uncaring, unfeeling cretin?' she rapped out before storming off, her gestures forming round her an exclusion zone fortified by the words pouring from her suddenly loosened tongue.

'Sile,' I called after her. 'SILE!' But it was useless. I doubt if she even heard me. I turned to Frazer and gestured with my hands to indicate my general lack of understanding of women and their moods and my total incomprehension of Sile in particular.

'Will she be all right?' Frazer asked. 'I mean, shouldn't you go after her or something?'

'Nah. She'll be okay. I'll give her time to cool off.'

His amused gaze tracked her as she rose up the hill towards Sonny's encampment. Shaking his head, he said, 'Rather you than me, mate.'

'What is all this stuff?' I asked, as I stood around watching Frazer and the others unloading the trucks. 'I know the outlines, but I've always been a bit hazy on the details of how VT equipment works.'

'This here is standard sound equipment; booms, radiomikes and so on,' he said. 'The basic technology's been around for centuries, long before VT. I think it even predates Euthuol; some of the diasporic worlds had retained the capability, or discovered it for themselves. But only Orth has the technology for the viewing-tank.'

'The wonders of Orth culture,' I said, mockingly. 'Semi-eternal youth and 3-D entertainment.' Frazer gave me a worried look. 'Oh don't mind me,' I said. 'Carry on.'

'Well, if you're sure.'

'Yes,' I apologised. 'Sorry.'

'My main problem is picking up a clear, uncluttered sound without the equipment straying into the camera fields. That can be tricky, especially if we're recording in an area that deadens vibrations. Apart from that we're more or less separate from the vision guys. They have to be really careful.

'Quadrax cameras must be set out in the exact 9:4 dimensions of the tank, otherwise the editing programme can't cope and the pictures come out a fuzzy mess. That sets a lot of limitations on where they can shoot. They've got to start rolling at the same time too or their longshots and closeups overlap and give multiple images. There's not much difficulty in a studio – the camera positions are fixed and each camera hardwired into the editor's console – but in the field it's a nightmare. The signals have to be phased correctly and matched to our sound inputs before they're 'waved to the editing truck and downloaded onto a bubble chip.

'At the same time there's a command system operating in the reverse sense, to take the director's instructions to the cameras. If the 'waving control is slightly out you get interference patterns buggering the whole thing up, and you don't know about it until you view the playback from the bubble chip.'

To make up for my earlier flippancy, I nodded sagely at various points during this disquisition (well I had asked), but then, once you've had explained to you, and understood, the intricacies of a Riemer-Tiemann 4X-2B drilling rig (core samples for the taking of) other miracles of technology hold little terror.

'Mm,' I murmured. 'Sounds complicated.'

'Not if you've had as much practice as we have.' He fiddled with a recalcitrant catch on one of the boxes he'd unloaded. 'Damn this thing. It sticks every time,' he muttered. 'Ah! Got it,' he added as it suddenly flew open. 'Whereabouts is this Sonny fella, anyway?' he asked. 'I haven't seen signs of unusual features on any of the guys round here.'

'He stays away from anything that might be called civilisation,' I said. 'Believe it or not that definition includes Roodsland quarry. He lives up over that hill.' I waved my arm vaguely in the direction of Sonny's lodge. 'That's probably where Sile went when she got into that huff. She'll have gone to warn him I suppose.'

'I hope she doesn't scare him off,' said Frazer. 'Chelsea won't be too pleased to have come on a wild goose chase. I've been on the receiving end of her bollockings more than once. It's not a pleasure, I can tell you.'

'He'll not stray far,' I soothed him. 'He's got some mystical attraction towards the outcrop beyond the quarry – tried to rope me into it, in fact. He treats the place like a sanctuary. I think you're safe from a tongue-lashing.'

'Good. I enjoy my job. I'd like to keep it.'

He squinted at the rocky, brush-covered hillside. 'Is there a road up to where we'll find him?' he asked.

'No,' I said. 'There isn't even a path. You're at the arse end of Copper here, you know. Civilisation disappears round the next bend.'

'Damn,' he said. 'Chelsea's not going to like that. We'll have to use her flier to get the equipment up. It'll waste time, and she hates hanging around.'

'Well, is there anything that's portable? We could maybe carry it up. It's not a difficult climb.'

'Not much,' he said, gloomily, 'but I suppose it would be a start. We'll need to scout the location for suitable camera positions, anyway, so we'll discover if that's possible.'

While Frazer and the vision director – a tall, loose-limbed woman named Dorka – were carrying out their reconnaissance, I took the opportunity to make my own investigations. I expected to find Sile at Sonny's lodge, laying out her soul to him, telling him what a miserable, unworthy convert I had turned out to be; but there was no sign of her. He was alone at his fireside, eyes unfocused, contemplating some elusive thing or other in that strange intense way of his. I treaded forward nervously, unsure of the depth of his meditations.

The greasy smell of dumbuck flesh soaked the encampment, rising like a miasma from the congealed remains in his cooking pot. The sharper odour of animal skin added to the blend, wafting from the coverings on his tent and the frame where his food was left to hang.

'Excuse me,' I said, hunkering down beside him. Absently I picked up a few loose stones from the ground around the fire.

His head turned slowly, like a sated predator disdainful of distraction. Impenetrable eyes regarded me levelly.

'Have you seen, Sile?' I asked into the silence. 'The

woman I was with, before,' I explained. 'She went off on her own. Has she been here?'

'The Rock welcomes Its Sons,' he said, nodding gravely to me. 'As It would Its Daughters,' he added. 'But none have sought Its grace today.'

'Damn,' I said, throwing the stones into the middle distance. 'I was sure she'd be here.'

'You are vexed,' he said. 'Sit, talk.' He waved a hand in invitation. 'The Rock listens to Its Children.'

'I really ought to go and look for her,' I protested.

'She will come to no harm. There are no dangers in these hills now. Sit,' he insisted. 'Unburden yourself.'

My squat had become uncomfortable; I was glad to change to a sitting position. 'I don't know that you'll want to hear what I have to say,' I cautioned.

'No matter,' he said. 'The Rock may decide to forgive.'

I frowned but found myself compelled by his curious manner; the disarming openness of his demeanour seemed to invite confession.

'I may have made a mistake – done something which will affect you,' I began hesitantly. 'It angered Sile anyway. She thought it would harm you.' I studied him to gauge his reaction but he remained impassive, staring again into the flames, face as inscrutable as the Rock he revered.

His shock of hair – still too incredibly white for me to come to terms with – hung limp and matted, strands crawling like ghostly fingers across his shoulders. His garments reeked with the aroma of dumbuck, an unsettling earthiness which contrasted with the invisible – because usually unnoticed – fragrances of the trimsuits, tops, trews or varied other apparel which Orth habitually wore. Not until I concentrated on them could I detect the clean, plastic emanations from my own clothing.

Being alone, I had to confront his *otherness* more closely. Previously Sile had always acted as a barrier between us, modulating the conversation, filtering my perceptions, accepting, without fuss, the impossible nature of his existence. The enforced intimacy with him entailed by her absence did not reduce my disbelief in his primitive condition, but only served to emphasise his strangeness. The thought that, perhaps prematurely, I would end my life in such a state filled me with apprehension.

'I didn't intend any harm,' I continued. 'It was before you took me for a Son. I told certain people about you. They will come and disrupt your home for a while. And later, there may be many others.'

'Men of Orth have come before, and never left,' he said, mildly. 'Their works are all around. I doubt there is more harm they can do.' His expression didn't change, as if reserving judgement.

'They will disturb you, clamber over your remaining hills, drive all the dumbuck away with their presence. What will you do for food, if that happens?'

'The Rock will provide,' he said, with calm assurance.

'As to that,' I warned, 'I'm afraid they will seek to have you give up your views and conform to theirs.'

'That will never be. While the Rock stands, so shall I.' He turned his face toward me, held my gaze. 'And the Rock shall stand so long as any of Its Sons remain.'

Was he testing me, or merely seeking confirmation of a suspicion? I felt the guilt rise, flooding my face with the ruddy stigma of my insincerity. I averted my eyes and mumbled, 'I guess.'

I heard him move and felt his touch on my arm pulling me towards him. He brought me close, his proximity revealing his body to have scents of its own. Unusual vapours trailed his movement – mature exhalations, ripened over weeks, maybe months; not like the vapid, deodorised effluvia of a quarryman or miner, nor the wistful lures I was accustomed to tracking over Sile's humps and hollows.

His grip, as before, was strong, the light in his eyes magnetic. His words were whispered, conspiratorial. 'Sons of the Rock are born, not made,' he confided. 'Unless you grow with the Rock, feel Its presence pervade your being, know Its gifts from childhood, to be a follower of Its ways is a mighty challenge: and even given those benefits, the path has proven too hard for most. I know you do not in your heart believe. You wished not to offend an old man, and to please your woman. Your vow was given under duress. Very well. I release you from it. You will leave this place soon, in any case. Better that the faith should die with me than be detached from its wellspring.'

The way he spoke, it seemed the most natural form of conversation; this talk of faith rooted in place and culture. His unbounded sense of worth, of the strength of things held on to for generations, was an alien concept to a young man brought up with the swiftly changing fads and fancies, the immediate gratifications, the reassuring monolithic universality that was Orth. To be sure, a few planets or cities – Mildenbeck, Femazonia, Kola – retained a local flavour, a frisson of difference; a mode of dress, say, or a style of architecture. But the same lifestyle, a standard set of assumptions, a similar list of pleasures, could be found throughout Orth. And those minor differences could themselves be the subject of a sudden craze over the other worlds and satellites. It was as if Euthuol brought with it not only prolonged youth but a deadening of activity. Accepting such a gift tended to be an unquestioning act. Few were willing to refuse the benefit because of an objection to the swamp of baggage trundling behind it.

Sonny's total failure to accept the norms of Orth culture set him apart. His resistance to what was considered an untrammelled good was an odd, almost subversive, peccadillo. But I couldn't decide if it was he, or I, who was the fool. His words made sense for him, and, there for a while, listening to him, for me. But his actions didn't. He hadn't been under the threat of a shortened lifespan when he refused Euthuol. What had he to lose? Then again, his powerful convictions gave him something to cling to when his world was buffeted by forces beyond his control. What did I have beyond a set of ill-formed doubts gained in a brief whirligig through a fragile childhood? If I had a vista of youth unbounded I also had the fear of losing it.

I never felt that I really penetrated the consciousness behind those old eyes; eyes that were at once a warning and a portent. They seemed to have seen all there was to see and to have no capacity for surprise. It was as if I were an actor in a shadowplay, flitting across the stage of Sonny's perceptions with as much effect as a puff of wind. And of as little account.

The immediate relief I felt at his words was soon tinged by anger. What was Sonny playing at? First he curses me with the task of preserving the relict of his religion; and now, with as scant consideration, relieves the burden. Bemused, I tried to stand. His skeletal fingers prevented me.

'It is not in your power to preserve faith in the Rock,'

he said, 'as it is not in mine. I was wrong to ask it of you. And you cannot feel the necessity as I do. My life has been spent here, enjoying Its favours, serving Its will. Your thoughts and destiny lie elsewhere. But the Rock surpasses all. It will stand or fall no matter what either of us may do. Forgive the devices and desires of an old man. I have no wish to lay on you a burden you cannot bear. Go your own way and seek the path of fulfilment for yourself.'

I have wondered since if what he said was just another way of manipulating me, a subtle means of nudging me to his will; but he seemed so genuine, incapable of artifice, that my misgivings began to ease. He was old and frail. Apart from Sile, I was the nearest thing he had to a friend.

I hesitated, unsure what to say.

'Go now,' he said. 'The blood in you is strong; let it course. Find your woman. Make peace and fulfil her. If I had your youth I would not let such a one run free.'

I grinned. 'Thanks for the advice,' I said.

As I was leaving a thought struck me. I turned back. 'Tell me,' I said. 'The initiation rite. Am I a Son of the Rock or not?'

He smiled then, the only time I saw that haunting face betray any light-hearted emotion.

'The Rock accepts all gifts, even of wayward souls.'

'But am I?'

'Whatever is written in your heart,' he said.

Maybe it was due to Sile's absence and the fact that I had to deal with Sonny on my own, or perhaps I was simply becoming accustomed to them, but despite his outlandish appearance and existence and the fears they still kindled in me, I was finding myself more comfortable with him, stumbling towards an appreciation of what his life was all about. As I came away I felt that, in some peculiar manner, strengthened by his beliefs and the hope for the future that they gave him, he may have been younger than me.

9

Chelsea Monday

'I couldn't talk to Sonny. I couldn't let him know how you'd let him down so soon after your promise.'

Sile was perched on the bed in our cabin. Her legs were crossed akimbo under her, her arms pressing down on them periodically as if she were performing some sort of training exercise. A slight puffiness round her eyes also betrayed a degree of distress.

She'd come back early in the morning to find me sprawled, fully clothed, in the chair where sleep had caught me while I waited for her to return. Her hair was tousled, her shoes scuffed and laden with Copper's red dust. She had discarded her shoes and socks to massage her feet while I splashed some water on my face to revive myself. A thin red line marked the gap where her socks and leggings had failed to meet.

'So what did you do, then?' I asked quietly.

'Just walked around.'

'All night?' I said. 'I was worried you know.'

'No need. What could have happened to me? Copper's not exactly a humming metropolis.'

'I don't know. Anything. You might have fallen, broken something.'

'I'm not as clumsy as you,' she retorted. 'Anyway. I wanted to be on my own. I needed to think. I was trying to work out why you'd done it.' She stared at me flatly, the sparkle her eyes usually held totally absent.

'Done what?'

'You don't know, do you?' she said. 'You really don't know.' She shook her head with a kind of bemused sadness, pity almost; then lifted her gaze to look at me. 'It'll kill him, Alan,' she said, matter-of-factly. 'He won't survive it.'

'That's a bit strong,' I said. 'How can a fleeting appearance on VT kill him? We don't know if Monday will even interview him. She might only want pictures. He is . . . strange, after all. Anyway, he's practically dead already.'

'Come on Alan! Grow up. You know how she works. She'll find some angle to make him seem even more disconcerting than he is. I think he deserves respect, not ridicule. How can some self-important, pushy busybody from glittertown be expected to treat him with sympathy? And even if by some miracle she does, think of the attention it'll bring. Copper will be inundated with hordes of people all wanting to see him for themselves, to talk with him. He'll be *pestered* to death.'

'Surely no-one will come all this way just to see Sonny,' I objected. 'He's too damn weird.'

'Oh they will, Alan. Believe me, they will. Sure, some folk will be repelled, think that he ought to be shunned or kept hidden; but there will be plenty eager to touch the hem of his difference. You know how often, and quickly, a craze sweeps Orth after it first appears on the tank. His life will be turned upside down. I don't think he'll want that. He ought to be left alone to die in peace.'

'If that's true then I'm sorry,' I said. 'I hadn't thought of it that way. But maybe he'll want the attention. It'll give him the perfect chance to promote his crazy religion. It might even bring some of his wanderers back to the fold.'

'It will kill him Alan,' she insisted. 'If you haven't managed to before then, it'll destroy whatever hopes he has left. He's hardly had any contact with Orth so far and that was enough to turn his world upside down. What's he going to feel like when he realises how big and unstoppable Orth culture really is?'

'I'm sorry,' I said, 'but it's probably too late now. If it makes you feel better, I told Frazer about Sonny at the Hole, before I'd become an honorary Son of the Rock. I wasn't breaking a promise. Not that I've actually made one, you understand.'

I knew then my stinted apology could come nowhere near consoling her. I think she'd begun to realise I wasn't the person she'd thought I was – had wanted me to be – and to suspect she wouldn't be able to change me. She'd be surprised if she could see me now, still – despite everything – interrogating mirrors about the nature and mechanics of ageing, pondering her influence on the course my life has taken. Still wondering if, maybe, the nudge she would give me was a conscious attempt on her part to manipulate me. If it was, then I guess it worked.

For the moment, all she did was give a kind of snarl of disgust at my grudging words and fling herself back on the bed. 'Go away, Alan,' she said. 'I want to be alone.'

*   *   *

The flier announced itself with a deep sonorous drone, building in pitch and amplitude to an ear-shattering shriek as it dropped out of the gathering cloud. The flutter of its rotors, stabilising the descent as it slowed for landing, could barely be heard above the roar. The relative silence as the lateral jets cut out was a delusion. I still struggled to hear Paczai's comment over the downblast of the chuntering blades.

'What?' I shouted.

'I could have done without this,' he yelled. 'We're behind schedule as it is, and with wages day coming up I didn't want any more distractions.' The pair of us were standing with hands ludicrously holding onto our hard hats, as if the wash of displaced air from the flier were about to blow them off, though it was hardly strong enough. Around the pad (a roughly cleared small area for emergency evacuations or unexpected visits such as this), other buffeted groups hovered in similar undignified poses, waiting to greet the new arrivals. Frazer's VT crew was prominent beside the off-duty quarriers.

'I shouldn't worry too much,' I replied. 'She's not likely to be a distraction to the work. She's here to film Sonny, not the quarry.'

'But she's a celebrity,' Paczai said. 'The men will want to meet her.'

'I suppose,' I acknowledged. 'I guess we could ask her to speak at some sort of get-together, but she may not have the time.'

'It might not be a problem,' he said. 'Don't forget this place will be deserted come wages day.'

'How could I?' I replied. 'I'm supposed to be leaving too.'

The flier had settled down gracefully, curtseying with

a hiss of hydraulics as its suspension took the strain. The remaining engine's note dimmed during its long diminuendo through the octaves. The blades bent as they lost momentum – their chatter reducing to an intermittent whup like a reluctant starter motor's – before finally collapsing. They sighed down like four deflating penises, surrounding the craft as if with some perfunctory protective skirt.

One of the VT crew scurried up to the flier and pulled at its door. After a short interval out stepped the figure of Chelsea Monday, OBN news's main reporter, familiar from countless tank appearances mediating Orth culture to viewers avid for new trends and experiences amid the otherwise seeming changelessness and stasis of their everyday lives, chronicler of peculiarities and oddities to those eager to imitate and extend them, single-handedly responsible for more crazes and trends than any other contemporary cultural icon. Her trade mark ribbonshades and sun hat (worn in even the dullest of conditions) had been the first aspect of her celebrity to be aped slavishly across the spiral arm. Wherever the influence of Orth – and the tentacles of OBN, portraying her rounded image in millions of viewing tanks – reached, sales of Monday dolls burgeoned, a thousand Chelsea trendies bloomed, child and adult replicas abounded. Later, the interest of the novelty thirsty had spilled over into the subjects of her attention. The nature of hyperspace travel and communications, with the accompanying delays and interplanetary longueurs, meant, sometimes, stumbling into an apparent time warp where the locals displayed all the flashings and accoutrements of a Chelsea trend long since abandoned in less remote parts; perhaps even a fashion whose vogue had been so brief that you had quite forgotten it (or so outré that to forget was a blessing).

Other VT stars had their partisans and devotees but none exerted the same influence as Chelsea Monday. She had made her name by ferreting out and doorstepping Leesa Layne, a former VT starlet who had dropped from public ken – giving rise to the odd rumour – several years previously. Chelsea – the familiarity had swiftly become ingrained – eventually wormed an interview from the hitherto elusive recluse. She proceeded to cajole the reluctant interviewee into bizarre revelations about her private life, involving early transvestism followed by regular sex changes, unusual *ménages* and exotic carnal appetites.

Chelsea had continued to seek out the strange and the oddball, descending – after a decent interval to allow the latest beneficiaries time to acclimatise to cultured ways – on the new life and civilisations of the gradually expanding sphere of Orth, exposing any strange quirks to the ever-hungry media desire for difference. Her piece on the Alban system of disfiguring criminals with indelible facial markings (an initial shock to a culture more used to the concealment of any such blemishes) had still managed to inspire a particularly long-running mania for cosmetic purple patches – inevitably dubbed 'beauty spots' – and had arguably paved the way for later experiments with unusual facial adornment such as the Femazon sisterhood had adopted.

She didn't ignore the unusual byways of more solidly Orth planets. Her documentary about the Femazons themselves had famously boosted both their membership and tourist trade as their peculiar attractions captivated, each in their different way, the widest spread of Orth humanity.

As far as I knew she hadn't yet got round to the Trevi on Mildenbeck, a manifestation of distinctiveness which, to me, cried out to be disseminated more widely; but I had meant to speak with her about it. Certainly, when I'd met Frazer I'd surmised Sonny would be a natural for her, and he had seemed to agree. But now, with Sile's reaction to her arrival, I had begun thinking about Chelsea's record. I hadn't yet realised that, for some, life in Orth became so stale that it was necessary periodically to reinvent it but it was finally, slowly, percolating through to me what Sile had seen instantly. Sonny wasn't – could never be – ready for any of this.

As Chelsea Monday strode across the landing area towards her technical crew, ribbonshades glimmering even in the dull light of the deepening overcast, her one concession to standard OBN garb the bright golden reversed N sigil that adorned her sun hat, I looked round guiltily to our cabin. Sile was standing by the door, arms crossed defensively as if in denial of the scene but yet unable not to watch. Her foot scuffed along the ground as she stared determinedly downwards, apparently intent on the patterns she was creating. A thin curtain of Copper dust hovered around her like a veil.

Paczai nudged me. 'Do you suppose she'll give me her autograph?' he asked. Escorted by Frazer and a flotilla of technicians, Chelsea Monday was striding towards us.

'From what I've heard,' I replied, 'she'll as likely chew your head off. Or something else.' I reduced my tone to a whisper. 'She's supposed to have a yen for outdoor types,' I confided. Paczai's demeanour immediately brightened, his mouth pursed and eyebrows raised in delicious expectation.

As the introductions were made I stole a glance at Sile. She regarded me evenly, cold and hard across the space that separated us. What did she want me to do? There was very little that was in my hands. Any mistake I had made in telling Frazer about Sonny was too late to remedy now.

'So where's this native?' Chelsea asked when the formalities were over. 'I don't see anyone out of the ordinary here.'

It was strange to hear that voice unmodulated by a VT set. The timbre was the same, but there were overtones which the tank did not convey; a kind of stretched whininess.

'Oh he's never been down here,' Paczai replied. 'He shies away from Orth and all its works.'

Chelsea tilted her head, the metallic coating of her ribbonshades refracting curious purple rainbows – yellows and greens strangely absent from the dancing images – as she gazed from face to face. Red and blue fractal reflections shimmered from the lenses. Her faded blue sun hat cast hardly any shadow over her hidden eyes. Behind her, the flier lay forlornly, its drooping rotors like a flop-eared quickrabbit. The jagged stripe OBN logo gave it a surreal air of abstract camouflage, designed to stand out rather than blend in.

A few strands of lank mousy hair strayed from beneath her sun hat's rim. She pushed them carelessly behind her ears. Her strong jaw-line jutted arrogantly. 'So when do I meet him? I'm a busy woman. I don't have time to waste.'

'He lives up yonder.' Paczai gestured vaguely at the nearby hill.

'Well let's go, then,' said Chelsea. 'Fetch a hovercab.'

Paczai and I looked at Frazer, barely suppressing our laughter. He shook his head at me warningly.

'I'm sorry. We're in a backwater here,' Frazer said apologetically. 'There isn't a road.'

She rounded on him. 'What do you mean, there isn't a road?'

'What I said. You can't take a vehicle up there.'

'We'll use the flier, then.'

'Sorry,' Paczai put in. 'No overflying the quarry. Regulations. There isn't a landing pad up there anyway.'

'Do you mean I'll have to walk?' she squawked, plainly horrified at the prospect.

'I'm afraid so.'

She hesitated for a moment, glanced at the flier, the crew, the assembled quarrymen, on the point of quitting; then strode ahead, up the hill. 'This is the last time I ever listen to one of your ideas,' she shouted over her shoulder at Frazer as she went.

I turned to look at Sile. She gave back my gaze as evenly as before. I gestured at the departing VT crew, shrugged impotently. She flicked her wrist dismissively and turned away. Slowly at first, I moved off to join the crowd following Chelsea. Contrasting with my mood, tiny bubbles of mirth were still occasionally bursting between them as I caught up.

Chelsea's pace soon slowed and she stopped dead when she remembered she'd no idea where she was going; whirled round to demand a guide. Frazer aided her for a while, pointing out the easiest path. Chelsea hobbled awkwardly among the stones, pausing frequently to catch her breath. From the angle I had as she laboured up the hill, one which she did not habitually present for a VT closeup, it was obvious she filled her OBN trimsuit all too well. I wondered if, perhaps, the rumours were true and the only exercise she normally indulged in was of the horizontal variety.

When I finally came abreast of Frazer, pulling him back gently from the wheezy tirade of abuse he was still suffering, I asked, 'Why did Paczai tell her she couldn't fly over the quarry? There's no rule about that.'

'I had him primed,' he explained, gleefully. 'I've been waiting for a chance like this for years. I wanted to see the look on her face when she realised she had to make some effort, put herself out for a change.'

'Are you sure it's been worth it? She's going to make your life hell, I'd guess, and she doesn't look as if she'll last long at this pace.'

'She'll get over it,' he said. 'Don't let her fool you. She's as tough as old boots, really. Lots of stamina. And she needs me. She won't make my life too unbearable.'

The noise we were making was certainly enough to warn Sonny of our approach and his camp appeared deserted as we broke into the clearing. A quartet of quadrax cameras framed the site. Sound equipment lurked beyond the fringe. A few wisps of smoke hung above Sonny's fire, rising sluggishly in the dampening air, fanning out into the lowering cloud base. A single bowl hung from the spit above the crackling logs. The skin was gone from the frame, probably to increase the pile inside the lodge. The flap covering the lodge's entrance was closed over but not tied down.

'Is this it?' Chelsea asked. 'Is this what I've come all this way to see? What a hovel.' She checked the camera positions, glanced at the recording decks and wandered across to the fire. She sniffed at the bowl's contents, wrinkled her nose in disgust. The aroma of cooked dumbuck mixed in with the less pleasant odours of the fibrous vegetables filtered over the clearing. She dipped a finger into the bowl and jerked it back again quickly. She repeated the experiment more cautiously, licking the finger afterwards. Her expression was one of grudging appreciation. 'She hasn't tasted the damned vegetables,' I muttered to no-one in particular.

'Where is he, then?' Chelsea asked. 'I don't see much sign of life.'

'I think you'll find that's rather the point,' I mumbled to myself. More loudly I offered, 'I'll see if he's in the tent.'

I moved over to the entrance. 'Sir?' I enquired. His thin voice replied, 'Enter.' I held up the flap and stood in the doorway. The overpowering animal stench rose to meet me, seeming stronger than last time. He was sitting on the pile of skins, the shadow cast by my body shielding his face. I let the flap fall and went in. The remaining illumination, seeping through the stitch-holes of the fabric walls, was surprisingly bright given the dull sky outside.

He greeted me gravely, as before. 'The Rock welcomes Its Son,' he said, bowing a little in acknowledgement.

I hesitated, embarrassed at the imminent disruption to his life, finally ashamed I had set it in train. 'The, em, people from Orth have arrived,' I said, haltingly.

'They have been here some days, I think. The dumbuck are disturbed. I retired here. No matter. They will leave soon.'

'This group wish to make pictures. Of you, your lodge, your food, your way of life. They will show these far away, encourage others to come. They also wish to speak with you, record what you say. Your words too they will take far away, repeat to others – perhaps to ridicule you. It may be that some will come to pay respects, even desire to become Sons of the Rock, but it is more likely that visitors will scorn you and mock your beliefs.

'I'm sorry, but I doubt there is little you can do to stop the picture making. It may be best for you to cooperate with them, say what you want to say. But even then you will have no control over the way you are presented. Forgive me for causing all this.'

'It is of no moment,' he sighed. 'The Rock wills as It wills. Its workings have ever been a mystery to me. I am an old man and must accept what befalls.' He straightened, breathed deeply. 'But we have more pressing affairs to discuss.'

He leaned forward, grasped my arm lightly. 'Tell me,' he said, softly. 'Are you reconciled with your woman?'

Already flushed with the guilt that Sile's unexpected reaction had thrust on me, his quiet solicitude was devastating. Facing a potential threat to the settled pattern of his life's gentle coda, a discord I had helped to bring about, he was more concerned for my wellbeing than his immediate predicament. The stirrings of respect and understanding that had been rumbling in my brain like a distant thunderstorm began to grow louder. Despite his grotesquerie, and its insistent reminders of my own unconquered – unfaced – fears, I had developed a degree of affection for him.

As if in sympathy I found my speech taking on his orotundities. 'Alas, no,' I replied. 'I am afraid I have displeased her too much for easy forgiveness.'

'A woman of spirit,' he said. 'I remember a few such.

With them,' he mused, 'you must weather the storm, let it break against you. They blow themselves out in the end.'

I grinned and said, 'Sile's storms are fierce indeed. I fear she may be gathering her strength. I may be in the eye of the hurricane with further blasts to come.'

'She cares for you, my Son,' he said. 'She would not rage so, otherwise.'

Sometimes, in the intervening years, I have thought that maybe he was as manipulative in his way as Sile. What better way to seduce me to his purpose than to pretend to empathise with me, to take on my troubles as his own? To offer me advice from the heart? But I have never managed to convince myself of it. Pretence was the last vice you could associate with him. His take-me-as-you-find-me attitude was no veneer of falsity, no inverted vanity. His whole experience proclaimed lack of artifice. His denial of Euthuol was, I suppose, the ultimate expression of that rejection of semblance. As such, it had become transubstantiated, something sacramental. Ageing does make a difference, does set you apart.

'Her anger is more with herself, I think,' I replied. 'She's wondering how she came to be mixed up with such a selfish, thoughtless idiot as me.'

'Do not be hard on yourself. I am sure you meant no malice.'

His forgiveness and understanding, while welcome, was misplaced; based on a misapprehension. He, who had rejected Orth on first contact and been ignored, the touchstones of his way of life marginalised as a result, made irrelevant, could not really conceive the depths of the larger culture's power, the insistent pressures created by its shallower manifestations.

'Have you decided?' I asked him. 'What shall I tell the picture-makers?'

'Let them do what they will,' he said. 'It means nothing to me.'

'They are waiting for you now, if you will come outside.'

'As you wish,' he said.

I offered him my hand, helped him to rise from the pile of skins. I stepped outside first and stood holding the lodge flap open for him. The VT crew was in a huddle near the fire, sycophantically clustered round Chelsea.

At the edge of the clearing a familiar figure hung back. I studied her demeanour carefully, hoping that there would be some break in her resolve, a glimmer of reprieve, but she glared at me relentlessly. Sile had come for no other reason than to witness the full depravity of my conduct, the culmination of my act of betrayal.

I supported Sonny with my arm as we waited for Chelsea. The impatience she had felt at the delay while I had talked to him was demonstrated as she pushed free of the group and strode towards us. A hushed silence fell as she came closer, breaths were held in anticipation of her reaction. Her involuntary expression of shock, open-mouthed as she absorbed the details of Sonny's appearance, was soon hidden behind her mask of professional detachment. The silence remained, throbbing with tension, as she examined Sonny minutely. All eyes save hers and Sonny's were fixed on Chelsea as she walked around the pair of us like a politician uneasily inspecting a guard of honour. His fastened on Sile, whom he acknowledged with a slight bow. The small movement distracted her momentarily, bringing a brief animation to her features as she smiled in return. She reverted to her belligerent stare as I glanced at her once more.

Chelsea walked round us once, then again, head traversing up and down, her ribbonshades strobing lilac as she scrutinised Sonny's body, lingering on each unusual aspect in turn. Her nose wrinkled as she caught the wafts of his ripe smell. She came between us and the fire, gazing full on Sonny's improbable face. He regarded her serenely as was his way, but his bearing silently put a question she could not dodge.

A muscle in her cheek twitched. She opened her mouth; shut it again, then paced backwards. She gazed at Sonny for a few more seconds, shook her head, snapped, 'No. I'm not doing this,' turned on her heel and walked off, down the hill.

10

Wages Day

A pandemonium of grumbling VT technicians followed in Chelsea Monday's wake, voices raised in agitated debate. Across it, through the flow, danced Sile in that poised way of hers, swaying with perfect balance between the obstructing bodies, elegantly bobbing over to where Sonny and I stood watching the departing throng. I was eager to join them to find out why Chelsea had opted not to proceed but I also wanted to make sure that Sonny was unperturbed by the fuss, and to have a word with Sile.

Relief was flooding through me. Chelsea's unexpected decision had given me the reprieve I needed. Sile would be pleased, I was thinking. Sonny's life would not be turned upside down now, not be exposed to the VT's prurient gaze, nor the subsequent intrusion of the masses.

Sile covered the last few paces slowly. She ignored me. 'Are you all right?' she asked Sonny.

He looked at us both in turn. 'The Rock wills as it wills,' he said, evenly.

'I think we needn't worry,' I said. 'Everything's going to be all right now.'

Sile glared at me. 'Is it?' she replied. I could see her anger was still hot, stoked by internal combustion, with no outlet since our last confrontation. The steam had to go somewhere. 'Or are you still the same heartless bastard you were yesterday?' she added.

Sonny put his hand on her arm. 'Peace, my child,' he said. 'Do not distress yourself. Accept the will of the Rock, as I do. Your friend here is a good man at heart, I'm sure. He meant no harm.'

'It didn't stop him being stupid, though,' she said. 'I don't want to be anywhere near him. I only came over to see you were all right. Now I'm satisfied you are,' – she turned to glare at me again – 'I'm leaving.'

'Would you at least stay and talk to him about it?' I asked her.

'No. You stay,' she replied. 'You're the reason all this mess happened. Clear it up yourself.' She strode off in the direction of the woods.

'But if he doesn't mind, why should you?' I called after her.

'Perhaps I can't stand hopeless idiots,' she shouted back, over her shoulder.

I looked at Sonny. 'This is going to be harder than I thought,' I said.

The argument had continued all the way down the hill. It was still going when I finally came within earshot.

'We can't use it. We can't use *him*,' Chelsea was saying. 'I've got my image to think of,' she went on. 'I'm not appearing in the same tank with anything as ugly – as disgusting – as that.'

'Let me do it, then. Put my byline on it,' said Frazer. 'Just a small piece. Everything is set up, for God's sake.'

'You!' Chelsea exploded. 'What do you know about doing a piece to camera?'

Frazer's view of her professional mystique was jaundiced. 'Come off it, Chelsea,' he said. 'I've seen you working. It's not that difficult. All I'll have to do is stand up and speak. Or not even that. I could just ask him questions with an over-the-shoulder shot.'

Chelsea paused in her descent, causing a hold-up in the line struggling down the narrow path. I cannoned into the crew member immediately in front. 'Sorry,' I mumbled, peering round her as she stuck her arms out for balance, steadying myself with a hand on her waist.

Chelsea was appraising Frazer closely. 'You seem to have all this worked out,' she said. 'How long have you been planning to get rid of me?'

'What?' said Frazer. 'Don't be ridiculous. It just seems a waste to come all this way for nothing. And if you won't do it . . . ?'

The technicians were slipping into a rough ring round the pair, quietly assessing the clash, wondering where they might have to jump next. It wasn't my concern so I hung back a little, not wishing to become involved. Beneath her sun hat the ribbon of Chelsea's shades flashed briefly, a line of pale lilac glimmering in the increasingly dull light.

I sensed a subtle balance of power lay behind Frazer's pause, unstated implications lurked in the gap. He stood up to her hidden gaze, steadily searching her face for a focus point.

Chelsea didn't hesitate for long. 'I'll think about it,' she said and restarted her downhill progress.

Frazer took it as a concession, levered for more. 'You won't regret it,' he said as we all surged after

her. 'I'll do a good piece. One you won't be embarrassed by.'

'I only said I'd think about it!' Chelsea snapped. 'And
I didn't say I'd let my name anywhere near it.'

'Sure thing, boss,' said Frazer. 'Anything you say.'

We filed out onto the broader sweep of the lower
slope. A rumble of thunder sounded in the distance,
the crew members quickened their paces.

The cloud had descended almost to the quarry's tip,
a dark shapeless mass stretching into infinity. Above
the workings, like a circle of fire on the dark ceiling
of the world, its base was lightened by the glow of the
lamps. A stream of men and vehicles was passing from
the quarry's mouth to the cluster of huts. Chelsea's flier
huddled forlornly, like a lost geep, totally exposed in its
landing area.

'Alan? You don't stop for rain do you?' Frazer asked,
indicating the homeward plodding quarriers.

'Sometimes,' I said. 'But not on this scale. Anyway
it's not raining.' I looked up at the sky again. 'Yet,' I
added. 'Every three months or so the place shuts down
for a few days,' I explained.

'Is that for maintenance?' Chelsea enquired.

'Not really. We can do most of that on the job. It's
only something really big, like some of the stuff at the
Hole, that would need special care and attention.'

'Why stop, then?' she asked. 'Why not keep running
all the time.'

'The men need the break,' I told her. 'A small
operation like this doesn't carry enough staff to justify
staying open. The Hole might; but even there it's really
a whole series of smaller workings lumped together.
Come wages day the men like to disappear to the
nearest spaceport to blow some of their earnings.'

Chelsea's journalistic instincts twitched. 'You said men,' she probed. 'Are there no women quarriers?'

'Not here,' I said and started to parrot the Orthrocks line. 'There are a few elsewhere. Not many women seem to want to do this kind of work but I think there's a woman-only group at the Hole. The company found the imbalance in mixed-sex squads to be disruptive,' I explained.

'Hmm,' Chelsea said, clearly unconvinced. 'How come your girlfriend gets allowed?' she asked.

'Special case,' I said. 'Only here for a few days. And definitely off-limits. Anyway; you're here.' I gestured at her VT crew. 'And this lot. There's no big deal. It's just a matter of ensuring efficiency,' I added primly.

Chelsea shrugged. A few heavy raindrops pattered down. We hurried towards the huts.

'So what do they do?' she asked.

'What do you mean?'

'The men. For relaxation?'

'Watch the tank mostly,' I said. We were approaching the common hut at the hub of the living quarters. 'You've got a few fans here.'

'Only a few?' She sounded disappointed.

'Well. You know,' I said, pushing open the door. 'They like to keep up to date.' The viewing-tank which gave the room its focus was showing an episode from the latest hit soap, a thrice-weekly dash of supposedly gritty realism set in a dreary inner-city area on one of Orth's more ancient planets. (Thrice-weekly at Orth's epicentre of course. Out there the discs were delivered en bloc weeks later, providing a diet of comforting pap among the more raunchy fare the workers actually preferred but which they'd sidelined in deference to the new visitors. It's probably still running somewhere, along with all the other half-remembered ratings busters of my youth, beamed through SHIFT relays to whoever has the necessary decoding receiver; endlessly recycled for the benefit of new viewers or those who'd forgotten how bad it had been the first time round.)

As Chelsea entered, a cheer rose from the assembled gathering, mingled with a few whistles and rude catcalls. She waved graciously to acknowledge the greeting, put on a dutiful smile and strode into the room. She was quickly surrounded by an unlikely clutch of burly acolytes, eager to bask however briefly in fame's reflecting gleam. I slipped out and set off to look for Sile.

The rain was hard and steady as I scurried towards our hut. It drummed on the roofs, bounced knee-high from the hard-packed ground and was already turning the dusty pathways into a greasy obstacle course dotted with shallow pools. I cursed as I skidded on the treacherous surface, slid to a halt by the hut door.

As I surmised, she wasn't there. I changed into some sturdier footwear, threw on a waterproof topcoat, grabbed one of Sile's and braved the elements again. By the time I found her, sheltering in the inadequate protection of a scrubby tree up on the ridge, we were both soaked through.

Rain had plastered her hair to her skull. Her leggings were sprinkled with glistening streaks where the rain had run down them. The excess weight they had accumulated had dragged her socks below her ankles. Her saturated Titefit tightened close, delineating her contours. The bottom of her rib-cage stood out sharp in a shallow inverted U. Breasts swelled against the fabric. Her nipples showed through, erect with cold. I thought of how they looked unconfined, like over-ripe berries sprouting from the darker skin of her aureoles, her breasts swinging above me; the feel of them on my tongue, between my lips. Lust stirred hopefully but I knew this wasn't the time nor the place. She rubbed a dribble of rainwater from her nose with the back of her arm.

'Here,' I said, handing her the coat I'd brought.

'Thanks,' she sniffled. I waited as she struggled to push her wet arms into it.

'It doesn't make any difference, you know,' she said.

'What doesn't?'

'This,' she said, tugging at the body of the coat. 'I still hate you.'

'I'm sorry,' I said.

'For what?'

'Everything,' I replied. 'Nothing. I don't know. What can I do, Sile? You seem to have set your mind against me. I didn't mean any harm, you know.'

'That's not the point.'

'What is, then?'

She paused for a moment, accessing the catalogue of offences. The rain continued to spatter on the leaves above, providing a percussive accompaniment to our discussion. 'You're thoughtless, and selfish,' she explained evenly. 'You're entirely self-centred. I know you've got problems, Alan, but why can't you think of others?'

'I do,' I said. Catching her sharp look I added, 'Sometimes,' in a lame attempt at humour.

It didn't work. 'I don't think I can take sometimes,

Alan,' she said, earnestly. 'I'm not that sort of person. I think I need more commitment. For me, it's all or nothing.'

Large raindrops were spilling from the overhanging branches, dripping steadily all over us. Several had fallen on my neck and started worming their way down my back.

I shivered. 'Come on,' I said. 'We might as well go back to the huts, get some shelter.' I turned to go.

She caught my sleeve, pulled me back. Stared at me as if performing some particularly difficult divination. Her expression was strange, inscrutable.

'I'm leaving tomorrow,' she said.

'I know. It's wages day. Everybody's leaving. Next stop Home.'

'No, Alan,' she said wearily. 'You might be going Home. I'm not. I meant I'm leaving you.'

'What?' I said. Adrenalin rushed from its glands, churning the nearby stomach muscle, constricting my throat in panic.

'I doubt you'll change, Alan,' she went on. 'I might as well give up on you now.' A straggle of hair darkened almost to blackness by the rain had flopped over her right eye. She pushed it back, wiped the moisture from both cheeks. 'It was a mistake. I thought I knew you but I didn't.' She shook her head sadly. 'It wasn't going anywhere.'

'But . . . But . . .' I croaked.

'It's not just Sonny,' she said. 'Though if things had worked out differently here . . .' Her sentence hung broken-backed, an incomplete bridge across the gap between us, summing up the 'ifs' and 'maybes' of our short relationship.

I finally found my voice. 'I thought we were good together,' I said. 'Something special.'

'Maybe we were for a while. But it's been missing lately. Ever since Maratak.'

'You never said anything,' I complained. 'And you seemed happy enough a couple of days ago, here, on Copper . . .'

'You were a different person, then,' she said. 'I see that, now. Don't you?'

'No,' I protested. 'I'm the same as I've always been. Maybe it's you that's changed. Or your perceptions. But I can tell you one thing. My feelings haven't.'

'It's no good, Alan. I've made my mind up.'

I tried another tack. 'But what will you do?'

'Go back to dancing. What else?'

'Will you at least come to Home with me? Please?'

'What for? It's over, Alan.'

'I love you, Sile. I don't want you to leave.'

'Don't pull that emotional blackmail stuff. You don't love me. You only love yourself. Or the inflated image you have of yourself. You'll get over me. Your sort always do.'

I thought at the time that she could have been right, if a bit harsh. Maybe I didn't love her. Not in this mood anyway. This was a side of Sile I hadn't seen before. One I didn't like. A cold, hard, calculating, implacable wall.

And she had seen through me to the essence. I *was* more concerned with my feelings than hers. I felt sick dread at the thought of losing her, her not being there for me. But that didn't necessarily mean I didn't care. I still do, all these years later. No-one else has taken her place in my heart. Or is that just me being sorry for myself?

I was glad of the rain on the long silent walk to the huts. It disguised the other moisture trickling down my face.

Music was playing in the communal hut; shafts of light from its windows speared the gloom outside. Dried and changed, I hovered at the door of our cabin, the party's noise muffled by distance and the intervening rain. I didn't feel in a party mood.

Sile had made it plain she didn't want my company, refusing to let me in while she freshened up and I got gradually more saturated. She had emerged eventually and made her way over to join the revellers. I think I was supposed to stay and suffer alone, but I needed to do something to occupy myself.

The noise blasted at me as I opened the door, loud pounding music from the VT underlaid by voices raised to compensate for the din. I couldn't see Sile at first; my eyes took time to adjust to the higher light levels. The tank's display medium was filled with ever-changing gobbets of colour, bright globules falling over each other, merging, elongating, splitting then remerging while other, darker flashes strobed through them in time to the music. The tables had all been pushed to the room's rim to clear an area for dancing. Dotted around like galactic clusters, small knots of interest centred on each of the women, dancing or not. I flicked my gaze over them. Sile was in a corner talking to Frazer and two other men from the news crew. She looked up, saw me, turned her back.

Near the VT, Chelsea Monday was attempting to dance, arms pumping up and down like a badly controlled marionette's. She was surrounded by a bevy of trimsuited groupies trying to echo her movements, with Paczai the imitator-in-chief. Her head moved jerkily, the epicentre of a purple haze of reflections blurring from her ribbonshades. She was still adorned by her perennial sun hat, which remained remarkably secure considering her gyrations.

I slipped between the groups of dancers, sidled over to Sile's huddle.

'Everyone having a good time?' I asked.

'It would be better if we had some stuff,' answered one of the men, a tall guy with dark skin sheened almost slate-blue and hair piled up in ropes. 'Even some booze would do.'

'Sorry,' I said. 'Strict rules. No intoxicants on site. Safety and all that.'

'Pity,' he replied. 'We could do with something to get things moving.'

'You could show her how it's really done,' I said to Sile, indicating Chelsea. 'Get a little practice in at the same time.'

'Professionals rarely perform except for money,' she replied.

'I just thought you might like to put on an exhibition,' I added.

'There are enough idiots round here making fools of themselves,' she said acidly, staring at me. Frazer and his two companions looked away.

'Fair enough,' I said. Sile pretended to be fascinated by her fingernails, which I suddenly noticed were painted a faint pink. The gap in the conversation lengthened as I tried to think of something to say. Eventually I mumbled some excuse and moved off to mingle with the crowd.

There was none of the rowdiness normally associated

with such a gathering. A few of the quarriers made occasional half-hearted attempts to proposition the female technicians but were easily rebuffed. For all I know a few of them might even have been accommodated, later, had Chelsea not curtailed the festivities. But the urgency was off them. The lack of intoxicants, coupled with the imminent prospect of leave and release at the *Merkins* took the edge from their ardour. Mine had been dulled by a day of argument and a glimpse of pink fingernail.

After a while, Frazer joined me.

'Lover's tiff?' he asked.

'Something like that,' I told him.

'She was asking for a ride back with us tomorrow,' he informed me.

'Oh?'

'To the spaceport,' he explained. 'I thought I'd better check with you first.'

'I don't own her,' I said. 'I guess it's up to you.'

'Ah,' he said. 'Right.' He paused and added, 'I told her we won't be leaving till late. We've still got the equipment to dismantle.'

'Is Chelsea letting you do the piece on Sonny?' I asked.

'I don't know, yet. She seems more interested in this lot.' He gestured towards the quarriers.

'I'd heard rumours,' I said.

'You don't want to believe everything you hear about her,' he said drily. 'Just most of it.'

The latest dance track was rumbling to an end, building to a raucous coda. Chelsea was still on the floor, her movements more frenzied now, tongue protruding, arms waving up and down, fingers wriggling like a monocrop rippling in the breeze. We watched her gyrations till the music stopped. She acknowledged her partner, waved away those in the queue for her attention, made her way off the floor and sagged down in a chair. Her face was red with exertion, fat beads of sweat stood out on her cheeks. She fanned herself lazily with one hand.

'Let's find out what she intends to do,' I said and dragged Frazer over to her.

'I'm not used to this,' she wheezed when we arrived. 'Are they always so energetic?' Her gesture encompassed the massed quarriers.

'Not when they're working,' I jested. 'But they need to let off steam. I suspect your presence has made them more than usually exuberant. Ask Paczai. He knows them better than me.'

Another dance rhythm thundered from the VT. I looked at the tank display which had now changed to a whorling series of harshly coloured fractals, a forest of fronds in mutating hues, pulsating in perfect synchronicity to the beat. I beckoned Paczai over.

'Is this your standard wages day party?' I asked.

'Not quite,' he confirmed. 'We don't normally have company.' Chelsea smiled graciously. 'The men are usually more quiet: saving themselves for their visit to the *Merkins*.'

'What's that?' asked Chelsea. 'The local night spot?'

Paczai laughed. 'Copper doesn't stretch to night spots,' he said. 'It's a travelling brothel,' he explained.

'It's a what?' demanded Chelsea.

'A travelling brothel. It staggers its runs round the mining planets to hit each of them on their particular wages days.'

'Do they all use it?' Chelsea's gaze darted over the men.

'Most of them,' Paczai said. 'There's not much else in the way of recreation on Copper.'

'But don't they have lovers? Sweethearts? Significant others?'

Paczai was dismissive. 'In this job?' he said. 'No. For out-of-the-way placements like this most of them sign up for yearly stretches. Not many relationships take that sort of strain. Getting away from one may be why they signed up in the first place. They're drifters really. I know I was. They come to enjoy it. They've usually contracted themselves for another year a few weeks after finishing a tour. The short break for wages day doesn't leave enough time for them to go back to their home planet, or to visit anywhere else, so they spend some of their money locally. Copper, like most other mining planets, has fuck-all in the way of amenities. The *Merkins* is just a response to a demand. She won't be the only ship in port, you can be sure. The hyperspacers know the wages schedule. The Hole will be emptying too, don't forget. It's a big captive market.'

'And this ship is here, on Copper, now?' asked Chelsea.

'Yes.'

She shouted to her crew. 'Team! Team! Here!' She waved at the VT. 'Someone get that thing off,' she said.

'What is it, boss?' Frazer asked.

'Hold on,' she said.

A chorus of groans greeted the sudden loss of sound from the VT. A clump of disgruntled quarrymen gathered near the empty tank. Residual fluorescence from the still-excited green liquid viewing medium gave their features an odd cast.

When her crew had assembled, Chelsea told them, 'Get the equipment packed. We're bailing out as soon as it's aboard. We've got work to do.'

'What?' Frazer said, 'But . . .'

'We'll need a few interviews with these miners first, though. Set up a quick voxpop here. We'll do it VT verité.' She addressed one of the trimsuited belogoed women, 'Did we bring any hand-helds?'

'I think there's some in the hovervan,' the woman told her.

'Check, would you. Quickly.'

'Okay, boss.' The woman was off and running.

'But boss,' Frazer said. 'You were going to let me do . . .'

'There's no time for that,' she interrupted. 'This is a big one. I can feel it. We've got to get back to the spaceport in time to catch this *Merkins*.'

Sile slung her baggage into one of the OBN team hovertrucks, managing to squeeze it between the VT equipment.

'Can I help?' I offered, but she ignored me. When she had finished stowing her stuff she climbed into the cab without a glance in my direction. The truck started with a hiss, gently sighing up to its running configuration. I scurried to Paczai's transvan and leapt in beside the other quarriers.

We made a strange convoy, the OBN pantechnicons in front blasting up curtains of spray as they glided over the puddles the rain had left in the uneven tracks, showering gobbets of red mud on the smaller more conventional Orthrocks transitters slithering behind on their wide wheels, striving to keep up, strung out like unsteady offspring following more proficient parents.

I kept staring at the middle truck, hoping to catch a glimpse of Sile, measuring the distance between us as it grew and ebbed with the twists and turns of the route. I felt out of place among the jokes and banter of my companions. Amid the relentless barrage of light-heartedness that continued all the way to the spaceport, I was a cold unyielding rock in the river of heated expectation of the joys awaiting there.

Chelsea's flier had put down beside the approach road. She was fretting and fuming impatiently as the convoy whined in, barely allowing the lead truck to stop before she jumped aboard and waved it on.

Progress was inevitably slowed by the increase in traffic. The spaceport environs were jammed by an accumulation of vehicles rarely seen on Copper. Normal deliveries were staggered; barring breakdowns two trucks were only occasionally to be seen in close proximity, and other traffic was effectively non-existent. But on wages days every available transport vehicle was pressed into service, all converging on the same destination, the distant but rapidly closing bulk of the *Merkins* and her attendant swarm of lesser craft.

The hovertrucks jockeyed to a halt by the spaceport apron. Crew members spilled down their sides like kids at a fairground. The quarriers' 'vans kept going. I caught a glimpse of Sile descending awkwardly from the middle truck as I was swept on by. I hammered on my 'van's side and shouted, 'Stop,' to the driver.

I was partway to my feet when the brakes hit. Inertia threw me forward in a bruised heap and a chorus of 'Hey!'s and 'Watch it!'s. 'Sorry, lads,' I apologised as I negotiated a tangle of legs to reach the exit. I swung the door shut and half-ran, half-limped past Chelsea, busy organising her crew, to where Sile was thanking her driver. The familiar shape of her dancer's muscles contoured her leggings. I thought of all the times they had knotted round me, drawing me into her. She bent over to pick up her bags. Her topcoat rode up. Her trim buttocks, separated and accentuated by the slash of overlapping Titefit, triggered a further attack of lust.

I extended my hand. 'Let me help,' I said. 'Please?'

She turned, scowled at me. 'Do you not know when to give up?' she asked.

'I guess not,' I said.

'You should learn.' She turned away.

I grabbed her arm. She looked down at where I had caught her, up at me accusingly. I let go.

'I just don't know what I've done,' I said.

'I made a mistake, Alan,' she explained. 'I thought you were like me. Felt like me. I was wrong.'

'How?' I said. 'Why?'

'Is this what you want for Sonny?' She gestured at the carnival surrounding us. 'Is this what you want crawling all over the Rock.'

'It wouldn't be like this,' I said. 'He's too distanced from mainstream Orth. No-one will make the trip out here just to see some freak, even one with a cock-eyed religion.'

'How can you be sure?' She indicated the crowds. 'This circus is on Copper, now,' she pointed out. 'And he's not a freak. At least not until you make him one. You're lucky she,' – she aimed at Chelsea, who was leading her crew off to record the gala, marching as to war with her technical battalions trailing behind her – 'has got some sort of problem about him, or they'd be on their way now. And nothing you could do would stop them.'

'It's not just her who's got a problem about him,' I muttered.

'And what does that mean?' she demanded.

'Have you forgotten?' I asked. 'My little secret?'

'Oh poor Alan,' she mocked. 'Traumatised by a tragic affliction.' She forestalled my response. 'But you didn't mean that anyway. You meant *I* have a problem with Sonny, didn't you?' She carried on before I could lie in denial. 'Well, all right,' she admitted, 'I have. I happen to like him the way he is. To think he should be left alone to die in peace.'

'So do I, now.'

'But you had to be told! Your little secret hasn't helped you not to be a self-centred bastard. It's probably encouraged it. Looked in any mirrors today?'

I winced. 'I can change,' I pleaded. 'You can change me.'

'Ha! I doubt it.'

'How can *you* be sure?'

'I can't. But I'm not willing to take the risk.

'Look,' she said, quietly. 'I've decided I want to dance again. It's not been enough for me, hanging around with nothing to do. You were always busy with some mining technique or other to oversee. It wasn't working for me.'

'But that would all change when I settle down to one job,' I objected.

'No it wouldn't. The pattern was set. It would be the same for ever, now. It's better to break it off. You do see that, don't you?'

'No, I don't. But I guess there's not a lot I can do about it.'

She waited, her silence an unspoken confirmation.

'I'll miss you,' I said.

'Yeah,' she smiled ruefully. 'Until the next one comes along.'

She offered me her hand. 'If you're ever at one of my shows,' she said, flashing me that wicked grin, 'come up and see me sometime.' I stared at her hand in confusion, wanting to take her in my arms and not let go. Finally my own hand reached out and shook hers.

'Goodbye, Alan,' she said. Then she came close, raised herself on tiptoes, put her other arm round my neck and hugged me. I clasped her tightly with my free hand, breathing in her intoxicating smell, better than any commercial drug, better than raki, even – a strange mixture of warm skin and sweet summer sweat – till she gently pushed away a little. She moved her head round and whispered in my ear, 'You're the best fuck I've ever had,' and kissed me there impulsively, a quick light brush, before pulling back.

'Then why . . . ?' She silenced me with a finger on my lips, then waved it admonishingly from side to side, stepped back, letting go the hands we still held, picked up her bags and scampered away through the crowds on those light-stepping dancer's feet, leaving me staring after her, wondering if I'd imagined the whole thing.

11

Dignity

I wandered the crowds in a daze. The various hucksters, hustlers and hangers-on which characterised the typical wages day pitch vied vainly for my attention, rapidly switching their efforts to the plentiful more amenable targets when they saw my disinterest.

As ever, Sile had managed to confuse me utterly. Had she really meant what she said or was she just letting me down gently, stroking my ego to make the parting easier to bear? I never could figure her out. If it was true it seemed to me a reason not to leave me. And if her regard for Sonny was so high why did she not stay around to try to protect him?

My emotions yawed between delight and despair. I glowed at the thought of her last words. Yet she had gone, left me; for the second time without a backward glance. The glow surrounded an emptiness deeper than anything I had felt during that first short parting on April and the misunderstanding that followed.

I have often wondered if her reasons were a blind even to herself; if she really left me because she was troubled by my genetic inheritance. Sonny was a given, she had not known him other than in his dotage on Copper and his frailties and extraordinariness were acceptable to her because of that. Maybe she couldn't face the prospect of watching someone she loved lose vitality, become ever more dependent, especially since, as was likely if I took Euthuol – and *everybody* (except Sonny) took Euthuol – it happened suddenly, and early. Or am I being charitable? The chances of our relationship lasting long enough for her to experience my change of life were small. Few Orth liaisons outlive a couple of years duration. When young, it is a matter of judging compatibility, weighing the factors, measuring your partner against an ideal. People may not exercise personal responsibility for their children but they still take care over their choice of parental partner. It is understandable that a certain amount of shopping around occurs. Still fewer Orth couples have both their permitted children to the same partner. After Euthuol, most relationships lack this intensity and drive, being, for the most part, fleeting dalliances. Novelty is, after all, the spring which waters the daily life of Orth.

Despite that, Sile and I had both been sired in an enduring association, and she may have thought ours was likely to last. If so, and she wished to procreate, I could see she might not want to pass my genetic risk on to her offspring, and so obliterated the possibility.

This has been a bitter train of thought to me over the years. After Sile, I could not trust anyone again. I never did have kids.

More likely she really did believe my character faults irredeemable and was truly irritated. Or maybe she was just tired of me. She had never indicated that she intended to stay with me long term. It was foolish of me to delude myself into thinking otherwise. I have not repeated the error. Youth and Euthuol offer up boundless possibilities; life snatches them away one by one.

The thoughts circled around, recurring and looping endlessly while I traversed aimlessly up and down the temporary alleyways of the spaceport, oblivious to the surrounding orgy of homage to the principle of pleasure. I'm still waiting for their resolution.

Only once did my interest stir. In a gap in the crowds I saw a bob of hair like Sile's near the entrance to one of the travelling ships. I quickened my pace, thinking she may not have boarded her flight immediately; pushed my way through the intervening bodies. I soon saw my mistake. The resemblance was superficial. This woman had rounder hips, sturdier legs. As she turned in my direction I made out her fuller face, and, closing to make sure, saw the red lips, the too-dark eyebrows, the smudges of artful colour on the cheeks and eyelids.

'Come on, dear,' she encouraged me. 'Come and join the fun.'

I backed away, retreating from this vision of a Sile fit only for my nightmares.

I circled round towards the *Merkins*, reckoning to catch Paczai or one of the quarriers, to find out where the transitter had been parked. Then I realised that I'd been so preoccupied with Sile during the departure that I'd left my bags at Roodsland. I headed for the spaceport buildings.

The two fly-by-night hire firms Copper ran to were closed. Nobody drives *out* on wages days. I trudged back to the *Merkins*, hung about the entrance lobby, enduring meaningful and gradually more menacing stares from the minders out front till I explained what

I was there for. It felt as though I wasted hours waiting for a face I recognised to turn up. Even then it was only some of Chelsea's technicians; and they were no help, scurrying off to some assignment or other.

I caught up with Chelsea's effort months later back Home, watching it hoping I would glimpse Sile. It was an outside chance but I thought maybe she might have been caught in the margins of one of the shots. I had no other record of her. I meant to send off for the disc if she had appeared, but there was no sign of her, nor me, in any of the broadcast cuts.

Chelsea had constructed a big production number out of it, merging it with her item on the Hole. She had interviewed some of the Roodsland quarriers, filmed the wild whooping exodus of the earliest decampers from the site, made off with the flier – a hastily rigged quadrax camera mounting slung below it – to capture the streams of men debouching from the Hole, arrowing to the spaceport. She followed it up by talking to the lassies (and a few lads) who worked on the *Merkins* and the various travellers who set out their stalls for the wages-day trade, the casinos, the drug parlours, the wide-tank VT multiplexes, the strip and clip joints, the karaoke haunts, the saunas, the massage clubs, the In-ships stuffed with petty merchants, the colourful barrowship 'captains' with their exotic sales talk, peddling (in amongst the VT-porn) tacky souvenirs, tawdry gew-gaws and cut-price goods of uncertain provenance – under guarantee of course (till you tried to have it honoured). Criss-crossing hyperspace between the mining and agricultural planets, these all converged on a scheduled wagesport like determined carnivores, eager to part the willing punters from as much of their electronic cash as possible in the shortest available time before passing them on to the next vulture in the chain. Certain planets were more favoured than others for such visits. Copper, with its plethora of mining operations and lack of indigenous distractions, tended to attract a larger gathering of vessels than a more mainstream world like, say, Helcynth.

In this company the *Merkins* was out on its own. A 'Nova' class liner, on their brief respites between planets its workers rattled around like the two balls in Astrakind roulette, rolling in their separate contra-parallel orbits; scarcely, if ever, ending next to one another. The first and best of the 'entertainment' ships, a cornucopia of every delight a tired or relaxed miner could want, on wages days the *Merkins* overflowed with enthusiastic clients. Within her huge decks she contained areas for harmless diversion and countless more rooms where straightforward, or baser, lusts and secret vices could be satisfied – rooms for which half the resultant thrill was in the finding of them, wending a way through her labyrinthine structure. Any ensuing fatigue could be slept off deep within her bowels in not quite spartan cubicles designed to be just barely comfortable so their occupants would quit them early and set off in search of further pleasures. On the apron of a spaceport she would tower over her parvenu rivals, surrounded by the smaller 'entertainment' fry like a sturdicow by hammertits; with the punters the flies they feasted on.

I suppose all that spectacle, the hustle and bustle of a wages-day gathering, has gone by now, like so much else. Or maybe not. The SHIFT mechanism must be close enough to a sun (or an equivalent mass) to access the required gravitational field strength. That would mean a lot of time-wasting ferrying from the typical mining planet, never mind one like Copper, so perhaps the entertainment ships still ply the hyperspacelanes, putting down at each successive rota point for a few days at a time, secure in their captive markets. I'm out of it now, and have been for a long time, so I don't really know. For sure there ought to be a demand still. The excavation operations haven't been wound down. Orthrocks continues to strip planets bare without a second thought.

At last two Roodsland quarriers strolled in, laughing and joking, looking like they were already enjoying the splendid time guaranteed for all that the *Merkins* promised. They directed me to where they thought I might find Paczai. He wasn't there and I veered off into the carnival mêlée again, randomly wandering the irregularly shaped lanes between the pitches, tracked by the pervasive smell from the food stalls, that peculiar spiced aroma that only seems to emanate from traders' kitchens.

I finally bumped into him by chance outside one of the casino ships, explained about my bags and the lack of transport and asked him for the keys to the transvan. He was reluctant at first but relented when I promised to return the 'van promptly. I was due to lift off the following morning anyway, I pointed out, so he needn't worry about being stranded.

It hadn't rained at all at the spaceport and the roads had more or less dried out near Roodsland with only a few stubborn puddles remaining, so the journey back was pretty routine.

Roodsland looked more like a crumbling tooth than ever as I jounced along the rutted approach road;

all side wall and no centre, the lack of activity, the isolation, emphasising the destruction worked to its innards. My bags lay where I had inadvertently left them in my rush to stick close to Sile when she left. They punctuated the space between the huts and the quarry like a misplaced apostrophe. Moisture had seeped up from the wet ground; dark irregular stains fringed with white efflorescences marked the extent of the damage. Thick, claggy red soil clung to them in a layer when I hefted them up. Disgusted, I carried them into the hut to check the contents and dry them off.

The deserted building echoed hollowly. Too fresh memories stalked the familiar scene. I retreated to the communal hut.

The blank viewing-tank stared dully at me. The absence of the usual noise, of people, in this habitually boisterous setting was disturbing. The unoccupied tables and chairs matched too closely my own mood. I plodded over to the tank, switched on its mechanism. The stirrer whirred into life, creating sudden shifting vortices in the liquid viewing medium. The beam generators at each corner arced up into life, sending shafts of yellow translucence through the green background. Static hissed from the speakers. Motes of light flashed where the odd impurity caught a beam's full intensity. Striations undulated slowly, densities evening out as the base plate warmed the viscous liquid and the stirrer whirled it to homogeneity. I shifted channels, pushing the buttons doggedly searching for a signal. Nothing but static and green iridescence greeted my efforts. I grabbed the topmost of the pile of discs nearby, slotted it into its hole. The thumping booming of a dance number shattered the equilibrium as I hit the right channel button. I snapped the tank off, started banging my head against its pliant surface, the sudden silence confirming my feelings of despondency.

I ventured outside breathing deeply, stood contemplating the quarry and the surrounding hills. Perhaps I just needed some company, an understanding shoulder, and Sonny was the only choice on offer, or maybe his strange imprecations were starting to affect me; but, over the ridge, I could feel the hill of the Rock exerting a curious pull, drawing me up to talk to him one more time.

The clearing appeared curiously uncluttered stripped of the VT paraphernalia and all the technicians. Sonny's trappings were still present of course, but they were not such an intrusion, sitting easily with the surroundings. His lodge, the fire roasting strips of meat which hung from the spit, the shimmer of slightly smoky haze rising above it, the empty wooden frame – even the partly dismembered carcase of what I supposed was a freshly killed dumbuck lying nearby – had come to seem perfectly natural, its solitude not as forbidding as the deadened ghost town of the vacant quarry settlement, and a sea of tranquillity compared to the bustle I had quit at the spaceport.

Sonny was not in sight. I trudged over to his square tent.

'Sir? Are you there?' He may have heard me approach. Almost as soon as I spoke he emerged, carrying a blanket. He accepted my arm to help him through the flap but waited till he straightened up before replying. His animal smell seemed less strong than before. My running around at the spaceport had perhaps brought out more of my own secretions than usual so I noticed his less. Or else I was accustomed to it by now.

'Welcome, my Son,' he said. It was a small thing, but I noticed his greeting had changed. Previously, he had always said it was the Rock which welcomed Its Son, as if he cared little either way; this time Sonny's reception appeared personal. It may only have been that he was becoming used to my visits, or just that he did not presume on friendship, that for him relationships took time to develop. Maybe it was part of his softening-up process to make me feel at ease as a Son of the Rock. If so, it was working. I took it as a sign of his favour. I needed some.

'I see you've made a kill,' I said.

'Yes,' he replied in his slow manner. 'The dumbuck begin to stray back when the men are absent and the noise gone.'

'So quickly?'

'They are creatures of habit and instinct, my Son. Only the greatest disturbances keep them from their age-old paths.'

'What do they feed on?' I asked, escorting him towards the fire. 'I would have thought they'd prefer scrubland to this kind of forested slope.'

'Anything young and tender,' he said. 'They take leaves from the lower branches as well as the under-growth. The dumbuck shunned what little open grazing Copper had,' he explained. 'Our carnivores were swift. Trees gave shelter and balanced the advantage. They may stray out more, now the predators are gone,' – he paused, sighed – 'but not in my time. Creatures of habit.'

'There can't be many of these left either,' I suggested, poking the dead animal with my foot as I passed. An aimless scurrying of hitherto hidden small creatures broke out immediately all over the carcase.

'Enough,' he replied. 'The Rock is good.'

I spread the blanket for him and helped him squat down by the fire. He adopted his usual cross-legged posture, I sat in a crouch, hugging my knees.

I kicked one leg at the fire. 'How did you keep this going through the rain?' I asked.

He regarded me strangely. 'I covered it,' he said. 'The embers remain candent for a good many hours.' When he asked, 'Do the men of Orth allow their fires to fail?' I realised he was amused.

'We use a different type of fire,' I replied. 'As I suspect you know.'

'Forgive an old man his jest,' he said. He gestured at the spit, 'We must share food again.'

I held up my hand in part restraint. 'No rituals, I hope?' I asked.

He stared into the flames. 'I fear the time for those is passed,' he murmured.

'Food, then,' I consented, before adding, 'but do you mind if I pass, on the vegetables?'

His expression didn't change. 'As you wish,' he said gravely. 'Does this meet your favour?' He indicated the hanging strips of meat.

The dumbuck flesh was as good as I had remembered, though this time of a different flavour due to the alternative method of preparation. The strips were hot, crisped on the outside but once through the layer of torrefaction, juicy and tender. We sat in silence for a while, chewing the lean meat.

As I was licking my fingers clean Sonny suddenly asked, 'Where is your woman? She is not here. And you have made no mention of her.'

I sat mutely, not knowing how to respond.

'If it is painful, do not speak,' he said.

'No,' I said. 'I need to.' I took a deep breath and continued, 'She has gone. She left for the spaceport this morning.' I looked up at the sky involuntarily. 'She'll be off-world by now. Somewhere up there.' The stars appeared sharp and bright with the competition from the quarry's floods absent. Crazily, I scanned overhead to see if any of the points of light were moving.

'Did you not follow her?'

'I tried to. She was too quick. I didn't know which flight she was on.'

'You will not see her again?'

'I doubt it.'

'That is sad, my Son. I had thought you suited, hoped you may have children together.'

'More Sons of the Rock?' I prompted.

He continued mournfully, 'I have little hope of that. What sway the Rock has over lands among the stars I know not. Its influence may not extend far beyond this place. In the presence of the Rock I can feel Its power but the effect wears off with distance. I doubt those not attuned to it could develop the faith.'

'Then why try to co-opt me?'

'An old man's conceit,' he said, wearily. 'An act of desperation. Do not judge me too harshly. I am the last of my kind.'

I thought back to the afternoon Sile and I had found him up above Roodsland, imperiously scorning Orth and all its works. Some of the light had gone from him since then. I suddenly saw him as perhaps Sile had from the start; not as a grotesque atavism, to be shunned and pitied, but as a lonely human being, battered almost into submission by forces outwith his control, but yet unbowed. The high summer of his life long since gone, its meaning all but faded away during autumn's slow decline, he still reserved in its winter a place for dignity.

These mist-covered mountains – so familiar, so strange – that I gaze upon when I tear my eyes away from the mirror, are a reminder that even in stable, relatively monolithic Orth, seemingly solid cultural manifestations, landmarks of a way of life, are subject to the forces of change. Existing in the shadow of the larger, more powerful culture, I guess the best the smaller ones can aspire to is to survive, somehow. Sonny had done well to keep his faith as long as this.

Without knowing quite why, I said to him, 'There is still you, and me to come after.'

He took my arm gently, not like the fierce grip he'd held me in on earlier occasions. 'Thank you, my Son,' he said, 'for trying to make an old man happy; but do not be bound by promises you made in haste. Soon they will not matter. I will be gone and there will be no-one to hold you to account. Go your own way. Find the path to contentment. Seek out your woman once more,' – it was hard to tell given his still largely indecipherable expressions but I think he smiled faintly here – 'or find one you can handle, and keep at ease.'

'Are there such creatures?' I asked bitterly.

'The joy, my Son, is in the finding out.'

'I'll pass on that one, for a while at least.'

'You are young, you still have time.'

Not as much as you may think, I reflected. 'I'm afraid I must go now. I doubt if we will meet again.'

'It is as it should be. You have your own destiny to fulfil.'

'I must thank you,' I said.

'For what?'

'Honouring me with your vocation. For not dismissing my ignorance. For your forbearance.'

'Your mind is not closed, my Son; unlike others of your kind. May the Rock remain with you always.'

'And with you,' I replied.

As I rose to leave he said, 'You will not forget this place.' I wasn't sure if he phrased it as a question or not, but I knew what the answer was.

'No,' I said. 'I won't.'

I descended the hill, a knot of disquiet building up gradually, moulding itself into an intense pressure on my back; as if I expected to suffer a blow. The sense of presence was so strong that I kept looking around, but of course Sonny was too slow and frail to have followed me and there was no-one else within kayem of here. It dissipated in a shiver of . . . Fear? . . . Apprehension? . . . Foreboding? . . . but undoubtedly Release . . . as I plodded across the open space towards the huts. Musing on Sonny's words the brief fanciful thought occurred that on entering Orth's furthermost outpost on Copper I had somehow emerged from the sphere of influence of the Rock. But I had never felt anything similar when I had made the same short journey before. I had, however, come to a grudging appreciation of Sonny and his quiet life, so perhaps it was merely a heightened form of the frisson experienced on any kind of parting. I was probably more susceptible to such feelings because Sile had just dumped me so spectacularly. Whatever, it seemed at the time a kind of ending, the final underlining of a footnote in my life.

My bags and their contents had dried out some by then. I hoisted them into the transitter and set off for the spaceport once more, accompanied by that strange mixture of euphoria and emptiness that Sile's enigmatic departure had stirred up in me, the swathe of the 'van's headlights a cocooning oasis of light fencing off the surrounding dark. I couldn't decide if Sile was an angel or a bitch, my attitude kept changing with the twists and turns of the road. Somewhere in there, too, was a confused set of feelings about Sonny. On the one hand I still pitied him, and the prospect of winding up like that, frail, friendless and alone, filled me with terror whenever I thought of it. On the other, he had shown me nothing but kindness since our original confrontation and had displayed a wisdom and serenity that mocked my fears.

The uncertainties stayed with me to the bright lights of the spaceport, while I parked the transvan, delivered Paczai the key and sauntered towards the berth where my flight out was waiting. My route lay past the *Merkins*. For some reason I stopped, found myself going in.

There was an element of revenge about it I'm sure. I wanted to get back at a woman, any woman, for the wrongs Sile had done me. But it was more complicated than that. I think that maybe I hoped I could fuck the whole rotten set of memories out of existence before I blew the red dust of Copper off my shoes for ever.

I brooded over the choice of 'partner' – all hideously overdone, nails and faces painted, who knows what else padded, filled or otherwise altered. I nearly left without sampling the goods but instead settled for the 'girl' that looked to have the least artificial adornment. As soon as we were alone I asked her to remove the cosmeticry.

'I'll only have to put it back on again, after,' she said.

'If it's too much bother . . .'

'No. No. You're paying. You get what you want.'

I watched her peel off lashes, nails, wig, the care with which she laid down each embellishment; saw her swab away at herself, revealing a plain, but far from unacceptable, face from beneath the layers; noted the reflex arrangement of the hair that followed her unveiling, a residual, determined prettification. The inevitable stirrings resulted when she began to disrobe, revealing her body, all the usual enticing bits in the correct places. I gave myself to the sensual signals she initiated as she straddled me.

She was a pleasant enough woman I suppose, but the process was functional, mechanical, her initial comments during the act – meant to be encouraging, stimulating – I found irritating and soulless. She was no Sile, though she knew a few tricks Sile hadn't. But she performed efficiently, taking a professional pride in her abilities, perhaps sensing in me more than the usual frustrations.

'What makes you do a job like this?' I asked her. 'Apart from the money?'

'Nice fellow like you,' she said, with what I presumed was a whore's insincerity, 'it's a pleasure. You wouldn't believe what some other folks ask me to do.'

'Like what?'

'You don't really want to know; it might put you off.' Her rhythmic rocking continued during the pause in her conversation. 'But the giving of pleasure isn't a mean occupation,' she went on, 'despite what many think.' She smiled down at me, caressed my cheek. 'It can even be a pleasure itself,' she added.

'Spare me the philosophy,' I said, rolling her over, roughly. 'See what pleasure you get from this,' and gave myself to the sensations of increasingly fulfilled lust.

When it was over she got rid of me with the minimum of fuss. Transaction over, it was back to the cold, hard business of making another sale.

The strange thing was it was Sonny's face, not Sile's body, that had kept drifting into my thoughts, distracting me from the joys of the moment.

Later, circling in orbit waiting for the hyperspace injection, gazing out of the observation lounge window, I could see the livid man-made scar of the Hole, looking from this distance like a large, blinded eye in the lined, craggy, ancient face of the planet.

I scanned my reflection in the plasglas, searching for latent creases, the grooves in the smooth curves of my skin, trying to imagine exactly how it would feel to be old. I shook my head wondering how long it would be before I'd be free of reminders of Sonny.

The steady push of the pulse-rod engines accelerating the ship to the injection point propelled the planet away, its shrivelled appearance shrinking and dwindling into the distance, then came the slight shimmer, the shivering apprehension between there and not-there that marks the space/hyperspace interface, and Copper and Sonny were behind me at last.

I thought I'd never see him again.

PART 2

Nor the Years Condemn

12

Promised You A Miracle

'You called me Sile, again,' she said.

Vazhni's tone was even. She seemed resigned, no longer angry about it, but that was just a front. I knew it still irritated her; hurt even, somewhere deep down. She had waited, bottling it up, till I had turned onto my back and we were both staring at the ceiling.

'Did I?' I asked, carefully. 'When? I'm sorry.'

'When you usually do,' she sighed. 'At the crucial moment; just when I'm beginning to think you've forgotten her at last.'

'I'm sorry, I didn't mean to.'

'No. That's the trouble. You never do.' She shifted onto her side to face me. I avoided her gaze, looking instead at her bare shoulders, the tumble of her breasts, the sweat-slicked flaccidness of enlarged aureole submerging each nipple.

'I don't know why you're so obsessed with her,' she went on. 'I mean, it was years ago. You should have forgotten her by now. She did dump you, after all.' I finally flicked a guilt-ridden glance towards her brown eyes. 'You could be a bit more considerate,' she complained. 'It's me who's here: not her. It's my body you're making love to.'

I couldn't explain – I couldn't even explain it to myself, never mind put it into words for someone else, especially someone who by rights ought to have been my sole preoccupation. Despite all my attempts to forget her, the many attachments I had formed in the intervening years, none had been able to drive her from my mind; no-one had ever had the same sparkle as Sile. I had been with Vazhni longer than most – perhaps because she put up with me – and had hoped for a while she might be the one to soothe the itch. She attracted me all right, she was fun to be with and I enjoyed her company, but something was missing. My spirits didn't lift every time I saw her, that peculiar fluttering was absent.

Though I suspected Vazhni didn't believe it, I had tried to forget, to put the memories behind me; but like a powerful scent, traces lingered. It was still Sile I thought of in my unguarded moments.

'I know. I'm sorry,' I said.

'Are you?' she asked. 'You don't seem to be. You keep doing it after all.'

'Maybe I just can't help it.'

'For goodness' sake. You're a grown man.' Remembering I had not yet had my youth shot, she corrected herself before I could interject. 'Well, maybe you're not, yet. But you're as grown as you're going to be. You've got a responsible job; a budget of millions. And in charge of, what is it? Fifty brilliant young engineers?'

'Oh more,' I boasted, airily.

'Quite,' she said, tone hardening. 'Don't you think it's time you put away childish things?'

'I've said I'm sorry. Can we let it drop, now?'

'No. Not until you stop doing it to me. I'm tired of it, Alan,' she ranted, raising herself on her elbow to give a better angle of attack. 'It's gone on long enough.' She punctuated each syllable with a finger poked at my chest.

I brushed her arm away but said nothing. She stared at me then lay down on her back again. 'And you're not the best fuck I've ever had,' she muttered towards the ceiling.

I made a mental note not to tell that particular story again. (But I have, of course. Another of my broken promises.)

'At least the others had the decency not to call out another woman's name when they came inside me,' she finished, quietly.

'Now who's not being considerate,' I said. 'Have I ever held your past against you?'

She turned to me once more. 'That's because none of mine means anything.' She shook her head. Her long flow of dark hair fell down across her shoulders, brushed across her cleavage.

'You're so gullible, Alan,' she said. 'She didn't mean it. Step into any whorehouse and you'll hear the same thing a thousand times a night.'

The remark stung, not least because the second bit was true. But I also resented Sile being compared to a tart. The image didn't fit with my perceptions; the flame inside still burned too brightly.

Vazhni grumbled on but I was no longer paying attention. Her comments had reopened the old, imperfectly healed wounds. To protect my feelings I shut myself off, clammed up. Maybe I had been a fool but I didn't need a reminder; the scab was one I picked at myself, obsessively, again and again. For sure Sile still had the capacity to twist my guts, but it wasn't primarily loss I felt. It was the exposure of my youthful naivety, the hint of gullibility. Vazhni had hit my weakest point; my uncertainty about Sile's true regard for me.

Compared to that, Vazhni's understandable disgruntlement was an irritant which I could easily block out. Her words bounced off my wall of silence and reflected back, reinforcing her frustration and annoyance. She soon lapsed into wordlessness, turning her back on me with a theatrical flourish, emanating icy shards of mute discontent as an echo to my performance.

I stared at the ceiling long into the night. When I finally switched out the light, images of Sile persisted, superimposing themselves through the darkness onto the faint fuzzy patterns fanning out from the chink in the curtains.

'Roodsland? Did you say Roodsland?'

'Yeah,' Barlett replied. 'It's somewhere on Copper, I think.'

'I know where it is,' I snapped. 'I've been there.' He gave me a hurt look, one of the don't-look-at-me, I've-done-nothing kind. 'Whereabouts at Roodsland?' I demanded, a bit less tetchily. I already knew the answer, had done as soon as I heard the word 'Roodsland'. But confirmation never hurts as much as uncertainty.

He scrutinised his printout. 'Doesn't say. Just Roodsland.'

'Find out, will you? I need to know.'

'Sure, boss. Is there some sort of problem?'

'No,' I said, then changed my mind. 'Yes.' Havered, 'There might be.'

He raised his thick eyebrows. On work matters I wasn't usually prone to indecision.

I clarified the situation slightly. 'I may have to go there,' I told him.

'Is it serious?'

'Probably not.'

'What's the fuss, then?'

'It's an old story,' I said. 'Partly personal. You don't need the details. Just make the arrangements.'

'When for?'

'As soon as possible.'

'By SHIFT, then?'

I hesitated for a moment. 'I suppose so,' I said. 'It'll be quicker.'

'Not by much. Copper's too far from mainstream Orth for its sun to have a SHIFT station yet, the last leg will still be by slowboat.'

I sighed. Subordinates, I thought. No initiative. Always dotting each 'i' and crossing each 't'. Still, I suppose he reckoned if he didn't check with me he'd be the one who'd suffer for it.

'Well make it the nearest SHIFT sun with a connection, then.'

'Right, boss. Whatever you say.'

He left, shaking his head in puzzlement at my strange behaviour.

I still couldn't quite take it in. Of all the sites in my sector why did it have to be Roodsland that had a motherlode of iridium ore?

I suppose I should have seen it coming. Ever since Orthrocks promoted me to Sector Manager with responsibility for the southern arc of the spiral arm a short Orth Standard year ago this had been a possibility. But the chance had been a remote one I'd preferred to ignore.

When, I thought selfishly, am I ever going to be free from reminders of that place? I had been carefully groomed for this position, or better. (Something else that never hurts, I reflected, is to have contacts in the business.) Now I had to wonder if I was going to make a complete and public fool of myself to match my private discomfiture over Sile. Though maybe that wasn't quite so private. Occasional veiled references suggested some of my subordinates were aware of my youthful dalliance. Not that their pasts would be entirely free of skeletons; but their unwanted bodies wouldn't have died in closets belonging to Orthrocks.

The problem was the SHIFT, and its ravening demand for iridium. A whole new market had opened up for Orthrocks with the advent of instantaneous transport between stars based on the theory of superstring harmonised integrated fields, sparking off a scramble for sources of the suddenly precious element it required. Survey teams were scouring the whole of the spiral arm for the high density readings characteristic of the metal. Now it seemed they'd been found at Roodsland. And I knew just where. Either I was going to have to break the spirit of my promise to Sonny or fail at my job.

But the choice wasn't real. If I didn't sign the order, my omission was sure to be brought to the attention of head office. I'd be disciplined; at best removed, at worst sacked, and someone else would authorise the Rock's destruction. I could only delay that outcome.

But maybe it wouldn't come to that. I might be worrying unnecessarily, which was another reason to see the situation for myself. I needed to be sure it was Sonny's Rock which was under threat. And if it was, I felt I owed Sonny some small gesture. The least I could do was tell him myself.

'Something's come up,' I said. 'I need to make a trip.'

Vazhni seemed to brighten at the news.

'Anywhere interesting?' she asked. 'Maybe I could tag along.' Perhaps she thought a change of surroundings might restore our flagging relationship.

'I don't think so,' I replied. 'Copper isn't the most enticing of planets.'

Her demeanour changed instantly. 'Copper? Wasn't that where . . . ?'

'Yes.'

'Oh,' she said. The silence sank around us like a blanket of snow. As she gathered her thoughts the seconds elongated; became tear-drops of time, falling slowly.

'Well,' she said eventually. 'Perhaps if I were to come with you it would help you to forget . . . You know, if you saw me there in the same places . . .'

Her voice trailed away into the vacuum of my lack of response. The truth was I was myself frightened of going. I couldn't be sure Sonny would still hold the same respect for me before I revealed the bad news to him. And afterwards . . . I wanted my memories of Copper intact, even the bad ones about Sile.

'And there was that peculiar man, wasn't there?' Vazhni went on, sounding now as if she were trying to convince herself as well as me. 'What was his name, again? I'd like to meet him.'

'Sonny,' I replied. 'And I don't think you would. His appearance is a bit of a shock. Even Chelsea Monday couldn't come to terms with it.'

'Well you survived.'

'Did I?' I mused. 'Sometimes I wonder.'

Vazhni snorted. 'Oh Alan,' she said, more confident now. 'Just because your *grande amoure* dumped you there doesn't mean the experience has to blight your life.'

She didn't understand. She couldn't: I hadn't told her about my honorary status as a Son of the Rock. She knew there was some tie to Sonny on my part, a residual affection, perhaps due to the association with Sile, but she wasn't aware of the responsibility I felt, the sense I had of being marked out, chosen, the pride I had begun to develop in it. And now most probably I had to oversee the destruction of the source of it all. And, as an all too likely consequence, of Sonny.

I shrugged. 'I suppose not,' I said. 'But if I must face up to it, I think I'll be better on my own,' I added. 'Having you there would probably be a distraction. It might not work.'

Her look of rejected bewilderment was almost enough to change my mind. A few more seconds and I might have relented, but her resolve broke first. Her shoulders slumped, her eyes lowered. 'Whatever you want,' she mumbled. I guess she thought if I was ever to break free of Sile this was probably my last, best chance. And if I didn't want her along . . .

She helped me pack, quietly. There wasn't much. My dress and work trimsuits, some more casual clothing, a scattering of toiletries, a few odds and ends. It's strange how removing so little can leave behind such emptiness.

Yet by the time I came to leave, Vazhni had achieved a kind of serenity. It was as if a barrier had fallen. She'd finally given up the struggle against Sile's memory and I think she found it a relief. The strain of fighting her unseen enemy had been removed and the sudden freedom was uplifting.

We both knew I wouldn't be back. There was no point. The relationship had been doomed from the start. Unfortunately neither of us had realised it till then.

What the hell. Easy come, easy go. I suppose it was for the best. I would only have hurt her the more.

I was unlikely to have stayed with her in the long term anyway: she insisted on shaving her armpits.

Ahead of the lugger the immense orange sun had dominated the sky for hours, an oppressive menace growing ever larger as we plunged down its steep gravity well closer to the SHIFT station. The fierce burning heat pouring from the star – terawatts of power on every measurable wavelength accompanying the solar wind through the considerably less than vacuum of such near stellar space – was a psychological more than a physical threat, dimmed as it was from its full glory by the shieldglass of the observation port. Fascinated by the closeup on such awesomeness, I had watched a huge prominence flick its fiery finger lazily across the photosphere, countless hectares of incandescent plasmic gas, at shorter range capable of crisping the lugger and all it contained in an instant, shimmering insubstantially in the convection currents of the roiling corona. The flare slid from sight as my immediate destination – the jumble of oddly shaped structures that made up the SHIFT platform, jutting from their parabolic base like the entrails of an orbital glued somehow onto a huge dish – had gradually cut into the radiation disc; the sweet silhouette swelling from the apparent size of a sunspot indistinguishable among the many till its irregularly truncated cone blocked off an arc of 130 or so degrees. Most of the platform's bulk was for shielding – direct exposure to the constant radiation at this distance rapidly disables normal tissue, and cells stabilised by Euthuol last only a little longer – but the subtle contours also had a deeper purpose.

The lugger slowly slipped from the arm of shade cast by this odd construction into the deeper penumbra of total shadow, the star's corona showing hazily as a brief yellow arc before it too was obscured. Maybe the extra shielding the SHIFT platform provided absorbed more of the radiation and my body had somehow recognised the change, but I shivered with relief, as if the physical shelter from the solar battering had somehow removed the lowering presence beyond the platform.

Pinprick lights, tiny beacons scattered across the structure, increased in intensity during the lugger's approach, resolved themselves into a skein of backlit viewports. More powerful satellights bathed the dock area as the lugger nosed in.

I disembarked, submitted my ticket for inspection. After collecting my luggage I followed the signs, moving along gridded catwalks, down assorted gloomy companionways barely wide enough for one person, deep into the bowels of the station. The claustrophobic confines contrasted with the wide expanses of more conventional reception buildings. There was no space here for the airy malls of ground- or orbital-based terminals nor for the gracious fripperies of the proud elegances that plied the hyperspacelanes. A new apprehension grew as, for the first time, I would experience, not the familiar slow transits of an interstellar cruiser, but instead the short, sharp disruption of the SHIFT.

A prickling of ozone mixed with a heavier bilious scent irritated my nostrils. Around me, the hum of machinery had intensified as the immense energies required to strip matter down to sub-quanta, hurl the information across the parsecs to be mirrored and reassembled, were harnessed and gathered. The integration of strong and weak nuclear forces, electromagnetism and gravity to corrupt the continuum sufficiently for a shift to occur is no simple achievement. A myriad curious devices – strange attractors and repellers, tronic accelerators, huge gravity lenses and other machines I also know in name only – were combining to focus the correct superstring harmonised integrated field theory parameters onto the SHIFT chamber. The strength of gravitational field required demanded the platform be so close to a sun. The clean simplicity of a hyperspace drive unit is, perhaps, easier to grasp; but this had the sense of raw power, of novelty, and the crucial advantage of unmeasurable, instantaneous, transition times.

I mistrusted the prospect of dissipation, feared the occurrence of a mistranslation. (The SHIFT has not yet suffered a loss but the possibility remains an unspoken dread.) I entered the chamber shaking, sweat-riddled. It was cramped, like a one-person escape hatch: the early symmetrical models could only project a small mass, no more than one adult, into the nine dimensions of the thirty-seven integrated fields. The large ships that tied the worlds and satellites of Orth in one cultural net still had a few more years trade, but have now in their turn been replaced. Only luggers and the like survive from the old ways.

The door slid shut and I was alone in the brightly lit cubicle. A list of instructions with appropriate diagrams decorated the far panels. I adopted the recommended position, legs spread, arms raised, palms pressed to the wall. There was a moment of darkness, a shimmer of unease like the slip between hyper and normalspace, and then the far door opened, spilling me onto a companionway identical to the one I had just left. I was momentarily confused, thinking the SHIFT had failed, then I realised that I had relocated, transcended light years in one fleeting instant. As the understanding struck, my fear gripped tighter, boiling over into nausea, and my stomach made its comment on the change, throwing its contents into the conduit provided.

It is a common reaction I know, many find their first SHIFT traumatic; but I was not consoled. I had hoped to avoid the indignity.

First stop was Argyros, or more correctly its sun. More correctly still I didn't actually stop – a swift transfer to a lugger at the receiving end followed by the long climb out of the sun's gravity well – till I reached Jefferson, one of the orbital satellites girdling the planet.

Positioned on the edge of mainstream Orth, gateway to the spiral arm periphery and a nucleus for the expanding wavefront of Orth culture, Argyros had been a commercial centre for centuries, its decently removed satellites a jumble of industrial workshops, foundries, spaceshipyards, ancillary fabricators, chandleries and the like serving the interstellar trade. But their last great days were all but gone. The shipping companies had become nervous about future prospects and new building orders had dwindled as the number of SHIFT outlets grew. The satellites were living on former glories and borrowed time.

Maybe it was just the confined environment, the concentrated hum of close-packed humanity, the intensely recycled atmosphere of an orbital, or maybe I was made more sensitive to it by my premonition of what lay ahead for Sonny but I thought I could smell the air of foreboding that hung about Jefferson in those days as soon as I stepped through the lugger's lock into the reception lounge. There must have been something different because I'd passed through such places before and never given the atmosphere a thought.

I handed in my luggage for processing and sought out a meal and some coffee while I waited for my connection. Strolling the endless treadmill of Jefferson's ever-curving-upward streets I was reminded of April, though the processes of genteel decay had not yet gathered the same force on Jefferson.

There was still some buzz while the last ship was on the stocks, residual activity on the malls – arched like upside-down rainbows cupping the orbital's hub, ceilings always cutting off the distant prospect – and in the drug parlours business was brisk as ever; but the spark of vitality was draining away. After the launch party for the final *Empress* the workers would decamp, the shutters go up, and only the ghosts of ships past would be left adrift among the mooring bays. In the meantime Jefferson struggled on, the remaining inhabitants breathing a peculiar kind of half life into its stuttering corpse.

There were a few scavengers willing to pick over the remains; carefully two-pieced business types scouring the orbital for assets to strip, offering knock-down prices for anything that could be moved; lawyers scrutinising small print for easy get outs; fly-by-nights taking advantage of the hastily improvised inducements the administration had granted to attract new investors, but intending to disappear when the tax breaks ran out. And, in the reception lounge when I got back, a cluster of beglittered trimsuits highlighted with golden chest flashes protecting their star performer from her usual scrum of admirers.

'Hello, Frazer,' I said when I had pushed my way to his side.

'Alan! Good to see you. It must be . . .'

'Since Copper,' I said.

'Yeah, and that strange old guy . . .'

'Sonny.'

'That's right. Whatever happened to him?'

'Nothing, as far as I know. In fact I should be seeing him again soon. I'm just on my way there.'

'Funny how Chelsea refused to do that piece on him,' he mused.

'Did she never tell you? It was something personal Sile seemed to think,' I said.

'Sile? I thought you two had split up.'

'We did.' I pre-empted his expression of regret. 'It's all right. I'm long over it,' I lied. 'What brings you to Jefferson?' I added.

'One of Chelsea's ideas. She's doing a series on the dying arts of Orth. This SHIFT thing has apparently killed the spaceshipyards' order books. She wants to document the construction process before it's gone for ever. We'll be recording the latest Empress's development from the drawing tank to launch.'

'Sounds like a load of fun.'

'It's a living,' he replied then added, 'Copper, you said. Still working for Orthrocks, then?'

'Yeah. Sector Manager, now.'

'I'm impressed,' he told me. 'But you always were marked out for higher things.'

'I suppose so. It didn't always feel like it.'

Frazer glanced over to where Chelsea's entourage

had begun making its collective way out of the reception lounge. 'Well, give my regards to the old boy,' he said.

'I will; but you might want to do that yourself. He could be an even better story for you, now.' Frazer waited, eyebrows arched.

'We've found iridium on Copper,' I explained. 'It's probably under Sonny's hill. I'm going to check that out. If it is it means he'll be thrown off the hill. At the minute it's my decision but Orthrocks won't let anyone stand in the way of an iridium mine. And where's he going to go? Who'll have him?'

'How do you feel about it?'

'I don't know,' I said. 'I suppose I've always felt kind of sorry for him.' I shrugged. 'But he was harmless. Now he's a barrier to progress, and there's nothing I can do.' I paused while something Sile had once said flashed through my head. 'It'll kill him if he has to move,' I added.

'It might not come to that,' Frazer consoled me. 'You still have to check, you said.'

'If it does, do you think you can persuade Chelsea to run with it?' I asked him. 'He is one of Orth's dying arts, after all.'

He grinned. 'Nice try Alan, but that's stretching it a bit.' He looked over his shoulder. The pack of technicians and hangers-on had disappeared. 'No promises,' he told me. 'But I'll see what I can do. I'll have to go, now. Let me know when you're sure.'

'Damn and blast!'

'What's wrong?' Paczai's latest successor, a thin and worried-looking man named Lemarry, became even more agitated. I couldn't blame him. In his position an unannounced visit from the boss, demanding to see the latest search results, wouldn't have been high on my list of desiderata.

'I was hoping it wouldn't be Sonny's hill,' I replied, staring at the figures. 'I don't suppose there's any chance of a mistake?'

'No. The readings are conclusive,' Lemarry said, 'and all double-checked. See for yourself.' He called up a map of the Roodsland area, laid it under the gravitic anomaly chart and lined up the markers. The chart's clustered peaks matched the tight map contours of Sonny's hill. Although the fit was not quite perfect, there was no doubt. The hill was doomed.

I looked at the damning overlay, remembering the miasmic face of the Rock, hacked out of the Hole by the laser cutter those not so many years before, hearing again its apparent cries of agony. Soon there would be no Rock left to protest Its passing: nor Sons to witness It.

Lemarry's relief melded with puzzlement. 'What difference does it make which hill it is?' he asked.

'None to you, or Orthrocks,' I replied. 'But it makes a deal of difference to me.'

'How is he these days?' I asked Lemarry, after a pause. 'Do you know?'

'Not really,' he replied. 'He's never bothered us much. And except for the surveying, we've kept out of his way.'

'I'll need to see him,' I said.

Roodsland had hardly changed I thought, walking across the broad ribbon separating the huts from the quarry entrance. Maybe the hill seemed a little smaller, the piles of rubble towering round its sides a little flatter, more filled in and overgrown so that the distinction between them and the hill itself was blurred, but the resemblance to a drilled-out uncapped tooth remained as striking as ever. The various outbuildings had sprouted some new companions, preliminary graders and sifters for the most part, adding their occasional roars and whooshes to the whine of vehicle engines and the rumbles and bangs from the main quarry. The painted rocks delineating the entrance appeared dustier, more weatherworn, but behind them the huge basaltic columns that I remembered still interlocked their immense fingers; though a considerable number of them had by now been prised loose, lopped off and carted away.

Tension built up in me as I made my way up the hill. The sense of premonition, of not being in control, had flicked on like a security light as I left the confines of the workings. The path I followed was so familiar, so burdened with memories, that the strangeness was heightened. I had expected some trepidation as I went to meet Sonny again – I don't suppose anyone is overly joyed to be the bearer of bad tidings – but nothing as strong as this. I felt somehow as if I had travelled back in time, that the ghosts of earlier days were watching me in my progress, and not approvingly. The echoes of the past redoubled as I found myself remembering the wave of emotion I had experienced the last time I had walked on the hill of the Rock, on my departure from Copper those eight OS years before. I had the bizarre thought that maybe the Rock did have a sphere of influence, that Sonny could distinguish a pull from this hill different from any other and that somehow this ability had been transferred to me. If the gravitic anomaly readings were due to a high iridium

content then the Rock was riddled with the stuff.
And if it could be detected instrumentally might not
the element's high density be fathomed by someone
specially attuned to it?

The idea seemed nonsensical, but was it possible that
Sonny could discern the small gravitational changes
involved? I certainly doubted that I had such a capability. I stopped (at the time it seemed for half an
eternity but it was probably no more than thirty seconds) pondering the question. No, I eventually decided.
It was too absurd. His attraction to the Rock could
only have been a mystical one. As to my feelings, they
were surely more attributable to mere apprehension.
And guilt.

I could smell woodsmoke, and the aroma of roast
dumbuck clinging to it, long before I caught sight of
the fire. Unsure of my welcome, feeling like a kind of
trespasser, I hesitated at the clearing's edge, almost
turned back. But I, too, was a Son of the Rock, I
reminded myself. He had made me one. I had a right
to be here; as well as a duty.

It would have been easier to have turned back;
never to have faced him, never to have confessed my
failure to live up to his hopes, my inability to protect
his heritage. To have left the job of demolishing his
faith forever to someone else. But, for once, I screwed
my courage to the sticking place and strode forward.
Besides, I told myself, it wasn't my fault if I was too
frail a vessel to carry successfully the burden he had
laid on me.

From its shrub-lined border the clearing was as I
remembered it, smoke from the fire spiralling upwards
over a piece of slowly roasting skewered dumbuck,

spits of fat sizzling as they splattered the hot timbers, the trellis with stretched dumbuck skin, Sonny's lodge square in the background; but as I approached I started to make out some differences, little signs of neglect.

The frame-stretched hide was torn and ragged, the barbecuing dumbuck was more fire blackened than the roasts I remembered. I removed the skewer from its supports, speared it into the ground by the fire.

A partly butchered dumbuck carcase lay mouldering near the tent, quivering faintly as Copper's equivalent of maggots beavered away. I caught a whiff of the rotting flesh. With a growing unease I noticed the lodge fabric was not as robust as before, there were a few frayed edges, some tattered joins; loose flaps of the covering fluttered in the breeze, tugging intermittently at the overall structure as they tensioned their neighbours, then relaxed, tensioned and relaxed again, in an irregular pattern. Sonny's care and maintenance had obviously fallen behind schedule. My sense of foreboding quickened as I stood before the tent flap and heard the sounds of ragged breathing from inside.

'Sir?' I called. There was an indecipherable answer.

I lifted the flap and gagged at the smell from inside. I had forgotten the overpowering stench that accompanied Sonny's presence. Steeling myself, I entered. He was lying on a pile of dumbuck skins stacked against the left-hand wall. His head was turned towards the light. I held my breath in an effort to avoid the smell but the particles which had got through tickled my memory. And there was something newer in the mix this time, I felt sure; a sweeter odour I couldn't place.

The flap fell back, reshrouding him in shadow. He remained still, not responding to the change in light level. As I crossed to his side my head brushed the overhanging strips of dried meat. Forced to breathe at last, I inhaled shallowly.

'Sir?' I announced myself again.

Watery eyes stared up at me. He feebly waved an impossibly gnarled hand in greeting.

'Do you remember me, sir? . . . Alan? . . . You once made me a Son of the Rock.'

There was a long pause while he continued to gaze at me. His long white hair, kept out of his eyes by a circular leather thong, straggled down past his shoulders, partly obscuring the pits and valleys of his face. The skin on his neck lay in loose folds. I wasn't sure whether it was the length of time since I had seen him that made his appearance seem worse than before or if there really were more lines and wrinkles than I remembered.

'The Rock welcomes Its Sons,' he croaked at last.

'Are you all right?' I enquired. 'Is there anything I can do?'

He extended his hand. I grasped it and was horrified at its paper-thinness, his all-but bare bones and tendons uncushioned by intervening flesh.

But my concern was not mainly for his welfare. My Orth conditioning had welled up. I found myself thinking it was no wonder the old were hidden away if *this* was how they were. My life experience still screamed to me that it was wrong, that to age was an abomination. And the intimations of my possible future were something I had neglected to face up to in the years since I had last seen him. I still shied away from its contemplation.

He levered against my extended arm, painfully hoisting himself to a sitting position with my help.

'I tire easily,' he said, after he had composed himself. 'And there is little remedy. I am done.'

My automatic surge of protestation against this assertion stilled in my throat. Even if he wasn't done yet, and my first impressions suggested that he was, my news would surely speed the process.

'But the Rock has been good,' he continued. 'It has brought Its last Son back to me.'

'Not for long, I'm afraid,' I said.

'A small benison is enough,' he affirmed. 'They are all that's left me, now.' He looked around, searching behind me.

'Where is your woman? The one with spirit? Is she not with you?'

'I have no woman, now, alas,' I replied. 'As for Sile, I told you she had left me. I said we'd be unlikely to pair up again.'

'I know,' he replied, 'but I had hoped . . .' He let the thought trail into silence. 'A pity,' he said, before nodding ruminatively. 'She could have kept you to a straight path.' His gaze turned quizzical. 'Still, a strong young man like you will not be partnerless long,' he said, patting my hand.

'I've had my moments,' I admitted.

'But then, all the men of Orth are young,' he mused.

'The women too,' I said.

'Ah yes,' he murmured, 'I suppose so.' He became lost in his thoughts for a moment.

Recollecting himself, he attended to the proprieties. 'You will eat with me, my son,' he said. I didn't interpret it as a question.

'Of course.'

'The fare will be poor I fear,' he said. 'I have little energy to spare for foraging.'

I gestured at the drying strips of meat hanging over my head. 'Looks like you still get the odd dumbuck, though.'

'My snares trap an occasional stray,' he said.

I began removing a selection of the greasy strips from the roofing poles.

'Some of those are not so fresh,' he told me.

I smiled, memories of unpalatable fibrous tubers colouring my response. 'Better use them then, before they start to rot. The roast outside is perhaps a little overdone.'

'As you wish,' he said.

I rummaged around for a bowl to place the slices in.

'Allow me, my son,' he said, attempting to rise.

'No. No. Don't bother,' I said. 'I'll manage.'

I bit into one of the strips to test it. The taste was fine but the texture a little tough. 'What do you use to soften these up?' I asked him.

'Water,' he said. 'In the skins.' He indicated a pair of gravid globular hides closed over with drawstrings. 'And heat.'

'No special ingredients? Magical herbs?'

'Dumbuck meat has need of no such embellishment,' he said.

I remembered the vegetables again. 'You could be right,' I murmured.

The water bag jiggled alarmingly as I picked it up, its contents squirming under my inexpert hands. I set it down again, undid the string. A faint tepid aroma rose from it – about two parts dumbuck, I thought, one part something I didn't want to contemplate too closely. 'How long has this been lying?' I asked.

'A week,' he said. 'Perhaps more.'

I sniffed the festering liquid again, shrugged. His culinary standards hadn't harmed me last time.

With some difficulty I sloshed a measure of the recalcitrant liquid into the bowl. A lot more cascaded down my trimsuit, splashed onto the floor.

'Sorry,' I said, then showing him the bowl asked, 'Is this enough?'

'A little more,' he said.

'You're just being awkward, aren't you?' I joked. 'You want to see how clumsy I am again.' But I juggled with the bag once more, with greater care this time, pinching the neck, holding it closer to the bowl. A trickle of water dribbled onto the meat, slowly drowning it.

'There you are!' I said, setting the bag down. 'I'll make a Son of the Rock, yet.' I picked the bowl up. 'I'll just carry this out to the fire. I'll be back in a minute.'

Outside I scrabbled around for some more sticks to stoke the fading embers then balanced the bowl precariously atop an impromptu triangle. I blew on the glowing sub-coals to encourage the flames. When I was satisfied the added fuel would catch I returned to find Sonny had manoeuvred himself off his bed and was staggering to the door-flap, swaying unsteadily. He was breathing heavily.

'Here. Here,' I said. 'Wait. Let me help. Give me your arm.' I supported him with my right arm round his shoulders, took his weight on mine. 'That's it,' I said. 'Steady. Steady.'

He could barely walk. The most he could manage was a slow shuffle. Despite my attempts to alleviate them his poor, tortured efforts at bending to get through the flap were painful to witness. Even when

we gained the unobstructed path outside his progress
was no better. It seemed an eternity till we reached the
fire's side.

At such close proximity the sickly smell which he
now exuded – a sweet, warm, foetid stench redolent of
neglect and decay – attacked my nostrils in waves. Was
this the odour of old age? An indicator of a sickness of
some kind, perhaps terminal? Or merely the result of
there being no-one there to look after him?

Perhaps as a necessary response to the wrinkled
future possibly awaiting me I recoiled from the belief
that it was intrinsic to his state. But whatever the
odour's origin I found myself resolving to do my best
to help him, to allow his last days in the Rock to be
lived as comfortably as possible. Too little, perhaps,
and late, but a sop to my newly aroused conscience.

The bowl's contents were bubbling away merrily
by the time I was sure he was sitting at ease. I sat
down opposite him, my arms loosely dangling over
my crossed legs. From time to time I stirred the bowl
with a stick, occasionally spearing one of the steaming
slices, presenting Sonny with the offering, or more often
gingerly nibbling one myself. His muscles quivered as
he accepted the food, a slow, jerky journey to his mouth
followed.

The meat was not quite so tender as my memory
of his concoction in Sile's presence would have it
but the cooking had softened it considerably from its
dried state.

We chewed in silence mostly, with only the occasional
murmur of appreciation for the delicate taste and texture
of lumbuck; me because I was putting off for as long as
possible telling him the purpose of my visit, Sonny, I
assumed, because his teeth were no longer very capable

of incisive action and his attention was focused on eating. He waited till the last morsel was sliding deliciously down my throat before asking, 'And what is it the men of Orth require of the Rock this time?'

The question shocked me with its suddenness as well as its perspicacity. I almost gagged in the act of swallowing.

He registered my discomfiture. 'I am not so old, nor so frail,' he admonished me, 'as to imagine that you came here solely for pleasure or sentiment. An ordinand Son of the Rock you may be, but I know you do not have It in the blood, as I do.'

'In making me a Son you did me a great honour,' I protested, 'though I confess I didn't think so at the time. An honour I didn't deserve. And still don't. I fear I cannot fully live up to it. But you're right. My journey here is more of a penance than a pilgrimage.'

'A penance, my son?' he asked, and I noted the more personal tone. But I wasn't sure if somehow he was gently mocking me.

'Your hopes for me were misplaced. I came to offer you my apologies.'

'I absolved you, once, from any obligation,' he remarked evenly.

'But I didn't renounce it, not formally. I let you hope. And I had selfish reasons, too.'

He dismissed my late-found scruples. 'None of that matters,' he said. 'You wanted to please your woman; that is understandable enough. But a tired old man, alone, has few real hopes.'

'I had no wish to be the shatterer of yours,' I said.

'Only follow your heart, my son, and my hopes will be fulfilled.'

'I don't think I can,' I said, and explained, 'I may be

unable to prevent you and the Rock being done a great
wrong.'

'How so, my son? What more can the men of Orth
do to the Rock and Its remanents?'

While I hesitated, partly to see if he would come to
the answer himself, I wondered about his use of the
archaism. Was it deliberate? It could mean the Rock
Itself, Its adherents, or both. Had he employed it to
avoid using Son in the singular, to keep me from
knowledge of his disappointment, his rejection of me
as a successor? Was it merely a rhetorical flourish, his
usual orotundity? A mispronunciation, even? Or was
I just too damned touchy? In any event he continued
to sit impassively, forcing me to address the point
at issue.

'There exist, in the ground, in the rocks, certain
substances of high value,' I began, hesitantly.

'I know the men of Orth think so,' he interrupted,
'and exert great efforts in convincing themselves, but
what value can be higher than the Rock Itself? The
great damage these men of Orth do with their misguided values, they know not.'

I accepted the implied rebuke without comment. In
his terms he was right. More than right. He had faith
to sustain him, not just a desire to exploit resources,
to turn a fast buck.

'One of these substances,' I continued, 'has been
detected here on Copper.'

'There have been many such, I think,' he grunted,
gesturing towards the quarry.

'Previously this one was not highly regarded,' I went
'but it has recently acquired a huge importance. Its
th has increased a thousand times.'

do not understand,' he said. 'Have its properties

changed in some way? If not, its worth is surely the same as ever.'

'It is an essential component of a newly invented device for transporting objects vast distances in an instant,' I told him.

He was silent for a moment. 'Do the men of Orth not travel widely enough already?' he then enquired. 'Have you not come from some insignificant speck or other in the night sky? A speck an unimaginable distance away?'

'Yes,' I conceded, 'but this new method avoids long tedious journey times.'

'I have never seen the need to rush from place to place,' he said, mildly.

'It is precious to some men of Orth. Without it I would still be days away from here.'

'You have used the device?'

'Yes. I made part of my journey through it.'

'And what difference did it make? Would you not have come here in any event?'

I laughed. 'It made me ill,' I admitted, grateful to delay the moment of confrontation. 'That's quite a common reaction, apparently.'

'Then the device is useless.'

'Not to people who require to transport goods urgently. Or to travel quickly.'

'At the risk of illness?'

'Perhaps my description was too strong. The side effects are short-lived.'

'Even so. You remarked upon it, the discomfort must be pronounced.'

'But bearable,' I said. 'The point is . . .' I hesitate once more.

'Yes?' His gaze fixed on me. I turned my face aw

'This substance we have been speaking of has been detected beneath – within, I should say – the hill of the Rock,' I mumbled.

'Aaah . . .' he breathed, in a dying fall. I looked up. His eyes had unfocused, gazing into infinity. He said nothing more. I didn't speak either, leaving him to whatever thoughts and memories occupied him. I stared all around the clearing, anywhere but at him, trying to locate a spot to focus on that would somehow assuage my guilt. My tension and discomfort grew while the silence stretched on, but I couldn't move. I felt obliged to stay, to be there to try to help him come to terms with the final ruin of his faith.

When he began to chant, softly at first, I wasn't really sure. I noticed his lips move but thought it was a nervous quiver. Then his intonations grew louder, his voice cracking at times, increasing in speed till he made a movement at last, punctuating his tempo with small motions from side to side. I remained still, cramped in my position lest I distracted him. I had no wish to disturb his communion with the Rock. The feeling drained from my legs and arms as pressure on their points of contact with the ground or each other increasingly restricted the blood flow through them.

His torrent of Cupric continued. I didn't understand the words, couldn't recognise them as similar to those he'd used on me, and Sile, that first time. But they till seemed eerily familiar, part of me somehow, as tapping into an essential core of being we might all, ns of Orth and Rock alike, share. But then maybe I s conditioned to accept them, having been exposed ady to his influence. I tried to ignore them, fought emptation to drown in the litany the way I had ime; yet some of their power still got through.

There were no comforting images of flying dolphins to fill my eyes, however. Just a staring, tortured face torn from a rock formation by the massed energies of a tight-frequency laser beam. A face whose movements and expressions matched Sonny's own.

Numbness spread to my brain as I struggled to shake off the vision. My consciousness retreated down a tunnel illuminated at the far end only by the light of his countenance, transformed into the image of his God. A transfiguration I had fervently not wished to see.

He came to, at last, his chant wound down. The vision I beheld of the Rock superimposed on his face expanded from the tunnel's vanishing point alarmingly, exploded across my sight for a moment then faded as his more familiar features reasserted themselves. I emerged from my daze as his eyes slowly focused on me. He held me with them, large, bloodshot, fluid-filled. 'The Rock is doomed, then?' he whispered. 'It will go the way of all the others?'

I turned my gaze away, stretched my legs, rubbed life into the numbed portions. 'I'm sorry,' I said, facing him at last. 'I wish I had not had to bring such news.'

'That I should not have seen this day,' he sighed.

'I will do what I can to prevent it,' I assured him, 'but . . .'

'But you will fail?'

'Almost certainly. One man against the demands of Orth? It's hardly an even contest.'

'You must follow your heart, my son,' he said. 'Follow your heart. The Rock, whatever is left of It, will show you the way.'

'I wish I had your faith,' I said.

13

Kiss This Thing Goodbye

'Does it have to be iridium? Wouldn't osmium or rhodium or some other metal do instead?'

'I'm afraid there's no alternative.'

'Are you quite sure?'

Barandra shrugged. 'I wish there was. The stuff's a pain to work or cast when it's pure. UOAL have tried all sorts of alloys but none of them work anything like as well and our labs haven't found a substitute either. It's got the perfect neutron capture cross-section, you see. At least, its less abundant isotope has; we have to separate it out first. Introduce other atoms into the mix and they reduce the effectiveness.'

'Shit,' I muttered.

It was the answer I'd been expecting but still somehow hoping not to hear. I'd left Copper with orders to Lemarry to make sure Sonny was kept well fed and comfortable in the meantime. (It was my budget and would easily stretch to it. Plus I didn't want Sonny's death on my conscience.)

The boom in Orthrocks' activities due to the SHIFT's need for iridium had induced a frenetic atmosphere.

R & D's endeavours had moved over from more conventional exploration to exclusive concentration on gravitic anomalies. Operations were screaming for more resources, moaning about being asked to do too much with too little: Personnel were already well into an all-fronts recruitment drive to satisfy them. Sales and Marketing were abuzz, thinking of all the ripe profits and bonuses to be plucked, pressing me for a quick go-ahead on any number of sites. I appeased them slightly by sanctioning most of the similar projects elsewhere but over Copper I'd managed to stall, despite the fact Sonny's hill seemed to be the most promising. In a break between scurrying round department heads in the sector offices, checking and rechecking, I'd somehow found the time to inform Frazer of the situation and suggested Sonny would not be around much longer for Chelsea to do a piece on him.

Instanta – a licensing operation involving the University of Orth (Aban Latur) and Stoneguy finance – had been set up to exploit the SHIFT's potential. Their research centre on Midian worked closely with UOAL and Reydel Baumwein, the harmonised field theory's eccentric deviser whom the Femazon sisterhood kept claiming as one of their own but who just as consistently denied adherence to anything but pursuit of the intellect and as a consequence would not tolerate trivial interruptions from mere mining engineers. I'd come to Midian to meet Barandra, the Science section chief and the main authority on the technology required – though his grasp on the thinking behind it was reputed to be almost as good as Baumwein's.

He was tall, tan-skinned, sporting the latest male fashion fad to sweep through Orth. A shaven head and eyebrows, not a scrap of hair allowed to remain above the lower jaw, which was marked with a razor sharp line of demarcation. It looked rather as if an irregularly shaped, impossibly shiny and smooth exotic fruit was ripening in some sort of hairy plant calyx. On him the stark effect was emphasised because elsewhere he was bristling. Hair covered his forearms and the backs of his hands with a dark mat, crawled over the rim of his Instanta trimsuit to mingle with his jaw beard, swarmed up his back to join the extended demarcation line between the overly hirsute and startling baldness. He might almost have been wearing a furry polo-neck under his workwear.

'It's curious stuff,' he went on. 'You get local concentrations like this one – which isn't unusual with relatively rare metals – but you can find a layer of it on most of the habitable-sized planets if you look hard enough – very thin, not enough to mine – and nobody's ever quite figured out why.'

'Wasn't it supposed to be caused by meteor impacts?'

'That's one theory. There's certainly iridium containing interplanetary debris in all the systems we've explored so far. It seems likely.'

'So,' I said, 'there would have been plenty just floating about for the taking aeons ago.'

'Probably, but we weren't around then, and neither was the SHIFT.'

'Well,' I said, 'we've got scoop-freighters quartering the spiral arm gobbling up every likely looking asteroid and it's still not enough to meet the projected demand. We're going to have to start exploiting the planetary sources sometime soon.'

He gestured towards his vidtank where a contour map of Sonny's Rock was revolving slowly. Vivid red blotches indicating areas high in iridium bespattered the graphic. 'Judging by the figures I'd say you've got a good viable motherlode here. I guess this pile won't be around for much longer. Except . . .'

'Yes?'

'Is there some sort of problem with extraction on planets?' he asked.

'No, no. I'd just wondered if there might be something else we could offer you instead,' I said feebly.

'No, it has to be iridium,' he insisted. 'I was worried for a second there. I thought there might be some reason you wouldn't be able to supply us.'

'Damn.' I didn't know how long I could delay it, now. I'd run out of excuses. Though Barandra's advice was unwelcome I had to bow to his expertise. I was going to have to make a decision soon. My last forlorn hope was that Frazer would act on the message I'd sent him and persuade Chelsea Monday to do a piece on Sonny that could sway public opinion in his and the Rock's favour.

'Raki,' I said. 'And leave me the bottle.' Then a bizarre desire overtook me, a cobweb from the corners of memory. 'Oh, and a Bulayma Grand.'

I took a seat and waited for the barman to bring over the order. At this time of day the bar was empty. There were the usual recreational drug-parlour paraphernalia scattered round the room, game tanks flashing their lurid invitations, the more discreet bulk of needlepak dispensers offering their different brands of 'Instant' hits – the usual Major Thoms and Easegoodes – a croaky corner; but even here, far from Copper, reminders of Sonny were inescapable. Chelsea Monday's familiar voice was floating from the speakers of the bar's viewing-tank. I glanced at it, scanning

the exterior shots of the orbital displayed there more
attentively when I realised I knew the place. The scene
changed to a construction bay where a large ship was
being prepared for launch, confirming it was Jefferson.
In the otherwise featureless vacuum around the ship the
spangled scintillae of the construction crew floated like
hoverflies at some unfathomable endeavour. Rendered
insignificant by the scale of the structure they attended,
their highly reflective suits scattered strange partial
rainbows as they twisted and turned in the satellights,
shimmering from one phase to another as their illumination changed during an occasional random dive.

My attention was distracted from this oddly beautiful display by the barman setting down a tray. Before
hitting the raki, I paused to say to myself, 'Well here's
to you, Sonny,' then raised my glass. The tingle hit
the back of my throat at once, the warm sensation
creeping through into my sinuses and on down into
my stomach.

My mind couldn't settle. I tried to shut everything
from it in anticipation of the oblivion to come. I puzzled
over the bits and pieces in front of me, the cradle and
the burner, sat there fiddling with the apparatus, trying
to remember how Sile had done it. For some reason
I couldn't quite fathom I wanted to get the ritual
correct.

The raki buzz dissolved slowly into my system and
I took another shot. This one was not so sharp, a slow
burn that was the more satisfying for being less intense.
I savoured the moment and refilled the glass. One more
swallow and I was settling nicely.

I adjusted the burner and took up the igniters. It
had been circular movements, I remembered. Gingerly
I waved the igniters in a broad sweep, bringing them

together in front of me. The gas took fire with a loud *whump*, roaring into flames which shot high into the air. I dropped the igniters in panic and scrabbled hastily for the burner control. When I had it about right I slid the burner under the cradle, watched the hot flame lick the cold glass. The white grains in the base glowed eerily through the red liquid, like a bloodshot eye in reverse. I poured another shot of raki and sat back to wait for the potion to boil.

Up in the tank Chelsea was delivering her piece from Jefferson. Behind her the vast looming background of the *Last Empress* was out of focus, as if her obsolescence were somehow manifest, her irrelevance as a transport medium of preference rendered visible.

The raki was beginning to numb my brain, my consciousness narrowing down to a small arc. I focused on the tank, trying to force unpleasant thoughts away. Meanwhile Chelsea wandered down spacious hallways, explored elegant staterooms groaning with plush fixtures and fittings, marvelled at the opulence of a huge ballroom lit by vast chandeliers. I giggled as I thought of the horribly cramped, squalid interior of the SHIFT chamber. At least in a hyperspace-liner there was plenty of room to be sick.

I let the Bulayma Grand come to the boil, adjusted the burner to a simmer. Before sampling it I consumed the last of the raki, holding the flavours on my tongue, breathing in its ragged vapour, allowing the alcohol to exert its numbing effect on my mouth.

I bent to the stems, sniffed. The warm gases seemed to slip straight through my nose into my brain. I flinched back, head reeling. Echoes of danderweed, boglily and fried Hometurtle tickled my awareness, fickle traces of the dysfunction the drug brought. As the local anaesthetic wore on I breathed in the fumes more deeply, relaxed into the sensations. Curiously, and against my expectations, there was no reminder of Sile in the experience. I had to concentrate against the drug's effects to remember her at all. Fleetingly I hoped that I might be about to forget her completely, but it was just that I was too blitzed to care.

Up above, Chelsea rambled on about the demise of the hyperspace-liner, the great orbitals, the honourable trade of shipbuilding and the end of Orth as we knew it. And I felt fine.

Deetox, I found, was wonderful stuff. A combination of metabolic accelerants and anti-pyretics, I didn't usually bother with it but this time I made the exception. Remembering my experiences on the *Strangeness And Charm* and that Sile had said that exercise helped I'd also taken the precaution of running all the way back to my hotel, the object of tolerant stares from the gentlefolk of Midian. They were used to stranger sights: research labs were scattered all around the place. I'd paused only to pop the D-pill before dropping off.

It was just as well. My message alarm warbled me awake to only the normal drowse, my head not feeling as if it had been hammered into oblivion. I hit the acknowledge button and Lemarry's already days-old news, even though SHIFT-beamed from the nearest access point to Copper, filtered through the Midian air.

I was nearly too late. Without the SHIFT I would have been; though, of course, in another sense I had never remotely been in time. Even SHIFTing as fast as possible, and its attendant miseries, cycling through the various intervening access points depositing less and less from my dwindling stomach contents at each stop – though heaving just the same – left me fretting more over whether I would miss the end of Sonny's story than my immediate discomforts. The final peaceful three-day hyperspace hop seemed interminable; the blinded, yet still staring, eye of the Hole when we made orbit, swelling hypnotically during the descent pass, an unblinking rebuke. I got down from the flier at Roodsland with a heightened sense of anxiety made all the worse by the presence of the OBN circus Frazer had brought with him.

I quizzed Lemarry immediately. 'How is he?'

'He's able to speak a little, but he can hardly move.'

'What happened? Does anybody know?'

'We called in the medic from the Hole. She thinks it's some sort of electrical overload in his brain. But she's never treated a case like this for anyone who's not had Euthuol. She's not really sure. Said it could be anything. We knew you wouldn't want him moved. She only had an emergency bag; without her usual equipment she was a bit lost.'

'So where is she?'

'There was an emergency at the Hole, a couple of quarriers crushed in a rock fall. Possibly damaged spines. She had to go back.'

'Poor sods,' I commiserated. Despite my exposure to Sonny's strangeness, as the good citizen of Orth I had been reared, the thought of physical disability, lack of perfection, was still capable of dismaying me.

'She said there wasn't much she could do for the old guy anyway.'

'So he's just lying up there all on his own?'

'I set up a rota. Someone looks in on him mornings

and evenings. Makes sure he gets fed. He can't take much that's not liquid, though. And . . .' He gave me an apprehensive stare.

'Yes?'

'The lads don't like it. It's not what they signed up for, nursing some old crank – no offence –' he inclined his head at that, raised his shoulders slightly, 'who by rights should be put away somewhere. They don't think it's right.'

'And what do you think?' I asked. I know it was unfair, but I was angry.

He turned his head away, embarrassed. 'It's none of my business,' he mumbled. 'I just do what I'm told.'

'Ah well,' I relented, my mind moving to other concerns. 'It probably won't be a problem soon.'

I gestured towards the assembled VT equipment and its wolf-pack of technicians. 'Right. What are we going to do about this OBN crowd?'

'That's up to you. It was you invited them here.'

'Yes, damn it. I wish I hadn't now. But I didn't know Sonny was going to . . . Shit. I suppose I'll have to negotiate something. In the meantime get that medic back here as fast as you can.'

I set off towards the group where Frazer was waiting, motioned him across.

'You know the situation?' I enquired.

'The old guy's been taken ill, I hear.'

'Yes. It might mean you've wasted your trip,' I warned.

'Maybe not. We can still do a background piece. An interview would have been nice, but it's not strictly essential.'

'That's good. I don't want to disturb him unnecessarily.'

I looked around. A certain kenspeckle figure was absent. 'When does Chelsea arrive?'

'She doesn't,' he said.

'What do you mean?'

'She still refuses to do this. She says it's obscene. Claims it would ruin her reputation to be connected with anything like it.'

'So why are you here? I mean, I thought you only worked with her. If she's not doing it . . . ?'

'I went over her head. Talked to the bosses at OBN direct. I got the go-ahead to do this on my own. You're looking at OBN's latest in-tank reporter. This crew is mine.'

'Congratulations.'

'Thanks.'

'Aren't you worried? It's a big step. I mean, I thought you were a sound man.'

'No. There's nothing to it. I've watched Chelsea do it scores of times.'

'So have I, but I still wouldn't attempt it myself.'

'Relax, mate. She makes plenty of mistakes. You only see the successful shots. It'll be a dawdle.'

'That's if I let you do it.'

'What?' The idea had obviously surprised him.

'Well, I don't know how bad he is or how your operations might affect him. I don't want his condition made worse.'

'If he's so far gone, we have to do it now,' he said. 'We might never get another chance. Come on, Alan. It was you that involved me in the first place. This is my big break you're talking about here. I can't go back and say I haven't got anything.'

'I'll think about it.'

'I might just go ahead and shoot anyway.'

That made me pause. It was something I hadn't considered. Ever since he'd told me Chelsea wasn't coming I had been hoping to fob him off cheaply. 'This is an Orthrocks site,' I responded, slowly. 'In my area. I decide what's allowed. Orthrocks is a pretty big company to get on the wrong side of,' I warned.

He gestured at his crew. 'And this is an OBN news team. We have resources too.' He let his implied threat hang. We both knew which of the two had most influence. Maybe the balance would change with the SHIFT and Orthrocks's ability to demand a high price for its services but I couldn't wait long enough for that.

'Let's not quarrel about this, Alan,' he said.

'So long as you get your own way?'

'What's your problem?' he demanded. 'I thought you wanted us to run a story on him.'

'I did. I do, I suppose. But with Sonny ill – dying for all I know – it doesn't seem right, now.'

'Well make up your mind quickly, will you? But remember, whatever you decide . . .'

'What?'

He pursed his lips, cast his glance over the nearby huts and then back, spread his hands in mock innocence.

'There are always stories to tell,' he said.

For a moment I wondered what he could mean. That I had once brought Sile here was hardly a well-kept secret and anyway not worth troubling over. But she had accompanied him back to the spaceport on wages day. While I thought Sile would not break a confidence I couldn't rely on it – where she was concerned I had always been confused. She had betrayed me once by leaving me, there was no reason to suppose she wouldn't have done it again. What might she have told him of my private fears, the intimate details of my medical history?

He may have been probing, remembering the unusual domestic arrangements of my youth, the sudden disappearance of my grandmother: adding two and two to make four. But it was more likely he knew nothing; he was bluffing on the assumption that everyone has something in their past they wish to remain there.

I frowned as if puzzled by his statement. 'I said I'll think about it,' I replied mildly.

The anxiety was stronger this time, mounting with each step up the hill. The sense of immanence, of ill-defined risk, the wheels of fate grinding slow and steady, was all pervasive. Tortured admonishing faces peered at me from every outcrop and crevice on the ascent, out of every tree in the woods surrounding Sonny's clearing. I suppose there was an element of auto-suggestion, a predisposition, a heightened awareness due to my knowledge of the deterioration of Sonny's condition, or maybe his ritual had gradually exerted its effect. I too now felt the pull that he did, had become more sensitised to it with each visit; but the Rock's influence on me seemed to be growing. While still intellectually dismissing the notion as nonsense, somehow, sometime, I had begun to accept the Rock as a physical presence. This burden had increased on making orbit round Copper and again on the flier to Roodsland, ratcheting up the disquiet I'd felt since the alarm call on Midian. But then I suppose I had never been truly at ease since I'd received word of iridium deposits on Copper.

Or did my apprehension stretch further back than that? Further even than the manifestation of the face of the Rock I thought I had imagined at the Hole? Had it not started from the moment I first saw Sonny and had that sudden reminder of my genetic inheritance; that terrible intimation of mortality?

In an attempt to ward off such thoughts I conjured up images of a light-footed dancer, nimbly picking her way from rock to rock. But that was just one more way of torturing myself.

There was something else wrong, something different that I couldn't quite identify. It wasn't till I entered the clearing that I realised what it was. There was no fire. The smell of woodsmoke that usually permeated the hill, adding its acrid tang to the local atmosphere – along with its usual more delicate accompaniment of roast dumbuck – was absent. The spit stood empty, stark and useless above it. The circle of stones that kept the fire in place held back only a residue of white ash mixed with a few larger blackened lumps. I stirred it with my foot, sending little columns of fine powder into the air, dancing and twirling in the shafts of setting sunlight filtering through the trees. Through them I saw his stretched hide frame tumbled over, dislodged from its usual position by some unruly wind.

The tent-flap was open, Lemarry's rota-man's attempt at ventilation. Nevertheless the stench inside was stifling, the sweetness I had noticed last time concentrated into something more putrid, drowning out any other smells from dumbuck skins or Sonny himself. The quarrier rose to greet me. I didn't recognise him but he would have seen me on my previous visit to Roodsland. Even if he was a newcomer he would have known who I was from my trimsuit flashes.

'He's been quiet, sir,' he said. 'No trouble. Sleeping a lot.'

'When does your shift end?' I asked.

'In about an hour.'

'On you go, then. I'll take over.'

'Thanks. Can't say I'll be sorry to get away from the smell.' He wasted little time in carrying himself off.

I glanced around, took in the Orthrocks-labelled assortment of energy and protein tetrapaks that Lemarry must have had provided for him. None of Sonny's usual fare – neither dumbuck nor fibrous tubers – was in evidence.

Alert for signs of discomfort, I approached his recumbent body. His sleep appeared to be fitful but my earlier disquiet began to dissipate now I could see he had been cared for at least tolerably and was, if not exactly well, then unmistakably still breathing. Harsh, ragged sounds dragged from his throat at irregular intervals; each one, it seemed, a terminal effort. I settled into the standard Orthrocks issue chair someone had thought to lug all the way up the hill and waited for him to awake.

Whether it was the disturbance of my entry or some more subliminal awareness of my presence that roused him I'm not sure but it was not long after that his breathing moderated and his eyes flickered open.

'Hello, sir,' I said gently.

He raised his head slightly, peered at me as if through a veil. 'You have come,' he whispered hoarsely. His head sank back onto its rest, his eyes reclosed.

'The Rock welcomes Its Son,' he sighed.

His hand fluttered towards me hesitantly. I took it, felt its paper-thin grasp, so weak compared to our previous encounters. I could almost feel the spirit ebbing from him.

'I couldn't let you be alone if . . .' I let the sentence drop. 'I feel responsible,' I explained. 'Guilty in a way.'

His other hand wavered across to cover mine. 'You have nothing to reproach yourself for, my son,' he said. 'You have shown an old man kindness he did not expect. If my time has come, I am ready to accept the Rock's will. Do not mourn my passing.'

'It hasn't come to that, yet,' I said. 'And needn't. I've sent for a medic to look you over again. I'm sure she'll be able to help you.'

He gazed at me reproachfully. 'I want none of your unnatural Orth remedies,' he said. 'They have done enough harm.'

'I promise you there will be nothing but treatment of your present condition,' I assured him. 'No Euthuol.'

I hesitated. What I'd thought of saying wasn't something I felt comfortable broaching even with him. 'I'll let you into a secret,' I said. 'I haven't taken Euthuol myself.'

The words seemed to have an immediate effect on him. Perhaps I only imagined his response but I felt his demeanour change. His grasp tightened, his pulse and breathing quickened.

'I knew I had chosen well,' he said.

I greeted this silently, not wanting to disillusion him.

'Lift me, my son,' he said. 'I wish to drink.'

I placed my arms under his, cradled his head in my left hand and pulled up gently. I shifted the burden to my right shoulder and adjusted the skins behind him, building them into a pile, holding my breath against the sweet rank smell of his slowly failing body. He sank back gratefully onto the support as I eased him down.

I fetched over a few of the tetrahedral drinks cartons while he lay gathering his strength.

'Is this okay?' I asked, offering him one.

'It matters little,' he said. 'None of these Orth confections has the savour of dumbuck or redroot. I cannot distinguish between them, except for sweetness. But they are all I am able to stomach.'

I fiddled with the plasformed spout at the corner of the tetrapak, held it against his lips. He dribbled in a pitifully small amount.

'Thank you, my son,' he said when he had done. He stared at the carton and sighed. 'We end as we began,' he said. 'Suckling naught but liquid. But that device is hard and cold, a poor substitute for the comfort of a woman's breast.'

'I could do with some of that myself,' I told him.

'Drink, then,' he said, evenly. 'I have had my fill.'

'No. No. I meant . . .' His quizzical gaze made me pause.

'You're not ended yet,' I said. 'Not if you can make jests like that.'

'My son, my son,' he said. 'You feel a lack. That is understandable; the young need companionship. Perhaps the old do too; though I am no good judge, I have been too long alone. But have patience. Your purpose will work itself out. The Rock sees all, knows all. What is planned, is planned. Let it come to pass.'

'Have I no choice, then?' I asked, thinking of my dilemma and the outcome I saw as unavoidable. 'Is everything laid out, inevitable?'

'The Rock tests us all, however we respond,' he replied, gnomically.

'I don't believe I know redroot,' I said, to steer clear of the subject of the Rock.

'You do, my son. You have eaten it: along with the dumbuck when you first accepted my hospitality.'

'That stuff! You should be grateful these drinks don't taste of it, then,' I said. 'It's awful.'

'You do not appreciate its qualities? Perhaps there is something in the relationship between a man and his environment which determines his tastes.'

'Mm. Maybe,' I mused, remembering April and the far-reaching effects of Beribbé.

'I was wondering,' I said. 'How well are you?'

'As you see,' he replied. 'I have fared better.'

'I know, but I must ask you this. Do you remember the people who wanted to take pictures of you, to show throughout Orth? The group Sile objected to so strongly?'

'Of course, my son,' he reproached me. 'As you reminded me, I am not quite ended yet.'

'Well, they have returned – except for the rude one. She declined again. If you don't feel up to it I'll try to put them off, I don't want you disturbed more than is necessary; but they may not take no for an answer.'

'What would they have me do? I am no longer capable of much.'

'They may be content with only a few pictures. Your lodge, your clothing, yourself. I doubt you will be asked to speak. In your present state it will mean allowing them in here, of course, but the disruption should be short.'

He lay for a moment, thinking it over, then pronounced, 'I can see little harm in this.'

'I'd rather have a medical opinion on that,' I told him. 'On the credit side, the exposure will make others in far-flung parts of Orth aware of the importance the

Rock holds for you, might encourage them to work to prevent Its demise. We'll have to be careful about that, though. We don't want hordes of tourists descending on you.' Then a particularly odd flight of fancy sprang into my head. 'Who knows,' I added. 'It may even bring lost Sons back to the fold.'

He was silent for a while. 'Do you think any of these are likely, my son?' he responded eventually.

I thought not, but I didn't tell him that. What I said was, 'It's worth a try.'

I also didn't tell him that it was the one slim hope I had left.

'I want a sympathetic treatment, mind. He's not to be ridiculed.'

'Yes, yes, yes,' Frazer replied. 'You've told me often enough. Don't fret. I know what I'm doing.'

'That's what worries me,' I said.

He spent his time fussing around, overseeing the final preparations for his grand début piece on Sonny, checking each 'wave guide, cable placing and camera angle obsessively, making sure the sound equipment was just right, every last detail was in place. I didn't remember such perfectionism when Chelsea had been in charge but I suppose he was taking more care than usual; he didn't want to cock up his chance for a brief splash of fame.

I was tagging along mainly to ensure that the process wasn't too intrusive and Sonny overstressed, but I knew I would have no control over the commentary Frazer would record later in the comfort of his editing suite back at OBN. As a result I took a small delight in turning the screw of his harassment a little whenever I could. He seemed oblivious to my barbs, however, surfing the crest of his wave of adrenalin, the embodiment of hyper.

We were standing together after one of the external shoots had been completed to his satisfaction and the technicians were setting up another, when out of the blue he said, 'I'm glad we could settle this as friends.'

My first reaction was anger. It wasn't friendship for him that had been the deciding factor. He surely didn't presume that? The second was that it might be his obscure way of apologising for his vague threat to me. There was still the element of doubt, however. He may only have meant that he was holding the threat in reserve.

I gave him a weighed response. 'I'm not sure I trust you media types, you know,' I told him. He dissolved into convivial laughter and, as I realised that I no longer cared, I joined in. My admission to Sonny that I hadn't taken Euthuol had lessened the inhibition I had long felt. At that moment I was indifferent as to who might know I may be genetically defective. Hell, I wasn't even sure of it myself, so what did it matter?

The medic from the Hole sickbay, a tight-lipped woman, rather too straight-laced for my tastes, had emerged from Sonny's lodge clasping her medpouch to her like a crown. Finding the source of the disturbance, she stared at us disapprovingly. We tried to compose ourselves.

'Here's trouble,' I said, as she came over.

'I thought you wanted the least upset,' she said. 'This sort of behaviour hardly qualifies.'

'Sorry,' I replied. 'We'll try to keep the noise down.'

'May I ask what was so funny?' she enquired.

'Nothing,' I said.

'Private joke,' added Frazer.

She stared at us suspiciously. 'I see. I'm glad certain people can find some amusement in this shithole,' she said.

'How is the patient?' I asked, shifting the conversational ground.

'Comfortable,' she replied. 'There's no difference in his condition. I'm wasting my time here,' she added dismissively. 'It's a disgraceful misuse of my abilities.'

'The Hole can do without you for a while,' I said. 'My flier's here ready for you if there should be another emergency.'

'You realise there's nothing I can do for him?'

'That's as may be,' I said, 'but I'd still like you to wait around till all this business is cleared up and things get back to normal.'

'As you wish,' she said. 'As long as I'm on expenses.'

'Don't worry. The files are in. I'll okay them at the end of the month. No problem.'

'Fine. Then if you'll excuse me, I'll get back to my rather overcared-for patient.'

'Walks away looking like butter wouldn't melt between her legs,' I said to Frazer as she moved off. 'Do you suppose she's ever ... ?' I asked. 'I mean, can you imagine anyone screwing that?'

'Oh, I don't know,' he said, watching her buttocks gently twitch the fabric of her Medix trimsuit. 'I'd give it a go.'

'But you'd fuck anything female,' I objected.

'Not quite anything,' he said. 'I'd draw the line at Chelsea Monday.'

'Is she female?'

Our renewed laughter temporarily halted her regal progress, and brought us a scowl to punctuate her retreat.

*   *   *

It was one of those bright, sunlit Copper mornings, a few balloons of cloud far off, no danger of rain, overnight condensation lifting from the surrounding vegetation in a fine shimmer of increasingly less tentative evaporation, the same unbroken weather as the day before and the day before that, back to the last periodic storm front a couple of months ago, that Frazer and I mounted the hill for the last time. The air was still cool, making the climb invigorating; the sun wasn't yet high enough to raise the temperature to throat-parching level as it would when the morning wore on. The trees on the plateau stood sharp and clear, swaying in the light breeze, leaves rustling their sibilant messages to each other.

Frazer paused for a moment to absorb the view through a gap in the trees, along the thin winding rivercourse in the valley to the higher hills of the headwaters beyond. 'You know,' he said. 'I'm getting to like this place. It reminds me a bit of Home. I'll almost be sorry to leave.'

'I know what you mean,' I said. 'But you surprise me. I thought you'd be anxious to get away, finish the stuff off. Be out there in glorious living 3-D full colour surround.'

'I am really. But so far it's all been familiar.' He glanced at Sonny's lodge, where some of his crew members were to-ing and fro-ing through the opened entry flap on various technical errands. 'The hard bit's still to come. I've been delaying my first straight-to-camera.'

He gazed up the valley again. 'To tell you the truth Alan, I'm shit scared. What if I'm no good? What if they don't like me?'

'I don't see why they shouldn't. Any fool in front of

a lens is as good as any other. You'll be okay. Whatever happened to "it'll be a dawdle"?'

'Bravado. I was trying to convince myself.'

We started walking across the clearing, stopped a few em away from the entrance. 'What about projecting an image of yourself?' I said. 'Like Chelsea with her hat and ribbonshades? Only not either of those. Choose something else.'

He smiled. 'Oh, yeah. Chelsea's hat. Remind me to tell you about that sometime. Thanks Alan. I hadn't thought of that. I owe you one.'

Although Sonny's table had been removed to provide more space, four mini-quadrax on tripods, a clutch of radiomikes, assorted lighting gear, ribbons of flexible ducting, two technicians and the medic made the lodge a claustrophobe's nightmare. I eased myself over the 'wave guides running through the entrance and squeezed past the gold-emblazoned chest of the nearest crewwoman whom Frazer immediately engaged in business talk. The air inside was less rank than usual, a through-current from a vent someone had opened at the rear of the lodge allowing the familiar odours to disperse a little.

Sonny was propped up on his bed, eyes closed, breathing hoarsely. His long, gaunt arms sprawled outside his coverings, strange pseudopodal animals ending in skeletal fingers like stranded starfish.

In a fair imitation of the caring professional the medic was taking some sort of reading from an instrument trailing a wire tacked to Sonny's body.

'How is he this morning?' I whispered to her.

'Stable,' she replied tersely. 'But I can't say what effect this activity might have on him.'

'It'll be over soon,' I said, 'And then you can get back

to whatever it is you do at the Hole.'

I peered down at him. 'Is he asleep?' I asked.

'I doubt it. Would you be?'

I leant over him and she removed the sensor with its intervening wire, stowed them in the medpouch balanced on her lap. 'Good morning, sir,' I addressed him, loudly.

Sonny's eyes flickered open, focused slowly. 'The Rock welcomes Its Son,' he greeted me.

'He's always speaking in riddles like that,' the medic muttered behind me. I ignored her.

I glanced at Frazer, received a nod. 'I think the picture takers are ready for you, now,' I told Sonny. 'Are you sure you want to go ahead with this?'

'If it is the Rock's will,' he said.

Frazer groaned. 'Is that a go or not?'

'It means he won't say no. It's up to us,' I told him.

'Right, then,' Frazer took over. 'Let's do it. Everybody out of shot, please.'

He stood back and I joined him. The two crew members finished their final checks and moved out of the area enclosed by the cameras. 'It's a bit cramped in here,' he told them. 'One of you had better go.' They exchanged glances. The nearest shrugged and left.

'Doctor?' he prompted. 'You're in shot.'

She rose from the chair slowly, looped the medpouch over her shoulder. 'Be as quick and orderly as you can,' she told Frazer. 'His condition is delicate. He needs as much rest as possible.'

'Don't worry,' he replied. 'He'll hardly know we're here.' A look of withering disdain crossed her pinched features. She left shaking her head.

'Why is it they have to talk in Medspeak?' I asked Frazer when she had safely gone.

'Don't know,' he muttered distractedly, moving to give the equipment feed indicators a quick check himself. 'I expect they feel it gives them more authority.'

'I'll just leave then,' I said. 'Let you get on with it.'

'Maybe you'd better stay. The old boy might need reassurance.' He pulled the chair out of the frame area and nodded to the remaining crewman. 'Lights,' he said.

The crewman went to the door flap, waved a signal to the recording desk. Sonny flinched as a harsh radiance from the various floods set around the quadrax perimeter bathed him in stark tones. His eyes closed and he raised his right arm briefly as if to ward the light off. His breath rasped slightly faster. Frazer waited till his eyes reopened and his breathing resettled to a low grumble before saying, 'Start recording.' The crewman signalled again. Tiny coloured lights began to strobe in repeating patterns across their condition displays as the cameras scanned the scene.

'Zoom in.' The crewman made a circular motion with his hands. The display patterns changed as the cameras' lenses whirred. At the same time their servoes panned them down slightly to keep their mutual focus synchronous. Sonny observed these gyrations unblinkingly, as if they were happening elsewhere.

'Okay. Cut.' The crewman chopped the air. The displays petered out and the floods cut off leaving patchy ghosts of deep purple after-image weaving over my retinas.

In the relative darkness a moan broke the silence. I blinked to clear my sight. Sonny's back was arched, his breath was escaping in an awful rasp. A look of horror and pain – a ghastly reminder of the tortured face of the Rock being torn from Its foundations – masked the ancient lines of his face. His body convulsed, legs thrashing briefly. Disturbed coverlets tumbled from the bed knocking over one of the mini-quadrax. The crewman leaped to catch it just before it hit. Sonny slumped down, head lolling, arms atwitch. An awful, breathless silence fell as his motions ceased.

'Medic!' I yelled.

She entered at a stooping run, unfolding her med-pouch awkwardly as she came. 'What's up?'

I jerked my head towards Sonny. 'Some sort of attack,' I said. 'Do something!'

She hopped past the crewman, scrabbled in her medpouch with one hand, grabbed for Sonny's wrist with the other.

I heard Frazer's steely voice as if out of a dream. 'Set them up again.'

'What?' I said, glancing round.

He was speaking to the technician. 'Set them up again,' he repeated. 'Hurry or we'll miss it.'

'You can't do that!' I objected as I realised his intention. The crewman paused, eyeing each of us in turn, flicked his gaze towards the activity on the bed. The medic was stooped over Sonny, hands kneading and poking at his body in some inscrutable medical function.

Frazer faced me squarely. 'It doesn't matter now, Alan,' he said. 'It can't affect him any more. This is exactly what I need. Don't you see? They can't turn stuff like this down.' He turned back to the technician. 'Set them up again.'

'But he might be dying!'

'I know that,' Frazer said.

'Tell him, doctor!' I shouted. 'Tell him he can't do this.'

'It doesn't bother me,' she panted, whipping a stethoscope from her medpouch one-handed, fitting it over her ears. 'As long as you don't get in my way.'

'Do it,' Frazer nodded at his crewman who immediately began resetting the quadrax. Frazer turned to shout through the flap, 'Quick! Lights! Mikes too! Start recording.'

A moment's delay and the floods flared again, throwing the medic's elongated shadow onto the lodge wall. The stethoscope's long tubing snaked down in a seductive arc, obscurely menacing. The quadrax displays scrolled once more, a kaleidoscopic jumble of meaningless lights.

As the medic worked on him, pumping his heart with the heels of her hands, my opinion of her upped by an order of magnitude. She may have been a snooty bitch but she seemed to know her job. Hypo poised, she was now pinching a vein in his arm, readying an injection, I guessed, of some stimshot or other.

Sonny's scrawny chest lay open to the world, a bag of stick-like ribs seemingly held in place by blanched tissue-paper skin. Sad, shrunken nipples punctuated the hairless pallor with a bizarre dash of darker colour. The medic slapped two small fabric-covered metal cylinders either side of his heart area, rapidly taped them in place, strung their leads to her medpouch. She thumbed a control. Sonny's torso jumped.

'Shit. This is marvellous,' Frazer breathed beside me.

I waited, helpless, thinking to myself Sile had been right. It had killed him. Or as good as. Even if it hadn't, I couldn't see him surviving the shock.

She pumped his heart again, listened through the 'scope. Her fingers fiddled inside the medpouch, pushed the pad. Sonny's chest heaved once more. 'Come on,' she muttered. She went back to the 'scope, her face intent, shook her head in frustration. 'One more time,' she said. I turned away. Frazer's hand clasped my shoulder.

I heard the jolt, the accompanying sizzle, felt Frazer's grip tighten, heard, 'Well done, my beauty.'

When I looked again she was grinning. Round the two electrodes on Sonny's chest patches of blackened skin flowered obscenely. The air of singed flesh filtered through the lodge. His breath came in shallow gasps, but it came.

She leaned back, sighed.

'Is he going to be all right?' I asked uncertainly.

'For the moment,' she replied.

'Right,' I said to Frazer. 'Cut this now. Leave him in peace.'

'Okay,' Frazer said. He motioned to the technician. A few moments after he left the floods cut out and the displays strobed to a halt. In the dark silence only the sounds of ragged breathing could be heard.

The medic returned to her ministrations, checking his pulse and breathing rate. After giving him another shot she restowed her equipment methodically.

'What's the outlook?' I asked.

'I've stabilised him for now, but he's still critical. I don't have the resources here to do any more. At the Hole sickbay his chances would be much better.'

'But can he be moved? Won't the journey kill him?'

'If he stays here he'll die anyway.' she said. In answer to my unspoken question she added, 'Within hours. A day at most.'

'And at the Hole?'

'Who knows? He's not taken Euthuol; there's no telling how far he's degenerated, his progression maybe won't be as rapid as in normal cases.'

'What do you recommend?'

'Fly him out. Unless you want a funeral tomorrow.'

'Can I have some time to think?'

'A few minutes won't make much difference,' she said. Frazer had already made himself scarce: when she had gone I was left alone with Sonny.

I couldn't face him at first. I was afraid. Not of Sonny – nor even the sudden, stark imminence of death – so much as what I would do. Could I remove him – albeit senseless and unseeing – from the place he held so dear, for the sake of a few more weeks of life? Yet I flinched from that starker alternative.

Guilt and relief were mingling with the fear in a strange cocktail of emotion. Temptation was strong. I could glimpse an escape from my dilemma. A terrible sense of impending freedom stalked my conscience, promising absolution, if only temporarily. Now there was the possibility to put through the inevitable decision on the Rock without affecting Sonny directly.

When I finally looked down at him it seemed a little easier. None of his usual presence was there. His animating spirit was absent as if, at the end, his devotion to the Rock had drained away leaving only a shallow-breathing husk.

I could see only the alien. A flaccid arrangement of lined and ridged leather parodying a human face, surrounded by a sparse collection of impossibly white strands masquerading as hair. Only a resemblance to what I took for humanity.

It may have been the drugs, of course, a peculiar side effect of the sedatives the medic had surely pumped into him shutting off his inner light, but this was not the way I wished to remember him. I pushed my way outside.

Frazer was off on the edge of the clearing organising some new camera positions. He'd obviously determined to film the outcome whatever I'd decided – either way it was good footage. The medic stopped pacing around Sonny's firepit and waited for me.

'Well?' she asked.

I shook my head. 'I'm not sure.'

The VT technician who'd witnessed her efforts to revive Sonny approached. 'Is it okay if we remove our gear from inside?' he asked. 'We'll try not to cause a disturbance.'

'No problem,' she said. 'I've sedated him for now.'

On the point of leaving, he hesitated. 'I was wondering. Why did you go to so much trouble?' he asked her. 'It hardly seemed worth it to me. I mean, the guy's near dying, right?'

She pointed at me, 'He might have fired me if I hadn't,' she said, drily. My protestations of innocence were eyed askance.

'No. You're right,' she told him. 'For a normal person in such an advanced state I wouldn't. It's better just to let them go.'

'So why, then?'

'Call it professional pride. It's an unusual case: a challenge.'

The crewman nodded, the silent appreciation of one practitioner for another. We watched him disappear into the lodge.

'With the monitoring equipment at the Hole I can keep him stable,' the medic prompted.

'I don't know,' I replied. 'He's spent all his life here. Is it fair to take him away?'

'It is if you don't want him to die.'

'He'll die anyway, sooner or later. With or without your intervention.'

'Yes. But it doesn't have to be sooner.'

Lemarry's solid form bustled across the clearing, hard hat a gleaming contrast to the bare-headed VT crew. 'I heard there's an alert,' he said. 'The old boy's had another turn?'

'Yeah,' I replied. 'We're thinking of flying him out to the Hole.'

'Can't say I'll be sorry,' he said. 'The lads hate this rota stuff.' He turned to the medic. 'With all due respect; they're not nursemaids.'

'Neither am I,' she observed.

Lemarry ignored the remark. 'I guess that means we'll be starting on this soon,' he said, jerking his head to indicate Sonny's hill. I could almost see the figures in his eyes. A grade promotion: more men, more responsibility, more pay.

'I suppose so,' I said. 'But haven't I done enough to him already? I brought all this on him.'

'How do you figure that?' asked the medic. 'He had his first attack before you arrived.'

'I invited OBN here. The extra strain was too much.'

'You don't know that. He might have had this shock at any time.'

'You didn't invent the SHIFT,' Lemarry put in. 'If you ask me that's what really stressed him out. The threat to his precious hill. Not to mention Orth luring away all his compatriots. You're not responsible for all the attractions of civilisation.'

'I guess not.'

The medic sensed me weakening. 'He'll be well looked after, you know,' she said.

'Will he be conscious? Aware?'

'It depends on his response.'

'I'd almost rather he wasn't.'

'We can tell him it's temporary. Till he recovers his strength.'

'I hope you're not saying all this just because he's a challenge,' said I.

'No. Really. He'll be more comfortable at the Hole. Believe me.'

'I doubt that,' I said. 'I doubt that very much.'

'Well, at least he'll be alive.'

I could feel the weight bear down on me; the crushing will of events. I felt helpless in the face of forces beyond my control, the inevitable unrolling of future pathways into tantalisingly broad sunlit uplands opening before me like a flower.

Like a door closing.

'Do what you have to,' I told her.

I watch the disc again, the pictures still not dulled by a thousand repetitions; see the heft and carry, his gaunt arms – nothing but bone covered in a pallid, floppy stretched stuff that didn't seem to resemble skin at all – raised in a feeble gesture of (. . . farewell? . . . protest? . . . resignation? . . . despair?) zooming in to a closeup on the mass of ridges and hollows that was his face, the sunken pits of his eyes, the slack drooling mouth, his white, white hair straggling like a cometary halo in the downblast from the flier. Follow the cut away, seeing the startling glimpse of my youthful self (triggering the question which mirrors now throw back at me so insistently) plodding along beside the stretcher, the stumble by the bearers which nearly pitched him off, the quick adjustment, the gentle deposition and slide, the closing door, the sudden, swift ascent, the chattering trip to exile and oblivion.

All gone, over so quickly. And nothing left behind to show he'd ever been. Except the constant action replay, scaled down and framed in a ratio of 9:4, of his final helpless, humiliating journey.

I raise my eyes to the hills, the holo hills of Home adorning the wall opposite the window and I think to myself how he must have felt, untimely ripped from his warm, cosy familiarity to wake up in a cold, antiseptic hell.

My hope is always it was farewell.

I fear it was despair.

I've often gone over why I allowed myself to be persuaded so easily. At the time I fooled myself into believing I had little choice, that I was helping to prolong his life, but there was always the niggle of guilt.

On one level it was simple enough, a humanitarian gesture designed to ensure his last days were spent in comfort. Despite my increasing respect for him, and my sympathies, cultural imperatives are not so easily thrown off. Mine were strong enough yet to insist his conditions and lifestyle were simply wrong. His was only one still, small voice to set against the chorus I'd been exposed to all my life.

Then again, I can't deny it let me off the hook of my promise to him. With him no longer in residence on the hill, my decision was easy: there was no obstacle left. Mining of the Rock could start at any time. And I jumped at it.

So did I remove him to give me no reason to refuse

permission? To rationalise my reluctance – cowardice might be more apt – to stand up to the demands of my job and of wider Orth? A fight that in my dazzling youthful certainty I knew I could not win; so would not start?

Was it that I still shrank from contemplating my future as a lined, craggy monster, shunned by the crowd, and was grateful for any opportunity to put unwanted reminders away?

The years have returned their solemn verdict.

Guilty. On all counts.

It has been a life sentence.

14

Keep Young And Beautiful

The old Home town looked the same, nestling reassuringly in the folds of two valleys. I had clicked off the landmarks one by one as, following the dips and hollows of the road, the hovercab made its meandering approach towards the bar of the loose curled T-shape formed by the town's sprawl along both rivers. Bowling down from the higher ground round the spaceport I was afforded a vista of the broader river fanning out slowly till it widened abruptly to estuarine size a few kayem in the distance. On its rural far bank a low range of Homegrass covered hills rose like a huge humpbacked sea mammal coming up for air. Geep and sturdicows dotted its green hide like speciated barnacles.

The road followed the river round the rocky promontory on the nearer bank before debouching into the roughly canalised ex-floodplain straddling the confluence where the main bulk of the town stood. The quarry cut its deep slash into the precise angle of the hillside, extending slowly backward with each succeeding year. Its restricted, vertiginously steep access was by-passed in seconds, leaving on the retinas the

picture of a confused jumble of seemingly ramshackle
buildings perched crazily atop one another as they
scrabbled for purchase on the incline. Once past the
bend the intervening bulk of towering rock hid it from
the town's view. Were it not for the periodic echoing
blasts sending clouds of slowly dispersing dust into the
atmosphere above the hill nor the one long betraying
declivity pulled down from the erstwhile summit like
a trembling lip it might almost have been possible to
forget the quarry's existence.

Below the stepped terraces of the crags above the
town and along the more rounded hills across the
narrower valley cotton-easter was strung out on the
middle slopes, decking them with patchy ribbons of
white fluff as if in welcome of a prodigal's return.
For me the effect was partly negated by the dark
green background of shrub, picked through in places
by the brown and grey of underlying soil and stone
scored along the hills, resembling the veins of minerals
I had seen lining the Hole. More or less resigned by
now to such episodic flashbacks, I shook my head to
remove this latest hallucinatory reminder of Copper
and the years-dead Sonny and concentrated instead on
the familiar twists and turns of the streets.

On my annual returns home things had always
looked cramped and smaller than my childhood memories would have them. Allowing for that as I scanned
the route ahead I nevertheless took note of some differences, a demolition here, a change of use there, a
'prime' development site displaying its gaudy invitations to the world. Through gaps between houses, the
sudden flash up side avenues, I caught glimpses of the
rash of new building that had sent probing tendrils of
urbanity into the clefts of the hills.

Mum and Dad were there to meet me as I stepped down from the hovercab. The relief I always felt at seeing her taut time-frozen face free of wrinkles had lessened over recent years but it was still a pleasure to see her well and sprightly. Dad was just Dad, a quiet background presence ever ready to support and protect.

After the hugs were over she said, 'You're looking tired, son. You've been away from your mother too long.'

'It's old age, Ma,' I joked, and regretted it as soon as I saw the look of shock which spread across their faces. I had miscalculated. Normally I wouldn't have made a remark in such poor taste, especially to her, but I'd thought maybe enough time had elapsed since she'd surpassed the age at which her mother had succumbed for her to be able to cope. Now, I guessed, she was waiting for the big one; if a wrinkle were to appear it would no longer be the prelude to a prolonged deterioration in conditions of enforced isolation but instead the harbinger of a sudden descent to oblivion. Which option was to be preferred was not obvious, and a decision I had as yet lacked the courage to face.

'What do you know of such things?' she asked in tones of dismay. 'We always took care to shield you from all that.'

'You'd be surprised,' I told her. I'd never found the right opportunity to discuss Sonny with her. Her reaction now suggested maybe that had been a fortunate oversight.

Dad's quiet authority then took over. 'Let's all go in, now, shall we?' he said, steering us swiftly into the house.

Later, in passing, he had a few quick words, 'Never

say anything like that again, son,' he admonished me. 'Not even in jest.' It wasn't necessary for him to elaborate.

'Sorry,' I said, 'I won't,' my ultimate destiny as ever forcing itself to the forefront of my mind. 'It's not such a bad thing, you know, old age,' I continued. 'It has a certain nobility.' I don't know who I was trying to convince, him or myself.

'That's as maybe,' he replied. 'But I don't think many would agree with that. Your mother's tranquillity is fragile. I don't want it disturbed.'

I watched her closely as I helped with the preparations for the party, her busying trivialities of assisting Dad with the cooking, folding napkins, fiddling with canapés, stocking up with drinks. My parents had always been desperately old-fashioned; they never knowingly let a sniff of more exotic drugs into the house. I guess that's one of the reasons why I ended up tippling raki.

She went about things with a kind of pernickety attention to detail that was a cover for her eternal preoccupation. Her thoughts never strayed far from the calamity that had befallen her mother. The spur of my presence and its reminder that her ancestry had condemned me and Sis to similar suspense sharpened her sense of guilt. For her, each year of life stolen from the jaws of uncertainty was, I realised, at best a brittle cause for celebration. Her victory over the recessive enemy that lurked in her chromosomes was indelibly tainted.

Just before the guests were due to arrive – colleagues from work mostly, with a scattering of neighbourhood friends – she stopped in front of the hall mirror to smooth down her glossy brown hair. Almost as a reflex she peered intently at the corners of her eyes, ran her fingers over her forehead and across her cheek ridges.

I came up behind her, caught her gaze. 'Habits die hard, I see,' I said.

She smiled at me nervously before inspecting herself again; turned sideways on to admire the still slim lines of her body — showed off to advantage by a figure-hugging tunic dress. Her long slim legs tapered gracefully inside her monochrome leggings. She faced the mirror once more. 'I never thought I'd get this far,' she said dreamily.

'Well you did, and I'm glad,' I said. I squeezed her shoulder. 'You're beautiful, Mum. Always will be.' She smiled more freely this time.

I leaned past her, checking my own reflection. 'You've got me at this too, you know,' I told her. 'A woman once told me I was such a vain so-and-so. She was only half wrong.'

'Pity,' she said wistfully. 'I always hoped you'd find a nice girl, settle down.'

'Oh, mother! No-one does that any more. No-one except you and Dad did it even when you were starting out.'

'I know, son. But your mother can always dream.'

Sis hadn't made it that year. She was way out on Belisario, pulling strings on a niche marketing ploy she'd got going to mass produce twee figurines based on local artefacts and sell her sanitised versions on. I consoled myself with the thought that at least there was some mining work involved for the raw materials.

Such enterprises are so much easier now the technology has improved. With the enlarged SHIFT chambers and more powerful transmission systems travel can be done in batches over longer hops. Nowhere in Orth is more than a couple of days away at most. Anyone can slap a fancy label on an otherwise nondescript product and distribute it throughout the co-prosperity sphere at a high mark-up. It does mean, though, that supplies of iridium have been pretty well exhausted. Orthrocks, they tell me, spends more and more money for less and less return. And shifting (without the emphasis) has become a commonplace.

I guess shipping goods these days is relatively hassle free, but I'd hate to be responsible for inspecting the SHIFT chambers after a batch of people has gone through, even if the cleaning is automated. Sometimes I've wondered if it's the characteristic smell of disinfectant and deodorant that requires en-suite vomitaria rather than vice-versa. Mind you, I've heard some people get off on the mix.

In the dim distance before such refinements even shifting by the many intervening jump points would have taken Sis a week, so she'd given it a miss. But she had sent a disc.

Mum slid it into the slot, touched the tab and the vibrant snow-flaked green fluid of the tank snapped from standby into its peculiar imitation of life. Sis was standing in front of a belt of peculiarly coloured trees, a lilting shade of blue. Her short dark hair was sharply shaped, framing her face, emphasising her resemblance to Dad. She was surrounded by a mass of gaily coloured figurines, crudely modelled I thought, from what I could see of the detail, and lacking subtlety in the painting. But I've never been wholly at one with the tastes of the great Orth public. I guessed she knew what she was doing.

Her broad shoulders were disguised by a well-cut

jacket which also obscured what may have been a tailored Titefit or some other no-nonsense upper garment. (She was touting for serious business. Not for her the garish sloganising popular at the time, the more or less blatant 'fuck me' T-shirts, the skimpy tops advertising the latest recreational drug, dance craze, some voguish popular pursuit, or otherwise emblazoned with arcana of various sorts.) A crisp pair of trews added to the effect which was rounded off by what Mum had always called sensible shoes, but these were elegantly styled. She had certainly dressed the part of the thrusting entrepreneur.

As soon as she spoke the illusion fell apart and she was Sis again.

'Hello Mum. Hello Dad. Hi Alan,' she said, accompanied by a manic wave and an ear-splitting grin. 'And everybody else who knows me,' she added.

'Well, here it is.' She spread her arms to encompass her collection of clay statuettes, twitched her eyebrows. 'Nice, aren't they?' She adopted an earnest expression, switched to a mock-serious tone, modulating her voice an octave or so lower. 'Available soon at an outlet near you.' She turned to somebody off camera, though to us it looked like she was talking to Dad's foreman who was in the corner of the room where her gaze was apparently directed. 'You know, sometimes I'm so inventive I could hug myself.' There was laughter, both outside the tank and in. Through it I just caught a thin, reedy voice from out of shot say, 'I'll do it for you.'

'Only if I let you, matey,' she replied to it, before turning back to face Mum, Dad and me, shaking her head, saying, 'Some people! No sense of decorum.'

She paused as if gathering her thoughts then continued brightly, 'Well, is it that time again? It doesn't seem like a year. Happy birthday, Mum. Sorry I couldn't be there. You and Dad make sure you have a good time. And keep that brother of mine off the booze. He never could handle it.'

'Ha!' I objected. 'She's one to talk.'

'I'm fine, Mum, and things are going well,' she went on. 'I've been busy, as you can see. By the time you get to watch this, these ought to be in the stores.' She gestured at the clutter around her feet. 'And I've been busy in more ways than one.' She jumped out of the frame, came back pulling a vainly protesting figure into shot by its arm.

'This is Harris,' she said. 'Say "Hello", Harris.' He could have endeared himself to me immediately had he said 'Hello Harris' in return but instead he merely shuffled in beside her, a weedy-looking guy with a shock of orange hair and an inane grimace, mumbling, 'Hi.'

'Where does she get them from?' I asked.

Sis had latched on to his arm, proprietorially. 'Harris has been helping me get things together out here,' she went on. I was about to make another facetious comment but she pre-empted me. 'Shut up, Alan. I know you're sniggering.' She turned to look at him and flashed a grin back at us. 'He is cuddly though, Mum; don't you think?'

'Oh no!' I said, curiously disgusted. 'But then Sis could always pick them.'

'Don't be so uncharitable Alan,' Mum chided me. 'He seems like a nice boy.'

Harris meanwhile at least had the grace to appear embarrassed. Mind you, I don't suppose he'd ever been dragged in front of a girlfriend's family and its assorted acquaintances before, even via the remote proxy of a

VT disc. Sis did have a knack of being persuasive. Both her projects would do well I had no doubt; until she took up other enthusiasms to replace them.

'I hope this finds you as it leaves me,' Sis wound up, 'and that Dad is behaving himself, as usual. Look after him, Mum. He needs you. See you soon. Bye.'

She gave Harris a sharp dig in the ribs and the pair of them began to wave madly, like demented puppets. The tank flickered briefly and hazed over once more into speckled green and white, their colour-reversed images dancing briefly on the spangled background.

'Silly, sentimental child,' Mum said into the sudden hiss from the speakers, but you could see she was touched.

It was while I was consuming some titbit in a quiet moment later, that Dad came over. 'That was nice of your sister,' he said.

'Mmm,' I said licking my fingers clean. 'What was?'

'Trying to boost your mother's morale like that.'

I looked at him closely, saw my grey eyes and trim nose reflected back, the precursor of Sis in his eyebrows and the frame of his face. But he had a faraway look, there was a pinched air to his expression. The strain he'd been living with for so long was beginning to affect him. The support he'd given so unstintingly had taken its toll, depleting his reservoir of quiet strength. I realised that Sis had been right. That support wasn't anything I had ever questioned, it was merely the nature of Mum and Dad's relationship. Something had kept them together all these years despite all the cultural inclinations to the contrary. It was a measure of his deep respect and affection for Mum that he had stuck around. I could think of no-one else who would

have done the same in the circumstances. But now
the support had to flow in the opposite direction. He
did need her; if for no other reason than to validate
his decision to stay. Without her his life would have
been empty.

'Yours as well,' I said. 'She cares for you both. So do
I. That's why she said it. She's not a fool, you know.'

'And neither is your mother,' he replied. 'She knows
the truth of things, who's the stronger between us.
She'll never be truly happy till she knows you're both
safe.' It was as if he was running on autopilot. The
veneer of capability he had cultivated for my mother's
benefit had become so engrained he couldn't take any
time out.

'I'm all right,' I assured him. 'I've still not taken
my youth shots. As for Sis, she's always been happy-
go-lucky. She'll put enough into her life to make it
worthwhile even if it is foreshortened.'

Someone had switched on the tank again. The stamp
and bluster of the intro music to OBN's news programme blared out from the speakers.

'But neither one of you has had any kids. Your
mother can't help but feel she's responsible for that.
I mean, but for – you know – she'd have loved grand-
children.'

'That's never been a factor as far as I was concerned,'
I told him. 'I've had such a lot to look up to, Dad; and
I've never met anyone suitable.

'Well, maybe once,' I conceded. 'I guess Sis hasn't
either. Look at that geek she's taken up with now.
Remember Mum and Sis are close in ways we're not.
I think they understood each other well enough.

'Sis was right in a way,' I went on. 'You deserve
a bit of looking after. Give Mum a chance. She's

maybe more resilient than you credit. It's been a long time.'

'It has,' he sighed, 'and you may be right. But I don't know if I can relax so easily.'

'Try Dad,' I said. 'For both your sakes.'

Inadvertently I let my gaze wander round the room. Mum was engaged in conversation with one of the guests, a woman I'd never seen before, dark hair styled in a peculiar pyramidal fashion, like a wedge perched on her head, with golden highlights marking each edge. She was clad in what I presumed was the coming fashion fad – all-black skin-tight leggings and exiguous top, exposing bare shoulders and midriff painted in fluo-rescent whorls to match her eyeflashes. Lemon-drop earrings completed the ensemble. A similarly-hued drink in her hand enhanced the effect. Mum looked utterly staid by comparison, but somehow reassuring. I caught her attention and smiled. She began to stroll towards us, companion in tow. Mum introduced her as a recently moved-in neighbour.

The woman looked me up and down as we made the usual polite noises, while I tried to ignore the nipples straining against the tight fabric across her chest. I forgot her name instantly.

'What were you two cooking up together?' Mum asked. 'I'll bet they were talking about me,' she added in an aside.

Dad winked at me, turned back to Mum. 'Of course Merle,' he said. 'What other subject could there be?'

'You'll need to tell me your secret, Merle,' the neigh-bour said. Her eyes flashed arrows of livid yellow as she blinked. Mum's startled expression faded into relief as the woman went on, 'I've never managed to inspire such gallantry.'

'Oh it's nothing,' Mum said too dismissively. She quickly cast around for another subject, fixed her gaze on the VT. 'Look, Alan,' she said, waving a bangled wrist at me. 'Isn't that Frazer Barber? You used to play with him when you were a boy, didn't you?' We all followed her gaze, shuffled space for a view. Mum and Dad gravitated together. I ended up next to the painted lady.

'Yes,' I said. 'To both.'

'He's done well for himself,' she approved.

The tank was displaying a huge wooden effigy of an aeons-obsolete type of spaceship from the diasporic age. Frazer was walking its length, delivering an apparently flawless piece to camera. How many takes it had required was another matter.

'If you ask me, he's just another Chelsea Monday,' the neighbour piped up. 'Look at that stupid trailing purple thong round his neck. It's like her ribbonshades thing, isn't it?'

I briefly imagined licking the navel at the centre of one of her yellow whorls, going on to lick something else; then repressed the thought. 'It's given you something to comment on,' I said. I declined to claim any credit.

'He's attracting attention to himself; away from the subject.'

'How do you think Chelsea Monday got famous?' I asked.

The tank showed a night scene now. Flickering light danced over the ship's hull, illumination from hundreds of flaming torches carried by the shadowed people in procession round it. The uncertain beams shone briefly on upturned faces. A ghostly, smeared out image of the tank's contents cast a lurid reflection from the ceiling above. There was a great concerted shout and the shadows lobbed their firebrands at the huge wooden structure, transitory arches of gold spanning the night sky. The ship must have been treated with an accelerant. It caught immediately, the innumerable small fires quickly merging into a giant conflagration.

'I don't think Frazer's the focus of attention now,' I murmured into a painted ear. The upper line of the woman's eyeflash followed exactly the triangular face of her stack of hair. Her body was angled towards me slightly, affording me the glimpse of a barely suppressed cleavage when I looked down. She smiled at me coquettishly, sipped at her drink.

A thunder of pyrotechnics erupted in the tank. An impossibly long shot whose framing Frazer's team must have spent an age in planning showed the explosions as weird scintillae scattered in the darkened volume over the ship, like startled jellyfish caught in a sudden unexpected radiance. The view cut to ground level. Smoke roiled and climbed above the burning wreck, cutting off with abrupt linearity where the viewing medium ended a few emmem below the tank's rim. A slight billowing betrayed the vortex created by the stirrer.

Through the appreciative murmurs of the audience in the room I discerned from Frazer's commentary that this spectacle was the decennial celebration by the inhabitants of Ophelia of the disaster which had befallen their pioneering ancestors and had almost caused their nascent enterprise to fail before it had begun: a bizarre commemoration of the original crash-landing transformed into a glorious affirmation of their eventual triumph over adversity.

'I suppose he carried it off okay,' the neighbour

said. Mum and Dad had drifted away leaving me alone with her. I had the vague notion that Mum may have set me up. But she was never usually as devious as that; and she knew my tastes so wouldn't have bothered. More likely the encounter was due solely to serendipity. Or its opposite, whatever that is.

'What?' I said. 'Oh, Frazer. Yes. He's good at it. At least as good as Chelsea. I've met her you know.'

'Really?' She turned to face me.

'Yeah. She's a queen bitch if you must know.'

Her eyebrows raised. 'Oh?' Luminous yellow half moons shone below them. Her heavy perfume filled my nostrils. I was uncomfortably aware of how long ago Vazhni had been, or even the few interludes since. 'Sounds like a wounded ego,' she probed.

'She's not my type,' I demurred.

'What is then?' Her tongue began teasing a perfect upper row of teeth.

'That would be telling.'

'Reticence, Alan?' she asked archly. 'I didn't expect that.'

I gave up the struggle to ignore the attractions on display. It *had* been a long time, and my aversion to artifice has on the odd occasion succumbed to the greater temptations of lust.

I leant forward. 'Do you want to fuck, then?' I asked.

She recoiled slightly. 'I wouldn't have put it quite so brutally.'

'Okay. For you I'll make an exception. I'll put it another way.'

'Aren't you the sweet-tongued charmer,' she said with heavy sarcasm.

'My sweet tongue has had a few compliments,' I said disingenuously.

'Is that so? I can put it to the test. But I warn you, I'm a devil when I'm disappointed.'

'Forget the disappointment. Just be a devil.'

Her grin suggested that was what she had intended anyway.

The paint continued below the black top and leggings, swirling round breasts tipped by red splashes tasting of thuleberry, merged into a thick arrowhead pointed at her crotch. Her saffrony pubic thatch was a different colour at the roots. My sweet tongue had a hard job stopping the bile rising: but, like I said, it had been a long time.

After, there came the inescapable two enquiries. 'Have you had your two kids?' and, 'How old are you?' In my case, on any extended liaison, there was usually a third – 'Who's Sile?'

'No and thirty-five,' I told her. 'A girl I knew some-where.'

'She must have made quite an impression.'

'Yeah, well. It's not something I talk about much.'

'You just did.'

'Heat of the moment,' I excused myself. 'An aber-ration,' I lied. 'I'm sorry.'

'That's all right. I've got a past myself.' After a few seconds she added, 'Perhaps you should talk more. Get her out of your system.'

'It's no good. Believe me, I've tried.' I lapsed into a broody silence.

She broke it with a thoughtful, 'I've got a daughter on Broomsvig and a son on Alta Plana.' It crossed my mind that she might be pitying me but at least that had got rid of one question. I took the bait. 'How old are you, then?'

She rolled on top of me, pushed herself up, firm breasts standing proud and round, elastic skin smooth and taut. She pulled a retaining clip from her disarrayed hair, tossed the loosed black and gold tresses back. 'I'm sixty-six,' she said.

Despite the shunning of any physical signs of ageing I'd noticed that for certain people the fact itself was a cause for perverse pride and celebration. There was an element of that to Mum's parties but she had a real reason to celebrate each passing year. For the rest it was another expression of the narcissistic nature of Orth culture. Look at me. See how old I am. And not a wrinkle.

Well bugger her. I could top that. Idly I tweaked a thuleberry flavoured nipple. 'I've not had my youth shots,' I said.

'You're joking!' From her expression you might have thought I'd just admitted to mass murder.

'No. I've never felt the need.'

She realised I was serious. 'But . . . I mean . . . Why not?'

'It's a long story. Complicated.'

'Just the same . . .'

'I may not ever get round to it.'

She sagged back on her heels. 'You don't intend to?' The thought plainly horrified her.

I shrugged.

'Aren't you afraid of getting old?'

'Were you?'

The question threw her completely. 'That was different,' she stuttered. 'I wasn't going to lose my looks.'

'None of that matters to me.'

'What do you mean?'

'I'm not interested in keeping up appearances. Don't you get tired of all this fashion business?'

'No. Why should I? It's amusing. Always something new.' She smiled tentatively. 'Like you.'

'Why bother? Why not let nature take its course?'

Through a long pause she stared at me uncomprehendingly.

'You're sick,' she finally announced. She started scrabbling around for her clothes. It didn't take her long to dress.

She left quickly, gold-flecked black tresses flaring.

'What was your name again?' I called out vengefully to her retreating back.

15

Move Every Mountain

The party was still in swing when I reappeared but I couldn't avoid Mum's attentions. Immediately she spied me she wended her way through the throng. 'What did you do to Erita?' she asked.

'Who?'

'Our new neighbour.'

'Oh. Is that her name?' I said.

'Don't be tiresome, Alan,' she said wearily. 'She seemed very upset.'

'I didn't do anything.'

'You must have. I couldn't get any sense out of her. She rushed off in a terrible state. You have been behaving yourself, I take it?'

'Of course. When have I ever done anything else? I'm glad if I upset her; she deserved it. I hope I put the fear of death in her.'

'Oh, Alan,' Mum complained. 'I wish you'd learn how to handle relationships. A bit of tact would be nice, especially when you're at home. Your father and I have got to live with these people.'

I was about to placate her with a show of contrition

but my attention was distracted by the chattering fanfare of OBN's news music erupting from the VT. The reversed-N news flash sigil rotated in the frame. As I watched, the head shot of an oddly wrong yet still hauntingly recognisable face blossomed in its place.

'Shit!' I caught my breath and strained to catch the announcer's words. 'Reports are coming in that the architect Cassandra Tybolt is dead.'

I sighed and my tension began to dissipate into a kind of relief. It wasn't Sile after all; but close enough, as was to be expected. The resemblance was marked. There were a few differences – the jaw-line was less pronounced, the eyebrows were less thick, the nose more so, and of course the hair was arranged in a later style, perhaps a little too severe, but the full lips and blue eyes were the same. Looking at them I could see where Sile's sparkle originated. I barely had time to take it all in before the face was swept away and the picture changed to a familiar one of a stepped curving building.

'Best known for creating the Crescent Pyramid on Shandra and the Triskylon on Vukoviab . . .' The blocky curvature of the image in the tank was replaced by an altogether airier confection – a twist-columned treble archway surmounted by a triple crown of slender metallic spines tapering gracefully skywards.

Mum couldn't help but notice my distraction. 'You didn't know her did you?' she asked.

'No. Not her,' I mumbled.

'Ah. I remember now,' Mum said. 'It was the daughter, wasn't it?' she prompted. 'The dancer.'

'Yes, Sile,' I said, as the memories flooded over me.

'I'd like to have met her,' I half-heard Mum say.

The announcer was continuing, 'She was killed following an accident during the construction of her design for Derdemden's new Metropolitan Opera House. One of the support beams for the new building is said to have slipped from its cradle as it was being hoisted into place.'

The flattened image of an amateur's attempt to disc the scene in its aftermath hovered in the centre of the tank. Tubular digits scrolled mirrorwise fore and aft.

It was ridiculous. I don't know what I thought I was doing. I was standing there gaping as if the woman had meant something to me. But of course it wasn't her that had me riveted. I think I had the crazy notion that I might somehow catch a glimpse of Sile if I kept my attention fixed on the display. It was an unexpected, brutal, reminder that I'd never managed to shake free of her memory.

The torrent of words washed on. 'Ms Tybolt's death was reported as being instantaneous. Several of the workers around her were injured. Most were released after a few hours but some have been retained for further treatment. Accident investigators are examining the site. A report will be sent to the office of the procurator coronal.'

The announcer's incongruous smiling face now filled the tank. 'We'll have more on this, including an assessment of Ms Tybolt's life and work, on our usual late bulletin after tonight's Backchat.' The signal segued into a trailer for a forthcoming 'major new' drama series. My eyes registered the images but my brain was on hold.

'Are you all right?' Mum's tone was solicitous, waking me from the dwalm.

'Yes,' I said, hesitantly. 'As okay as I'll ever be, I guess.'

'I wish I could meet her,' Mum said. 'I'd give her a piece of my mind.'

'Don't worry yourself,' I tried to assure her. 'I get by, don't I?'

'How are things in the rest of the spiral arm?'

Dad's foreman, Flotta, one of that broad-shouldered type which Orthrocks seemed to attract in disproportionate numbers, always felt constrained to talk shop. Despite the fact we had met several times over his years on Home I guess he was sensitive to me being the son of his immediate boss. He was clearly uncomfortable talking to a Sector Manager, even though our responsibilities lay in different Sectors.

'Oh, you know,' I replied off-handedly, over the background gabble from the other guests. 'Orthrocks grinds on as usual.'

'They're looking up, here, of course,' he gushed. 'We've just processed the data on the extended grav-an survey. It looks like there are viable deposits of iridium running through the crags all the way along to Squat Thrust.'

With my mind running on the death of Sile's mother I was hardly paying Flotta any attention. I was still hoping that somehow or other I would glean from the coverage some news of Sile herself. Even a glimpse of her to see if she remained at all like the woman I had known would have satisfied me for the moment. Of course it would set all the old feelings churning away again (if that hadn't happened already) but I figured I could cope with that. And somewhere in the middle of that turmoil lingered the desire to meet her once more. If I ever did, I was determined to get it right next time.

Flotta continued oblivious to my preoccupation, 'There's some on the far side of the valley too.'

Somehow a little of his meaning managed to filter through the ball of confusion lodged in my brain. 'What did you say?'

With a puzzled air, he complied. 'There's some on the far side of the valley.'

'No! Before that.'

'There's workable iridium all the way along the crags,' he repeated, puzzlement growing.

Now he had my undivided attention. But surely he couldn't mean . . . ? Not the hills of Home!

I had a sudden darkening vision of the myriad broad pathways that had once blossomed in front of me narrowing down to just the one. 'You're certain?' I asked.

'Of course. I wouldn't make mistakes about anything so important.' His tone was now tinged with resentment. I wasn't having a good day.

'No,' I stammered. 'I didn't mean to imply . . . I knew there had been some surveying but I hadn't been expecting mineable iridium.'

'Well it's there whether you were expecting it or not. And it's a nice, juicy seam.' I'd noticed this corrupting effect of iridium before, but more increasingly of late. It wasn't the metal itself but the mere thought of it and its promise that was enough to twist the hearts and minds of otherwise normal people out of true. It was like seeing Lemarry all over again; money signs popping into his eyes. Flotta was almost drooling.

'Can I see the figures?'

He looked at me sharply. 'Now, do you mean?'

I nodded.

'I suppose I can access them for you. If I can use your father's link?'

'I'm sure he won't mind.'

As Flotta barrelled away I set off in search of Dad, and confirmation. I found him talking to three of his cronies, Hometown citizens of long-standing. Loud bursts of laughter had just broken from the group as one of them completed some witticism.

I interrupted the merriment rudely. 'Why didn't you tell me about this, Dad?' I demanded.

'What's the matter, son?' He sucked me into the circle by slipping his arm round me, muttered to his companions, 'He's always in a state about something,' turned to me. 'Tell you about what?'

'These new survey results.'

'There's nothing to tell.' His voice was carefully neutral.

'Flotta seems to think there is.'

The pressure on my back increased warningly. 'Ah, well. You know Flotta,' came the measured response. 'Ever the enthusiast. Relax, Alan. It's your Mum's party. We don't want to be discussing business in front of friends.' His smile had an undercoat of steel. 'This can wait till morning.'

'But I've asked Flotta to show me the figures.'

'When? Where?'

'Just now. On your link.'

He sighed in a bemused fashion. 'I suppose I'll have to come and set your mind at rest.' He said to his companions, 'Excuse me a moment, will you.' They chorused assents.

'Well, Alan,' he said, steering me across the room, the picture of affability. 'I don't know what you're making all this fuss about.'

Once the door to his study was shut he rounded on me. 'What in Orth do you think you're playing at?'

'What?' I replied. An embarrassed Flotta hovered in the background, pretending to busy himself setting up the link.

'Have you no sense? Don't you realise the impact this is going to have?'

'So it's true, then?'

'Of course it's true.'

'That's why I wanted to talk about it.'

'But not in front of the neighbours!' he burst out. 'We don't want them going off at half-cock. These are delicate matters, with ramifications. The ground has to be prepared. We should move slowly.'

'I don't believe this,' I said. 'It sounds like you don't care.'

He shook his head. 'You've lost me.'

'About those neighbours you seem so keen to avoid upsetting. About what happens to the hills.'

He regarded me with slightly amused tolerance; as if I was a child again. 'It's work, Alan,' he stated baldly. 'It's what we do.'

'But . . .' I floundered, realising I lacked the information to take my protests further. 'I'm in the dark here.' I brushed Flotta from the numbralphic controls. 'Let me see what we've got.'

I scanned the contents of Dad's minitank, the clusters of orange where the gravitic anomalies, small but easily detectable with the highly tuned equipment now in use, lay, the red spheres highlighting confirmed iridium deposits measling the volumes within the hills' gridded contours. The pattern suggested a meandering layer of iridium following the Southerland crags, more intermittent concentrations along the Kiproch ridge to the north. The numbers scrolled up the tank's edge, delineating the extent of the finds. The layers were only emmem deep in places but they were tens of em wide. Feeding in likely results from future spotcores would probably strew the images with livid red pools.

'Who authorised this?'

'I did, of course.'

'Why, Dad? You must have known the consequences. I mean, iridium! Orthrocks can't let findings like these slip by.' My conscience about Roodsland and what I'd suffered to befall Sonny's hill was colouring my appreciation of the figures.

'I hadn't dared hope they'd be as good as this,' Dad replied. 'But we needed something. The present quarry's running down, Alan. There's no future here for your mother and me without it. You know how she loves living on Home.'

'There's no future here with it,' I declared. 'When this lot,' I nodded at the tank, 'is being extracted there won't be a here worth living in. And not a lot left afterwards. The place will be unrecognisable. Mum won't thank you for that.'

'That's a chance I'll have to take. I've always had a hankering to run a really big operation. Till now I've only been able to do that through you.'

The symptoms were all too familiar. With a sick despair I realised even my father wasn't immune to what I would always think of as Lemarry syndrome.

Another thought struck me. 'Does Mum even know yet?'

'Of course. All the reports go through her.'

'So how did you square that?'

'She understands. Your mother has worked for Orthrocks all her days. She'd have made a good career of it if she hadn't wanted to stay on Home with me. She's wasted on the admin here. I should have listened to her, sworn everybody to secrecy.' He glared at Flotta briefly. 'She had an idea you'd not respond well.'

'She was right.'

The layouts were all there, estimated seam widths, projected yield ratios, volumes to be processed, equipment requirements – even down to the laying out, and in, of roads – the accompanying traffic projections, a laughably cursory environmental impact study, compensation assessments (on the low side naturally, Orthrocks knew what it could get away with), local worthies' egoes and accounts to be massaged, the necessary palms or other portions of anatomy to be greased. The body of a full-blown planning application was before me in embryo, only fringe details and grace notes were missing.

While Dad and Flotta waited silently for my reaction I stared at the data hanging before me, trying to will the figures away. To me the activities of Orthrocks had always seemed inevitable, necessary even. I had never seriously questioned them. Now for the first time they threatened to impact on me directly.

On Copper I had had doubts, but they were thin and fragile, though bolstered for a time by Sonny's influence. They had begun to fade with his demise. With this threat to my childhood haunts those feelings were revivified, in a stronger form. I could now perceive Orthrocks differently; a wayward monster – like something out of one of Sile's beloved pre-diasporic myths, or Sonny's *stravaigants* before they were tamed – well-meaning but misdirected, careless of the havoc it might cause. And I felt even less power to alter its ravening course now, than when I had proved unable to divert it in the past.

As I sat there working through the implications, all

else for the moment forgotten, the minitank's autoclock had been quietly tumbling diced numbers. Its flickering finally caught my eye. 'Shit!' I said. 'Now I've gone and missed the late news.'

A restless night's slow passing later I was up on the hills. A brief coffee and a couple of left-over canapés had fortified me against the early morning chill. Overcoming my tiredness, a strange brew of adrenalin and haste propelled me up the narrow cleft that led to the first vantage point. I broke into the more open shrubland of the middle slopes, prepared myself to wade through knee-high cotton-easter.

Beyond the vale the sails of small pleasure craft – sailboards, dinghies, yachts – were already plying among the scattered islands of the tree-shrouded lake, catching the early morning wind, dotting the notoriously treacherous surface with a patchy coat of many colours. Squat Thrust was hunched over the shimmering blue waters like a baleful amphibian readying to leap. Partly hidden by the houses and shops scattering out from its banks like an unruly fungus, the outflow leaving the lake ran straight towards me for a kayem or so then concertinaed into a meandering series of sluggish loops through the less populated area of the widening vale, before funnelling into the canalised stretch intended to protect Hometown proper where a thundering rush took it over the ancient ford down to a graceful sweep into the confluential embrace of the main river. Deep swirls and eddies pushing past the central dredged channel of the larger waterway testified to the helter-skelter pace of that final constricted charge. A flock of swannecks paddled in the waters on the upper side of the ford, like a luminous white eyot sparkling in the morning light.

Running my fingers through the filmy cotton-easter strands of the scrubby knee-high plants clothing the craggy hillside I abandoned myself to memories. Here was where Gran, Sis and I had walked the never-ending holidays of my misplaced childhood. There I had pedalled my bicycled steed, huffing and puffing against the magic dragons of my juvenile imagination. A little further on was the spot where Sorene Lerbu and I had frolicked in the autumn mists what now seemed like a long lifetime ago. A different lifetime, even.

In an unguarded comment when my future appeared to hold nothing but delight and fulfilment, I had once told Sile that she would like this place. Now that time had rewritten every line of that future more radically than I had thought possible even the lingering promise of that moment was lost to me. Can the mature citizen, I still wonder, fail to look back on the days of his or her youth without disbelief of the person they once were?

Sile would never see any of this, now, I reflected. And nor would anyone else, unless they were quick.

I looked down over the familiar features of Hometown, along the crags, up to Squat Thrust and the hazy mountains beyond, trying to imagine the scenes to come. It wasn't difficult, I had enough experience of the exploitation of territory, whether virgin or clasped already in the great hand of Orth's co-prosperity.

The town would survive, even prosper. Some would protest but the pool of potential sufferers of Lemarry syndrome was large enough to ensure the project would go through.

But the Kiproch hills across the vale, the Southerland crags where I stood. All this was doomed: like the blasted wreck that was all that remained of the hill of the Rock on Copper. No complaint of a concerned local could prevent it. Devastation would walk along this ridgeway. And call its trespass progress.

I was unaccountably saddened. Perhaps it is only the prospect of loss that brings forth the realisation of how precious the familiar can be; the comfort there is in the known. In my travels I had scarcely given these hills a thought. I had not considered my attachment to them to be particularly deep-rooted. Yet now they were to be taken from me all had changed; changed utterly.

The revelation was a shock and a rebuke. How much more dreadful his loss must have been for Sonny, whose whole being was bound up in the rocks and land and sense of place.

My guilt and shame gnawed at me with rekindled vigour.

'No. No! Not the hills of Home!'

'Why not, Alan?' Dad replied reasonably. 'Why not, when so many other hills have gone the same way?' Then he turned the barb. 'A lot of which you've been responsible for, I might add. What's so special about these ones?'

We were in his office at the quarry, for his monthly progress meeting. A phalanx of grim-faced Orthrocks-trimsuited bodies was ranged in the discussion circle. Flotta, a couple of his assistants, someone from the area office, Dad. As a visiting Sector Manager I had a right to sit in. I was the only one arguing against the proposals.

'You can ask that after living here most of your life?'

'What difference does that make?' he said. 'I came here for the quarry. So, I'm sure, did these people,' he indicated the local employees. 'What you're saying is you would affect their livelihoods for the sake of some crazy notion of . . .' He took on a puzzled air – 'You know, I'm still not sure what.'

'Neither am I,' I muttered to myself. 'I've had a few days to think,' I said to the others. 'I've had enough. I've seen too many places destroyed like this. It can't go on.'

Dad's voice took on a worried tone. 'But how can you stay with Orthrocks if you feel like that?'

'I don't know. Maybe I can't,' I said.

'And just what are you going to do to stop it?' the area officer put in. 'This isn't your sector. You have no jurisdiction here.'

'That's a good question. And one I don't have a ready answer to. Perhaps I'll organise the local opposition,' I said mischievously. All their voices raised in a discordant unison of disbelief and outrage. Dad's face registered dismay.

I made calming motions with my hands, allayed their fears with, 'It doesn't matter. It's all futile anyway. I know there isn't a hope of preventing it. I may do nothing; as usual.'

Mum was doing her admin thing in the site office when I came out. 'You missed the funeral, Alan,' she greeted me.

'What funeral?'

'Cassandra Tybolt's. It was on the midday news.'

I feigned indifference. 'Oh, did I?'

'Yes. It was a lovely ceremony.' She waited.

'Go on, then,' I relented. 'You're obviously desperate to tell me about it.'

'It was a bit understated for an architect, I thought. Nothing flamboyant, no floral representations of her buildings on top of the coffin or anything like that, but I suppose they gave her a good enough send off.' She paused again. We both knew the subject was entirely different. Had she seen Sile or not?

'Yes, mother?' I prompted.

'That woman you've never managed to forget. You know. The daughter.'

'Yes, mother,' sarcastically.

'Not much of a looker, is she?'

I smiled tolerantly. 'Stop winding me up, mother. Now I know you didn't see her. You wouldn't have said that if you had.'

'I don't like you being unhappy,' she explained. It was an apology of a kind.

'I know,' I said, then, 'Why didn't you tell me?'

She was prepared for it. 'I thought that was up to your father.'

'But you could have softened the blow. Explained maybe. I thought you loved the hills. I never expected you'd agree to their destruction.'

'All I ever wanted was your father,' she reflected, 'and after that a happy and healthy family. But your Dad alone is worth more to me than all the hills of Home.'

'I guess I can understand that,' I told her. 'It's sort of the way I feel about Sile.'

'That's entirely different,' came the brusque response. 'You know my opinion. Forget her. She's forgotten you.'

At the time I resented her cruel-to-be-kindness. I know she was only thinking of my long-term welfare, but the remark had nevertheless elicited the old hurt.

'It's not as easy as that,' I replied. 'As you, of all people, should realise.'

Still, I suppose it was nice of her to try.

16

Whatever's Written In Your Heart

One man; against the might of Orth . . .

I jumped before I was pushed. I contacted Frazer, told him what I was prepared to do, called in the favour. I reckoned he owed me at least twice over so that didn't bother me in the slightest.

'I can't promise you an easy ride,' he warned me.

'I don't want one,' I told him, foolishly.

He agreed to set things up, started to put in a word here and there, twisted a few arms, did some gentle persuading. Whatever, a couple of weeks later I found myself sweating under the studio arcs in front of a live audience inside OBN's main complex on Sutra, surrounded by quadrax cameras of all shapes and sizes, trying to compose myself for a talk with Orth's latest broadcasting sensation, Perland Dene, and, eventually, who knew how many millions besides.

Dene's dress was conventional, as you might expect of a VT host. The only mark of individuality to sully the blandness of his OBN trimsuit was a flaming orange chest tag proudly proclaiming his name. A loose fringe of otherwise unexceptional brown hair flopped over one eye as a concession to trend setting.

In his intro I was given a big build-up – graduate of Eilay, first-class honours at mining academy, one of Orthrocks' senior management team, all that stuff. I found it difficult to follow at times due to his effete style of pronunciation. When he said my name I wondered briefly who was this Awan he was talking about. It was one of the affectations which I detested in those who liked to think of themselves as an elite in Orth. But they seemed many and I was few; and they had virtually unlimited access to OBN. Over the years I had got used to it.

It's different now shiftbeaming has ensured more or less untrammelled instantaneous broadcasting throughout the coprosperity sphere. ISB's network of retransmit stations may have been slow to grow but it has allowed wider varieties of voices and opinions to express themselves.

Dene finished up by telling his audience that I had a startling secret which tonight for the first time I was willing to have revealed. 'Alan,' he said, 'is in his thirty-fifth year, and has never been administered Euthuol.'

He waited till the astonished gasps in the studio and the buzz of talk that followed them had abated a little then began his questioning.

'So. Alan. How have you managed to escape Euthuol?'

'I haven't escaped it,' I corrected him. 'I've just never taken the shots.'

'That's rather a fine distinction, if I may say so, and it doesn't answer my question. Could you perhaps tell us some of your reasons?'

'I suppose I've never felt the need,' I replied.

'Come now, Alan,' he said. 'Never felt the need? How can any citizen of Orth be unaware of the need?'

He'd been well briefed. I knew, I'd done the briefing. But I realised he had to approach it from the audience's point of view. They would have found my answer more than a little strange.

'Bad phrasing,' I said. 'It's more like I've never found an opportune moment.' He let that pass.

'You haven't fathered two children, I take it?' he continued.

'No. Not even one. But the point is obvious. The rules are strict. After two children I'd have had to take Euthuol.'

'So is it children you have an aversion to?'

'Indeed not. I've always thought it a pity that most people in Orth take so little to do with their children.'

'Thanks, Alan,' he said. 'I just wanted to establish the point before we go any further.'

'On the other hand,' I put in, 'I'm not overly bothered about extending my bloodline.'

'I'll come to that precise point later, if I may,' he said.

I had to admire his technique. He was softening the crowd up nicely. I could see him teasing all the strands, layering them together, laying the net of logic that would suddenly snap them into a different perspective when he popped the big one.

'Is it perhaps Orth women you object to?' he went on to ask. 'Do none meet your high standards?'

'No. It's not that either. But I've not had many sufficiently stable relationships. I did meet one once,' I admitted, 'whom I might have considered fathering children on. But it didn't work out. I haven't seen her in years.'

'And what would she think of your peculiar circumstances?'

'I don't think they're peculiar,' I said. 'In fact they
are actually natural,' I asserted. 'Whereas, if you think
about it, Euthuol isn't.' I felt the audience bristle. 'And
since you ask,' I went on over the increasing murmurs,
'I think she wouldn't have objected.'

'Well it seems not many of the citizens here would
agree with that,' he said. 'Perhaps, after the break, we
can explore your circumstances further.' He bestowed
a smarmy grin on the space between the two nearest
quadrax cameras. 'Don't go away,' he told his distant
viewers. 'We'll be right back.'

As the truncated theme music rolled over the artifici-
ally whipped-up applause stimulated by a huge flashing
sign dangling safely above the shot he leaned towards
me. 'It's going okay,' he said. 'Keep it up.'

He began to engage in technical badinage with
the stage crew and production staff. Despite his
encouragement I still felt tremors of nervousness. I
tried to distract myself by watching the floor manager
positioning the show's other guest, a theatrical act
featuring a strange-looking woman of whom I had
never heard. She was dressed in a cut-down version of
an orthodox trimsuit exposing a long expanse of leg
curiously exaggerated by improbably short leggings
that barely reached her knees. Her hair was pulled
back severely from above a pair of heavily drawn
arched eyebrows into a series of floppy spikes held
in place by interlinked bows of ribbon. Further facial
make-up enhanced the size of her eyes and made a
deep red seemingly amateurishly applied slash of her
mouth. She resembled a startled owl caught in the act
of eating a kill, a smear of blood still across its face.

A semi-circular array of sound and vision projectors provided her sole backing.

On Sutra, I surmised, the fashion fad Erita was following on Home was already doomed. I ruminated gloomily on the bizarre sight a clutch of the inevitable imitators of this new style would make if they were ever to be gathered together somewhere. The imperiously flashing sign and the sound of the theme music brought me heart-flutteringly back to reality.

Dene noticed my agitation. 'It's okay,' he reassured me, 'you're not on yet. And don't worry. You're doing well.'

He turned to the side. 'Welcome back,' he said to empty space. 'We'll get back to the subject of the very interesting talk we had during part one in a moment. But first a former member of the *Sweet Peppers*, a lady who since going solo has enlivened the entertainment scene with a distinctive blend of music and performance. Premiering her latest stylistic creation, "Rotten Neoteny", ladies and gentlemen, Mercy Boaks!'

The strangely garbed woman activated her control console and sidestepped back into the semi-circle of apparatus. A series of wails began to emanate from the speakers. Shafts of light from the vision projectors punctuated the wails in syncopated time. She stood at their focus, bathed in alternate beams of violet, green, red. When she opened her lips a strange chirruping sound came out, squeaking discordant notes from between clenched teeth, gradually transforming into a succession of bass gurgles like she had just opened her mouth and let her belly rumble.

As the syncopated shafts lost their colour, fading down to ever paler cones of light, a stage mist began to creep around her, swirling up to cover knees, thighs,

torso. Finally only her head bobbed above the grey
swell which veiled her, like the enigmatic marker of
some forgotten shipwreck booming out a mournful
warning.

The sounds she made seemed purposeless to me,
lacking in power or affect, but the rhythms held a
faint, ill-remembered echo of Sonny's litany, as if they
too tapped into the same deep well of common ancestry
that united the diasporic worlds. For an instant I even
imagined I could see a school of flying dolphins.

Darker images flashed onto the mist from the all-but
hidden projectors, surrounding the dimmed outlines of
her body with spectral shadows which leaped at her
menacingly then retreated; one moment obscuring her,
the next all but vanished, then swarming around her
again like tormented acolytes forever prevented from
attaining the object of their veneration. These figures
faded in their turn as her voice rose through the octaves
again, each successive swooping movement of their
arms rendering them less substantial and apparently
propelling them deeper into the ground. The mist fell
slightly with them, dropping to below her shoulders;
then, as her ululations took on a more pleading tone,
appeared to rise once more.

My initial reaction to this spectacle had been one
of disdain at its lack of conventional musicality but
I had gradually been won over by the bravura of her
performance and I was now thoroughly engrossed.

It soon became clear that it was her head that
was sinking. Apparently cast adrift from whatever
anchor had been holding it in position up to now,
it appeared to be buffeted back and forth across the
stage by waves of grey mist, rolling from one crest to
another as if helplessly, disappearing from view – to

an abrupt cessation of sound – as it was occasionally swamped, to reappear moments later with a burbled scream. The mist's turbulence increased and the head's movements became more and more erratic and uncontrolled until eventually it seemed to lose the will to continue the uneven struggle and, with a few final despairing whoops, sank into the mist.

Despite the peremptory promptings of the flashing sign a stunned silence followed this astonishing performance. It was eventually broken by a first few unsure handclaps which catalysed an outburst of genuine applause growing to a tumultuous roar. The mists dispersed, revealing Mercy sitting cross-legged, head bowed, gales of acclaim washing over her the way, moments before, the grey waves had. She rose slowly, acknowledged the plaudits with a shy smile and made her way across to the conversation area.

After the mutual greetings Dene asked me, 'What did you think of that, Alan?' over the dying applause.

'Amazing,' I replied. 'I've never seen anything like it.' Mercy nodded appreciatively.

'Well then, Mercy,' Dene turned to her. 'Everyone seemed to like it.'

'Thank you,' she said and waved to the crowd, who started to woo and yay once more.

'Tell me where you got the title from,' Dene said when calm was restored. 'What is "Rotten Neoteny"?'

'Well,' she replied in a slow drawl. 'Had to call it something.' A few souls laughed. She shrugged. 'I thought the words have a nice sound.'

'Is the piece symbolic in some way?' Dene persisted. 'Can you tell us what it means?'

'I ain't sure. It just is. Let other people read into it what they like.'

'Perhaps our viewers will let us know their thoughts.'
He glanced to the side. 'The number to contact should
be showing in your tanks in a moment.'

He tried to penetrate her reticence again. 'What
about your equipment? Anything interesting we should
know about?'

She afforded him little explanation, 'It's basically
a cut-open VT,' she said, 'with a few additions of
my own.'

'Well you've certainly come up with a novel concept,'
he conceded and tried for more fruitful ground. 'But
let's turn to a less professional matter; what did you
make of Alan, here?'

She scanned me up and down for a moment. 'Looks
okay, for a pervert,' she announced to general laughter from the studio audience. Dene glanced at me
expectantly.

I waited till there was reasonable quiet. 'And have
you taken Euthuol yourself?' I asked her sweetly. There
were some startled oohs from around the studio.

But Mercy was unruffled. She had obviously decided
to handle me less carefully than she had Dene. 'I'm too
young just now, honey,' she said. 'But I'll take my shots
right after my second kid just like everyone else.' She
looked out at the audience. 'Give me a few years, yet,
and the right man or two first.'

'How about Alan?' Dene interjected swiftly. 'He's
not fathered anyone, or so he says.' He played to the
crowd. 'Wouldn't that be nice, folks? Alan and Mercy
getting it together?'

I looked at him in alarm as the few shouts of woo and
yay dribbled away against a general lack of enthusiasm.
What was he doing?

I scanned Mercy hurriedly. She was studiously flicking

away an invisible patch of dirt from her cut-down trimsuit.

'I don't think so,' I demurred when Dene turned back to me. 'We've only just met.'

'Mercy?' he asked.

'He ain't my type, honey,' she said laconically.

'He may not be anybody's type after today,' Dene asserted. 'As we may find out shortly. But you will definitely be performing another piece for us, later?'

'That's right,' Mercy replied.

'I'm looking forward to it. Thanks for talking to us, Mercy.'

'My pleasure,' she said.

'Ladies and gentlemen,' he signed her off, 'Mercy Boaks!'

When the applause accompanying her immediate departure had died down he resumed his interview with me.

'I noticed you seemed a little coy there, Alan.'

'Forgive me,' I said. 'I don't usually get urged into a relationship in front of a huge audience,' I said.

'But there's more to it than that, isn't there? We've not heard the real reason why you've never taken Euthuol.'

I pondered that for a moment while registering how cleverly he'd set it up. What was the real reason? Mum? Gran? Sonny? A half-baked notion of winning Sile back by becoming what she always wanted me to be?

'You can call it cowardice, if you like,' I offered.

'Cowardice? That's a strange term to use. What is there to be frightened of? I think you'd better explain.'

'For me,' I said slowly, 'Euthuol may have the opposite of the intended effect.' I could feel the crowd all waiting expectantly for the unfolding of this strange premise. 'I have,' I went on, 'a significant chance of ageing prematurely if I have the so-called youth shots.' A sigh made up of alarm and confusion tinged with pity, came from the audience.

'How is that possible?' Dene prompted.

'A quirk in my genetic inheritance,' I replied. 'My chromosomes may carry a gene which expresses a protein causing Euthuol to misbind to the relevant active sites, changing them drastically. Far from preventing ageing, Euthuol then in fact accelerates it. The cells seem to stabilise for a while but then wear out quickly. Not as devastatingly as with a normal subject admittedly, but not at the end of a long lifetime, either. It all happens earlier. Much, much earlier.'

'I see,' Dene said. 'Not the most alluring of prospects. But I noticed you said your cells "may carry". Are you not sure?'

'No. I can't be. It's a matter of probabilities.'

'It's not something I've ever heard of before,' Dene said in a dubious tone.

'It's not common. Most potential sufferers prefer to keep it quiet. You wouldn't know unless it had occurred to a recent ancestor.'

'I take it in your case it did?'

'My grandmother,' I said. 'She took Euthuol as normal but began to age long before the end of her fourth decade.' The moan of sympathy from the audience was muted. This wasn't a subject the majority of them was happy to contemplate. 'I'm told it's possible to survive several years under these conditions,' I went on, 'but, as you will appreciate, no-one wants to know or see you. She lost the will to live. My mother took her shots before the problem came to light. Mercifully she has been spared a similar fate – she seems to have suffered no ill effects – but she could have passed the susceptibility down to me.'

'So how significant is the chance you told us about earlier; of you being genetically unsuited to Euthuol?'

'It depends to a large extent on my father's genome, but it could be as high as one in four.'

'I would have thought you could know more precisely. Isn't everyone's genetic make-up on record?'

'Only in the crude form required for resolving disputed parenthood cases. No-one can tell me. No-one's allowed to look into it because of the ban on genetic tinkering.'

'Of course,' Dene nodded. 'How do you feel about that?'

'I understand it and I guess I have to accept it. Nobody wants to produce a situation where Euthuol might be made ineffective for the mass of Orth's population which wants to make use of it; but the ban forbids any artificial alteration to human genetic material, even to relieve cases such as mine.'

'I'm sure I speak for all those watching when I say I sympathise with your predicament,' Dene said. 'But the risk is surely small when weighed against the potential gain?'

'That's easy for you to say.'

'I realise that; but you surely intend to?'

The low-angle quadraxes whirred in for a closeup. 'Take Euthuol, you mean?' My question teased him and everyone else – including me, or so I thought at the time.

'Yes.'

'No,' I replied. 'I don't.'

Despite the long preamble, the logic of my situation hadn't made it through. A shocked intake of several hundred breaths in unison filled the studio air. There were even a few boos and catcalls. I began to realise a little of what Sonny must have felt, faced time after time with the blank incomprehension of every youthful new face he met.

'I think what people may not have grasped sufficiently,' I said, waving away Dene's attempt to interject, 'is that if I do have this peculiar genetic disposition and take the shots, the rather unfortunate corollary is that I would die earlier than I would if I hadn't been treated at all. On balance I think I'm better off taking my chances on ageing naturally.'

'But that's unprecedented!' Dene protested. 'No-one from Orth ever does that.'

'No-one from Orth, no,' I agreed. 'Until now.'

Dene abruptly swivelled into professional mode, 'Well, I guess that's as good a time as any to take a break,' he said to the unseen millions. 'We'll be back with more of Alan in a minute. I'm sure you won't want to miss it.'

The theme music swelled again and the audience slavishly followed the imperious flashing command. Dene jubilantly jabbered out over the applause, 'Great! Brilliant! I told you you were doing fine.'

'I wish I felt it,' I said.

The audience sank down into a curious grumbling static as knots of people began to engage in debate. A few shouts punctuated the general racket. One man, more persistent than the rest, rose from his seat and approached the main studio floor, jabbing his finger towards us. 'This is disgusting,' he shouted. 'The man's an obscenity.' A few voices called, 'Sit down', and, 'Shut up', but there were more growling agreement. Most sat bemused, wondering, I guess, if this were

some part of the entertainment. I stirred agitatedly in
my seat preparing to defend myself but Dene motioned
me to remain. 'It's okay,' he reassured me. 'We'll deal
with it.'

'You're a disgrace, Dene,' the oncoming man said,
as the heavier among the studio crew moved in on him.
'This is an outrage,' he continued as they hustled him
away. 'It shouldn't be allowed.' The returning theme
music was almost lost amidst the uproar. The floor
manager and crew were making frantic calming signals,
the sign had reverted to a commanding 'QUIET!'

'Welcome back,' Dene said. 'As you can probably
hear, feelings are running high in our studio audience.
There are mixed reactions to tonight's guest's declara-
tion of his intention never to take Euthuol.' He waited
briefly till a degree of order had returned.

'Now, Alan,' he asked me. 'How do you justify to
all the people watching this rejection of Orth norms?'

'If they don't know they haven't been listening,' I
declared. 'I would have thought that the fact that
acceptance of the norm might lead to my premature
death would be enough to give anyone pause.'

'Nevertheless, as you have seen, there are clearly
some you haven't convinced.'

'I would turn the question round. I do not intend
to transgress any of Orth's laws. How can anyone
justify a demand for me to use a potentially dangerous
substance merely because that is the usual custom?'

'But you would be compelled to if you had children.'

'Agreed. But if I make the free choice to forego
children – incidentally saving them the anguish I have
had – and to live my life my way, adding no additional
burden to Orth's cosmopolity? It may not suit others'

sense of propriety but surely no-one will force me to take Euthuol against my will? That would not be part of the Orth culture I know.'

'It's a valid comment, but as far as I'm aware the situation has never arisen before.'

'But it has. I've seen it.' I stretched the point. 'On the diasporic worlds. And it's something the majority in Orth remained resolutely unaware of. Or if they ever were made aware they promptly forgot.'

'Surely Euthuol is everyone's birthright as citizens of Orth, whether born into it or not? Aren't we morally obliged to share what benefits our culture has to offer rather than keeping them to ourselves?'

'It isn't my birthright,' I stated baldly into the almost perfect silence that had fallen as the studio audience waited for the next words to fall from the lips of the apparent madman before them. 'And it isn't the birthright of the dispersed humans on as yet unreclaimed planets. The sort of people in front of whom we dangle this miraculous mirage of an ever-youthful future, dazzling them with visions of paradise; visions I doubt we fulfil. People like the poor bedraggled inhabitants of April, brought up out of their isolated misery I'll admit, but cast down again almost within a generation; like the *émigrés* from Alba, the forgotten Sons of Copper. The list is as long as the roll of re-embraced worlds.

'We exploit them ruthlessly,' I ranted, happy at last to get down to my purpose. 'We show them scant respect. We trample over their customs, mock their traditions, twist the minds of their young with our temptations, seduce them to our ways with gaudy ephemera, all so that we can appropriate their land, rip up their hills and fields, strip them bare of anything we find useful or even merely diverting.

'And we think nothing of it. Less than nothing. We think that anything else is an affront to the natural order, that ours is the best, the only, way to do things. Never for a moment does it occur to us that other people, other customs, are as worthy as our own. Because if we did it would stand in the way of our hallowed coprosperity.

'We tolerate difference only in so far as it doesn't threaten us or our perception of what life should be. Only if it accepts, explicitly, what we ourselves stand for.

'And what we do in the furtherance of those beliefs is simply wrong. The people here, or watching, who would force me to take Euthuol are wrong too.'

As this speech had unfolded I became aware of the full extent of the effect Sonny had had on me. It wasn't so much that the sentiments I expressed were essentially his – they had been working on me for a decade and a half – but that I had adopted some of his rolling cadences to lay them out. It was as if I knew that, to act as his advocate, which is what I had at last become, in some way I had to embody him. I could see now that my decision to renounce Euthuol, which in my rude blindness I had thought to be recent, was a necessary step towards the fulfilment of that process. Until that culmination, reflecting his speech patterns was the closest I could get.

'But, Alan,' Dene's voice penetrated the disbelieving silence that had greeted my words. 'You are a senior employee of Orthrocks. You yourself have overseen the exploitation of vast reserves and resources from the sorts of planets you have just been talking about.'

'I know. And I've come to bitterly regret it.'

'But you had no apparent qualms at the time. You

carried out your duties effectively. So effectively you gained rapid promotion.'

'I did have doubts, from the first,' I said. Damn the man! He'd never hinted at this line of questioning. And damn my naivety in not foreseeing it.

'But these . . . doubts,' he persisted, 'were not enough to prevent you doing your job.'

'Alas, no.'

For the benefit of his wider audience Dene speared me with a piercing look. The low-angle quadraxes angled in again. 'Isn't the truth,' he asked, 'that you were more than happy to act in Orthrocks' interests? That it was only when your home planet became the subject of extensive quarrying plans that your doubts surfaced? That you resent what you have imposed on others inflicting itself on you?'

I knew I'd lost them the second he said it. I didn't need to hear the confirmatory cheers and waytogos. Here, at last, was a picture they could understand; someone out to protect his own, covering his tracks with a show of altruism. And Dene had reestablished his control. They would take his side no matter what I said. Well; Frazer had warned me.

Nevertheless, I tried. 'That was only the final push over the brink. It crystallised for me what I'd always felt subliminally, made me fully aware of what we as a culture do. The way we ride roughshod over weaker or less resilient obstacles in our path.'

'I hardly think that after what you've admitted today,' Dene responded icily, 'you can consider yourself to be a part of Orth any longer.'

The sally pricked me to anger. 'So that's to be the way of it,' I said. 'If you're not for me, you're against me. If you're against me, you're not of me. So stands exposed the great myth of Orth inclusivity.'

It was a mistake. But then so was my earlier ranting when set beside Dene's cool professional manner. I had hoped to persuade rather than confront. I hadn't intended my disillusion with the direction Orth culture had followed to come out in such strong terms. I was too transparent, lacked the necessary dissembling skills.

'I would say that any exclusion involved here was strictly self-inflicted,' Dene said smoothly. 'You're the one who has turned against the advantages Orth offers.'

'I'm the only one describing the disadvantages,' I cavilled.

'So everyone is out of step but you?'

'Maybe,' I replied. 'Who knows? Unless I can present people with the contrary viewpoint no-one ever will.'

'Who knows indeed,' Dene preened himself, swivelling in his chair. 'Well, that's all we've got time for I'm afraid. My thanks to Alan for coming along . . .' – the customary applause had a distinct lukewarm texture – 'but before we leave you tonight, another creation from Orth's latest performing sensation, Mercy Boaks!'

A genuine wave of enthusiasm rippled through the crowd as the arcs faded to establish the correct atmosphere. A thin pulsating beat began, lights flashing stroboscopic synchrony, gradually overlaid by weird skitters of high-frequency sounds. A sudden ecstatic crash of noise heralded her vocal contribution and she was off in a sequence of aural swoops and howls.

Amid the squeaks and rasps I sat contemplating all my burned boats. An uncertain future, a wrecked family, a lost career. The show may not play to wide audiences everywhere but it would certainly cause a stir on Home, and anywhere Orthrocks had a presence. I couldn't escape the consequences. Nor expected to.

It would only have been a matter of time, anyway. A company like Orthrocks wasn't going to want as a Sector Manager someone who so obviously flouted the norms of Orth culture. As soon as the lines and wrinkles arrived, the patches of grey, it would have been out, here are your cards, close the door behind you, the security codes have all been changed – even if I had kept my nose clean, my head down and hadn't started campaigning against the company's activities. Going public about my disillusion with it only hastened that end.

I imagined the scene at Home when the disc of the show would be broadcast; the paroxysm of shock my mother would endure, her secret shame exposed to everyone who knew her. I hoped my father would be able to get her through it, that she could forgive me. I've never been so wasted.

Dene startled me into awareness, grabbing my arm and whispering, 'Better get off now while Mercy's still performing. Before another member of the audience decides they want to take a pop at you.' Of course that may not have been necessary, the one that had, could have been a plant; Dene knew the sorts of tricks to maximise his ratings. But I scuttled off obediently.

I moped around the hospitality suite, after enquiring in vain for raki and in consequence being reduced to drinking something much less palatable, a Sutran concoction originally derived from a local root crop, production of which had long since been farmed out to an agricultural world. I had briefly considered a Bulayma Grand, but I had no Deetox, didn't want to risk further ridicule at asking for it and couldn't face the vicious prospect of the hangover. Staring up at the ceiling tank laying forth its cut down, brightly laundered version of reality in the form of the late news which immediately followed Dene's show, I missed the quick familiar buzz the raki would have given. It would take some serious knocking back of this local brew before I gained the inebriated state I sought.

Everyone in the place was giving me a wide berth, probably hoping that the taint wasn't spread by an airborne vector. I really should have said, 'Fuck them', and left, but I wasn't yet ready to face the outside world. I needed the false fortification of drunkenness first.

As I was raising my second glass of the miserable pisswater I had been palmed off with, the doors of the suite swung open and the diminutive figure of Mercy Boaks swept in, surrounded by the bubble of her totally female entourage. A towel was draped round her neck. Her eye fixed on me for a moment. I held it while I knocked the drink back and only then switched my gaze away.

Dene's puff-chested swagger had followed her in, trailing his own retinue of flunkeys. He ignored everyone, disregarding guest and colleague alike with an imperious disdain, and headed straight for the intoxicants display. I settled down to the business of getting myself blazoned.

It was several minutes later, well into my third refill, that I felt a presence at my side. I looked up and saw Mercy, toying with a tumbler full of some brilliant blue liquid. A red circle of gamabo fruit hovered halfway down it.

'You ain't ever been told it was dangerous to go

hitting on your own?' she said. Her speaking voice seemed more mellifluous than it had under the studio lights, a far remove from the weird twitterings and groans of her performing persona.

'Frequently,' I replied. 'But I never paid them any attention.'

Her laughter surprised me. 'I guess I deserved that,' she said. There was no excess of muscle on her stick-like arms and legs despite her likely punishing rehearsal schedules, and her small breasts gave only a slight swell to her trimsuit upper.

'No,' I said, reassessing her. 'No, you didn't. It was ungracious. At least you're willing to talk to me.' I gestured at the small army of people casting towards us suggestive glances – disapproval or apprehension in various degrees. 'Aren't you frightened the madman's mark will rub off?'

'Who cares?' she replied. 'I'm off the leash for a while. I'll do what I like. Talk to whoever.'

'Sit down. Please,' I invited her. She put down her drink, slipped into the seat opposite me with a sinuous grace. Memories of another supple body flitted in with her. 'What is it with dancers?' I thought. I tried to look beyond the stage artifice still misadorning her face, but the mask was too thick. A patina of sweat beaded the exposed flesh below her neck. She mopped at it, pulled the trimsuit fabric out, blew down onto her tiny breasts.

'Shouldn't you be gladhanding your way around, hobnobbing with contacts and the like?' I asked her. 'Instead of wasting your time with me?'

'I've an agent does all that grovelling shit,' she said, fanning herself with one arm of the towel. 'It's what I pay her for, and she loves it.'

'So what makes you want to talk to a social out-cast?'

'Curiosity.'

I smiled wryly. 'Killed a large variety of feline mammals, I hear. I take it you're not in their number.'

'I sure hope I ain't.'

'That would be a change,' I said.

'You sound bitter, honey.'

I grunted. 'Experience does that to you,' I said. 'How old are you?' I enquired.

She sipped at her blue liquid; swallowed. 'Nineteen,' she replied.

'Nineteen!' I marvelled. 'Don't I seem to you like a strange creature from another dimension. All this talk of refusing Euthuol?'

'Because I'm nineteen? Honey, you'd be strange whatever age I was.'

'Story of my life,' I said, swigging another mouthful from my glass.

'Shouldn't let it get to you,' she admonished me. Surprised at the unexpected remark I cocked my head in query.

'What you did tonight?' she asked. 'On the VT and all?'

'Yes,' I said, guardedly.

'That sure took courage.'

'Ha!' I said. 'It was just talk. Talk comes cheap. Can you imagine what it's going to be like going through with it? When the lines and wrinkles come, when my hair goes grey a bit at a time? When all this,' – I took a hold of the skin at my neck – 'hangs in folds and bags? When my face has so many ridges it resembles a mountainside?'

'Is that what happens?' A fearful insecurity had crept

into her voice, over her face. I dreaded it tipping over into pity.

'Yeah. You can see it starting now, if you look close enough.' I pointed to the incipient tracery round my eyes.

My harshness worked. She declined the offer, sat back in her seat, hid herself behind her drink.

'It's your choice,' she said.

'No,' I told her. 'It isn't. I've never had a choice.' I sighed. 'It only took till now for me to realise it.'

She sat forward once more, said earnestly, 'Despair don't sit easy on you.'

I shook my head. 'It's more like acceptance,' I said. 'I've given up trying to fight it,' I expounded. 'It's too strong.'

I swirled the contents of my glass, performing the hopeless divination of the aeons, a gesture going back almost to humanity's first encounter with fermented fruit on whatever primaeval world we evolved. 'It's not so bad, gazing on old age,' I told her, and looked away. 'When you get used to it.'

'Thinking of your grandmother?'

'No. Someone else. Long ago and far away.' The, 'and thought about it every day since,' which I added, touched uncomfortably on self-pity. 'It's a long story,' I said to forestall further enquiry.

She hooked the circle of gamabo out of her drink with a deft sweep of her forefinger, pinched it in half using her thumb and popped it in her mouth. Something about the action nagged me.

She seemed so young, so assured. Untouched.

Memories drifted in. I had been like that myself once. I caught myself wondering if I could relate to someone in her state any more or if I was separated from it all for ever. I suppose now, underneath, she was in panic like everybody else. I know I was. I still am.

'Do you wear that stuff on your face all the time?' I asked her. 'Or just when you're working? I can't help wondering what you look like without it.'

'It's working gear. I'm a sweetfaced kid really.'

I found a playful smile on my lips. 'I don't suppose you fancy a fling with the sort of man your careparents warned you about?'

She looked at me with mock suspicion. 'Honey, I thought you said you didn't with women you hardly know.'

I rolled my wrists dismissively. 'It was only a stray thought.' More eagerly I added, 'I make exceptions in special cases.'

She reacted warily, as if it had only just occurred to her I might be serious. 'And you say that to all the girls, right?'

'No. I'm usually a bit more direct.'

If her startled eyebrows could have raised any further they would have. 'Well, I sure am flattered, honey.'

'I sense a "but", coming here,' I said, smiling resignedly.

She grinned broadly. 'Like I told Dene. You ain't my type.'

'That's a shame. I'd have liked the chance to find out if you're mine. Ah, shit. I'm lonely and far from home and I may just have made the biggest mistake of my life. What's one more?'

'Don't be too hard on yourself, honey. We can't always get what we want.'

Her sense of inclusion seemed misplaced. 'I'd have

thought you'd be in line to get virtually anything you wanted.'

She looked over to where her entourage was busily making merry. 'Most about,' she said. 'But not quite everything.'

'You can have my thanks, anyway,' I said to her. 'You've cheered me up.'

She laughed; brightly, unaccountably, as if something had cut loose. It could have been a signal. 'Well, honey,' she said eventually, 'that's sure the first time I've turned a man down and it's cheered him up.' It was my turn to laugh.

Over her shoulder I saw one of her escorts making a purposeful approach. 'It looks like you're in demand,' I said.

She glanced back then offered me an apologetic smile. 'My agent,' she said. 'It's leash time again.'

She finished her drink. 'Nice talking to you. At least I'm allowed the odd whim.' As she rose to go I caught her wrist. She looked down at it wearily then raised her eyes in a slow challenge. I let go. Her integrity restored, she heard me out.

'Could you ever renounce Euthuol?' I asked. Her agent's breath fizzed dangerously.

Mercy considered for a moment before delivering her rueful verdict. 'I ain't that brave, honey.'

She said it matter-of-factly, but there was a core of truth to the remark, a burdened inevitability, that for me invested it with wistful irony. It conjured up visions of Sile, forever young and beautiful in the crucible of my memory and, surely anointed by Euthuol, likely to remain so for real. The two images, one long gone but honed to sharpness, one actual, fused. 'Maybe you are my type after all,' I said.

The two women in front of me grinned at each other. 'Ain't no chance of that,' Mercy told me. She put her arm round her agent, who shrank slightly from the contact. 'This is my type,' she said. Then she spread her hands wide in apology, and added, 'Trouble is, she's straight,' and shrugged as if to say who can account for any of it?

I stared at her in shock. 'But what about that banter with Dene?' I asked. 'That "right man or two" business?'

'P.R., honey,' she said, as if to an imbecile. 'Can't get by without it.' The comment stung. In that area, as I had just found out, I had a lot to learn.

'But ain't it the truth?' she went on, to my obvious puzzlement.

'Only thing wrong with Orth,' she explained. 'You'd think that being able to cross light years in a fraction of a second would mean we could sort it, but no. To make a child I still need a man.'

'Ah,' I said. 'Of course. But . . .'

'Yeah, honey?'

I shook my head. 'Nothing.'

I smiled and watched her go, my eyes following her lithe childlike body across the room while I reflected that the solution to her little dilemma was related to mine, and blocked for exactly the same reason.

In bed that night, alone in a cold hotel room which was making unsteady circles round me, I went over our encounter. As I remembered her delicate consumption of the slice of gamabo I realised it was the practised ease with which she'd done it that I'd registered, the ritualistic aspect. Perhaps a Bulayma Grand would have been the perfect accompaniment after all. The merest of actions was still enough to stir Sile's ghost in my heart. It helped to explain the resonances I had felt all through our chat.

There were similarities, I guess. They were both young when I met them, both performers, and they had both reached out to me. But how could I have confused them?

More to the point how could I have misinterpreted Mercy's intentions? It was easy now to see she was just one tormented soul seeking some sort of comfort with another.

Maybe I was blinded by the fact she approached me. Perhaps I was so dejected I mistook any interest for a sexual one. But whatever black mood I was in I should have picked up the signs.

Perhaps it was that I just didn't care any more, that I was so desperate for a relationship with a woman that I couldn't be bothered with all the preliminary fencing. It had worked with Erita, after all, but I'd subsequently blown that one right out of the quarry. Whatever, it seemed my maunderings since Sile had taken a downward turn. Perhaps to settle my inner pangs I should give up on women completely. Or try to find Sile again.

I was possibly more sensitive to such thoughts as I had just separated myself so conclusively from all of Orth and set out on what I expected to be a long, lonely road. But Mercy knew the deepest, darkest thing about me (for someone who hadn't been on the receiving end of my cries at the crucial moment) yet she still had come to talk to me. I had needed that, whatever her motive.

My thankfulness for this first, welcome, indication that

I might not suffer universal rejection was shattered by the hovercab driver who ferried me from my hotel to the spaceport the next morning.

'Did you see that sicko Perland Dene had on last night?' he asked.

I grunted non-committally.

'Boy, they sure breed 'em weird in some parts of Orth. If you ask me they should isolate 'em on some far out planet and leave 'em to rot. Perverts like that shouldn't be allowed to bother us decent folks.'

'I didn't ask you,' I said mildly, 'and I'd be grateful if you kept your opinions to yourself.'

'Okay, pal,' he bridled. 'Don't take the 'ump. I was only making conversation.'

'Yes,' I said drily. 'Well we're all entitled to our opinions but I'd much rather you didn't burden me with yours.'

He harrumphed a grudging response and muttered something under his breath, while the hovercab stuttered in its progress.

For the rest of the short and I'm sure deliberately bumpy journey he managed to contain his urge to communicate, completing the trip in a surly silence. Miraculously, he even forswore commenting on the driving habits of his fellow road users, despite the doubtless many provocations.

'Thank you,' I goaded him as I paid him off, taking great delight in doling out the exact fare he'd requested. 'I enjoyed the repose.' I smiled at him insincerely. 'I've got your number. I'll make sure I mention you to all my friends and associates.'

'My pleasure, pal,' he growled as he violently engaged the hovercab's drive before whirling away in a cloud of Sutran dust.

The honours ended about even, though. I'm fairly certain he charged me over the odds.

I made the rounds, retravelling, in shifted time, the route of my youthful Grand Tour. The hotel on April, to my relief, had a different manager. At each stop, I contacted the local VT agency, offered myself for interview, attempted to hone my technique.

I noticed a rash of Mercy Boaks lookalikes spring up round me as her startled owl image caught the fashion consciousness. Unfortunately not all her imitators had the childlike body to match, nor the graceful carriage.

I took care, on the way, to visit what seemed like every hole-in-the-wall theatre and over-opulent Terpsichore the head- and backwaters of Orth had to offer. If Sile was still dancing I never saw her.

For all I knew she could have been dead, odd diseases strike, accidents happen in the best-regulated societies – though it would have been a strange kind of coincidence that separately struck down both her and her mother in such a similar way. Or her schedule and mine might have been out of synch and she was halfway around Orth somewhere dancing for the delight of someone else's eyes, while I was searching for her in the spiral arm. I supposed she could have been shacked up incognito, incommunicado wherever, with some other poor misguided soul she'd managed to beguile the way she had me.

Wherever she'd managed to hide herself it wasn't for lack of looking that I failed to find her. I must have scrutinised hundreds of 'forthcoming attraction' ads and a similar number of programme notes, flattered scores of dozy stage door jobsworths, accessed countless dance company schedules, all without success.

Eventually I came to the conclusion that she'd given up dancing again.

Nor did I lack a high profile. Fifty or sixty local chat-show hosts was the minimum to numb my brain. I mentioned Sile in passing to each one but to no avail. My nights and my bed remained resolutely empty.

I didn't dare to contemplate the thought that she might deliberately be eluding me. I was her champion too now as well as Sonny's.

My other campaigns got nowhere. Orthrocks continued to strip iridium from every known source, and I met with amazed incomprehension, unveiled hostility, whenever I questioned the merits of Euthuol.

I developed my P.R. skills, ranted and raved less than I had with Perland Dene, presented my case more soberly. But people remained unmoved; there was some piece to the puzzle of convincing them that I had not yet upturned, something missing. Until I found the key, whatever was written in my heart was doomed to stay locked inside myself.

17

Alive And Kicking

Victories are seldom won without cost. Take my mother, whose relief at escaping the direr consequences of Euthuol was always marred by the fear that she would pass on her mother's susceptibility. She spent the latter years of her life in a bitter regret which her treacherous son could only aggravate.

Or Sonny, who ground out his lonely life so long waiting for a redeemer and yet held on to his faith; not letting it shatter even when his chosen one seemingly rejected him. Who, in the end, died alone, apparently friendless, denied the comforting unction of his dreams' fruition.

Mine has been neither a short nor an easy road and I too have had my victory, for which I was grateful at the time, though I see now it was petty and incomplete.

Life extracted its payment as it always does. My account was settled by the once simple process of ageing. I may have paid in full, but the price was a necessary one.

Inside I feel no difference from my younger self; it is only when I try to exert myself beyond my usual bounds that the blithely forgotten hazards bother me. But I do not mourn the fading of my more youthful vigour, rather I welcome it. I welcome it all. The processes came upon me slowly, giving me time to adjust, but even without that none of it would have shocked me. I have seen it all before. More than once.

You must forgive me if I seem to ramble, my memory is no longer what it was. My earliest recollections shine sharp and bright, like a well-adjusted viewing-tank, but ask me what happened yesterday, last month, or last year and my mind becomes confused. Things blur, time shifts, as you get older. The chronology of more recent events becomes obscure. At least, that has been my experience.

As I write this, taking the occasional rest, gazing from my window to the streets below – the now familiar streets which seem to radiate out from the small lawned dun on which my house perches like a primitive fortification – and beyond them to the distant hills whose resemblance to the Southerland crags brought me to make a home in this place, I have just celebrated, if that's the correct word, my eightieth birthday.

I had no party such as Mum would have had. No Mum come to that; no Dad, no Sis. No family around me. No Sile either, but I have given up hope of her long since. Just Frazer and a VT film crew, my memories and a consoling raki or two. It's how I wanted it.

The SHIFT's gradual extension in range and scope made my missionary travels round the coprosperity sphere easier, though no less disagreeable. As the chambers expanded to accommodate ever more bodies, batch transmissions became the norm, the ante-rooms filling up with gaily-bedecked would-be travellers in search of 'exotic' experiences – safely sanitised at their eventual destinations by the replication in large degree of the sights and sounds they were already familiar with on their home worlds – who made inane conversation and imbibed copious quantities of intoxicants as an inadequate preparative. The chambers themselves, despite their increased size, seemed overcrowded due to the number of bodies, the subsequent communal heaves in the rather less lavish vomitaria one of life's more dubious pleasures.

Occasionally I returned to Home, with ever more reluctance as I observed the changes, but not once in all the visits did I have contact with Mum or Dad. Year on year I saw the Southerland crags reduced in height, stripped open like a side of sturdimeat to reveal the delicacies inside, cotton-easter wisps one year draped on the lip of the cut like the frothing drool of a diseased dog, the next even that sad reminder of former days was obliterated. Squat Thrust was gradually flattened, first to a single elongated trapezium, then to an indiscriminate bulge in the foreground of the as yet untouched mountains beyond. The Kiproch hills on the western bank had even their meagre dimensions diminished till they no longer obscured the vista up the main river. I was glad I'd managed to take a few holos of the hills before it all started, at least I would have something to remember them by.

Sis kept in touch. She had a child with the dreaded Harris and after he failed to withstand the strain of parenthood another to someone equally vacuous and with even less staying power. She gave up the struggle herself not long after, leaving the day-to-day charge of her children to a carephanage, like normal people.

When the message dropped into my tank the tell-tale flagging its point of origin was a perplexing surprise.

The approaches were crowded. Even the provision for dedicated access roads Orthrocks had built into its plans had failed to anticipate anything like this volume of traffic. The overspill clogged the main boulevard, snarled up the familiar streets, brought movement to a standstill.

A continuous pall of gritty dust hung over Hometown and its environs, laying its grimy load on any exposed surface. The constant back and forth of vehicles of all kinds stirred the deposits, the passage of hovercabs blasted the silty floccules over the rooftops and houses lining the streets. Unsightly smears streaked the buildings where overhangs protected them from rain, giving them an air of dowdy neglect. The newer shopfronts wore strident gaudiness like a uniform, contrasting with the more down-at-heel appearance of the older establishments. Several large drug parlours had been slung hastily into newly cleared prime sites to avail themselves of the increased daily trade.

As I passed over the bridge straddling the ancient ford I noted the absence of the swannecks which had graced the vale's waterway for as long as records existed. Unable to tolerate the noise and disturbance they had decamped for more tranquil water pastures. The river itself had been colonised by a tenacious waterweed dragging at the fast flow, bordering it in a livid green that flicked and waved like a siren's invitation.

My grim-faced father met me at the door. 'So, what's the damage?' I asked, after his rather formal greeting.

A flicker of disapproval darkened his features further. 'Your flippancy always was one of your least endearing traits,' he sighed.

'It's how I cope,' I told him.

'There's a time and a place, Alan. This is neither. Your sister's ageing is well advanced.'

For a brief irrational moment on receiving the message I had felt a surge of rage and relief, thinking that it would have been safe for me to take youth shots after all. But my higher awareness had swiftly overriden such unthinking naivety. The odds were the same as they'd always been. Sis's affliction confirmed them as one in four. That she had fallen victim changed them not at all. For me to take Euthuol would still have been to play the deadliest form of genetic roulette.

I had had the whole journey to formulate some sort of response, but I still struggled. 'How's Mum taking it?' I said.

'How did you expect?' he replied. 'Badly. She's upstairs with her now.'

On the upper floor a door clicked. I moved to the stairwell, looking up. Mum stood on the landing, tissue clutched in one hand, gripping the bannister tightly with the other. She was muttering something.

I climbed towards her, Dad behind. Mum was quivering, pale face trembling. Her only steady points were at her feet and where her hand clutched the rail. 'It's my fault. It's my fault. It's my fault,' she was whispering, over and over. She looked at me wordlessly, her tear-filled eyes a pleading mixture of grief and disbelief.

I took her outstretched hand. 'How long have you been like this?' I asked.

'It comes and goes,' said Dad. 'I think your arrival's triggered it again.'

'It's all my fault,' she said again.

I put my arm round her. 'Don't be silly, Mum,' I said. 'How was it your fault? You weren't responsible for the package of genes you passed on any more than Gran was. You could as easily blame Dad as yourself. He must be a carrier.'

She stiffened, pushed me away. I tried to appeal to Dad for support but they had both turned withering looks on me. It was obvious to me that this was the way they had mutually agreed to get through the ordeal, probably without even speaking about it.

Their closeness had often had a conspiratorial quality. I saw now that Mum derived a curious kind of strength from her dependence on Dad and in turn she would allow nothing to detract from it, and he was happy to play along. To suggest any faults in him was to call all that into question.

'You always were an ungrateful child,' Mum said. Conscious that I had been rejected and no further solace would be sought from my direction I walked away.

Sis was in her old room, one back from where Gran had been. I looked down on her suddenly fragile body as she smiled up at me and I didn't know what to say. From my experiences with Sonny I thought I had known what to expect but this was different. This was someone I had known young, in the same surroundings, and that at once exaggerated the shock but also tempered it. The sags and folds of her wizening face seemed like an elaborate disguise which somehow failed to conceal the familiar features underneath.

'How do you feel?' I asked.

'Tired,' she said. 'Permanently tired.' The bright vibrancy of her nasal timbre had gone. A weary fatalism had replaced it.

'You don't look so bad, you know,' I tried to reassure her. 'I've seen worse.'

'Don't patronise me, Alan,' she said with some of the old spirit. 'I know I've not got long.' That would have been a normal response when ageing struck, as the worn-out cells destroyed themselves rapidly – I wouldn't have seen her in time. But Sis had been afflicted way too early. Had her cells been untouched by Euthuol they wouldn't have reached that critical state. The misbinding on her active sites would still make them deteriorate outrageously compared to mine but she could survive for years if she had wanted to enough. Gran, I reflected, had apparently suffered a similar accidie. Perhaps it was a side effect of the main disorder. Or maybe to contemplate life in Orth as a hideous specimen was simply unbearable. I knew I was destined to find out one day but that was still a distant prospect.

I remember wondering if I would lose the will to live when the signs and portents came upon me. Sonny hadn't, of course, but Sonny hadn't been brought up in the ways of Orth.

'If it's any consolation,' I told her, 'this will come to me soon as well. Maybe not soon enough and not as quickly. But soon.'

'Don't feel guilty,' she pressed me. 'You mustn't feel guilty. One in the family is bad enough.' She lay back, stared at the ceiling. 'I'm not bitter. I've a lot to be grateful for.'

'Like what?'

'Harriet,' she said, reprovingly, 'and Jarvis. Keep a

brotherly eye on them for me, will you? Mum and Dad won't always be around.' She smiled wistfully. 'Tell them to beware the lures of miracle drugs.'

I grinned. 'Of course. But why are you here? Why at home?' I asked. 'Isn't it a bit depressing?'

'When I told Mum, she insisted,' Sis said. 'She didn't want me going to an Elder Hospice, like Gran. It's her penance,' she explained. 'Twice over.'

'Sometimes I think she deserves one,' I said.

I managed back for the funeral, six months later. It was not a happy occasion. The pillar of smoke from the crematorium chimney had hardly begun its steady wind-dispersed climb to add to the pall from the frantic activities of iridium extraction a few kayem away when I got into an argument with Mum over Sis's child-care arrangements.

'Be reasonable Mum,' I said. 'What else could she do but give them up?'

'I didn't hand my children over to strangers,' Mum said disapprovingly.

'But you had Dad to help, plus Gran for a time, before . . .'

'She might still have entrusted them to me. I could take care of them.'

'Perhaps she thought you'd done enough,' I said.

'What's that supposed to mean?' Mum snapped, sensitive to the least whiff of criticism.

'I only meant maybe she thought you'd done your share,' I hastened to soothe her. 'That you deserved a rest. She wasn't entirely happy with you taking it upon yourself to look after her at the end.'

'But I was glad to do it,' Mum said.

'I know. She just thought you'd had enough worry.'

'The stupid child,' Mum said. 'It was my responsibility.'

'Perhaps if you hadn't thought of her as a child . . . ?'
I let the sentence trail away into the cold wastes of her
disapproval.

It was peculiar to see a small version of Harris
walking around the reception room. On Sis's daughter
though, that same shock of carrotty hair was improved
immensely by being curled and ringletted and framing
a face only five years old. A face, moreover, unlike
the adults present, apparently incapable of projecting
a sombre mood. She seemed a composed little girl,
taking an alert interest in the goings on, yet apart
somehow, moving around in a bubble of her own.
For myself I can't quite remember far enough back,
but I suppose all adult life is unutterably strange to
children.

'Hello, Harriet,' I said to her. 'Remember me? I'm
your Uncle Alan.'

She stared at me gravely for a moment. 'Are you
the one who hasn't taken Euthuol?' she asked with a
strangely comical mixture of openness and solemnity.

'That's right.'

'How does it feel?'

I smiled at her lack of guile. 'I don't know. Have
you ever asked anyone who's taken it how it feels?'

'No.'

'Well, then. They'd probably say the same as me. No
different from before.' She nodded sagely.

'Tell me,' I said. 'Did they ever let you see your
mother? I mean, since she became ill?'

'No,' she said.

'I thought so. She didn't want to leave you, you
know, but she couldn't possibly have looked after you.'

'I know.' A glimmer of sadness showed for a moment. 'She did think about you all the time.'

'It's okay,' she passed it off. 'I've got lots of friends at the carephanage.'

'Have you?' I said. 'That's good.' During those few sentences I'd shared with her I'd realised I was nervous. I was suddenly glad that I'd never had kids of my own, apart from the genetic danger. I wasn't used to them and I had no idea of how to speak to her. In the end I decided to come right out with it.

'I need to tell you something, Harriet,' I said. She just stared at me curiously, head half-cocked.

'Ageing isn't as bad as they say,' I went on. She frowned. 'But . . . You do realise you're going to have to be careful when you're older?'

Her expression cleared. 'About Euthuol you mean? They told me about that at the carephanage.'

'Yes. And about having children of your own.'

She shrugged. 'It's no big deal.' The poor kid had a lot to learn.

'I think you'll find it is. Tell you what. I promise to come and see you when I start to look old. Show you there's nothing to worry about. So you can make your own mind up.'

'Harriet?' a commanding voice interrupted. 'Take Jarvis just now and play with him, will you? I need a rest.' The man who'd spoken crouched to lay down the toddler he had been carrying in his arms.

'Must I?' Harriet complained. 'I was talking to my Uncle Alan.'

'Yes. Now run along.' Harriet waved at me solemnly and I smiled back. Jarvis put out a trusting hand which she took tenderly and I watched them both depart, his curious waddle beside the more assured stride, equally curious in its way, of his half-sister.

'Do you think that's wise, talking to her like that?' the man said. He was dressed in an institutional trimsuit made of a fabric patterned in pink and blue swirls with some sort of curlicued logo I didn't recognise on the front.

'And who might you be?' I asked him.

'One of her careparents,' he said stiffly. 'And Jarvis's.'

'She's my niece,' I pointed out. 'I'll talk to her about whatever I want.'

'The less she has to do with her family the better as far as I'm concerned,' he said.

'Oh really. And what's wrong with it?'

'Apart from your particular unOrthly attitudes there is the question of ancestral upbringing.' The distaste in his voice was evident. 'To be too close to one of your real parents is unhealthy. To have both of them is downright irresponsible.' Supercilious prat.

'Yeah, yeah,' I retorted. 'We're all freaks in my family. I suppose you would know,' I added heatedly, 'and it's not just professional jealousy on your part. Why did you bring them, if you feel like that?'

'Terms of the care agreement,' he replied. 'It's quite specific. Wherever possible all family gatherings are to be attended.'

'I'm glad my sister had the sense to see to that, if you're typical of what they'll be exposed to. I take it you can't stop me seeing them?'

'No.'

'Good.'

I hit the rounds again, convinced I had a clinching argument. There was no way I was going to touch

Euthuol now. With my sister dead before her time who could question the rightness of my decision to renounce the shots?

I could blush now at the hopeless naivety.

It made no difference. I still met with incomprehension and hostility. Sis's death was an unfortunate accident to my interlocutors, who sallied blithely on in the safe knowledge that it couldn't happen to them. Euthuol was an article of faith, the small matter of its few insignificant victims could not be allowed to disturb it.

I had long despaired of the unequal struggle against Orthrocks. I had not fully given up trying but it was such a juggernaut that I no longer seriously expected to prevent its depredations, at least in the short term. All I could do now was attempt to save Orth's soul. And my own.

I did discover I wasn't quite alone. Every so often, in contrast to the vast amount of poison mail which I learned to distinguish rapidly from its opening infelicitations, and dumped without further perusal, a message would drop into my tank from someone whose mother or father, sister or brother had suffered some mysterious ailment or other for which there was no cure, and had been hustled away to die. Despite my never having heard of most of these maladies before – nor since – many of them were no doubt real, and not cases of a massive cover-up of Euthuol intolerance as some of my correspondents suspected. The small fraction that were admitted to be connected with youth shots meant a fair number of carriers did swim in the human gene pool but they still represented only the tiniest of drops in a planet-sized ocean among the teeming millions that inhabited Orth.

The saddest missives came from bewildered lovers

whose partners, sometimes of many years standing despite Orth's general inclination to short-term relationships, had inexplicably faded away at the ripe old age of forty-two or three or so.

Mostly these communications were anonymous, the ones that weren't invariably contained a plea that the name of the sender be kept secret along with the dear departed's. Failure to conform to the notional Orth ideal of youthful perfection was still the weakness that dared not reveal itself too overtly.

After Sis died I felt a perverse sense of duty to keep in contact with my parents – we had a lot of shared experience, even if there was more we didn't share and I was about all they had left apart from each other. But any attempts at a full reconciliation fell on the altar of Orthrocks brutal landscapings.

'Well you got your empire Dad,' I once said to him. 'Does it make you happy?' He mumbled something non-committal.

'Are you proud of all the reconstruction?' I persisted.

'What do you mean?'

'It's what some of my cynical acquaintances on Home call your iridium workings.'

'It was necessary, boy,' he growled at me.

'Was it?'

'You know it was,' he said, but he looked as if he didn't believe it.

My mother's suspicions of my unorthodoxy didn't help. Despite the twin tragedies that had dominated her life she could not see herself as a victim, only as a perpetrator, and refused to listen to a contrary opinion. She withdrew into herself and started to become reclusive.

Once, on one of her increasingly rare outings, I came upon her in the centre of town. 'Don't talk to me here,' she said, glancing around guiltily. 'Just look at you,' she said, viewing my receding hairline with unconcealed repugnance. 'Why do you always have to draw attention to yourself?' She tried to push past me. 'I don't want to be seen with you,' she said.

I grabbed her arm, turned her to face me. 'Look at the sky, Mum,' I said, indicating the overcasting pall. 'Look at the hills. Is this what you wanted?' I pointed, 'Do you see it? Kiproch disappearing fast,' jerked my thumb over my shoulder, 'Southerland no more.'

She didn't answer, just marched off up the street away from my unseemly presence. What hope did I have if I couldn't even convince my own mother?

I began to settle into a dull, grudging acceptance that things were never going to work out for me, that I was doomed to linger in obscurity till I died, friendless and alone, just like Sonny.

To avoid witnessing the continuing despoliation that was befalling the hills of Home I set up house temporarily on Helcynth. The first flecks of white appeared in my hair, droopiness began to tug at my jowls. Now it was no longer only close quarter encounters that drew disbelieving, disapproving stares. The tracery round my eyes filed out, the sags under them deepened. When I pinched the skin there with my fingers, several seconds elapsed before it returned to its normal configuration.

The greyish flecks merged into white streaks, the stares turned to scowls. Open-mouthed citizens gaped incredulously, nonplussed careparents hustled their charges out of sight along with their perplexed questions and rudely pointing fingers. I experienced a cold formality during the necessary ordinary everyday exchanges.

I knew it had got bad the day I noticed a passerby detach himself from a group up ahead and advance on me purposefully. He stepped in front of me, preventing my passage, held my gaze contemptuously for a second or so and, slowly, deliberately, spat at my feet. His fellow guardians of public decorum cheered in derision. I stared at them as forcefully as I was able, trying to project an air of calm bemusement. 'If you don't mind,' I said, evenly. He then stepped aside and waved me on with a sarcastic bow. I held my ground for a moment before continuing on my way, ostentatiously avoiding the patch of phlegm. I ignored the catcalls that followed on behind.

It was after that I allowed my beard to grow but the expedient afforded me only a brief respite. As soon as the grey showed up strongly, messages from 'concerned citizens' routed through public access points to avoid flagging their origin began to drop into my tank inviting me to leave Helcynth for my 'own good', before I 'joined with its dust forever'.

The SHIFT further extended its ethereal tentacles into the coprosperity sphere as the technology developed and miniaturised. SHIFT chambers of various sizes catered to the trading and transport needs of planets, orbitals, systems large and small. The installation of modulated relays on VT dedicated satellites in close solar orbits allowed shift transmissions of tank signals across the spiral arm in real time. Nowhere in Orth was now more than a few communication minutes from the nearest relay and therefore from anywhere else. ISB slowly replaced OBN as the dominant mediator of cultural life. The capacity to flood the whole of Orth with simultaneous images produced ever swifter and briefer eruptions of fashion mania. Admen and manipulators of all sorts exploited the opportunity voraciously.

Frazer's star rose as he joined the newly integrated network. 'The Worlds and Satellites of Orth' with which he'd made his name had been straight reportage but now he turned his hand to the less journalistic pursuits of the satirical interview and exposé. His neck continued to sprout a variety of knotted decorations.

Chelsea Monday had long since assumed a similar more sedate role, anchoring OBN's main bulletins. Under the studio lights she dispensed with her trade-mark ribbonshades and sun hat, opting for a crown-like elaborately plaited curl to emphasise her queenly sta-tus. The 'Chelsea Swirl' enjoyed a brief vogue but ISB's inroads into the VT market gradually eroded her eminence. In an effort to boost her dwindling celebrity profile she then joined the host of rent-a-mouths doing the chat-show circuit.

I followed the arc of Mercy Boaks's cometary career with a special interest – she had shown me some compassion, after all. It had a common trajectory, a dazzling apparition heading an extended fantail of lookalikes for a brief season before her place in the sun was taken by the next PR-conscious hopeful in the long line and her imitators willingly transformed themselves into the semblance of their latest curious object of desire.

I watched her decline into obscurity with a twinge of sadness. I hoped she found some way to be content in her protracted retirement. The even quicker demise of her successors, on the other hand, gave me nothing but a grim sort of satisfaction.

As for Sile, she might as well never have existed.

*   *   *

The lowest point came on Balnestra, it must be twenty-five or so years ago now – before Mum's death finally gave her release from her self-recriminations. I was there to make yet another appearance in my regular rounds of local VT stations. Dispirited by the inevitable unproductive outcome I had declined the customary cab back to my hotel. I needed some air and hoped the late night stroll would clear my head.

The group of hangers-out in the sit-outery of the Easegoode franchise ignored me at first, then I saw one of them nudge another, say something. Interest rippled through them as four other pairs of eyes followed his gaze. 'Hold on, mate,' one of them shouted over the background pulse of music from inside. I increased my pace. 'Come and have a drink or something.'

'No thanks,' I riposted, quickly. 'I'm in a hurry.'

I hurried by, glimpsing them rise out of the corner of my eye, two of them downing the remainder of their drinks in one gulp. Chairs clattered to the ground. Down at the end of the street the winking entrance to my hotel was tantalisingly far away, the distance between here and there frustratingly empty. I slowed again, hearing the sound of running footsteps approaching. The confrontation was inevitable.

I felt a hand on my shoulder. ''Ere mate, don't be rude, now. 'Old hard,' a different voice said. I stopped and they surrounded me.

'What's with all this strange gear, mate,' the one in front of me said, indicating my appearance. 'You trying to start some sort of fashion? I don't think it'll catch on,' he leered. 'It's ugly,' he added, pushing his face into mine. He recoiled at the closer view.

Their laughter was ugly too, uncontrolled. A night hitting at Easegoode's had removed too many restraints.

'I would have thought so once,' I admitted.

One behind pulled at my hair. 'What's this? A wig?'

'No, it's all my own.' I attempted self-deprecation. 'What there is of it.'

'It's a funny colour,' he slurred. 'Set of colours,' amending himself.

''Ere mate, have you got a disease?' asked the second voice again. 'I 'ope it's not catching.' The laughter was louder this time.

'It's a natural condition,' I assured him.

'Not on Balnestra, it ain't,' said the leerer.

'It was, once.'

'Never. I'd 'ave 'eard about it.' They seemed to take it in turns.

'It would have been before Balnestra was absorbed into Orth.'

Comprehension hit slowly. 'What? You mean you ain't had youth shots?' Disgust crawled across the features of the leerer.

''Ow old are you, then?' – the second again.

'I forget,' I said, turning towards him. 'About fifty-five?' I hazarded.

The fifth voice took its turn. 'I suppose that means you can still have children,' it said thoughtfully.

'I haven't taken Euthuol,' was all I admitted to.

'That's 'orrible!'

'You perv!'

The leerer snarled, 'You ought to be in a hospice, looking like that.'

'What for? I'm not dying.'

'I wouldn't be too sure about that, mate,' came the original voice as the first fist struck.

I didn't feel much after the initial punches; I was too shocked. I collapsed quickly, rolled into a ball, steeled myself against the kicks. I may have been lucky they'd been hitting all night, their aim was pretty erratic. Most of the blows were glancing ones. Or perhaps they were just inexpert, there wasn't a lot of street brawling on Balnestra as a rule. Some time after my left leg was broken, I lost consciousness.

The procurator's investigator, clearly uncomfortable in my presence, claimed he wasn't used to interviewing people in hospital. He pronounced himself baffled. Never had a case like it, he said. I suspect he didn't even bother talking to the staff at Easegoode's. I got the impression he wanted to sweep the incident under the carpet to avoid damaging the tourist trade. Well, I'd get my own back.

Broken limbs, I found, do not heal quickly when you're about fifty-five. I had to suffer the massed attentions of a bunch of medics and parameds agleam with ultra-white trimsuits and freshly scrubbed time-frozen faces, all eager to update their CVs with a touch of clinical exotica.

'How long before I'm up and about again?' I asked one of them.

'I don't know,' she replied with alarming honesty. 'Can't tell. None of us has ever treated anyone this old who hasn't taken Euthuol. Weeks certainly. Maybe months. There's not much in the literature; one obscure report. And the trauma there was organic rather than physical.'

'How am I going to stay sane in here for weeks?' I moaned.

'I don't know,' she said. 'I sometimes wonder that myself.' Then, just to cheer me further, added, 'But we've got ISB.'

I spent tedious days hoisting myself every so often from

position to position to avoid sores, staring vacantly at the tank in my room, skating through the channels trying to find something that I didn't remember from decades before or watching endless mindnumbing trivia shows just to pass the time: anything to avoid thinking about my situation.

The tiresome routine was broken by an unexpected visit. 'Oh Alan, Alan,' Mum greeted me. 'What are we going to do with you?'

'Nothing, I hope. Hello, Dad. Thanks for coming and all that, but . . . what are you doing here?'

'I've come to look after you,' she said as if it was the most normal thing in Orth to burst suddenly out of seclusion and jump halfway along the spiral arm, dragging your partner with you. I suppose it pandered to her late-found view of herself; always a stalwart in a crisis. Whether the objects of her ministrations wanted one or not.

'I don't need looking after,' I grumbled.

Silently she inspected the light-casts immobilising my arm and leg, the yellowed bruises, the extensively stitched lacerations, the myriad abrasions.

'All right,' I conceded. 'I need looking after. But the medstaff here are trained for it.'

'Your sister didn't need medstaff.'

'This isn't like Sis, Mum,' I told her, gently. 'I'm going to be all right.'

'How can you say that? Just look at you! Well, you wouldn't listen to your mother,' she said in reproof. 'I hope this has brought you to your senses and you'll stop all this nonsense.'

'What nonsense?'

'This ageing business.' Her nose wrinkled in distaste.

'How can I stop it? It's already started. Even if I took Euthuol I'd still be stuck like this. Tell her Dad,' I appealed to him, forlornly. When the fancy took her she could equal a force of nature. In such moods he knew better than to interrupt.

'You could wear a wig,' Mum breenged on. 'And cosmetics so that your face looks a bit more decent.'

'Mum,' I said with a grimace. 'You know I've always hated stuff like that.'

'It doesn't have to be heavy; a little powder, some highlighter to alter the angles.'

'No! Certainly not. The most I'll go to is a beard.'

'Mmm,' she said. 'I suppose that might do.' She shook her head. 'I was so careful,' she sighed. 'Where did I go wrong?'

I humoured her by letting her fuss around for a few days. She was more wearing than the interminable proddings and pokings from the medics. When she was satisfied I would come to no more harm I persuaded Dad to take her off Home again. I wish I hadn't. It was the last time I saw her alive.

I could now shuffle about with the aid of a crutch, which helped break the monotony, but my horizons were still limited to a couple of corridors in either direction and every so often it was back to the delights of ISB, which gave me the chance to witness Frazer's celebrated last encounter with Chelsea Monday.

The story he tells about it now – whether he'd planned it all along or it was just that her haughtiness got to him – depends on the mood he's in; but I'll say this, Frazer was always a meticulous organiser and his resentment of her had smouldered for years. She came on in her OBN studio trimsuit – blue with the sigil picked out in bright yellow – looking a little plumper than I remembered; but that may have been the distorting frame of the tank. From the outset she treated him with disdain, wasting no opportunity to remind the viewers that he had once been hers to control – in her words, 'a mere sound engineer' – and that her pedigree in the tank was much longer than his. He just smiled routinely and allowed her to roll-call all her past triumphs and the various cock-ups of his she could recall during shooting. There weren't many of hers, that was partly the basis of her early reputation, so I guess she thought she was on safe enough ground. It was when they discussed her move to passive reporting that he began to worry her.

'You know,' he said. 'I miss the ribbonshades and sun hat. Why did you abandon them?'

'They weren't appropriate, I needed something different. Everyone was tired of them.'

'It wasn't because they were tired of you, then?'

She glared at him as if it was beneath her dignity to contemplate such a thing. 'All of us in the public eye need some small distinguishing characteristic,' she said. 'You're known for one yourself.' She indicated his current neckwear, a florid green winged effort about ten cee-em wide. 'Though it's not something I remember from your days with me.'

'I'm glad you noticed,' he said.

'I could hardly avoid it.'

'I've got a pair here,' Frazer said, rummaging around in his desk. 'I don't suppose you could remind us all of how you used to look?' A few cheers from his studio audience greeted his request. 'They've been cut at the back so you can slide them on.'

Chelsea shrugged, took the violently strobing lens-strip. She settled it across her eyes, prised it out over her ears and allowed it to snap onto the back of her head. Turning to the audience she gave them a triumphant smile. Various whoops and yells surfed the applause.

'It doesn't look right without the hat,' Frazer said. Chelsea's beam vanished. 'I suppose you've got that as well,' she said, warily.

'Sure,' he replied and tossed it to her. She fingered it carefully, running it around in her hands.

'Put it on then,' he prompted.

'I'm not sure it will still fit,' she said, smiling. 'I've got longer hair now.'

'I noticed,' he said, as Chelsea squashed the sun hat onto her head. 'I could hardly avoid it.'

It didn't sit properly. Her curled plait pushed it up, away from her ears. She gave a disappointed moue to the audience, spread her hands resignedly.

Frazer said, 'But that's not the real sun hat, is it? I've got the real one here.' Chelsea's face froze.

He produced an identical looking hat from underneath his desk, holding it upside down, carefully. 'Go on,' he urged. 'Take it.'

'But it still won't fit,' she protested.

'It used to. Has your head size changed?' This sally elicited some stray laughs.

'Not as much as yours,' she muttered.

Frazer gave her a steely grin, stood up and walked over to her, still cradling the hat. 'I think if we make a few adjustments,' he said, 'we'll find it fits perfectly.'

Chelsea made a half-hearted attempt to rise which he stopped with a firm hand on her shoulder.

'My turn now,' he said. She seemed to shrink into her chair. 'Let's see. If I take out this here, and here,' he went on, removing various pins and grips which restrained her plait, 'I should . . . It's not coming out.'

'No.' It was almost a whisper.

'Ah. I see now,' he said. 'It's not real.' He slid the curl down off her head. A gleaming dome of hairless skin lay underneath. With the sole adornment of her ribbonshades it looked as if a gift-wrapped egg perched on Chelsea's shoulders. Stupefied gasps greeted the revelation.

Frazer turned over the sun hat, letting the strands of hair it concealed fall into view. Gently he set it over her domed nakedness, draping the hair carefully down around her neck.

It had been cruel, but it was riveting VT. Frazer attempted some amends by asking her about the circumstances, teasing from her, encouraging her unaccustomed haltering tones, the story of her adolescent disease – she was apparently utterly hairless – and a lifetime of prosthetic headwear. Frazer's dominance was so complete he even got her to peel off her false eyebrows. Though there was a strange dignity about the action that reminded me of Sonny I nevertheless discovered there was a limit to my preference for the real over the feigned. She looked like a peeled grape.

But he'd destroyed her. In that one moment of disclosure Chelsea's long career was gone. Her next news broadcast was a nightmare of fumbled lines and misread scripts. She recovered her confidence quickly but her authoritative aura had disappeared for good.

For a few brief weeks the cult of Chelsea Monday was reestablished. A rash of sun hat wearers occupied the streets again. The joke was that every so often the hat would be removed in an extravagant sweep and revealed to have several lengths of lank hair attached to it.

She was taken off-air well before this fad died down,

even though her bosses must have known about her condition all along. Ridicule was not the accepted lot of an OBN anchor. Perhaps if she'd had the nerve to brazen it out, made an asset out of necessity and adopted hairlessness as an image, it might have been different; but I know how hard it is to go against prevailing opinion. I guess those same bosses wouldn't have allowed her to, anyway.

I hadn't had a boss to please for years, apart from jockeying to appear on disparate VT shows. As I ruminated on the affair during my long convalescence, the lesson I took from it slowly gelled. By the time I left Balnestra for ever I had shaped the notion into a new tactic.

18

Justified, And Ancient

Count the days into years.

I look in the mirror every morning – as I have done ever since I can remember – and the tale of my life is writ large, the lines of battle prominent. My hair (what's left of it) is mostly white now, with a few steely black strands lingering stubbornly on to give an illusion of greyness – though to my credit I keep it in a tidier fashion than did Sonny. My back complains when I bend over, which is no longer often. My eyesight fades with the years. My breath is shallow, my walk slow. I take great care when entering or leaving a shower cubicle. And the skin . . .

I flex my fingers and the tendons on my arms stand out bold, the underlying veins form a river system of blue gnarls. Small irregular brown patches darken the otherwise pallid backs of my hands and swell to larger ellipses on my arms. The delicate tracery round my eyes has become a mountain range, the once taut, supple covering over my jaws and cheek-bones is reduced to jowls and sags. For a short while after the incident on Balnestra I regrew my beard to help hide the healing wounds, and, to my shame, tinted it.

Yes, I let discretion overrule my still-nervous endeavours and lapsed into the insistent narcissism of Orth. How could I not? My culture demanded it.

Sile had derided the trait but as with my mother, so with me. I see no point in denying it. The precise point at which legitimate fear for oneself trips over into excessive self-regard is difficult to pin down but I am and will remain an unreconstructed narcissist. Why else would I have spent all my years fretting about my appearance?

Now, through the repeated self-scrutiny the condition insists on, every wrinkle is so easy to place, so familiar and strangely comforting. And, perhaps surprisingly, a source of pride. Sometimes I feel it is a combination of Sonny and the face of the Rock which stares back at me through the mist from my morning ablutions. Which is, perhaps, fitting.

I came back to Helcynth to find my place ransacked. The viewing medium of my smashed tank had ebbed onto the floor and dried to a sticky, blackening goo. The glutinous liquid had been used to cover the walls in graffiti – gems of wit such as 'Queer Go Home' and 'Fuck Off Pervert', together with the comparatively lyrical but insidiously menacing 'Keep Helcynth Pure', and 'Orth Young, Orth Beautiful'.

The desire for a respite from such attentions while I looked around for a new home (I was determined never to live on Helcynth again; I have set foot neither there nor Balnestra since I left) partly figured in my decision to regrow the beard. The relief it provided was welcome, though I made sure it was only temporary.

I floated through a sea of what I had now begun to consider as interchangeable time-frozen characterless Orth faces. Not a vestige of the lives they had lived could be traced on most of them. Everywhere I looked were the same bland visages, the same meaningless sense of dress, the same cosmeticry, the rapidly tedious ubiquitous fashions instantly spread by ISB's shift-beamed channels and replaced as soon by the next vapid observance, the essential rigidity and conformity of Orth culture only emphasised by its confusing carousel of churning enthusiasms. I longed for the real spark of individuality that its denizens presumably thought they were displaying by their eager graspings at each new mode to shine through the gloom of uniformity and point to the clearer skies of true diversity and tolerance. I never imagined I would be able to provide that beacon myself.

I still had the minefields of two more funerals back Home to negotiate before the visits became too depressing and, after a long search, I settled on the nearest approximation I could find, here on Alcluith, on the little dun with its watery protection in the form of the stream which dribbles round its base in an irregular three-quarter circle, and its glorious views to the occasionally mist-clad and mercifully unravaged mountains beyond the city.

Dad hung on for a few years after Mum's death, not knowing quite what to do with himself. He made some tentative attempts at reconciliation doomed to failure by his lack of sympathy with my chosen path.

When Dad's turn came, all the locals regarded me warily. Even though some had known me since birth they were lost for a polite reaction to the ever-whitening

hair and greying cheeks, the unapologetic wrinkles, and
perhaps confounded by the presence among them of
the VT celebrity at the centre of a burgeoning cult, the
weirdest enthusiasm that Orth had ever seen.

I'm still not quite sure whether it was the ageing or
the mysticism that did it. Or the boost to my profile
gained by appearing on Frazer's increasingly popular
show. Perhaps it required the combination of all three.
Knowing Orth's inveterate habits, without Frazer's
help I'd likely still be waiting for my sanctification
to begin.

'Alan has done a brave thing,' he said in his introduc-
tion. 'Maybe a foolhardy one. He has dared to question
the foundations of Orth culture, the fulcrum round
which everything else pivots. He has not taken Euthuol,
an understandable decision given that – through an
extremely rare genetic defect – he was likely to die
prematurely if he had. But, perhaps more profoundly,
he has also shunned any cosmetic concealment of that
fact, nor has he allowed himself to be hidden away
in a hospice, but instead proceeds openly about his
business, challenging conventional views about what
is acceptable in Orth and what is not, what faces a
citizen may be allowed to show.'

He turned to me. 'Is that a fair summary of your
outlook, Alan?'

'More or less, though I wouldn't describe myself
as brave.'

'I'm sure you've been asked many times before, but
why? Why subject yourself to all the hassle that must
come with such extreme unconventionality? Why no
cosmetics? Or remedial surgery? Why no hospice?'

'In my opinion that question ought to be reversed.
Why should I disguise myself? Why should I enter a

hospice? I'm a fully capable, functioning person. I'm not ill nor – despite what some may think – deranged. I'm a danger to no-one. Why should I hide myself away for who knows how many years just because others may dislike my appearance? If they are disturbed by it they should look within themselves. If they're afraid, it isn't actually me they fear.'

'Your appearance is what makes visible your divergence from Orth norms. Let's start with that. Your hair seems thin and has lost colour. Will that progress further?' We smiled knowingly at each other. Our experience with Sonny gave both of us a reference point but his viewers likely had no strong memory of it even if they'd seen his original broadcast.

I managed to surprise Frazer, just the same. 'First may I say I hope you're not going to play about with it to see if it's a wig.' The amount of laughter which this remark produced encouraged me. Despite my long experience under studio arcs this was the first time in the sweat of the rectangular pool enclosed by quadraxes that I began to feel I wasn't on the verge of losing an audience; that they might actually be with me.

'To answer your question, I don't know,' I said after the chortles faded. 'It may stay like this or the hair loss may continue. The transition to white will accelerate, though.'

'And what about the lines on your face?'

'These?' I queried, placing my index fingers to the sides of my eyes, then waving them contemptuously. 'These are mere mounds and hollows compared to the hills and crevasses that might appear.' A groan of horror relieved with some sympathy greeted the revelation.

'Are there any less obvious signs of your aboriginal state?' Frazer continued.

'I can't run as fast as I used to,' I admitted, to a further flutter of amusement. 'I get short of breath more easily,' I added.

'I couldn't help noticing you walk with a limp, now. Is that part of it?'

'No. I have the good people of Balnestra to thank for that. They took such exception to my appearance that a group of them attacked me. I had to spend several weeks in hospital waiting for my bones to knit together again. I'm not quite sure they did, properly.'

Frazer took his cue from the various members of the audience who had shown disapproval of my assailants. 'I hope we all agree that violence is not the sort of thing a responsible citizen of Orth should resort to,' he said.

'We all know it happens,' I said. Then I took a risk. 'I think it was my potency that bothered them more than anything. The thought that looking like this I could still father children.'

'That's no excuse for them,' Frazer blustered.

I shrugged. 'It was only a more extreme variant of the attitudes I continually come up against,' I said. 'The disbelief, the malevolent stares, the abuse. Some might say I had it coming.'

'And yet you are undeterred. Defiant even.'

'To some extent I have no choice. Shuffle them how I will, the genetic cards I have been dealt leave me with a poor hand.'

'Are you reconciled to that?'

'It doesn't bother me now.'

'But it used to?'

'When I was younger. It's been with me a long time.'

'There's something I think the viewers will want me to ask. How does it feel to grow old?'

'Compared to what?' I rejoindered. 'To someone who has taken the shots? I can't tell you, I don't know. The life I have is as much as I can understand.'

'So tell us about that. How do you feel, now?'

I thought for a moment and shrugged. 'I feel no differently from when I was young,' I said. 'I may look in a mirror and see a different face but inside I still have the image of myself I had as a youth. The only real difference is in people's reactions to me. Now, I get looks of shock and outrage, abuse at times. I used to be regarded as quite handsome, as you may recall. I turned a few heads in my time.'

'Would you say, then, that beauty is not in the eye of the beholder but rather in the mind of the beheld?'

'I don't think so,' I replied. 'Beauty isn't the point. I wouldn't argue that I am beautiful, for instance. I just think that, provided it doesn't affect anyone else adversely, everyone has the right to live how they will, to grow old gracefully if that's what they want, and not to be abominated for it. To be left alone and in peace.'

'Those are rather airy-fairy, wish-washy sentiments, aren't they?'

'Are they? Isn't anything else a kind of cultural authoritarianism? Social dictatorship? An unquestioning exaction of the tribute due to a hegemonic society? The moral equivalent of beating someone up? Physical assaults are not the only ones to leave scars.'

'These are deep waters you're treading, Alan,' Frazer warned me.

'And dangerous currents,' I replied. 'I know.'

'You could easily hide away from it all, disguise yourself, or retire,' he said. 'You don't. What is it that keeps you going? What drives you? It can't simply be that you feel you have no choice.'

I hesitated. For all my preoccupations, with Sonny, with my treacherous genes, with the hills of Home, I hadn't really considered the point deeply.

'I am a Son of the Rock,' I found myself saying, to my astonishment; and in that moment Frazer's debt to me – and Sonny – was expunged, and mine to him established. For the first time since, perhaps, roaming the cotton-easter clad hills of my carefree childhood, or since Gran was hauled away on that hospice trolley – certainly since Sonny had laid his strange burden on me – I felt free.

It seemed, too, that the atmosphere in the studio at large changed. Bodies stiffened, heads craned. A buzz of interest, a whiff of fascination spread through the audience.

'Could you explain that?' Frazer asked, launching me into that long, rambling peroration which took in the usual subjects, the hills of Home, the quarries on Copper, Orthrocks widespread depredations; ones I had hitherto neglected, Sonny, the hill of the Rock, the mystical unions that form between people and the places where they live, those bonds of attachment which lead to a sense of belonging; and ones which I had completely ignored, the Rock's tortured face, the long history of Its Sons and Daughters, their gradual wasting away so that I was now, as far as I knew, the surrogate last of their kind. 'Why should these smaller cultures cringe before ours?' I asked at one point. 'Why should they be made to feel inadequate because ours is bigger, brighter, more alluring – and more wasteful – than theirs?'

I ended on a descending note. 'I am wary of the

element of coercion in Orth's prestige and power. That it's a cultural imperative. That the underlying aggression it betrays is a sign of insecurity. That our relationships to each other, to our resources and to other cultures are unbalanced. That we have lost our way and there is no easy road back. Once before, humanity lost touch with its wider self through a too-rapid expansion. I fear the same may happen again, only this time the collapse will be more extreme.'

The audience heard me out in silence. When it was over the silence remained. Frazer's winding-up remarks struggled to achieve an upbeat tone. The applause over the end credits seemed muted, reflective.

Liberty and release. Free to be whatever I . . .

To grow old gracefully. Not to give a damn. To say what I liked, when I liked. To look in a mirror and be content. I returned to Alcluith thinking no more of it than that.

A small crowd had gathered in front of the gates of my house, barring entry. My newly lightened mood darkened a little as I wondered if the demons that had assailed me on Helcynth were about to strike here as well. As a precaution I directed the hovercab driver to swing round to the back. There was a short, steep walk involved, but it felt safer.

A 'reply-awaited' message flagged with the procurator's logo was queueing in my tank. Warning of anonymous threats? Offers of protection? I struck the read button. The logo rearranged itself, assembling its various parts into one of Orth's bland time-frozen faces, smooth neck rising from an epauletted dark green trimsuit.

'I wonder if you would contact this office as soon

as possible, sir,' the woman proc said, 'on the number displayed. The matter is pressing, but not urgent.'

Intrigued – I had intended to contact them anyway – I keyed in the thirteen digits. The face dissolved as another, male this time but equally characterless, different shoulder flashes on the 'suit, materialised in its place. 'Procurator's office. How may I help you?' As I gave the reason for my call the proc began fiddling with his control panel.

'Thank you for calling,' he said. 'Is there something wrong with your set, sir? I don't seem to be picking up vision.'

'I always use voice-only. I'm not a great believer in hitech.'

'Ah. Well, sir. You noticed a group of people around your entryway?'

'Yes, I had to detour to avoid them.'

He looked puzzled for a moment, consulted his datatank, then said, 'I wonder if you would mind asking them to disperse? They're liable to cause an obstruction.'

'Me? What have they got to do with me?'

'It's you they claim to want to see,' he explained.

'I know nothing about them,' I told him. 'Isn't it your department's job to disperse crowds?'

'We thought a word from you would be less . . . confrontational.'

'You have details of what happened to me on Balnestra?' I asked.

He scrolled through his datatank again. 'Yes, sir. But this is not Balnestra. We don't think these people represent a danger.'

'Nevertheless, I'd prefer a few deputes present. Would you send a hovercar over?'

'As you wish, sir. Would you keep the link open? We'll patch you into our net so that you can assess the situation for yourself.'

'I suppose so,' I assented. I hit retain and started scanning the rest of my t-mail – bill reminders mostly, and 'unrepeatable' offers on a variety of junk merchandise.

A few minutes later the wirble-warble of a patrolcar fluttered over the dun, dopplered down as the vehicle came to a halt. I struck restore and listened in to the conversation. The procurator's logo hung in the tank, dark green and glittering silver.

'Now then,' came a depute's voice in imitation of innumerable dire VT dramas. A hovercar door slammed. 'What are you all waiting here for? A glimpse of the madman across the water?' I could imagine the officer's malicious grin.

I wandered to the window. Down below, intermittently green-swept by the 'car's rooflights, the small crowd was forming a circle round the depute. Their shuffling sound preceded a deeper reply. 'We have come to see the Son of the Rock,' the new voice said, quietly. What trickery is this? I thought.

'The fool on the hill, d'you mean?' – the depute again. She was clearly enjoying herself.

'Please do not refer to him in that manner,' said someone else in yet more soft tones. 'It is not fitting.' There were murmurs of agreement. My cynicism began to waver.

'What if he doesn't want to see you? You can't stay here, you know. You'll have to move on.'

'We wish only to talk. To seek guidance in the ways of the Rock. We will disperse if he wishes it.' The earnestness was plain. I was stunned.

'Sarge?' The depute's voice was louder. 'Did you get that?'

The beep from the tank alerted me. The logo was shattering once more, rejigging into the procsergeant's features. 'Sir?' he enquired. 'Sir?'

I jolted myself to awareness. 'Yes?'

'There really doesn't seem to be too much of a problem, sir. We would appreciate it if you could have a word. Send them away peacefully.'

'Yes, yes,' I mumbled. 'Of course. But . . .'

'Yes, sir?'

'Could your officer stay awhile. Just in case?'

'Naturally, sir. She won't leave till you're happy with the situation.'

'Thank you.'

I thumbed the tank off, stood for a while watching the green glow die, gathering my reeling emotions. Could this be genuine? And the truly appalling thought: if it were, was I worthy of the mantle I had so suddenly assumed? Adrift on a cloud of confusion and self-doubt, I slowly descended to greet my new-found acolytes.

Release and liberty. To forge necessity into an asset, and with what rapture! To flaunt myself openly. To accept and adapt. To be a bemused father figure to a flock of discontented questing souls.

Sonny never said it would be easy.

I am a Son of the Rock. *I am a Son of the Rock*. Such simple words with which to change the course of a life, to fulfil its destiny. A moment before they slipped into my head, I had not even contemplated uttering them. Until they spoke themselves I had not fully realised their truth. After, I could not conceive of any other way to describe myself, the many paths I could have followed had finally coalesced, flowed into one.

Frazer's show percolated into many of Orth's nooks and crannies but ISB's network had yet to achieve blanket coverage. I still had a few rounds to do to get my unforgettable face fully known, to maximise my unanticipated celebrity.

'I am a Son of the Rock,' – on Nova Ventura, to ripplings of applause. 'I am a Son of the Rock,' – on Rosario, to delighted cheers. 'I am a Son of the Rock,' repeated like a mantra now at every opportunity, riding a wave of recognition and enthusiasm. On Alta Plana, on Cliftonhalle, on Mildenbeck, Shestri, Barat Marata, on Trevi, on Home, on Wemadeit, on Midian, Novymir, Jefferson. Everywhere and nowhere. Anywhere they would have me (except Helcynth and Balnestra). On all the worlds and satellites of Orth; preceded, through the ethereal workings of the SHIFT, by my new-found fame. 'I am a Son of the Rock,' and I have started for myself, unexpectedly, gloriously, a cultish fad.

I was bemused by the first imitators, descending on me at Alta Plana with their greyed-up hair and crude 'ageing' masks. After so many years of being shunned in public, of expecting every approach to be a prelude to an abusive tirade, of accepting exposure only through the relatively safe medium of the VT, it was still a concept I found difficult to grasp that I could be an object of desire, however obscure. In my youth I had had far too little difficulty with it, but I was older now, I hoped wiser. The notion sat on me uncomfortably. Desire and I had parted company a long time before.

I endured the pawing hands stoically. They imagined they were touching the hem of godhood, the tortured face of the Rock, and who was I to disabuse them? I was a mere channel, a conduit between them and whatever it was they sought.

I eyed the women with particular askance, there was so much reminder in them of Sis and of how I imagined Gran at her end. The men were laughably pale imitations of Sonny and poor ones even of my own less-advanced state. Their carriage was too grand, their bearing too upright; the stabilised cells of the Euthuol-treated body do not produce the metabolites which waste the organs and joints, at least not until their catastrophic descent into chaos and decay. For a long time, till they learned to develop the correct stance, I was surrounded by adherents whose presence only advertised their vigour and highlighted my declining powers.

Roll with it, I told myself. Embrace it.

The element of chicanery involved pained me. All my life I had reacted against bodily artifice, things feigned, and yet here were people who sought to become like me but could only do so by adopting disguise and subterfuge.

I accepted them. I even gave them my blessing. Without it there was no possibility of my acceptance in the wider coprosperity sphere. Only as one in a wide scattering of faces which looked like mine could I hope to walk freely again, if walking freely is what I had ever managed to do since I left Copper.

In some there was a deep spiritual longing, a desperate urge to find meaning in a hedonistic age. Many times I was called upon to explain the mysteries of the Rock. My protestations that I knew no more than the poor supplicants themselves tended to be greeted with a renewed zeal on their part, as if they believed I was holding something deeper back, that they had to prove themselves somehow more worthy of a higher revelation.

Attitudes fractured. With the growing numbers of my followers came the wider acceptance I craved, but in some quarters grudgingly and only to appearances. My hate mail reduced to mere complaints. Look how you like, ran the gist of most of them, but do not tamper with the foundations of Orth. The struggle to overcome the strongly entrenched beliefs of generations remained as complex as ever.

The strangest complaints came from outraged ex-inhabitants of Copper or their descendants deploring me mentioning their ancestral religion – to which they no longer adhered – in the same breath as the decadence and obscenity of rejecting Euthuol. I forbore to reply to these misguided idiots.

I found myself making ever more frequent visits to small enclaves of oldsters whose numbers rose steadily on each round. I lodged in their meeting houses and the term, I felt, had a certain appropriateness. I made the designation official.

It was in the Astrakind lodge, I think, that one of them called me 'father' for the first time. It somehow seemed natural despite my childless state. Had I not sparked off a new line of Sons and Daughters?

But some of my fellow travellers were undoubtedly more attracted to cult trappings, to the superficialities of my message rather than the substance. Certainly I came across the strangest misconceptions.

I remember one follower removed his two offspring from the local carephanage for the day in order to receive my blessing. The girl and boy reminded me of Harriet and Jarvis, though a year or so younger.

After I had mumbled something suitable over their heads the girl startled me by asking, 'Must we renounce Euthuol, father, as you have done?'

'No, no, my child,' – I had settled happily into the part by now – 'Whoever gave you that idea?'

'My truefather,' she said, glancing uncertainly in his direction.

'Don't let it worry you,' I told her. 'You have a free choice. Remember, to renounce Euthuol may be to renounce children. I would not forbid you from becoming a parent.'

Harriet and Jarvis themselves grew up with an amused view of their strange uncle, dropping in on them from time to time with his now only slightly odd appearance, telling tales of faraway lands and distant days, of strange customs and practices, of their mother when she was young, of blue-remembered hills, and of a sparkling-eyed, lithe dancer named Sile.

The final irony was when the representatives of Orthcosm came to me with their offers of a franchising operation based on the 'Old Look'. I could have taken the money, I suppose, (in my days as a mining engineer I had done worse) but I could not have squared it with my conscience. I turned them down, but I knew I couldn't prevent them marketing the stuff anyway. Wigs – grey and/or receding – eyeliners, special foundation powders, moulded facefits in boxes flashed 'carve your own furrows' hit the shops. Soon the worlds and satellites of Orth were hardened to the sights of the aged – whether artificial oldsters, made-up, or those real ancients emboldened out of hospices by the unaccustomed climate of acceptance – tripping down their streets and alleyways. I barely merited a cursory glance.

Something else I knew, though only as a vague worry at the back of my mind, was that it couldn't last. Nothing that reeks of fashion in Orth ever does. It could only ever be a passing fad. One more order of the day. A quick shimmer on the surface of Orth life and then away.

What the VT could elevate it could also strike down. I only had to remember the grim lesson of Chelsea Monday, the brief career of Mercy Boaks – too high, too far, too soon – to realise that. The tank's fickle caress could be curse as well as blessing.

But I was determined to exploit the moment as far as possible, to effect some form of change so that, at the least, this vogue might leave behind a benign legacy even if its old soldier should fade away.

The Old Look never remotely approached a monopoly on style, the normal flux and reflux of street life always had it competing with alternative fashion statements. Its first few brave stalwarts had to endure some ridicule and hostility before the sight became too commonplace to merit close attention, only one decorative fragment among the constant kaleidoscopic gyre of Orth's casual wardrobe. Successive waves of fashion threw out their creations into the spiral arm for the citizens to make of them what they would. There was even a mode, promulgated by ClothesOrth, which commandeered the institutional trimsuit as a form of leisurewear, backed up by an advertising campaign juxtaposing weirder aspects of Orth life with the utterly banal. I suppose they might have tried outrage to attract customers if I had not already succeeded in comprehensively trumping anything a creative director could come up with. The garment itself was plain and logoless but nevertheless proclaimed ClothesOrth as loudly as the real workwear endured by employees of OBN, Orthrocks, ISB, UCAL, MedOrth and the rest marked their status. Why people should voluntarily subsume their character and style in someone else's and become walking billboards displaying the fact has always been a mystery to me. Orthodoxy and I have made at best only idle companions. If the role hadn't been thrust on me I would have been a poor choice to lead a cult. I've never really comprehended the instincts of the herd. But maybe only the unwilling should be figureheads, they may do less damage.

The VT offers dwindled, of course, but I didn't want to risk overkill anyway. Still, I was too busy doing the rounds of the Rock's new Sons and Daughters, who had flocked to the lodges I had set up across the western spiral arm, to appreciate the drift.

It was brought home to me on Bindematsu when I noticed a passer-by giving me more than the usual brief glance. He was bedecked in a style which brought to my mind the carved faces of the Alban migration. I guessed his modification was as surgically reversible as those had been. (It is one of the more depressing aspects of a long life that you see what others regard as exciting new trends and developments as mere retreads; an uninspired stirring of the same old ingredients into more or less familiar forms.)

Unlike the scarifications of that long defunct craze, his mutilations were based on the native customs of Kuros, the latest diasporic world to receive the benefits of coprosperity. A carved loop of bleached animal bone pierced his nose and curled round to penetrate each ear. Another, gleaming whitely as he bared his teeth, projected through his lower lip at two points and curved up fiercely towards the first. His face appeared trapped inside a cage of tusks. His fluted headdress and flowing cape provided slightly jarring finials.

As I passed he called out to me derisively, 'Hey! Oldster! Don't you know the old look is outmoded. That was last year's fashion.' I had difficulty deciphering the comment at first as the fragment of bone inside his mouth affected his ability to form words properly. At my quizzical response he made his meaning clear with a mocking gesture. Dismay rose in me. I had thought I had made my escape from hostility.

'At least I can speak properly,' I spluttered, 'and this,' – I grabbed my thinning strands of whitened hair – 'is real. As are all these.' I traced my wrinkled brow and wizened cheeks. 'Can you say as much for your get-up?' I asked him angrily. He seemed dumbstruck; either by my vehemence or the still outrageous notion that someone might elect to undergo irreversible disfigurement. I stormed away before he could respond, bothered not so much by his comment as by my reaction.

It was that nagging fear that had prompted my outburst: the sudden shifting of my subconscious apprehension into sharp focus. Was my success, little as it had been, to be over quite so soon? Had all I strained for for so long been for nothing? Were the Sons and Daughters of the Rock doomed to follow the path of all Orth enthusiasms to swift replacement? Or to suffer death by a thousand slow lapses? To survive purely in the minds of those who witnessed them and then only as a dimly remembered epiphenomenon which even its adherents would barely recall?

As I strode those narrow winding streets on Bindematsu, the raucous cries of the indigenous swooping seabirds filling the air, their stark eyes agleam with the prospect of forage, I thought on the slight decline in numbers, the absent faces in the lodges throughout the western spiral arm, the drought of invitations onto VT shows. I realised interest had waned, the descent had already begun. I had been too busy to notice, riding the wave of my small celebrity, swept away by the twin delusions of adulation and pride. Ah, Sonny, you would have been rightly dissatisfied.

So. Humbly and contritely begin again. Swim against the tide of Orth culture.

'I am a Son of the Rock,' on Kuros, but too late. It would perhaps have been too late the moment the splorecraft shimmered out of hyperspace into the glare of Kuros's sun to home in on the perfect white and blue jewel orbiting around it. Certainly too late a few days on, when the SHIFT station had been set up, and the bland, characterless faces of the fashion vultures poured through.

Or perhaps too early. The lure of Euthuol is a hard one to resist. Let it lie, and come back when you can.

'I am a Son of the Rock,' reverently, on Vukoviab. 'Its servant in all things.' On Ophelia, Paramatang and Baltazaar. Anywhere they would have me (except Helcynth and Balnestra).

'I am a Son of the Rock.' No more triumphantly or wantonly, but instead discreetly and soberly. All along the spiral arm, cajoling, encouraging, bolstering. Falling slowly.

Numbers stabilised for a while, the odd convert, the lodge attendance losses only a dribble. But the stream of Orth life was always going to bear the Sons away.

I should never have expected more. That the cult of the Rock had flowered even so briefly was the miracle I had unbelievingly, impossibly, promised Sonny, made flesh. Sometimes, when it was at its height, I didn't quite believe it myself. I'm not sure I'd believe it even yet, if I didn't have the discs and the daily evidence.

The faces remain, no longer shocking in their lack of smooth flawlessness. Just one more lifestyle accessory to be lifted from the stock shelf of Orth's merry go-round come-around, and worn till boredom sets in. Throw it away and pick another. Or keep it carefully stashed somewhere. It will always crop up again. Echoes like dust.

But it seemed I had started something. The bounds of acceptability had altered. And Frazer, as ever, was quick to tongue the new zeitgeist.

His guest, a man he'd introduced as Ruadhys Inlov, appeared outwardly unremarkable, with a typically time-frozen indeterminate face framed by an unexceptional hairstyle: unlike me whenever I had visited the tank, whose looks could not be easily disguised, nor wished to hide them. The puzzling normality of the encounter – Frazer was apparently unable to elicit anything but utterly banal responses from his interviewee – was only explained when he asked the man to display his right hand.

At first glance nothing seemed amiss. The close-up however showed it had a thumb, yes, but only three fingers. The pinky had been neatly excised at the lower knuckle. A patch of smooth scar tissue marked the absence.

Murmurs of distaste could be heard from Frazer's audience. A few souls in the lodge-house where I was watching the relay shifted uncomfortably.

'What happened to make you like this?' Frazer asked.

'I had the finger removed,' Inlov replied evenly.

'Was it damaged, then, or diseased?' Frazer enquired of him.

'No,' was all he said.

A wave of disgust and revulsion rolled through the audience and swept the lodge, but I could feel also a tingle of interest in that commotion, a sudden sharp alertness missing a few seconds before.

'Why?' asked Frazer.

'Why not?' Inlov replied. 'It's my body. I can do what I like with it. If people can flout Orth convention with white hair and lined faces why can't I remove a finger if the effect pleases me?' The discontented rumbles grew louder.

'Those apparitions you mention are cosmetic for the most part,' Frazer argued. 'What you've had done seems a little more . . . drastic.'

'It's only a finger,' Inlov said. 'Hardly more drastic than body piercing. It's not as if it's an arm or a leg.'

'And may I ask what happened to your finger? Was it thrown away or . . . ?'

'It's in cryogenic suspension. I've been assured there's no reason it can't be replaced in the future if I want it back.'

'So this is just a piece of dilettantism, a kind of dabbling?' Frazer said. 'Not a serious endeavour?' But the relief flooding his audience was against him. And the mood in the lodge. If the process was reversible it could be seen as artistic, and attractive. I knew then that the cult of the Rock was doomed to decline more rapidly than it already had.

'The pain was real,' Inlov said in reply, to a shudder of sympathy bordering, in some cases, on ecstasy. 'So too is the disability, however temporary.'

Frazer swung with the new, lighter atmosphere. 'So how long will you persist with it?' he asked.

'Oh, I don't know. Till I get bored with it, I guess. Or until something else grabs my attention.'

Thus joined the ranks of oldsters in the streets, adding to those with caged faces or ClothesOrth trimsuits, and all the other fads which jostled for attention, the concept of the aesthetic mutilation. Mutees abounded, first lacking fingers or thumbs, then with hands or whole arms docked, lopped, truncated, or legs shortened at ankle, knee, thigh. Fingerless palms were waved gratuitously in the faces of the unaltered. Hirpling pedestrians unashamedly displayed their stumps or emphasised them by careful pinning of sleeves or trewlegs, which could also be left to flap uselessly as a badge of honour. In a further refinement, jewels were set in the centre of the amputation scar or arranged around its edges. Nerve-activated display lights able to convey short messages replaced the jewels in those more daring still.

Ever more bizarre bodily mutilations accrued to the list, most of which I found nauseating, good clean-living Orth citizen that I was. Sculpted limbs; grafts of various sorts – an extra head was a popular choice, geep or wisemonkey usually, eyes blind, interface carefully tailored to prevent cross-circulation of the blood – or occasional legless small animals incorporated into the shoulder; transparent body panels giving a view of pulsing veins and organs, or the rhythmic contractions of peristalsis. Empty eye sockets were left to gape sickeningly, maybe filled with livid green or purple gel, or now and then plugged with an eyeball-sized PortaVee screen, wires drooping round to a tiny disc reader affixed behind the ear. Sometimes it seemed that the only real strangeness was the 'normal' unaltered smooth Euthuol complexion.

I found myself wondering; what was it about Orth that the populace needed such things? Were their lives so devoid of meaning that they simply had to have diversion to remind themselves they were alive? Perhaps the Sons would survive after all, if belief in the Rock could assuage such aimlessness.

And was it me who had changed things? Or was the axis of Orth's kaleidoscopic fashion swirl simply ready to tilt in a new direction and I happened to nudge it at the critical moment?

The new Orth that I had partly shaped was as little to my taste as the old. I withdrew gradually from extended contact with the lodges, leaving the everyday running of the cult to younger, stronger hands, and slipped into a long twilight of semi-retirement taking in the view from the hill, my vigil punctuated by the occasional visit from a lingering devotee of the Rock or a travelling VT crew with nothing better to do than pester an old crusader: and Harriet and Jarvis dropping in from time to time.

My Sons and Daughters dwindled from the streets slowly, keeping the flame of the Rock alive for a while longer before returning to virtual obscurity, though the odd 'old' face still crops up in the tank from time to time in crowd scenes or voxpops. I suppose I should have kept a measure of control, been truer to Sonny's wishes, but I was old and I was tired and I had nothing more to give. Let the remaining elders do with it what they would. I had never sought the burden, never believed in the power of the Rock, despite my visions at the Hole and the strange frissons I experienced round Sonny's hill. But the pebble I had thrown into the sea of Orth culture had become like, yes, a rock; and stood against the whirling tides, occasionally submerged but clinging on stubbornly nevertheless. And I was content.

Frazer has gone, and taken his crew with him, another item on a decayed icon of Orth culture – currently residing in the 'Where Are They Now?' file – safely stored on disc. The sun has set behind the distant hills, the stars cast their meagre gleam over the trees, over the land and the city. One of those faint points of light, I know, shines on Home but which it is I couldn't tell you. The lamps of the city are twinkling in response, their shimmering decoration climbing like a fairy light imitation of cotton-easter up the otherwise darkened slopes of the green hills far away over the rooftops.

Looking back on my long lifetime has been a strange experience. What a wide-eyed, innocent, *confident*, youth I was. Brash to the point of arrogance. So different from the vaguely troubled, more tolerant – I will not say wiser – man I have become. But I have made my peace with the universe, and Orth.

In the end it was the SHIFT, of course, that made the change. Not Sile. Nor Sonny. Nor my unjoined battle with the danger lurking in my genes. (I still do not know if I have the defect. Only by taking Euthuol could I have found that out, and I was never prepared to run the risk.)

To me, everything felt manageable before the SHIFT – except for Sile – but I concede the possibility that the mists of nostalgia are colouring my ancient perceptions and that I may be fooling myself. After all, I've spent a lifetime doing that, one way or another.

Without the SHIFT I would have remained with

Orthrocks, happy to gouge out the faces of planets far and away, troubled no doubt by occasional twinges of conscience about the peculiar old man I had left to die alone on Copper, and the odd yearning for a long-lost lover, but never seriously questioning my role. (And I could have been dead long since.) Without the SHIFT the hills of Home would lie proud and tall against the sky, swaddling Hometown in their protective embrace. Without the SHIFT the bounds of Orth would not have been drawn ever tighter, the lingering vestiges of diversity within the coprosperity sphere smoothed out, blanketed over by ISB's mounting domination of the ether. But equally, without the SHIFT the Sons of the Rock would not have known their brief resurgence – nor Sonny his vindication, labelled posthumous.

This window, with its panoramic view, is where I take my simple pleasures. Sipping down raki (I've lost count by now) I gaze each afternoon to the distant mist-shrouded slopes which bear such a haunting resemblance to others I have known, trod, and seen demolished. The view is little comfort. It brings back too many memories.

Of endless childhood afternoons walking cotton-laced hills with my grandmother; and the pain her legacy bestowed. Of Roodsland quarry with its accompanying thoughts of Sonny; whom I failed, but whose astonishing faith sustained him to the end. Of Sile, whom I also failed, and then fulfilled her wishes for me far, far too late.

I look at the planes and angles of the distant rock, their juttings against the sky, the declivities cutting through them, the runnels of eroded gullies, the sparse covering of shrub giving way to lusher slopes below, merging finally into the bright roofs and walls of the city outskirts. I suppose these foreign hills are fair enough, and pleasant in their way. But however fair and green they may be, they are not the hills of Home. All that remains of those lies in holo effigy on the wall behind me.

But these mist-covered mountains are home for me now. The only home I will know, till I no longer know anything.

Would it have been harder to have taken Euthuol and possibly faced an earlier death? A lifetime considering that was still not enough time for me to come to an answer. Was I a coward, taking the easy way out? I only ever really made one decision in my life, and that was not to make a decision at all.

Doubtless, under the impetus of Frazer's latest free-lancing efforts – retirement doesn't satisfy him, he only continues them to give himself something to do – the 'Old Look' will flicker up again like a not quite tamed brush fire. I can always hope that, like a distorted reflection of the awful fascination it has held for me since I first beheld the tortured face of the Rock screaming against its dissolution, its chic glister – just one of the many jostling, periodically 'rediscovered', styles available to the fashion-conscious Orth citizenry – will bring for others, if only slightly, a lessening of the ordeal of premature ageing my grandmother and sister endured, and the loathing and regret for it which blighted most of my mother's life.

I would like to believe so. But it is probable that, like the other passing fads of Orth, the imitations I have spawned will eventually fade away in the collective memory, to become a historical footnote which no-one will remember having known. Who tipples Bulayma Grand these days? Or remembers a VT reporter named Chelsea Monday? Or a performance artiste called Mercy Boaks? Where, for that matter, are the journeyman interstellar hyperspaceships which once dominated the commerce of Orth? All gone – shifted, if you will.

So much change, and so little. The massive Orth juggernaut rolls on, unmoved by such passing fancies, absorbing and digesting all in its path, reconstructing them in its own image.

But, thinking back on my weary life each morning, I look in the mirror. And it throws back the question, 'Just what is it about him that is so shocking?'

After all; he's only an old man. And I see at least one every day.

Epilogue

Get It Right Next Time

Life is full of surprises, even in such a comparatively stable culture as Orth. There has been the coming of the SHIFT, the reconstruction of Home, the demise of the spaceways, the Sons' re-emergence from their redoubt of one (though I cannot forget their subsequent dying fall), the gradual acceptance – the active embrace – of trends which would once have been considered unmentionable obscenities. And, this morning . . .

'Hello,' she said. I stood there speechless, gazing at twins whose flawless, unlined faces looked back at me from slim, lithe bodies.

'You look like you could do with some company.' This was spoken by both of them, obviously rehearsed. I stared back and forth dumbstruck.

'Who is it?' Harriet called from inside.

They looked at one another. 'Oh, obviously not,' the one on the left said.

'I'm not quite sure,' I shouted to Harriet. 'I *think* I know,' I said, doubtfully. I shook my head. 'I don't believe this.'

'Believe it, Alan,' that still-haunting voice said. She squeezed my hand. 'Be sure.'

And I was.

'You'd better come in,' I said as Harriet came to see what the trouble was.

'Mmm,' that same voice said appreciatively. 'Who is this, Alan? Not lost your touch with the ladies, then?'

'Harriet is my sister's daughter,' I explained. 'Some touch. I haven't had a woman in about forty years.' A look of shock crossed her face, mixed with concern. 'What a waste,' she said, then frowned. 'Not on my account, I hope.'

'It's all on your account,' I replied.

'We'll need to do something about it, then,' she said, briskly. And I knew I was lost.

'Where have you been for most of my life?' I asked, with just a trace of bitterness. She stared at me, for once uncertain. 'I . . .' she mumbled; started again, 'Alan . . .' Then my resistance wavered and I opened my arms wide. She moved into them, I clasped myself to her, and stepped back sixty years.

This morning. It was only this morning.

Her smell seemed different. A patina of time, of unshared experience, overlay her inner core. But underneath the familiar scent lingered. The same old stirrings I had thought lost rose in me. It hurt: it had been so long. So long. My joints have stiffened, my juices ceased to flow. But my urgings strove to wake my moribund desire from its long sleep.

'Uncle Alan?' Harriet asked. 'What in Orth's going on? Who is this woman?'

'This,' I said, through gritted teeth, holding back the years of pent-up longing threatening to engulf me, 'is Sile.'

'Oh,' said Harriet. 'I see.'

When I finally let her go Sile gave me the ritual Orth greeting along with that still-mischievous grin. 'Well, Alan. You haven't changed much.'

I smiled ruefully. 'Not much,' I said. 'Just every way possible.' I made sure I held her gaze. 'Except one.'

'I'm sorry, Alan,' she said. 'How was I to know?' I let it pass, escorted the pair of them in, sat them down. Harriet set herself down beside me, balancing the situational equation.

Sile had noticed my flickering glances, assessing her companion. The resemblance was close but not exact. If I'd had to rely on memory, of course, I might not have known the difference. Sixty years is a long time to hold a vision in your head and the only reminder I'd had in all that time was the also subtly different face of Cassandra Tybolt, and that in a dimly lit viewing-tank almost as long ago.

'This is my daughter, Devi,' she said. Harriet's breath hissed in sharply.

'How do you do,' I said. I couldn't think of anything else. A churning apprehension was building in my gut. Why was she here, unless . . . ?

'Pleased to meet you,' replied Devi. 'Mum's told me so much about you.' Her voice was pitched a little lower than her mother's.

'Really? Now why is that, I wonder?' I said. I turned an anxious look on Sile. 'She's not . . . ?'

'Relax. She isn't yours,' she said, and shook her head. 'You always were quick at jumping to conclusions.' I was too relieved to react to the comment. For an awful few moments I had been thinking I had spent my early lifetime only one mistake away from an enforced shot of Euthuol. And then where would I have been, if not dead? Not here; not like this, certainly. Probably awaiting with dread the first grey hairs and wrinkles.

Then a worse thought occurred.

'She isn't . . . Don't tell me she's Ruddy's?' I said in horror. Sile's great peal of laughter rang out, filling the low-ceilinged room.

'There you go again. You never did believe me about him, did you?'

'I had good reason,' I protested.

'No you didn't. You were just being childish.'

'Why not?' I sulked. 'It's what I'm good at.'

Sile turned to Devi. 'I told you he was impossible,' she said.

'So why are you here, then?' put in Harriet.

Sile looked at her shrewdly, 'It's been a long time. I have fond memories. I wanted to see Alan again before it's too late. For both of us.'

Harriet waited for Sile to fill the gap. So did I.

'Partly to apologise,' Sile continued, and my mind thought my ears had misheard – Sile apologise! That would be a new experience – 'and partly, Alan, to see how things stood with you.'

'Stood? In what way, stood?' Harriet demanded.

Sile glanced at her quickly and then back to me. 'Well. To see if you were in a relationship, Alan; and if not, to see how things went between us this time.' Then I *knew* I must have died and gone to paradise; or else some serious prankster's version of hell.

'You've had sixty years to apologise, to start again,' Harriet said. 'Why wait till now?'

'Isn't that rather obvious?' Devi put in.

'Well she's not been celibate, that's for sure.'

'Now, now children,' I interrupted. 'Settle down. I'm

sure Sile had her reasons.' Then I added to no-one in particular, 'She always did. Refreshments, anyone?' I asked sweetly. 'I'm sorry, Sile, we don't have any Bulayma Grand.'

Sile reacted with amazed delight. 'How did you remember that? I haven't had one of them in . . . You know, I can't remember.'

'But you hardly used to touch anything else,' I reminded her. I caught Devi's eye, shook my head in mock sorrow. 'See these people that suddenly come crashing into your life again and shatter all your illusions . . .' She grinned; so like her mother my heart spasmed. You wait all your life for the woman of your dreams, I thought, then two come along at once.

'I don't suppose I need to ask what you think of her,' I said to Harriet as we skittered about the kitchen fixing coffee. Everyone had decided to keep a clear head.

'I think she's a bossy cow,' she replied bluntly. 'But you always did need someone to organise you.'

I sighed. 'You wouldn't make such blithe comparisons if you'd known your mother, you know,' I told her.

She ignored me. 'You're just going to let her waltz in and take over your life again, aren't you?'

'I don't know. I guess so. Why not? I reckon I deserve some joy, don't you?'

'Are you sure you're fit for something like this? You're not used to it.'

'No, I'm not. But I'm going to do it anyway.' I shrugged. 'I'll just take it one day at a time.'

'One day might be all you have,' she said darkly.

'Let's hope it's a good one, then.'

* * *

'Sixty years, Sile!' I said to her, when we were finally alone, after I'd made it clear I'd play along.

Devi had asked, 'Are you sure you're okay with this, mum?' Sile had said yes and her daughter had departed uncertainly, with a sideways glance at me. Harriet had managed to conjure up some tact and disappeared as well.

'Sixty years!' I said, 'And not a word. It's not as if I was anonymous, exactly. I've been in more VT studios than there are stars in the spiral arm. I dropped enough hints. At least in the early days.'

'I was busy. I had another life,' she explained. 'What do you want me to say?'

'I don't know. Sorry seems desperately inadequate. I had another life too, but that was all played out before the quadraxes, in public view. What have you been doing all this time? Did you keep on dancing? Who's Devi's father?'

She hesitated, shell-shocked by this mini-barrage. She said, 'He was a good man.' She sighed in recollection. 'I made his life a misery at times, but he put up with me. I danced when I could, kept my hand in. Time was passing, so I had Devi, and then Kannon.'

'Kannon?' I queried.

'My son.' I nodded. Of course. There would have been two.

'I wanted them to grow up with both parents, the way I had. I made sure I kept him interested so he wouldn't stray.'

'I can imagine,' I said.

'Living with someone for so long,' she mused, 'you either get tired of them or grow much closer. In the end Vern and I came to fit like a well-tailored trimsuit. But I never quite forgot you, Alan. Not that I could. You kept popping up to remind me. Devi and Kannon couldn't believe I knew someone from the tank.'

'So what changed?'

'Vern died,' she said simply. I said nothing.

'It was sudden of course,' she continued, 'and it left a gap, but it meant that phase of my life was over.'

'And I'm supposed to fill the gap?'

'No. No-one can. But I do owe you an apology and I've no ties apart from Devi and Kannon – who can look after themselves. So if you want to have another stab at it . . .'

One day at a time . . .

I look over these notes, made hastily at the time, when I was still confused and delighted in equal measure – when I wanted to get it all down while it was fresh in my mind, frightened somehow that if I didn't record it immediately, give it semi-permanent form – my late-found joy would vanish as suddenly as it had appeared. Perhaps it was just that I was overwhelmingly aware of Sile's past unpredictability but it was a strange apprehension none the less.

Eighty-two brings many fears, but re-establishing a sexual relationship after an interruptus of sixty years is not, I think, usually one of them. I was scared; like a virgin.

Would my frail body betray me? Was it still capable of physical response? Was I any longer fitted to pleasure after such long abstinence?

Thoughts of Sile's possible deep strange needs also plagued me. Had she, for all his outlandish appearance, actually been perversely attracted to Sonny all those years ago? Her anger with me a cover for her necessarily sublimated feelings? And had she only sought me out now because I had aged in my turn? If so, I reasoned, then it was all to my advantage. I didn't want to probe her motivations too closely.

Against that, I had mirrored Sonny's looks, if not his lifestyle, for decades. She could easily have found, and made a play for me at any point in all those years. Maybe, and not for the first time, I was misjudging her and it was just as she said.

Then again, perhaps she was as lost and uncertain as I was and sought her consolation in laying the ghosts from her past. Whatever her reasons it didn't – doesn't – matter. I was more than willing.

'It's just as well you've had the shots,' I joked feebly. 'I'm still potent, you know. But almost terminally rusty.'

'Let's see what I can remember, then,' she said.

What goes through the mind of a woman in the prime of her vigour when she makes love to a man who is physically much older? When her firm flesh is pressed to his fragile, almost worn-out body? Especially if she is unused to it, has not had the experience of seeing that body age slowly? Is it pity, disgust, some exotic, aberrant sexual pleasure? Or does she simply switch off, perform the act mechanically? Get through it as best she can?

She was gentle with me, but seemed assiduous enough. My hands once more exploring her body, her scent in my nostrils again, the hormones coursing at increasing pace along my veins, threw me back through time and space to that cubicle on the *Strangeness And Charm*. Called on April, Helcynth and all the stops to Copper. My memories whispered treacherously across the years that her eagerness had diminished, her vitality was eroded. The lustful zest was gone.

Perhaps it was only the effect of age; for we had both changed. She now had a lifetime of experience to bring to the encounter, instead of at most a few years since losing her virginity.

I cried out when the locked up, held-in passions of too many years finally released themselves, clutching her to myself desperately. She stroked and caressed me, soothed my troubled breast, kissed me, whispered, 'It's all right. I'm here now. I'm here now,' as I lay and wondered when she would leave me this time. Unlike that first time, she did not insist on an immediate repeat bout, contenting herself with holding me till my overwound body relaxed.

'Caught you!' I said one afternoon, as she scrutinised herself in the hall mirror.

'What?'

'You always used to complain about me doing that.'

She considered her reply for a moment. 'You were twenty-two and loved yourself. I merely pricked your conceit occasionally.'

'I was twenty-two and loved you. You tore my conceit apart. You left me; remember? Despite that, after all these years I'm still crazy about you. Whose was the bigger conceit?'

'Let's not argue, Alan. At our age life's too short. When you were young you were a vain bastard and such a pig brain. But you've redeemed yourself. I never thought you had it in you to let yourself age naturally. Or campaign on Sonny's behalf.'

'Neither did I.'

'And you did it all for me?'

I looked at her in puzzlement. 'Whatever gave you that idea?'

'Well,' she explained, 'you knew my interest in old things, ancient cultures. I assumed you were trying, in a roundabout way, to win me back.'

'If I had been, then it worked in the end. You're here. Now. But your assumption is wrong. I didn't do it for you, I did it for Sonny.'

'But you didn't even like him!' she complained.

'Not at first. But you weren't there when I had to go back, again and again. When I had to choose between him and my job, and chose wrongly – or maybe it was rightly, who knows now with all that's happened since? When I had to destroy all that was left of his world. I was his last hope and I betrayed him. I owed him. You'd left me high and dry. I owed you nothing, after that.'

'Well what about now?' she asked, slipping her arms through mine, turning her face up to be kissed. 'What do you owe me, now?'

'I'm old,' I said. 'I'm treating each day as a bonus.'

'I've been wondering,' I said to her, another day. 'Did you mean what you said? Or is it something you tell all your lovers?'

'What?'

'You once told me I was the best fuck you ever had.'

'Did I?'

'Yes.'

'Trust a big-headed sod like you to remember something like that.'

'Don't I have anything to be big-headed about?' I asked her, grinning.

She eyed me archly. 'You're obsessed, that's all.'

'I'm not. I've just got a lot of catching up to do,' I said, drawing her towards me.

Later, she said, 'Did I really say that?'

'Of course. I wouldn't make it up.'

'When?'

'On Copper, as you left. On wages day.'

'I must have meant it, then. I don't say things I don't mean.'

I heard the door open and close, the sound of someone entering the main room. I came out of the kitchen and she was sitting there, back towards me. I came up behind her. 'Hello,' I said, bent over to kiss her, flinched as she jumped away.

'I'm sorry,' I said. 'I thought it was your mother. You're so alike.'

'No. It's me,' Devi said, standing up.

'If it's Sile you wanted I don't know where she is. She went out a while ago and I guess she's not back yet. I thought you were her.'

Devi's continuing silence was odd. A cold misgiving started to form. 'How did you get in?' I asked.

As she fumbled in a pocket of the loose-fitting jacket covering her torso it swung open revealing a trim breast pushing against her Titefit. A blast of lust at this reminder of her mother momentarily confused me.

She thrust a keypad at me. 'You'd better have this back,' she said. Her varnished fingernails sobered me as much as her words. Sile had been scrupulously artifice-free since her reappearance. 'Mum won't be needing it any more.'

'What?' I stammered. 'Why not? I thought . . .' I snapped suddenly into anger. 'She's done it again, hasn't she? At least last time she had the decency

to tell me herself. Where is she? Let me talk to her.
I'll . . .'

My outburst alarmed Devi. 'Calm down,' she said.
'It's not like that. I'm afraid I'm not coping very well
with this.' She took a deep breath. 'Mum's going into
a hospice.'

My anger was abruptly shifted. Concern rushed to fill
the vacuum in my stomach. 'What's wrong? Is she ill?'

'An Elder Hospice,' Devi said, slowly, clarifyingly.
'Her time has come.'

Relief and apprehension make strange companions.
We wouldn't have long now, I thought, but at least I
would be with her. Could succour her as I failed to
succour Sonny. 'Which one?' I asked. 'The one in the
city or out at Drimn?'

She shook her head. 'She told me not to tell you. I'm
afraid she doesn't want you to see her again.'

'Why in Orth not? Look at me for goodness sake!
It won't disturb me! I know about ageing. I wrote
the book.'

'I can only guess at her reasons,' she said. 'But
she's always had that small streak of vanity.' Her
voice and gestures tantalised me. So many reminders
of her mother. 'It's not just you,' she assured me. 'She
doesn't want any of us to see her again. Only strangers
to witness her end. She warned me you'd try to find
her if you were told where she is. All I can say is she's
off-planet. There's no point searching. You know how
it is. It'll be over in a few weeks.'

I sagged into the chair, thwarted even at the last by
Sile's unpredictability, and damnable wilfulness.

'I'm sorry,' Devi said. 'I know how much she meant
to you.'

'No you don't,' I replied. 'No-one does. Not even

Sile.' I looked up at her standing there, thinly powdered face shining in the afternoon light slanting through the window, dust motes dancing in a halo around her. This is what I'll remember, I thought, strangely. This moment now. But I'll put Sile's unpainted face over hers.

'Thank you for coming,' I said. 'It can't have been easy for you.'

I stood up slowly, pushing for purchase against the chair arm. 'May I?' I asked, extending my creaky arms to her. She let me hug her, coldly, her arms at her sides. Her smell was all wrong, and barely detectable under a discreet but annoying perfume. 'For your mother,' I whispered.

'I don't suppose you'll keep in touch?' I asked, when I disengaged a moment later.

'I don't think that would be a very good idea,' she said dispassionately.

'No. No. I suppose not.'

A few seconds later she was gone. My late-found joy had lasted even more briefly than the heyday of my almost forgotten Sons.

I'll admit it took a while but in the end I think I understand. I had flirted with the insidious thought that nagged at me even before Devi left, that Sile had simply grown tired of me again as she had on Copper. But the funeral was rather elaborate for a charade, so I guess things were as they seemed.

Whatever Sile's reasons for her concluding departure – vanity, fear, or simply the instinctive huddling away that was ingrained as a response in Orth citizens of my generation when the signs and portents came – her impulse had been correct. An old and lined Sile, that lithe, lissom body decrepit and incapable, all that vitality reduced to helplessness, would have been too much to bear; even if only for the final day or so it would have lasted – and certainly in the days beyond. The other memories would have been indelibly sullied, the bright vision that once delighted my youthful sight – and so recently burned away the feathery cobwebs of my decline – clouded over and tarnished.

They are all gone now. All the movers and shakers of my life. First Sonny, then Sis, Mum and Dad followed too quickly. Then, much later, Sile. And now it is Frazer's turn also. His obit filled the tank last night, complete with clips from his greatest triumphs. In full living colour the ghosts of people and times lost stalked once more across my vision.

I begin to wonder in my rambling, incoherent way if Sonny was more right than he or I ever knew. That he saw Euthuol as a menace was beyond question. That his conviction was deadly accurate is a thought that would never have occurred to a normal citizen of Orth. For who could doubt the benefits of prolonged youth, burning bright the candle of life? Albeit with a short, sharp extinction at its end.

Yet, of all my youthful friends and acquaintances, I alone – who never took the shots – am left to tell the tale. To fall slowly into the dying of the light.

I try not to think about Sile and the cruel ironies which brought her to me so late and took her from me so soon. I have spent too much of my life wishing it away.

But what else is left to me now? However much I fight it, every afternoon as I take my abiding pleasure and sip down raki, I think about Home; and the distant hills dim as my eyes brim with thoughts of Sile, forever young and beautiful.